TERRY BROOKS

ARMAGEDDON'S CHILDREN

Every legend has a beginning

orbit

www.orbitbooks.co.uk

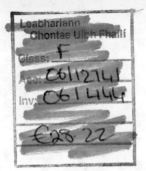

ORBIT

First published in the United States by Del Rey Books, an imprint of
The Random House Publishing Group
First published in Great Britain in 2006 by Orbit

A CIP catalogue record for this book
is available from the British Library.

HB ISBN-13: 978-1-84149-478-4
HB ISBN-10: 1-84149-478-X
C-format ISBN-13: 978-1-84149-479-1
C-format ISBN-10: 1-84149-479-8

Printed and bound in Great Britain by
Clays Ltd, St Ives plc

Orbit
An imprint of
Little, Brown Book Group
Brettenham House
Lancaster Place
London WC2E 7EN

A member of the Hachette Livre Group of Companies

www.orbitbooks.co.uk

For Judine.
My best friend in all the best ways.

1

H E I S F A S T *asleep in his bed on the night that the demon and the once-men come for his family. They have been watching the compound for days, studying its walls and the routine of the guards who ward them. They have waited patiently for their chance, and now it has arrived. An advance party is over the walls and past the guards. They have opened the gates from the inside to let in the others, and now all are pouring into the compound. In less than five minutes, everything has been lost.*

He doesn't realize this when his father shakes him awake, but he knows something is wrong.

"Logan, get up." Urgency and fear are apparent in his father's voice.

Logan blinks against the beam of the flashlight his father holds, one of two they still possess. He sees his brother dressing across the way, pulling on his shirt and pants, moving quickly, anxiously. Tyler isn't griping, isn't saying anything, doesn't even look over at him.

His father bends close, his strong features all planes and angles at the edges of the flashlight's beam. His big hand grips his son's shoulder and squeezes. "It's time for us to leave here, Logan. Put on your clothes and your pack and wait by the trapdoor with Tyler. Your mother and I will be along with Megan."

His sister. He looks around, but doesn't see her. Outside, there is shouting and the sound of gunfire. A battle is being fought. He knows now what has happened, even without seeing it. He has heard it talked about all of his life, the day their enemies would find a way to break through, the day that the walls and gates and guards and defenses would finally give way. It has happened all across the United States. It has happened all over the world. No one is safe anywhere. Maybe no one will ever be safe again.

He rises quickly now and dresses. His brother already has his pack strapped across his back and tosses Logan his. The packs have been sitting in a corner of his bedroom for as far back as he can remember. Each month, they are unpacked, checked, and repacked. His father is a careful man, a planner, a survivor. He has always assumed this day would come, even though he assured his family it would not. Logan was not fooled. His father did not speak of it directly, but in the spaces between the words of reassurance were silent warnings. Logan did not miss them, did not ignore their implications.

"Hurry, slug," Tyler hisses at him, going out the door.

He finishes fastening his boots, throws his pack over his shoulder, and hurries after his brother. The shouts are growing louder now, more frantic. There are screams, as well. He feels curiously removed from all of it, as if it were happening to people with whom he had no connection, even though these are his friends and neighbors. He feels light-headed, and there is a buzzing in his ears. Maybe he has gotten up too fast, has rushed himself the way he does sometimes without allowing his body to adjust to a sudden change.

Maybe it is just the first of many adjustments he is going to have to make in his life.

He knows what is going to happen now. His father has told them all, taking care to use the word *if* rather than the word *when*. They are going to have to escape through the tunnels and flee into the surrounding countryside. They are going to have to abandon their home and all their possessions because otherwise they will be caught and killed. The demons and the once-men have made it clear from the beginning that those who choose to shut themselves away in the compounds will not be *spared once their defenses are breached. It is punishment for defiance, but it is a warning, too.*

If you want to survive, you have to place yourself in our hands.

No one believes this is true, of course. No one can survive outside the compounds. Not as a free man or woman. Not with the plagues and poisons in the air, water, and soil. Not with the slave camps to take you in and swallow you up. Not with the Freaks and the monsters running amok in cities and towns and villages everywhere.

Not with the demons and once-men seeking to exterminate the human race.

Not in this brave new world.

Logan knows this even though he is only eight years old. He knows it because he is dreaming it, reliving it twenty years later. His understanding of its truths transcends time and place; he embraces the knowledge in the form of memories. He knows it the way he already knows how things will end.

He is standing with Tyler in front of the trapdoor when his father reaches them, ushering his mother and sister into place. "Stay together," *he tells them, glancing from face to face.* "Look out for each other."

He carries a short-barreled Tyson 33 Flechette, a wicked black metal weapon that when fired can tear a hole through a stone wall a foot thick. Logan has seen it fired only once, years ago, when his father was testing it. The sound of its discharge was deafening. There was a burning smell in his nose and a ringing in his ears afterward. The memory stays with him to this day. He is afraid of the weapon. If his father carries it, things are as bad as they can possibly be.

"Jack." *His mother speaks his father's name softly, and she turns and takes him in her arms, burying her face in his shoulder. The shouts and screams and firing are right outside their door.*

His father lets her hold him for a moment, then eases her away, reaches down, and flings back the trapdoor. "Go!" *he snaps, motioning them in.*

Tyler doesn't hesitate; carrying the second of the two flashlights, he goes down through the opening. Megan follows him, her green eyes huge and damp with tears.

"Logan," *his father calls when he sees his youngest hesitate.*

In the next instant the front door blows apart in a fiery explosion that engulfs both his mother and his father and sends him tumbling head-over-heels down the stairway to land in a twisted heap on top of his sister. She screams, and something heavy falls on the dirt floor next to him, barely missing his head. In the waver of Tyler's flashlight he looks down and sees the Tyson Flechette. He stares at it until his brother jerks him to his feet and snatches up the weapon himself.

Their eyes meet and they both know. "Run!" Tyler grunts.

Together the three children hurry down the long dark corridor, following the beam of the flashlight. In the darkness ahead, other flashlight beams and flickering candles appear out of other tunnels that join this one, and the sound of voices grows louder. He knows they all come from homes close to his own. The tunnel was the joint project of many families, spearheaded by his father and a few other men, a bolt-hole in case of the unspeakable. Quickly the tunnels are packed, and people are pushing and shoving. Tyler, fighting to keep Megan in tow with one hand while wielding his flashlight with the other, shouts his name and shoves the Tyson Flechette at him.

Logan takes it without thinking. His hands close over the cool, smooth metal of the barrel and work down to the leather-bound grip. Curiously, the weapon feels right in his hands; it feels like it belongs there. His fear of it dissipates as he cradles it to his chest.

Ahead, there is a convergence of lights, and a wooden stairway leads upward. People are pouring out of the tunnel and up the steps into a night filled with flashes and explosions and the sounds of death and dying. He can feel the heat of an intense fire as he gains the opening. As he breathes in the night air, he can smell the acrid stench of smoke and charred timbers.

He has just paused to look around, not three steps back from Tyler and Megan, when an explosion rips the earth beneath him, flinging him backward into the night. An eerie silence descends over his immediate surroundings. Everything he hears now is distant and strangely muffled. He cannot see at first, cannot even move, lying on the ground clutching the flechette as if it were a lifeline.

He rises with difficulty, dazed and in shock. He sees bodies strewn everywhere on the ground in front of him, all around the tunnel opening, dozens and dozens of crumpled forms. He climbs to his feet and staggers over to where Tyler and Megan lie still and bleeding, their eyes wide and staring. He feels his chest tighten and his strength drain away. They are gone. His whole family is gone. It happened so fast.

Sudden movement catches his eye as a knot of dark forms converges on him from out of the darkness. Once-men, wild-eyed and feral, their faces the faces of animals. Without thinking, without even knowing how he remembers what to do, he snaps off the safety on the Tyson Flechette, whips up the barrel, and fires into their midst. Dozens of them disappear, blown backward into the night. He swings the barrel to the right and fires again. Dozens more fly apart. He is exhilarated, become as maddened as they are, as consumed by bloodlust. He hates them for what they have done. He wants to destroy them all.

Then he sees another figure, an old man standing off to one side, tall and stooped and ghost-gray in a cloak that hangs almost to the ground. His eyes are fixed on Logan, peering out from beneath a slouch-brimmed hat, and in those eyes is a cold approval that terrifies the boy. He does not understand what it is the old man approves of, but he does understand one thing. Without ever having come face-to-face with one before, he knows instinctively that this is a demon.

The demon smiles at him and nods.

A hand jerks him about sharply and whips the flechette out of his hands. Eyes as hard and black as obsidian stare out of a face streaked with grease and sweat. "Good enough, boy, but it's time to leave now. Let's live to fight another day!"

He takes Logan's arm and begins to run with him into the darkness. Others with faces painted in the same way join with him, shepherding the strays they have gathered from the ruins of the compound. A rear guard forms up to protect their retreat, weapons firing into the waves of once-men that seek to reach them.

"Run, boy." The man who holds him shoves him away.

Fighting down the pain he feels in his gut, struggling to hold back his tears, he does. He does not look back.

● ● ●

THE MIDMORNING SUNLIGHT blinded Logan Tom when he opened his eyes, and he blinked hard to clear away the sleep as he

peered out through the windshield of the Lightning S-150 AV. The
Indiana countryside, empty of life, spread away to either side of the
little copse of elms he had pulled into the night before. The highway
he had followed west toward Chicago stretched back the way he
had come and ahead the way he must go, cracked and weed-grown
and littered with debris. His gaze shifted. Fields fallow and dried
out from weeks without rain formed a broken brown patchwork to
the south. North, about half a mile off, a farmhouse and barn sat
abandoned and derelict in a small grove of oaks turned wintry and
leached of life.

On the four horizons, nothing moved. Not even feeders, and
feeders were everywhere there were humans to consume.

He reached over for the staff, gripped it tightly for a moment,
then ran his hands slowly along its polished black length, feeling the
reassuring presence of the runes carved into its surface.

Another day in the world.

He checked the gauges of the AV, a cursory examination of several banks of lights that glimmered a uniform green in the daylight
brightness. The red lights were dark, reassuring him that nothing had
approached the vehicle during the night. He would not have slept
through their audible warnings in any case, but it didn't hurt to
make sure. The assault vehicle was his favorite weapon against the
things that hunted him, and he relied on her the way you relied on
a best friend. Not that he had ever had a best friend. Michael had
been his last real friend, but mostly he had been Logan's teacher. It
was Michael, a genius with anything mechanical, who had acquired
and modified the AV. When he was gone, the Lightning had become
Logan's, a small legacy from a man larger than life.

He thought momentarily of his dream, of that last night with his
family, with his childhood. Twenty years ago now, but it seemed an
eternity.

Don't dwell on it. Don't give power of any kind to the past.

Satisfied that nothing threatened, he glanced at the solar battery
readings. Full power. He was good to go. Solar had its advantages in
a world in which the climates had been so drastically altered that
the sun shone 350 days a year all the way from the equator to
Canada. When you crossed the Mississippi, there was nothing but

desert until you reached the mountains, then more of the same after that until you got close to the coast. The ozone layer had mostly burned away, the polar ice caps all but vanished. Temperatures had risen everywhere, and the land that had once been Middle America had turned stunted and dry. Old news; it had happened more than thirty years ago. So lots of sunshine was the forecast for today, tomorrow, and the next few centuries.

Rainfall? Six to eight inches a year in the wet spots.

Logan Tom wondered if anyone would ever again see anything that even resembled the old world. He thought it possible his descendants might, one extrapolated from the raw conditions of the present. But the world his parents and grandparents had known was gone forever, as dead as the moral and social fabric that had failed to hold it together. No one had thought it possible. No one had believed it could happen.

No one except the Knights of the Word, who had dreamed the nightmare and tried unsuccessfully to prevent it. Men and women conscripted to the cause, champions of and believers in the need to keep the magic that bound all things in balance.

For there *was* magic in the world, born out of the time before humankind, out of the world of Faerie, out of an older civilization. Magic that infused and sustained, that reached beyond what could be seen or even understood to tie together in symbiotic fashion all life.

Magic over which both the Word and the Void sought to exercise control.

It was an old struggle, one that dated all the way back to the birth of humanity. It was a struggle for supremacy between shadings of light and dark, between gradations of good and evil. Logan Tom didn't pretend to understand all the nuances. It was enough that he understood the difference between a desire to preserve and a determination to destroy. The Knights, as servants of the Word, sought to keep the balance of the world's magic in check; the demons, as creatures of the Void, sought to upset it. It was a simple enough concept to grasp and one easily embraced if you believed in good and evil— and most humans did. They always had. What they didn't want to believe, what they tried repeatedly to dismiss, was that whatever good and evil existed in the world came from within themselves and not from some abstract source. It was easier to attribute both to something larger than what they knew, what they could see. A refusal to accept that it came from within was what had ultimately undone them.

The Knights and the demons understood this truth and sought, respectively, to reveal or exploit it. Both were born of the human race, evolved into something more by becoming what they were. Until the beginning of the end, humans hadn't even known of their existence. Many still didn't. Knights and demons were the stuff of urban legend and radical religions. No one saw them at work; no one could pick them out from other humans. Not until they had begun to reveal themselves and their cause. Not until the balance was tipped and the steady, purposeful destruction of all humankind a reality.

How hard it was for them to see the truth even then, when it was staring them in the face.

Even after the plagues had killed half a billion people, no one had believed. Even after the air was so polluted and the water was so badly fouled that it was dangerous either to breathe or drink, no one had believed. They had started to believe after the first nuclear weapons were launched and whole cities vanished in the blink of an eye. They had started to believe when the governments of countries collapsed or were overthrown, when chemical warfare attacks and counterattacks decimated entire populations. Enough so that they began turning what remained of their cities into walled compounds. Enough so that they retreated into a siege mentality that hadn't abated as a way of life in thirty years.

It got worse, of course. When food and water started to dwindle, survival hinged on controlling what supplies remained and on acquiring new. But few knew how to forage adequately in a world poisoned and fouled so badly that even the soil could kill. Few knew how to develop new sources, and the demons got to those who did. A reticence to share with those less fortunate settled in, and the compounds became symbols of tyranny and selfishness. Those within were privileged, less threatened by hunger and thirst and sickness. Those without, some already beginning to change as their bodies adjusted to the poisons and the sicknesses that infected them, were labeled enemies for no better reason than that they had become different from everyone else.

Freaks, the regular humans called them. The street kids had given them other names—Lizards, Croaks, Spiders, Moles. Mutants. Abominations. They were called that and much worse. Infected by radiation and chemicals, they were the monsters of his time, banished to the ravaged land outside the walls of the compounds and left to their fate.

Logan Tom looked out across the Indiana flats, reached for the AV's ignition, and turned it on. The engine purred softly to life, and he felt the thrum of her metal skin vibrate beneath his seat. After a moment, he engaged the clutch and steered out from the trees back onto the cracked surface of the road, heading west.

The real enemies were the once-men, humans subverted not by radiation and chemicals, but by false promises and lies that went something like this: "Do you want to know what it will take to survive? A willingness to do what is needed. The world has always belonged to the strongest. The weak have never been meant to inherit anything. You choose which you want to be in this life. By your choice, you are either with us or against us. Choose wisely."

Demons had, of course, been telling those lies and making those false promises to humans for centuries. But those to whom the demons whispered were more willing to listen now. The world was a simple place in the aftermath of civilization's destruction: either you lived within the compounds or you lived without. Those without believed those within weak and afraid, and they understood fear and weakness instinctively. They had been culled from the remnants of broken armies and scattered law enforcement bodies, from failed militias and paramilitary organizations, from a culture of weapons and battle, from a mind-set of hate and suspicion and ruthless determination. Once they embraced the propaganda of the demons, they fell quickly into the thicket of resulting madness. They changed emotionally and psychologically first, then mentally and physically. Layer by layer, they shed their human skin; they took on the look and feel of monsters.

Outwardly, they still looked mostly human—apart from their

blank, dead eyes and their empty expressions. Inwardly, they were something else entirely, their humanity erased, their identity remade. Inwardly, they were predatory and animalistic and given over to killing everything that moved.

They were once-men.

Logan Tom knew these creatures intimately. He had seen good men who had changed to become them, some of them his friends. He had watched it happen over and over. He had never understood it, but he had known what to do about it. He had hunted them down and he had killed them with relentless, unshakable determination, and he would keep hunting and killing them and the demons that created them until either they were eradicated or he was dead himself.

It was the task he had been given in his service to the Word. It was, by now, the definition of his life.

He was not, he understood, so different than they were. He was their mirror image in so many ways that it frightened him. He might claim to occupy the moral high ground, that he was only doing what was right. He might rationalize it in any way he chose, but the result was the same. He killed them as they killed others. He was simply better at it than they were.

He drove west at a steady thirty miles an hour, careful to avoid the deeper cracks and potholes that had eroded the highway, steering past what looked to be the burned remains of fence posts used for fires and piles of trash blown in from the now empty farms. He hadn't seen a single soul since he had left Cleveland yesterday. There were several compounds there, larger than most and heavily defended. The demons and the once-men were just now beginning to attack these, having wiped out almost all of the smaller enclaves. Soon enough they would eliminate the bigger ones, as well. Would have done so by now, perhaps, if not for the Knights of the Word.

If not for him.

Were there still others like him? He had no way of knowing. The Lady did not tell him in his visions of her, and he had not encountered another Knight in two years. He knew that at one time, others had fought as he did to stop the demon advance, but they were few and many had died. The last Knight he'd encountered had told him that on the East Coast, where the damage was the worst, they were all dead.

Midday came and went. He passed out of Indiana and into Illinois as the sun eased slowly toward the western horizon until eventually the skies began to turn a brilliant mix of gold and scarlet. His smile was bitter. One thing about air pollution: it provided some incredibly beautiful endings to your days. If you had to live in a poisoned world, you might as well enjoy the scenery.

He stopped the Lightning in the center of the highway and climbed out to watch the colors expand and deepen, taking the black staff with him. He stretched, easing the aching and stiffness he had developed in the confines of the AV's cab. He had grown tall and lean like his father, exuding a rangy kind of strength. Scars crisscrossed his hands and arms, white slashes against his darker skin. He had sustained worse damage, but nothing that showed. Most of it was emotional. He was hardened from his years of service to the Word, by the pain and suffering he had witnessed and by the sense of aloneness he constantly felt. His face, like his father's, was all edges and planes, a warrior's face. But his mother's gentle blue eyes helped to soften the harshness. Compassion reflected in those eyes, but compassion was a luxury in which he could not often afford to indulge. The demons and their kind did not allow for it.

He stared off into the distance past a broken line of crooked fence posts to where the darkness was beginning to creep over the landscape. A failing of the light had already turned the eastern horizon hazy. As he retied the bandanna that held back his long dark hair, he watched the shadows from the posts lengthen like snakes.

Then suddenly the late-afternoon breeze shifted, carrying with it the stench of death.

He followed his nose down the side of the road until carrion birds rose in a black cloud from the drainage ditch that had concealed them and he could see the remains of the bodies on which they had been feeding. He peered down at them, trying to reconstruct what had happened. Several families traveling on foot, he guessed. Dead several days, at least. Caught out in the open, dispatched, then dragged here. Hard to tell what might have gotten them.

Something big and quick. Something I don't want to run into just now.

He returned to the Lightning, climbed back aboard, and drove on, following the fading light. The sky west was clear and still bright, so he left the headlights off. After a time, the moon came up, a narrow crescent off to the northeast, low and silvery. Once, the light revealed something moving through the blasted landscape, crouched low on all fours. Could have been anything. He glanced down at the AV's readings, but they showed nothing, banks of green eyes shining up at him.

It took him less than an hour to reach the town. He was nearly all the way across Illinois, come to a place he had never been to before. But the Lady had made it clear that this was where she wanted him to go. She had visited him in his dreams, as she often did, providing him with directions and guidance, giving him what brief relief he found from the constant nightmares of his past. Once, another Knight had told him, they had dreamed of the future that would come to pass if they failed in their efforts to prevent it. Now there was no reason to dream of the future; they were all living it. Instead he dreamed of the darker moments of his past, of failures and missed opportunities, of losses too painful to relive anywhere except in dreams, and of choices made that had scarred him forever.

He hoped that after his business here was finished and it was time to sleep again, the dreams might let him be for at least one night.

Houses began to appear in the distance, dark boxes against the flat landscape. There were no lights, no fires or candles, no signs of life. But there would be life, he knew. There was life everywhere in towns this size. Just not the sort you wanted to encounter.

He eased the AV down the debris-littered highway toward the town, past broken signs and buildings with sagging roofs and collapsed walls. Out of the corner of his eye, he caught a glimpse of movement. *Feeders.* Where there were feeders, there were other things, too. He scanned the warning gauges on the Lightning and kept driving.

He passed a small green sign off to one side of the road, its lettering faded and worn:

WELCOME TO
Hopewell, Illinois
Population 25,501

Twenty-five thousand, five hundred and one, he repeated silently. He shook his head. Once, maybe. A hundred years ago. Several lifetimes in the past, when the world was still in one piece.

He drove on toward his destination and tried not to think further of what was lost and forever gone.

2

HAWK WALKED POINT as the Ghosts emerged from their underground lair beneath what had once been Pioneer Square and set out on foot for midtown Seattle. It was an hour before midday, when trade negotiations and exchanges usually took place, but he liked to give himself a little extra time to cushion against the possibility of encounters with Freaks. Usually you didn't see much of them when it was daylight, but you never knew. It didn't pay to take chances. As leader, it was his responsibility to keep the others safe.

The city was quiet, the debris-littered streets empty and still. Storefronts and apartments stood deserted and hollow, their glass windows broken out and doors barred or sagging. The rusted hulks of cars and trucks sat where their owners had abandoned them decades ago, a few still in one piece, but most long since cannibalized and reduced to metal shells. He wondered, looking at them, what the city had been like when vehicles had tires and ran in a steady, even flow of traffic from one street to the next. He wondered, as he always did, what the city must have been like when it was filled with people and life. Nobody lived in the city now outside the walls of the compounds. Not unless you counted the Freaks and the street children, and no one did.

Hawk stopped the others at the cross streets that marked the northern boundary of Pioneer Square and looked to Candle for reassurance. Her clear blue eyes blinked at him, and she nodded. It was safe to continue. She was only ten years old, but she could see things no one else could. More than once, her visions had saved their lives. He didn't know how she did it, but he knew the Ghosts were lucky to have her. He had named her well: she was their light against the dark.

He glanced momentarily at the others, a ragtag bunch dressed in jeans, sweatshirts, and sneakers. He had named them all. He had tossed away their old names and supplied them with new ones. Their names reflected their character and temperament. They were starting over in life, he had told them. None of them should have to carry the past into the future. They were the Ghosts, haunting the ruins of the civilization their parents had destroyed. One day, when they ceased to be street kids and outcasts and could live somewhere else, he would name them something better.

Candle smiled as their eyes met, that brilliant, dazzling smile that brightened everything around her. He had a sudden sense that she could tell what he was thinking, and he looked quickly away.

"Let's go," he said.

They set off down First Avenue, working their way past the derelict cars and heaps of trash, heading north toward the center of the city. He knew it was First Avenue because there were still signs fastened to a few of the buildings eye-level with the ornate streetlights. The signs still worked, even if the lights didn't. Hawk had never seen working streetlights; none of them had. Panther claimed there were lights in San Francisco, but Hawk was sure he was making it up. The power plants that provided electricity hadn't operated since before he was born, and he was the oldest among them except for Owl. Electricity was a luxury that few could manage outside the compounds, where solar-powered generators were plentiful. Mostly, they got by with candles and fires and glow sticks.

They stayed in the center of the street as they walked, keeping clear of the dark openings of the buildings on either side, falling into the Wing-T formation that Hawk favored. Hawk was at point, Panther and Bear on the wings, and the girls, Candle and River, in the center carrying the goods in tightly bound sacks. Owl had read about the Wing-T in one of her books and told Hawk how it worked. Hawk could read, but not particularly well. None of them could, the little ones in particular. Owl was a good reader. She had learned in the compound before she left to join them. She tried to instruct them, but mostly they wanted her to read to them instead. Their patience was limited, and their duties as members of the Ghosts took up most of their time. Reading wasn't necessary for staying alive, they would argue.

But, of course, it was. Even Hawk knew that much.

Overhead, the sky began to fill with roiling clouds that darkened steadily as the Ghosts moved out of Pioneer Square and up toward the Hammering Man. Soon rain was falling in a soft, steady mist, turning the concrete of the streets and buildings a glistening slate gray. The rain felt clean and refreshing to Hawk, who lifted his angular face to its cool wash. Sometimes he wished he could go swimming again, as he had when he was a little boy living in Oregon. But you couldn't trust the water anymore. You couldn't be sure what was in it, and if the wrong thing got into your body, you would die. At least they had the rain, which was more than most of the world could say.

Not that he had seen much of that world. At eighteen, he had lived in exactly two places—in Oregon until he was five and in Seattle since then. But the Ghosts had a radio to listen to, and sometimes it told them things. Less so these days, as the stations dropped away, one by one. Overrun by the armies of the once-men, he assumed.

Once-men. *Madmen.*

Sometimes they learned things from other street kids. A new kid would show up, wandering in from some other part of the country to link up with one of the tribes and provide a fresh piece of news. But wherever they came from, their stories were pretty much alike. Everyone was in the same boat, trying to survive. The same dangers threatened everyone, and all you could do was decide how you wanted to live: either inside the compounds like a caged animal or out on the streets like prey.

Or, in the case of the Ghosts, you lived underground and tried to stay out of the way.

It was Owl who knew the history behind the underground city. She had read about it in a book. A long time ago, the old Seattle had burned and the people had buried her and built a new city right on top. The old city had been ignored until parts of it were excavated for underground tours. In the wake of the Great Wars and the destruction of the new city, it had all been forgotten again.

But Hawk had rediscovered it, and now it belonged to the Ghosts. Well, mostly. There were other things down there, too, though not other street kids because other street kids respected your territory. Freaks of various sorts. Lizards, Moles, and Spiders mostly—not the dangerous kind, though he guessed they could all be considered dangerous. But these kinds of Freaks ignored them, stayed away from their part of the underground, and even traded with them now and then. These kinds of Freaks were slow-witted and shy. They could be bad and sometimes scary, but you could live with them.

The Croaks were the ones you had to be careful of. They were the ones who would hurt you.

Something metal clanged sharply in the distance, and the Ghosts froze as one. Long minutes passed as the echo died into silence. Hawk glanced at his wingmen, Panther and Bear, the former sleek and sinewy with skin as black as damp ashes, the latter huge and shambling and as pale as snow. They were the strong ones, the ones he relied upon to protect the others, the fighters. They carried the prods, the solar-charged staffs that could shock even a Lizard unconscious with just a touch.

Panther met Hawk's gaze, his fine features expressionless. He made a sweeping motion with his arm, taking in the surrounding buildings, and shook his head. Nothing from where he stood. Bear had a similar response. Hawk waited a few minutes more, then started them forward again.

Two blocks short of the Hammering Man, at the intersection of

First and Seneca, movement to his left stopped Hawk in his tracks. A huge Lizard staggered out from the dark maw of a parking garage, its head thrown back. It moaned as it advanced up the street toward them, its approach erratic and unfocused. Blood soaked through dozens of rents in the thick, plated skin. As it drew closer, Hawk could see that its eyes had been gouged out.

It looked like it had been through a meat grinder.

Lizards, Moles, and Spiders were mutants, humans whose outer appearance had been changed by prolonged or excessive exposure to radiation and chemicals. Moles lived deep underground, and the changes wrought were mostly in their bone structures. Spiders lived in the buildings, small and quick, with squat bodies and long limbs. Only the Lizards lived out in the open, their skin turned scaly, their features blunted or erased entirely. Lizards were very strong and dangerous; Hawk couldn't think of anything that could do this to a Lizard.

Panther moved over to stand next to him. "So what are we doing? Waiting for that thing to get close enough to hug us? Let's blow like the wind, Bird-Man."

Hawk hated being called Bird-Man, but Panther wouldn't let up. Defiance was too deeply ingrained in his nature.

"Leave it!" Panther snapped when he didn't respond quickly enough. "Let's go!"

"We can't leave it like this. It's in a lot of pain. It's dying."

"Ain't our problem."

Hawk looked at him.

"It's a Freak, man!" Panther hissed.

Bear and the others had closed ranks about them. Their faces were damp, and their hair glistened with droplets of water. Their breath clouded in the cool, hazy air. Rain fell in a misty shroud that obscured the city and left it shimmering like a dream. No one said anything.

"Wait here," he told them finally.

"Shhh, man!" Panther groaned.

Hawk left them grouped together in the center of the street and walked toward the stricken Lizard. It was a big one, well over six feet and heavily muscled. Hawk was slender and not very tall, and the

Lizard dwarfed him. Normally, a Lizard would not intentionally hurt you, but this one was so maddened with pain that it might not realize what it was doing until it was too late. He would have to be quick.

He reached into his pocket and extracted the viper-prick. Tearing off the packaging, he eased up to where the Lizard lurched and shuffled, head turning blindly from side to side as it groped its way forward. Up close like this, Hawk could see the full extent of the damage that had been done to it, and he wondered how it could still even walk.

There was no hesitation as he ducked under one huge arm and plunged the viper-needle into its neck. The Lizard reared back in shock, stiffened momentarily, then collapsed in a heap, unmoving. Hawk waited, then nudged it with his toe. There was no response. He looked down at it a moment more, then turned and walked back to the others.

"You just wasted a valuable store on a Freak!" Panther snapped. His tone said it all.

"That isn't so," River said quietly. "Every living creature deserves our help when we can give it, especially when it is in pain. Hawk did what needed doing, that's all."

She was a small dark-haired twelve-year-old with big eyes and a bigger heart. She had come to them on a skiff down the Duwamish, the sole survivor of a plague that had killed everyone else aboard. Fierce little Sparrow had found her foraging for food down by the piers and brought her home to nest. At first, Hawk hadn't wanted to let her stay. She seemed weak and indecisive, easy prey for the more dangerous of the Freaks. But he quickly discovered that what he had taken for weakness and indecisiveness was measured consideration and complex thought. River did not act or speak in haste. The pace of her life was slow and careful. *She's like a deep river, filled with secrets,* Owl had told him, and he had named her accordingly.

Panther was not impressed. "Nice words, but they don't mean spit. We don't live in the kind of world you keep talking about, River. Most of those creatures you want to help just want to see us dead! They're nothing but frickin' animals!"

Bear leaned in, his blunt, pale face dripping rain. "I don't think we should stand out here like this."

Hawk nodded and motioned them ahead once more. They spread out in the Wing-T without being told, disciplined enough to know what to do. Panther was still muttering to himself, but Hawk paid no attention, his mind on the dead Lizard. If there was something in the city that could take on and nearly kill a Lizard that size, then they needed to be extra careful. Up until now, there hadn't been anything that dangerous to contend with, not counting Croaks. He wondered suddenly if maybe a pack of them had done this, but quickly dismissed the idea. Croaks didn't inflict that kind of damage. No, this was something else—something that had either crawled up out of the deeper parts of the underground or come into the city from another place.

He would ask Owl when they returned. Owl might be able to learn something from one of her books.

They reached the Hammering Man and paused for a quick look, just as they always did. The Hammering Man stood frozen in place, a flat black metal giant with one arm raised and the other outstretched in front of it. The raised hand held a hammer; the outstretched hand held a small anvil. It was a piece of art, Owl said. The building behind it had once been a museum. None of the Ghosts had ever seen a museum except in pictures. This one had long since been looted and trashed, the interior set afire and the windows broken out. The Hammering Man was really all that was left.

Hawk drew them away and turned them uphill toward the city center. The streets were slick with mud and damp. Climbing the sidewalks was slow and treacherous. Candle went down twice, and Bear once. Panther frowned at them and kept going, above such failings. He had worn his hiking boots for better traction. Panther always wore what was needed. He was always prepared.

In another place and time, he might have been leader of the Ghosts. He was bigger and stronger than Hawk, and only two years younger. He was more daring, more willing to take on anything that threatened. But Hawk had the vision, and they all believed that without the vision, you were lost. Owl was wise, Candle blessed with infallible instincts, and Bear steady and strong. Panther was brave. Chalk was talented, Sparrow fierce, and Fixit inventive. All the Ghosts had something that Hawk didn't, but Hawk had the one thing they all needed, so they followed him.

Two streets up, they found the Cats waiting, ten strong, at the appointed meeting place at the intersection of University and Third. Their home was in one of the abandoned condo buildings some-where on the north edge of the city, although Hawk was unsure which one. This was neutral territory, uninhabited by any of the other tribes, a gathering place for all wishing to do business. Trades were how they all lived, each bringing something to the bargaining that the others needed. The Cats had a source for apples and plums. Fresh food of any sort was rare, and the demand for all of it high. Where the Cats found such food was a mystery, although Owl said she thought they must have discovered a small rooftop garden with the apple and plum trees already in place and had simply taken ad-vantage.

Whatever the case, you needed fresh fruit to stay healthy. Owl had studied up on it and told them so. Much of what had once been the diet of their civilization was gone—nearly everything that had been grown on the farms. The compounds still grew their own food, but they were having only mixed success, given the soil and water they had to work with. Most of what the street kids ate was pre-packaged and made edible by adding water and heating. There were certain canned foods you could still eat and bottled liquids you could drink, but these were fast disappearing. Stores of all kinds had long since been raided and cleaned out, and only a few useful ones remained, their locations carefully guarded secrets. The Ghosts had discovered one a couple of years back, and still carried out and stockpiled what they needed from time to time.

What they had brought to trade at this meeting was as precious and as hard to come by as fresh food and was the sole reason the Cats might be willing to give up a portion of their own stash.

"You're late, Hawk," called out Tiger, the Cats' big, muscular leader.

They weren't, of course, but Hawk didn't argue. This was just Tiger's way of marking his territory. "Ready to deal?"

Tiger was wearing his trademark orange-and-black-striped T-shirt beneath his slicker. All of the Cats wore some piece of clothing that was meant to suggest the kind of cat from which they had taken their names, although some of them were hard to decipher. One kid wore pants with vertical blue and red stripes. What was he supposed to be? Panther liked to make fun of them for working so hard at being something they clearly weren't. Real cats were small and sleek and stealthy. The Cats were a jumble of sizes and shapes and might as well be called Elephants or Camels. He was a better cat than they were, he was fond of saying. They didn't even have a "Panther" in their tribe. Besides, they had only started calling themselves Cats and taking cat names after they found out about the Ghosts.

"Ain't nothin' but a bunch of copycats," he would declare, sneering at the idea.

Hawk met Tiger alone in the center of the intersection while the others on both sides stayed where they were. Trades were rituals, marked by protocol and tradition. The leaders met first, alone, talked through the details of the trade, came to an arrangement, and settled on a time and place to make the trade if it wasn't to be done that day. This time both sides had come prepared to trade immediately, having done so often enough before for each to know what the other needed. The Cats would bring their apples and plums and the Ghosts would bring a valuable store to offer in exchange.

"What have you got for us?" Tiger asked, anxious to get to the point of this meeting.

Hawk didn't like being rushed. He brushed back his ragged, short-cropped black hair and looked back down toward the water and the Hammering Man, thinking again of the dead Lizard. "Depends. How much you got for us?"

"Two boxes. One of each. Ripe and ready to eat. Store them in a cool place and they'll keep. You've done it before." Tiger hunched his shoulders. "So?"

"Four flashlights and solar cells to power them. The cells have a shelf life of thirty years. These are dated less than twenty years back." He smiled. "Wasn't easy finding them."

"They still make them twenty years ago?" the other asked suspiciously.

Hawk shrugged. "It says what it says. They work. I tested them myself."

Tiger looked around, maybe searching, maybe killing time. "I need something else."

"Something else?" Hawk stiffened. "What are you talking about, man? That's a fair trade I'm giving you."

Tiger looked uneasy. "I mean, something more. I need a couple of packs of pleneten."

Hawk stared. Pleneten was a heavy-duty drug, effective mostly against plague viruses. No one outside the compounds could get their hands on it unless they happened to stumble on a hidden store. Even then, it usually wasn't any good because it had to be kept cold or it would break down and lose its curative powers. Unrefrigerated, its shelf life was about ten days. He hadn't seen any pleneten in all the time he had been a Ghost.

Except once, when Candle caught the red spot, and he'd had no choice but to ask Tessa.

"It's for Persia," Tiger said quietly, looking down at his feet. "She has the splatters."

Red spot. Like Candle. Persia was Tiger's little sister. The only family he had left. He wouldn't be asking otherwise. Hawk could sense the surfacing of the other's desperation, radiating off him like steam leaking through metal plates, white-hot and barely contained.

Hawk glanced back at the other Ghosts. All expected an exchange to take place and would be disgruntled if it didn't. The fruit was a treat they had been looking forward to. Some of them would understand, some wouldn't.

"Make the trade," Hawk told the other. "I'll see what I can do."

Tiger shook his head. "No, I want the pleneten first."

Hawk glared at him. "It will cost you a lot more if you don't make the trade now. A lot more."

"I don't care. I want Persia well again."

There was no reasoning with him. But Hawk would lose face if he gave in to what was essentially blackmail.

"Make the trade now," he said, "and you can have the pleneten for nothing."

Tiger stared at him. "You serious?"

Hawk nodded, wondering at the same time if he had lost his mind.

"You can get it? You give me your word on it?"

"You know you got my word and you know it's good. Make the trade or you can forget the whole thing. Find someone else to get you your pleneten."

Tiger studied him a moment longer, then nodded. "Deal."

They touched fists, and the deal was done. Both signaled to their followers to bring up the stores, the Cats the boxes of fruit, smaller than Hawk would have liked, but still sufficient, and Candle and River sacks containing the cells and flashlights. The stores were exchanged and their bearers retreated to their respective positions, leaving the leaders alone.

Hawk looked up at the sky. The rain had passed and the clouds were breaking up. It would get hot before long. He shoved his hands in his pockets and looked at Tiger.

"Came across a Lizard down past the Hammering Man on our way here," he said. "A big one. It was all torn up. Dying. What do think could have done it?"

Tiger shook his head. "A Lizard? I don't know. What do you think did it?"

"Something new, something we don't know about. Something really dangerous. Better watch your back."

The bigger boy pulled back the edge of his slicker to reveal a short-barreled flechette hanging from his belt. "Found it a few weeks back. Let's see anything get past that."

Hawk nodded. "I'd be careful anyway, if I was you."

"Just get me that pleneten," the other growled, dropping the slicker back into place. "Tomorrow, same time, same place."

"I need three days."

Tiger glared at him. "Maybe Persia doesn't have three days."

"Maybe that's the best that I can do."

Tiger stared him down a moment longer, then wheeled away to join the other Cats. They slouched off up the street in a tight cluster and didn't look back.

Hawk watched them until they were out of sight, thinking about the bargain he had just made, wondering how he could justify asking Tessa to risk herself yet again when he knew the danger of doing so.

3

CHENEY WAS CURLED up in one corner of the big common room between the old leather couch and the game table, his massive form most closely resembling a giant fur ball, when Owl rolled her wheelchair through the kitchen door and crossed to the bedroom to check on Squirrel. She was aware of one pale gray eye opening as she passed, registering her presence before closing again. Cheney saw everything. She had found the wolfish, hulking guard dog unnerving when Hawk first brought him home, but eventually she got used to having him around. All of them had by this time, even the little ones, all but Panther, who really didn't like Cheney. It was something in Panther's past, she believed, but he wasn't saying what that something was.

In any case, Cheney was important enough to their safety that it didn't matter what Panther thought. Hawk had realized that from the beginning. Nothing got close to their underground hideout without Cheney knowing. He could hear or smell anything approaching when it was still five minutes away. Even the Freaks had learned to stay clear. Although the Ghosts had come to accept him, they were wary of him, too. Cheney was just too big and scary with all that bristling hair and those strange patchwork markings. A junk-yard dog made out of thrown-away parts. But a very large junkyard dog. Only Hawk was completely unafraid of him, the two of them so close that sometimes she thought they were extensions of each other. Hawk had taken Cheney's name from one of Owl's history books. The name had belonged to some long-dead politician who'd been around when the seeds for the Great Wars had been planted. Owl's book described him as a bulldog spoiling for a fight. Hawk had liked the image.

She rolled the wheelchair up the ramp Fixit had built for her and eased herself into the mostly darkened bedroom. Squirrel lay tan-gled in his blankets on his mattress, but he was sleeping. She glanced at Sparrow, who was reading by candlelight in the far corner, keep-ing watch over the little boy. Sparrow looked up from her book, blue eyes peeking out from under a mop of straw-colored hair.

"I think he's doing better," she said quietly.

Owl wheeled over to where she could reach down and feel the boy's forehead. Warm, but no longer hot. The fever was burning it-self out. She exhaled softly, relief washing through her. She had been worried about him. Two days ago, the thermometer had registered his temperature at 106, dangerous for a ten-year-old. They had so few medicines to treat anything and so little knowledge of how to use them. The plagues struck without warning, and any one of them could be fatal if you lacked the necessary medicines. There were vac-cines to protect against contracting most of the plagues, and Hawk had gotten a few from Tessa, but mostly the street kids had to rely on luck and strength of constitution to stay healthy.

The danger of sickness or poisoning was the primary reason that people lived in the compounds. In the compounds, you could mini-mize the risk of infection and exposure. But the compounds held their own dangers, as Owl had found out firsthand. In her mind, if not in Tessa's, the dangers of living inside the compounds clearly outweighed the dangers of living outside.

Which was why she had decided five years ago to take her chances with the Ghosts.

Before that, she had been living in the Safeco Field compound along with two thousand other people. When the Great Wars had escalated to a point where half the cities in the nation had been wiped out and the remainder were under siege from terrorist attacks and plagues and chemical poisonings of all sorts, much of the population began to occupy the compounds. Most were established within existing structures like Safeco, which had been a baseball park decades ago. Sports complexes offered several advantages. First, their walls were thick and strong and provided good protection, once the entrances were properly fortified. Second, they could hold thousands of people and provide adequate storage space for supplies and equipment. Third, all contained a playing surface, which could be converted to gardens for growing food and raising livestock.

At first, the strategy worked well. The measure of protection the compounds offered was undeniable. There was safety in numbers. A form of government could be established and order restored within their walls. Food and water could be better foraged for and more equitably distributed. A larger number of people meant more diversity of skills. When one compound filled up, those turned away established another, usually in a second sports complex. If there was none available, a convention center or even an office tower was substituted, although none of these ever worked quite as well.

The biggest problem with the compounds began to manifest after the first decade, when the once-men started to appear. No one seemed certain of their origin, although there were rumors of "demons" creating them from the soulless shells of misguided humans who had been subverted. Urban legends, these stories could never be confirmed. Some claimed to have seen these demons, though no one Owl had ever met. But there was no denying the existence of the once-men. Formed up into vast armies, they roamed the countryside, attacking and destroying the compounds, laying siege until resistance was either overcome or the compound surrendered in the false hope that mercy would be shown. When word spread of the slave pens and the uses to which the once-men were putting the captured humans, resistance stiffened. But the compounds were not fortresses in the sense that medieval castles had been. Once besieged, they turned into death traps from which the defenders could not escape. The once-men outnumbered the humans. They did not require clean water or good food. They did not fear plague or poisoning. Time and patience favored the attackers. One by one, the compounds fell.

This might have discouraged those hiding in the compounds if there had been anyplace else for them to go. But the mind-set of the compound occupants was such that the idea of surviving anywhere else was inconceivable. Outside the walls you risked death from a thousand different enemies. There were the Freaks. There were the feral humans living in the rubble of the old civilization. There were the armies of the once-men, prowling the countryside. There were things no one could describe, crawled up out of Hell and the mire. There was anarchy and wildness. The humans in the compounds could not imagine contending with these. Even the risk of an attack and siege by the once-men was preferable to attempting life on the outside where an entire world had gone mad.

Owl was one of the people who believed like this. She had been born in the Safeco Field compound, and for the first eight years of her life it was all she knew. She never went outside its walls, not even once. In part, it was because she was crippled at birth, deprived of the use of her legs for reasons that probably had something to do with the poor quality of the air or food or water her mother ingested during pregnancy. After her parents died from a strain of plague that swept the compound when she was nine, she was left orphaned and alone. A quiet and reclusive child, in part because of her disability, in part because of her nature, she had never had many friends. She began living with a family who needed someone to care for their baby. But then the baby died, and she was dismissed and left without a family once more.

She began working in the kitchens of the compound and sleeping in a back room on a cot. It was a dreary, unrewarding existence, but her choices were limited. In the compounds, everyone over the age of ten worked if they wanted to remain. If you did not contribute, you were put out. So she worked. But she was unhappy, and she began to question whether the life she was living was the best she could hope for. She began spending time on the walls, looking at the city, wondering what was out there.

Which was how, five years ago, she had met Hawk.

A growl sounded from the common room. Cheney, head lowered, ears flat, and hair bristling, faced the iron-plated door that opened onto the outer corridors of the underground city. He didn't look like a fur ball now; he looked like a monster. His muzzle was drawn back to expose his huge teeth, and the sleepy eyes of a moment earlier had turned baleful. Owl rotated away from Squirrel and moved her chair back down the ramp and into the common room, where lamps powered by solar cells gave off a stronger light. Sparrow was already there, standing next to Cheney, gripping one of the prods. Sparrow was small, and the big dog, even crouched, stood shoulder-high to her. Owl maneuvered over to the door and waited, listening. Moments later, she heard the rapping sound—one sharp, one soft, two sharp. She waited until it was repeated, then reached up and released the locking bars and unlatched the door.

Fixit and Chalk pushed through, soaked to the skin and looking like drowned rats. Cheney quit growling and took himself out of his crouch. Sparrow lowered the prod.

"He fell in the storm sewer," Chalk announced, gesturing at Fixit.

"Then he fell in trying to help me out," Fixit finished.

"You were supposed to be on the roof," Sparrow pointed out, her blue eyes intense. "The roof is up, not down, last I heard."

"Yeah, yeah." Fixit brushed the water from his curly red hair and shook himself like a dog. Both Cheney and Sparrow backed up. "You can't do much with solar cells when it's raining. We switched out the collectors from the catchment system, threw in the purification tablets, and were done. Then we decided to forage for stores. Found a big stash of bottled water two blocks south. Too much to haul without help."

"It'll take all of us and the wagon," Chalk added. "But a good find, right, Owl?"

"Better than good," Owl agreed.

He grinned, then looked around. "Where are the others, anyway? Aren't they back yet?"

Owl shook her head. "Soon, I expect. You better get out of those clothes and dry off or you'll end up like Squirrel."

"I'd have to be pretty stupid to end up like Squirrel," Chalk declared, and Fixit laughed.

"It's not funny," Sparrow snapped. She crossed to confront them, not as big as they were but a whole lot more unpredictable. "You think it's funny that he's sick?"

"Stop it, Sparrow," Chalk said, turning away from her. "I didn't mean anything. I want him to get well as much as you do. I was just teasing about how it happened."

"Well, tease about something else," Owl suggested gently. "What happened to Squirrel was an accident."

Which was true, so far as it went. It had been an accident that he had cut himself on a piece of sharp metal and that the cut had become badly infected. But he had brought it on himself by trying to salvage a box of metal toy soldiers that Hawk had told him not to touch.

"Besides which, where do you get off calling anyone stupid?" Sparrow demanded.

Chalk was so fair with his pale skin and white-blond hair that he almost wasn't there. Now he flushed with the rebuke and spun angrily back on Sparrow.

"Let it alone, Chalk," Owl said, intervening quickly. "Just go change your clothes. You, too, Fixit. Sparrow, you go back into the bedroom and sit with Squirrel. Let me know if he needs anything."

There were a few more pointed looks and some grumbling, but everyone did as asked. Owl was the mother, and you don't argue with your mother. She hadn't asked for the position, but there was no one else to fill it, and as the oldest female member of the tribe she was the logical choice. Most of them could barely remember their real mothers, but they knew what mothers were and wanted one. Hawk provided leadership and authority, but Owl gave them stability and reassurance. In a world where kids believed that adults had failed them in every important way, other kids were the best they could hope for.

Owl wheeled toward the kitchen, beginning to think about din-

ner. Cheney was back in place between the leather couch and the
game table, eyes closed, flanks rising and fall slowly beneath the
thick mass of his patchwork coat. Owl watched him for a moment,
wondering if he was dreaming and if so what he dreamed about.
Then she angled herself into the makeshift work space that served as
the food preparation area and began rolling out prepackaged dough.
Tonight she would serve them a special treat. Hawk would be bringing back apples, and she would make pie. They lacked electricity, but
could generate sufficient heat to bake from the woodstove Fixit had
built for her.

She thought about the boy for a minute. An enigma, he defied
easy categorization. He was a talented craftsman and mechanic; he
could build or repair almost anything. He had constructed the
makeshift appliances in the kitchen and the generators and solar
units that powered them. He had rebuilt her wheelchair to make it
easier to maneuver and laid down the ramps that allowed her to
reach all the rooms. The catchment systems on the roof were his.
Using scrap and ingenuity, he had constructed all of the heavy security doors and reinforced window shutters that kept them safe. He
claimed to have learned his skills from his father, who was a metal-
worker, but he never talked about his parents otherwise. He had
come to them early, when he was not yet ten but already knew more
than they did about making things.

Now, at fourteen, he was old and capable enough to be given responsibilities reserved for the older members of the tribe, but he had
a problem. As he had proved repeatedly, he was unreliable. He was
fine when he was working under someone's supervision, but terrible
when left on his own—prone to forget, to procrastinate, even to ignore. Sending him out by himself was impossible. The last time they
had done so, he hadn't come back for two days. An old broken-down
machine had distracted him, and he had been trying to find a way
to make it run again. He didn't even know what it did, but that
didn't matter. What mattered was that it was interesting.

His closest friend was Chalk, which made a sort of sense because
they were polar opposites. Chalk was easygoing and incurious, unin-
terested in why anything worked, only that it did. He liked to draw
and was very good at it—hence his name. But he was not a dreamer,

as so many artists tended to be. He was practical and grounded in his life; his art was just another job. Fixit was something of a mystery to him, a boy of similar age and temperament who could make everything run smoothly but himself.

Inseparable, those two, Owl thought. Probably a good thing, since each boy had a steadying effect on the other and neither was much good alone.

She was midway through the piecrust assembly when Cheney scrambled to his feet and stood facing the iron-plated door once again. This time he did not growl, and his posture was alert and unthreatening. That meant Hawk was coming.

Her hands covered with pieces of dough, she called to Sparrow to open the door. Moments later Hawk and the others surged into the room, laughing and joking as they hauled in the boxes of apples and plums and deposited them in the kitchen where some could be separated out and the rest put into cold storage. Chalk and Fixit reemerged, Sparrow wandered out, and soon all of them were gathered in the common room exchanging information on the day's events. Owl listened from the work space as she finished with the crust and began cutting up apples, watching the expressions on their faces, the excited gestures they made, and the repeated looks they exchanged, taking pleasure in their easy camaraderie.

This was her family, she thought, smiling. The best family she could imagine.

But when Panther started talking about the dead Lizard, the good feelings evaporated and she was reminded anew that she lived in a world where having a family primarily meant having safety in numbers and protection from evil. The word *family* was just a euphemism. The Ghosts, after all, were a tribe, and the tribe was always under siege.

She finished with the pie, adding cinnamon, sugar, and butter substitute, stuck the pie in the baking oven, and started making their dinner. Forty minutes later, she gathered them around the work space on their collection of chairs and stools and sat them down to eat. They did what she asked, she their surrogate mother, and they her surrogate children. So very different from her days in the compound, where she had been merely tolerated after her parents died.

Here, she believed, she was loved.

When dinner was over, Bear and River cleared the table, and Sparrow helped her with the dishes. They used a little water from the catchment system, just enough to get the job done. They were lucky they lived in a part of the world where there was still a reasonable amount of rainfall. In most places, there was no water at all. But you couldn't be sure it wouldn't be like that here one day. You really couldn't be sure of anything now.

She had just finished cleaning up when Hawk wandered over to stand next to her. "Tiger says that Persia has the red spot," he said quietly. His dark eyes held her own, troubled and conflicted. "He wants me to get him a few packs of pleneten. I agreed. I had to. Otherwise, he wouldn't have made the trade for the fruit."

"She must be pretty sick. He needs the trade as badly as we do." She folded her hands in her lap. "Will you try to get the pleneten from Tessa?"

He shrugged. "Where else would I get it?"

"We have some. We could give him that."

"We need what we have."

She exhaled softly. "Tessa may not be able to help. She puts herself in danger by doing so."

"I know that."

"When do you see her again?"

"Tomorrow night. I'll ask, see what she can do."

She nodded, studying his young face, thinking he was growing up, that his features were changed even from just six months ago. "We will help Persia even if Tessa can't," she said. "She's only eleven."

Hawk smiled suddenly, a wry twist of his mouth that reflected his amusement with what she had just said. "As opposed to fourteen or sixteen or eighteen, which is so much older?"

She smiled back. "You know what I mean."

"I know you make good apple pie."

"How many other apple pies have you tried besides mine?"

"Zero." He paused. "Can we have our story now?"

She put away the dishes and rolled her wheelchair into the common room. Her appearance from the kitchen was their signal that story time was about to begin. The talking stopped at once, and everyone quickly gathered around. For all of them, it was the best time of the day, a chance to experience a magic ride to another place and time, to live in a world to which they had never been and some-day secretly hoped to go. Each night, Owl told them a story of this world, inventing and reinventing its history and its lore. Sometimes she read from books, too. But she didn't have many of those, and the children liked her made-up stories better anyway.

She leaned back in the wheelchair and looked from face to face, seeing herself in their eyes, a young woman just a little older in years, but infinitely older in experience and wisdom, with brown hair and eyes and ordinary features, not very pretty, but smart and capable and genuinely fond of them. That they cared for her as much as they did never ceased to amaze her. When she thought of it, after her years alone in the compound, she wanted to cry.

"Tell us about the snakes and the frogs and the plague that the boy visited on the evil King and his soldiers," Panther suggested, leaning forward, black eyes intense.

"No, tell us about the giant and the boy and how the boy killed the giant!" Chalk said.

Sparrow waved her hands for attention. "I want to hear about the girl who found the boy on the river and hid him from the evil King."

They were all variations on the stories she had been told as a child, stories that she remembered imperfectly and embellished to demonstrate the life lessons she thought they should know. Her par-ents had told her these stories, reading them from a book that had long since disappeared. She thought she might find the book again one day, but so far she hadn't.

Owl put a finger to her lips. "I will tell you a different story tonight, a new one. I will tell you the story of how the boy saved the children from the evil King and his soldiers and led them to the Promised Land."

She had been saving this one, because it was the resolution of so many of the others involving the boy and the evil King. But some-thing made her want to tell it tonight. Perhaps it was the way she was feeling. Perhaps it was simply that she had kept it to herself long enough. The stories lent strength and promise to their lives when everything around them was so bleak. The gloom weighed heavily on her this night. Persia's sickness and the dead Lizard were just today's darkness; there would be a fresh darkness tomorrow. The stories brought light into that darkness. The stories gave them hope.

She could feel the children edge closer to her as she prepared to speak, could sense the anticipation as they waited. She loved this moment. This was when she felt closest to them, when they were connected to her by their love of words and the stories made from them. The connection was visceral and alive and empowering.

"The evil King had forbidden the boy and his children from leaving their homes for many years," she began, "even after he had suffered over and over again for his stubbornness. No one could reason with him, even after the snakes and the frogs and the deaths of all the firstborn of his people. But one day the King awoke and decided he had endured enough punishment for his refusal and ordered the boy and his children to leave forever and not return. Why should he refuse them permission? What did he hope to accomplish? If they wanted to leave, then they should be allowed to do so. His Kingdom would be better off once they were gone."

"Took him long enough to catch on," Panther declared.

"Bet he changes his mind," said Sparrow.

"He did change his mind," Owl continued. "But not until the boy and his children had packed their few belongings and set out on the road that would lead them to the Promised Land. They walked and they walked, stopping only to eat and sleep. They traveled as swiftly as they could because they were anxious to reach their new home, but they did not have even an old cycle to ride on or any kind of car. So even though they had been gone for a week, they really hadn't gotten very far.

"This was when the evil King changed his mind about letting them go. He had thought about it a lot since they left. He didn't miss them or anything, he just felt like they should have been made to stay where they were. He felt he had been weak in letting them go. Thinking about it made him furious, and so he called his soldiers together and went after them. He had war machines and carriers in which to travel. Nobody walked; everybody rode. The King and his soldiers traveled very fast, and they caught up with the boy and his children in only two days."

She paused, forcing herself not to look at Hawk, not to let him see in her eyes what she was thinking. "The evil King did not know about the boy's vision of the Promised Land. He did not know about the promise the boy had made to his children that he would lead them there and they would live happily ever after. Only the children knew this, and they believed in the vision. They believed in the Promised Land and in the happiness that waited there."

"Like us," Candle said softly. "We believe in Hawk's vision."

Everyone looked suddenly at Hawk, and Owl said quickly, "That's right, we do believe in Hawk's vision. Just as the children in this story believed in the vision of the boy. But the evil King did not believe in visions. He only believed in what he could see with his eyes and touch with his hands. He did not believe in tomorrow. He only believed in today."

"What happened next?" Bear asked.

"The boy and his children reached a river that was too wide and deep for them to cross. Before they could find a way to get around it, the evil King and his soldiers appeared behind them in their war machines and carriers. The boy and his children were trapped. There was no place for them to go, and they knew they would be taken back to their prisons or killed."

"They should fight!" Panther shouted excitedly.

"They should try to swim!" exclaimed Bear.

Owl shook her head. "There were too few of them to fight and the river was too fast for them to try to swim. But just when it seemed that all was lost, that there was no hope for them, the boy held up his arms and the waters of the river parted in front of them, pulling back on either side to form a path across."

"How did it do that?" Fixit asked doubtfully.

"It did it because the river knew of the boy's vision," Owl said. "Rivers are deep in knowledge and hold many secrets. This one knew the secret of the boy's vision. So it let the boy and his children cross over to the other side where they would be safe."

"What about the King? Didn't he try to follow?" Panther was still looking for a fight to take place.

"He did. He took all of his army in their war machines and carriers and went down the same path the boy and his children had taken, determined to catch them and bring them back. But the boy lifted his arms a second time and the waters collapsed on the evil King and his soldiers and drowned them all, every last one."

There was a momentary silence as the children digested this. She gave them that moment, then said, "So the boy led his children away from the river and after two more days, they reached the Promised Land."

"What was it like there?" River asked, huddled on the floor next to Candle, her knees pulled up to her chest.

Owl leaned back in her wheelchair. "That story must wait for another night. It's time to go to bed now." She looked around at the disappointed faces. "Practice your reading until you get sleepy, then blow out your candles. Sweet dreams."

She rolled her chair down forward, stirring them to action. They climbed to their feet grudgingly, some asking for another story, some saying they weren't sleepy, but no one really arguing. Hawk was moving around the room, turning off the lamps, one by one, all but the tiny one that illuminated the heavy entry door. In the old days, one of them would have stood watch all night. Cheney took care of that now.

As the others trudged off to the bedrooms they shared, Owl paused to watch Hawk reach down and ruffle Cheney's thick coat around the neck and ears. The big dog lay quietly, letting the boy pet him. Owl always found herself waiting for the day Cheney would take off his arm.

Candle stopped by her chair and looked her in the eye. "That was *our* story, wasn't it, Owl?" she asked quietly. "The boy's vision was Hawk's vision."

She didn't miss much, this one, Owl thought. "Yes, it was," she said. "But it happened to the boy and his children, too."

Candle nodded. "Except that the vision in the story isn't real, but Hawk's vision is. I know it is. I have seen it."

She turned and walked toward her bedroom, not looking back. Owl felt her throat tighten and tears spring to her eyes.

I have seen it.

Candle, who saw what was not entirely clear to the rest of them, had seen this.

Alone in the common room, Owl sat quietly in her wheelchair, staring into space and thinking, and did not move again until the rest of them were in bed and fast asleep.

4

THE LADY CAME to Logan Tom for the first time in a vision. Even now, he could remember the details as clearly as if the meeting had taken place yesterday. He was alone by then, Michael and the others gone, traveling north toward the Canadian border. He had stopped for the night on the shores of one of a thousand lakes that dotted that region, somewhere deep inside what had once been Wisconsin. The day was gone and night had settled in, and it was one of those rare occasions when the skies were clear and bright and free of clouds and pollution. Stars shone, a distant promise of better times and places, and the moon was full and bright.

He had gotten out of the Lightning and was standing at the edge of the lake, staring off into the moonlit distance, pondering missed chances and lost friends. He was in a place darker than the night in which he stood, and he was frightened that he might not find his way out. He was riddled with misgivings and guilt, wrapped in a fatalistic certainty that his life had come to nothing. His wounds were healed, but his heart was shattered. The faces of those people he had loved most after Michael—his parents and his brother and sister—were vague images that floated in hazy memories and whispered in ghostly, indecipherable warnings.

You have to do something. You have to find a purpose. You have to take a stand.

He was eighteen years old.

A sudden movement in the darkness to his right caused him to glance down the shoreline. A fisherman stood casting into the waters, not twenty yards from where he stood. He watched as the rod came back and whipped forward, the line reeling out from the spool, the filament like silver thread. The fisherman glanced over and nodded companionably. His features were strong and lean in the moonlight, and Logan caught the barest hint of a smile.

"Catching anything?" Logan asked him.

But before the fisherman could reply, there was a noise off to his left, and he wheeled about guardedly. Nothing. The shoreline was still and empty, the woods behind the same.

When he looked back again, the fisherman was gone.

A moment later, he saw a tiny light appear somewhere far out over the water, little more than a soft shimmer at first, brightening slowly to something more definable. The light, diffuse at first, gathered and then began to move, drifting toward the shoreline and him. He stood watching it come, even though he knew he should move away, back toward the AV and safety. He didn't even bother to shoulder the flechette, letting it hang useless and forgotten from its strap across his back. He couldn't have said why. His training and his instincts should have made him react quickly and decisively. Self-preservation should have been his only concern.

Yet the light held him spellbound—as if he realized even then that it was the beacon that would provide him with the direction he sought.

When it was no more than a few yards away, bright enough that he was squinting against its glare, one hand up to shield his eyes, it began to fade, and when it was gone, the Lady was there.

She was young and beautiful, her skin so pure and clear that it seemed to him, in the white cast of the moonlight, he could see right through her. She was dressed in a diaphanous gown that hung in soft folds about her slender body, white like her skin, her long black hair in stark contrast where it tumbled about her shoulders.

She stood several yards offshore—not in the water but upon it. As if it were solid ground, or she weighed no more than a feather.

"Logan Tom," she said.

He stared, unable to reply. He did not think he was hallucinating, but he had no other explanation for what he was witnessing.

"Logan Tom, I have need of you," she said.

She gestured toward the sky, and when she moved her garments rippled like soft shadows and revealed that her perceived translucency was real. She was a ghost—or at least more ghost than human.

"You are meant to be one of mine, one of my brave hearts, one of my great ones. I see it in the way you are revealed by the stars, as immutable and shining as they are. Yours is to be a path of great accomplishment, a path no other has taken before. Will you walk it?"

He started to say no, to back away, to do *something* to break the spell she had cast over him. But even as he made the attempt, she pointed toward him and said, "Will you embrace me, Logan Tom?"

In that instant he heard in her voice a power that he had not thought existed. It wrapped him in chains of iron; it bound him to her as nothing else could. He saw her for what she was; he recognized her vast, ancient power. The stars overhead seemed to brighten, and he would swear ever after that he saw the moon shift in the sky.

He dropped to his knees before her, not knowing why, just doing so, hugging himself against what he was feeling, lost to everything but her last words: *Will you embrace me?*

"I will," he whispered.

"Then you will become my Knight of the Word. As he was, once upon a time."

She pointed to his right, and when he looked the fisherman was back, standing on the shore, casting his line. He made no response to the Lady's gesture and did not turn to look at Logan Tom. It was the same man, but this time Logan understood instinctively who he was and what he was doing there.

He was the ghost of a Knight of the Word.

"It is so," said the Lady.

Logan blinked, then looked back to her. *What do you want of me?* he tried to say, and failed.

Yet she heard him anyway. "The efforts of my Knights to keep the balance of the Word's magic in check have failed. The balance is tipped, and the Void holds sway. Yet this, too, shall pass. You will help to see that this happens. You shall be one of my paladins, my Knights-errant, my champions against the dark things. You will do battle on my behalf and in the name of the Word. Your strength is great, and few will be able to stand against you. In the end, perhaps none."

He licked his lips against the sudden dryness. "I don't know if . . ." His voice shook. "I don't know how to . . ."

"Give me your hand."

She moved closer to him, gliding across the waters, her own hand extended. She approached to within a few feet, and her closeness caused him to shudder. He could feel the heat of her presence, an invisible fire that brightened so that everything else disappeared. He stood alone in the circle of her magic, of her power.

He reached out and took her hand in his own.

Flesh and blood met heat and light, and the contact was sharp and penetrating, and it sent shock waves coursing through Logan's body. He gasped and tried to wrench free, but his body refused to obey him, standing firm against what was happening to it. The shock waves rose and fell, and then disappeared in the face of sudden strength that began to build from within him. He was reborn then, made whole in a way he could not explain, but that embodied fresh determination and courage.

Visions of the future filled his mind, and he saw himself as what he could be, saw those he would impact and where he must go. The road he had been set upon was long and difficult, and it would exact much from him. But it was a road that burned with passion and hope, so bright with possibility that he could not even think now of forsaking the trust that had been given to him.

The Lady released him, a gentle withdrawal of her touch that left him suddenly empty and oddly bereft.

"Embrace me," she whispered.

Without hesitation, he did so.

● ● ●

A SUDDEN LIGHT bloomed in the darkness of the trees off to
his right, causing him to blink, and his memory of that first meeting with the Lady vanished. A second later the light became a fire
burning hot and fierce. No one would light a fire at night in the open
unless it was meant to be a signal.

He squinted against his confusion. Had he dozed off while waiting to discover who he was supposed to be meeting? He wasn't sure,
couldn't remember. One moment he had been thinking back to his
first meeting with the Lady and the next the light had appeared. He
took a moment to reorient himself. He was sitting in the AV, parked
by the side of the road. Ahead, a broken iron crossbar sagged to one
side and the road stretched away through a wide swath of moonlight
to a heavy wood before branching left and right a hundred yards farther on to run parallel to the Rock River. He couldn't see the river,
but he knew from the maps he carried that it was there.

A scarred wooden sign set off to one side reassured him that he
was where he was supposed to be. Sinnissippi Park. His destination.

He turned on the engine and eased the AV ahead past the broken
gate and up the cracked surface of the blacktop road. As he neared
the fire, he saw a solitary figure standing close to it, a silhouette
against the light. He slowed the AV to a crawl and peered in disbelief.

It couldn't be . . .

O'olish Amaneh. Two Bears.

He stopped the Lightning where she was, killed the engine, and
reset the alarms. He took his staff from where it rested against the
seat beside him, opened the driver's-side door, and climbed out.

"Logan Tom!" the last of the Sinnissippi Indians called out to
him. "Come sit with me!"

Two Bears spoke the words boldly, as if it did not matter who
heard them. As if he owned the park and the night and the things

that prowled both. Signaling that nothing frightened him, that he was beyond fear, perhaps even beyond death.

Logan lifted his arm in response. He still didn't believe it. But stranger things had happened. And would happen again before this was through, he imagined.

Cradling the black staff in his arms, he walked forward.

As he drew closer, Logan Tom could see how little Two Bears had changed in ten years. He'd been a big man when Logan first met him, and he hadn't lost any of his size. His strong face and rugged features showed no signs of age, and the spiderweb of lines at the corners of his eyes and mouth had not deepened. His copper skin glistened in the firelight, smooth and unblemished where it stretched across his wide forehead and prominent cheekbones. No hint of gray marred the deep black sheen of his hair, which he still wore in a single braid down his broad back. Even his clothes were familiar—the worn military fatigues and boots from some long-ago war, the bandanna tied loosely about his neck, and the battered knapsack that rested on the ground nearby.

When he reached him, the Sinnissippi took Logan's hand in both of his and gripped it tightly. "You have grown older, Logan," he said, looking him up and down. "Not so young as you were when we met."

"Didn't have much of a choice." Logan gestured with his free hand. "But you seem to know something I don't about how to prevent that from happening."

"I live a good life." Two Bears smiled and released his hand. "Are you hungry?"

Logan found he was, and the two moved over to where the fire burned in an old metal grill with its pole base set into a slab of concrete. Nearby was a picnic table that had somehow survived both weather and vandals. Plates and cups were set out, and eating utensils arranged neatly on paper napkins. Logan smiled despite himself.

They sat down across from each other. Though he had offered it, Two Bears made no effort to prepare any food for them. Logan said nothing. He glanced around the clearing and the wall of night surrounding it. He could not see beyond the glow of the fire. He could not see the AV at all.

"You are safe here," the other said, as if reading his mind. "The light hides us from our enemies."

"Light doesn't usually do that," Logan pointed out. "Is this an old Sinnissippi trick?"

Two Bears shrugged. "An old trick, yes. But not a Sinnissippi trick. The Sinnissippi had no real tricks. Otherwise, they would not have allowed themselves to be wiped out. They would still be here. Eat something."

Logan started to point out the obvious, then glanced down and saw that his plate was filled with food and his cup with drink. He gave Two Bears an appraising look, but the big man was already eating, his eyes on his steak and potatoes.

They ate in silence, Logan so hungry that he finished everything on his plate without slowing. When he had taken the last bite, he said, "That was good."

Two Bears glanced up at him. "Picnics used to be a family tradition in America."

Logan grunted. "Families used to be a tradition in America."

"They still are, even if you and I don't have one." The black eyes looked toward the road. "I see you still drive that rolling piece of armor Michael Poole built for you."

"He built it for himself. I just inherited it." Logan stared at the impenetrable black, seeing nothing. "I think of it as my better half."

"The staff is your better half." The Sinnissippi fixed his gaze on Logan. "Do you remember when I gave it to you?"

He could hardly forget that. It was several weeks after the Lady had appeared to him and he had agreed to enter into service as a Knight of the Word. He was waiting to be told what he must do. But she had not reappeared to him, either in the flesh or in his dreams. She had sent no message. He was frozen with indecision for the first time since Michael died.

Then O'olish Amaneh, the last of the Sinnissippi, arrived, a huge imposing man carrying a black staff carved from end to end with strange markings. Without preamble or explanation he asked Logan his name and if he had accepted his service to the Word, then said that the staff belonged to him.

"Do you remember what you said to me when I told you the staff was yours?" Two Bears pressed.

He nodded. "I asked you what it did, and you said it did exactly what I wanted it to do."

"You knew what I meant."

"That it would destroy demons."

"You could not take it from me fast enough then. You could not wait to put it to use."

He remembered his euphoria at realizing what the staff would enable him to do in his service to the Word. He would do battle on behalf of those who could not. He would save lives that would otherwise be lost. He would destroy the enemies of the human race wherever they threatened. In particular, he would destroy the demons.

He would gain the revenge he so desperately wanted.

It was all he'd wanted then, still so young and naïve. It was the natural response to his rage and pain over the losses he had suffered—of home, family, friends, and way of life. The demons and their minions had taken everything from him. He would track them down, dig them out of their warrens, expose their disguises, and burn them all to ash.

He had been adrift in the world and seeking direction. The Lady had shown him the way. Two Bears had given him the means to make the journey.

"Are you still so eager?" the Sinnissippi asked softly.

Logan thought a moment, then shook his head. "Mostly, I'm just tired now."

"I hear your name spoken often," the other continued. "They say you are a ghost. They say no one sees you coming and no one sees you go. They only know you have come at all by the dead you leave in your wake."

"Demons and their kind."

Two Bears nodded. "They speak of you as they would a legend."

"I'm not that." He shook his head for emphasis. "Nothing like it." He straightened and eased back from the table. "How are things in the wider world? I don't hear much."

"There is little to hear. Things are the same as they have been for many years."

"The compounds still resist?"

"Some do. Fewer now."

"America the Beautiful. But only in the song."

"She will be beautiful again one day, Logan. Cycles come and go. One day the world will be new again."

He spoke with such confidence, with such conviction, that it made Logan's heart ache with his need to believe. Yet everything he knew from his travels, everything he had witnessed, said otherwise.

He shook his head doubtfully. "What about the world right now? What about other countries? What about Europe and Asia and Africa?"

"It is the same everywhere. The demons hunt the humans. The humans resist. Some humans become once-men, some slaves. Some stay free. The struggle continues. What matters is that the human spirit remains strong and alive."

"Then we are improving our chances of winning?"

The big man shook his head.

"Then what exactly *are* we doing?"

"Waiting."

Logan stared at him. "Waiting on what?"

The obsidian eyes pinned him where he was. "That is what we are here to discuss." He rose, his big frame straightening. "Walk with me."

He started to move away from the fire and into the darkness. Logan hesitated, hands tightening on the staff. "Wouldn't it be better if we talked here?"

Two Bears stopped and turned. "Are you afraid, Knight of the Word?"

"I'm cautious."

The big man came back and stood in front of him. "A little caution is a good thing. But I do not think you will need it this night. Come."

He started away again, and this time Logan reluctantly followed. They moved out of the circle of the firelight and into the darkness. At first, Logan could barely see. When his eyes adjusted to the darkness, he realized that they were moving toward the river and the woods that bordered it. He could smell the sickness of the water, even here. The Rock River had gone bad on this stretch decades ago, poisoned first by chemicals and then by dead things.

He glanced off through the trees, searching for hidden dangers, but found only skeletal trunks and limbs. Somewhere distant, he heard an owl. It surprised him. He seldom heard birds these days. Save for the carrion birds, he almost never saw them. Like the animals and fish, their populations had been decimated by the wars.

"The Lady didn't tell me why I was to come here," he said, catching up to the other. "I assumed it was to be another demon hunt."

The big man nodded. "Your assumption was wrong. The truth, Logan, is that you can hunt and kill the demons until you are too old to walk, and they will still prevail. There are too many of them and too few of us. The world has been sliding down a steep slope for many years, and the climb back will be long and slow and painful. A new path must be found."

"What do you mean?"

"I mean that killing demons will not restore the world. Humankind is fighting a war it cannot win."

They walked on without speaking for a time, their footfalls barely audible in the deep silence. Logan tried to absorb what he had just heard and could not make himself do so. Had he just been told that the human race was finished, that no matter what anyone did—the Knights of the Word included—it was over? He could not accept that, he decided. He could accept almost anything else, but not that.

"Are you saying we should just give up?" he asked finally.

The Sinnissippi glanced over at him. "If I tell you to give up, will you do so?"

"No, not ever."

"Then I will not ask it of you."

They reached the bluffs overlooking the Rock. Below them the river wound through its broad channel, silvery and sleek in the moonlight, its clean look belying the reality of its condition. Stunted clumps of dead trees lined the banks on both sides. On the far side, houses sat dark and empty. Once people lived in those houses, families with pets and neighbors and friends, and on nights like these they would laugh and talk and watch television and then sleep peacefully, knowing that when they woke, their world would not have changed.

Logan leaned on his staff. He was hot and stiff, impatient and tired. "What are you trying to tell me? Because I'm not understanding."

Two Bears sat cross-legged on the rocks at the edge of the bluff and peered out across the river. Logan hesitated, then joined him, setting the staff on the ground beside him.

"Look around, Logan." The big man made a sweeping gesture. "This park was beautiful once, a haven watched over and protected by a sylvan, a gathering place for creatures of magic. But it is dead and empty now. No sylvan watches over it. All the sylvans in the world are gone. They were destroyed along with their forests. What will it take to bring them back? What will it take to make the park beautiful again?"

Logan waited a moment, then said, "Time."

"Rebirth." Two Bears looked directly at him. "Do you know what lies in this park? My ancestors. Almost all of them, buried in the earth, right over there."

He pointed to a series of dark mounds visible through the trees not far from where they sat. Logan wondered where this was going.

"I have strong memories of my people, but stronger memories still of a little girl who now also rests here. I met her in this park almost a hundred years ago, when I was younger than I am now." He smiled. "She lived in a house close by the entrance. She was a friend to the sylvan who tended the park. The park was her playground. When she was in it, she was at her happiest. She was followed everywhere by a spirit creature, a huge wolf dog born of magic. The creature, it turned out, was a part of her. Bad and good, it was a part of her. She was the most important human being of her generation, but when I met her, she was still just a girl."

One eyebrow lifted quizzically. "Her name was Nest Freemark. Do you know of her?"

Logan shook his head. "No."

"I found her first, but two others were searching for her, as well.

One was a Knight of the Word named John Ross. The other was a demon. One had come to save her, the other to subvert her. She possessed great magic, Logan. She was the linchpin to the future of the world, able to change the course of history because of who she was and what she might do. She didn't know any of it. She discovered a part of the truth of things over the course of the next fifteen years, but she did not ever know the whole of it."

"Why was she so important?" Logan caught sight of a pair of feeders lurking in the trees and forced himself to ignore them. "Is she the reason we're here?"

Two Bears nodded. "She rests in the cemetery just over the rise, behind the burial mounds of my people. She has been gone from the world for a long time now, but her legacy lives on in the form of a child born to her in the fall of her thirtieth year. It was her only child, a child she hadn't even known she would produce. It was born of magic, a creature of enormous power, her gift to the world we now live in because it is that world's best hope."

"Must be a rather old child by now," Logan observed.

"Almost eighty, but still only a child. It is not a human child—at least, not as we think of human children. It began life as a gypsy morph, a creature of a very powerful, wild magic. Gypsy morphs can assume any shape, take any form. No two have ever turned out exactly the same. Only a handful of morphs are conceived in a human lifetime, and most are never even glimpsed. But John Ross trapped this one on the Oregon coast, and after it had gone through its changes and taken the shape of a small boy, he took it with him to this town to find Nest Freemark. Its purpose in life was to become her child, born to her in the aftermath of the battle that took Ross's life. The morph entered Nest Freemark in one form and emerged in another. Only she knew its origins and its secrets. Only she knew what it really was."

He paused. "Knowing what it was, she kept it apart from the rest of the world, living mostly alone. It stayed with her for a time—we don't know how long exactly—and then it disappeared. I kept waiting for it to resurface, but its time had not yet come. By then, the world was drifting toward anarchy and the seeds of the Great Wars had begun to take root. I searched for the child without success;

wherever it was, it was well hidden. Very few can hide from me, but this one did. I could not track its magic because I could not define what it was. The magic of each gypsy morph, like the morph itself, is unlike that of any other. Wild magic is unpredictable; it may turn out to be either good or evil. The demons sought to capture and make use of this morph, aware of its potential. But Nest Freemark saved it."

Logan looked out across the river. "You're about to tell me that it's reappeared, aren't you?"

Two Bears nodded. "Its time is now, after all these years. Its purpose is known. The Lady has divined it. But it is still a child, still in a child's form with a child's mind. It will know what to do when it is time, but not how to survive until then. It must have help for that. It must have a protector."

Logan sighed. "That would be me?"

"Whoever goes to the aid of this child will be attacked from all sides. The demons will do anything to destroy it or to stop it from fulfilling its purpose. I know of no one better able to withstand the demons than you, Logan. The Lady has made her choice. I think she has chosen well."

The owl hooted softly, closer now. Sylvans had once ridden owls, Logan remembered. Six-inch-tall fairy creatures with long life spans and tiny bodies made of sticks and moss, their given task was to care for trees and plants. He had never seen one. Were they really all gone?

"What makes this child so important? What is it supposed to do?"

Two Bears leaned forward and rested his elbows on his crossed legs. His copper face dipped into shadow. "It is going to save humankind, Logan."

"That's a tall order." He tried to keep the incredulity from his voice. "How is it going to do that?"

The Sinnissippi considered his answer for a moment. "I told you earlier that the climb out of the abyss would be long and difficult. What I did not tell you is that only a few would make that climb. Most will perish in the effort. The demons have won their war against the old world, and no amount of retribution is going to change that. The evil has penetrated to the core of civilization. A fire is coming, huge and engulfing. When it ignites, most of what is left of humanity will vanish. It will happen suddenly and quite soon."

"Sounds biblical." Logan shifted his weight toward the other man. "You're telling me the demons have managed to get their hands on nuclear weapons and intend to use them? On a massive scale?"

The black eyes glittered from out of the shadow of the heavy brow. "What the demons either do not appreciate or do not care about is that it will prove indiscriminate in its destructiveness. Bad and good alike will be consumed. Most of the demons will perish, too."

"That part sounds pretty good. But the morph can prevent all this in some way?"

"No one can prevent it. Nothing can stop it. But the morph has the means to survive it, the means to transcend the destruction and allow a handful of the world's inhabitants to start anew."

"How is it going to do that?"

The Sinnissippi rocked backward slowly. "By opening a door that leads to a safe place."

"For a chosen few?"

"For a scattering of men, women, and children who will find their way to you."

"The remnants of humankind."

"Some. Not all will be human."

Logan hesitated on hearing that, but decided not to pursue it. "Where will the child find this door?"

"The child will know."

Logan felt a keen sense of frustration. Nothing about any of this seemed very clear. "One problem. If you can't find this child, how am I supposed to? I don't have the skills for that."

"You won't need them. You will have its mother's help." He climbed to his feet. "Come, Logan. We will walk some more."

He led the way through the trees and past the burial mounds toward the remains of a wire fence that had long since rusted away into orphan posts and twisted ends. Logan followed the Sinnissippi in silence, but his eyes kept scanning their surroundings. He was still unconvinced that they were as safe as the big man seemed to think. He had spent too many years looking over his shoulder ever to think of himself as being safe. The habits of his lifetime could not be put aside easily.

On the other side of the fence, they found the cemetery. Rows of stone markers in various stages of decay poked up through heavy weeds. Some of the markers had fallen over completely. Many had been vandalized, their inscriptions so badly defaced that they were unreadable. Logan didn't know how cemeteries were supposed to look. No one had used cemeteries since before he was born. But he could envision how this one would have appeared if it had been kept up. It made him sad, thinking of so many lives forgotten. Still, he supposed, you carried your memories of the dead in your heart. That was the safest place for them.

Two Bears took him onto the bluffs, into a smaller section of the cemetery that was divided from the larger by a cracked and buckled blacktop road. They walked through the weeds and grasses and marble and granite stones to a pair of massive oaks. A plain, unadorned marker sat by itself in front of the trees.

The big man stopped and pointed at the marker. Logan stared at the writing. It read:

MARION CASE

Born September 2, 1948
Died March 21, 2018

"Who is Marion Case?" Logan asked.

In response, Two Bears swept his hand in front of the stone, and the old writing melted away to reveal new.

NEST FREEMARK

Born January 8, 1983
Died July 29, 2062
FAST RUNNER

"I disguised it after the wars began, to hide it from those who might do damage even to the dead," the Sinnissippi said quietly.

"Even in her bones, there is great power. Power that should not fall into the hands of the wrong creatures."

Logan glanced over. "What does the inscription mean? *Fast Runner?*"

"She was an Olympic champion in the middle-distance events. She won many times. Even though it wasn't her most important legacy, it had special meaning for her. I came back after she died, buried her, and set this stone in place. I knew her work wasn't finished. But this is where she belongs. Sit with me."

He lowered himself to the ground over the grave site, crossed his legs, and folded his arms. Glancing about first, Logan followed. "What are we doing?"

O'olish Amaneh didn't answer. Instead, he put a finger to his lips to signal for silence. Then he closed his eyes and went very still. Logan watched him, waiting to see what would happen. After a moment, the big man began to chant softly in a tongue that was unfamiliar to Logan and must have been the language of his people. The chant rose and fell, filling the silence with its rolling cadences and sharp punctuation. Logan picked up his staff and held it in front of him, ready for anything. He had no idea what to expect. He worried that the sound of the chanting would bring things he would just as soon avoid.

But nothing appeared, not even the feeders he had seen earlier. After a few anxious moments, he began to relax.

Then tiny lights rose out of the earth, out of the grave itself, and danced on the air before him. The dance went on, the lights spinning and whirling and forming intricate patterns. The dance grew frenetic, and suddenly the lights flared a brilliant white, dropped to the earth like stones, and disappeared. The chanting stopped. Two Bears continued to sit without moving, his breathing quick and labored.

Logan blinked to regain his sight, blinded by that final surge of light. When he could see again, Two Bears was looking over at him. "It is done. She has given us what we need."

He reached down, scooped a scattering of white sticks from the grave, and slipped them into his pocket before Logan could determine what they were. Then he rose and started away. Again, Logan followed obediently.

They returned to the fire and the picnic table, where they seated themselves across from each other. The intensity of the fire had not diminished, even though neither of them had been there to feed it. Logan glanced around the clearing. Everything was as they had left it.

"This is how you will find the child," Two Bears said suddenly.

He laid a piece of black cloth on the surface of the table, spreading it out and smoothing it over. When he had the wrinkles brushed out and the material squared, he reached into his pocket and removed the white sticks, holding them out for Logan to see.

The white sticks were human bones.

"The bones of Nest Freemark's right hand," O'olish Amaneh said softly. "Take them."

Logan decided not to ask the other how he had gotten the bones out of the coffin and the body of Nest Freemark. Some secrets you didn't need to solve. Instead, he did as he was asked, accepting the bones and holding them cupped in the palm of his hand. He was surprised at how light and fragile they felt. He studied them a moment, then glanced questioningly at the big man.

"Now cast them onto the cloth," the other ordered.

Logan hesitated, then scattered the bones over the cloth. For a moment, nothing happened. The bones lay in a jumble, their whiteness stark against the dark surface. Suddenly they began to jerk and twist, and then to slide across the cloth and link together at the joints to form fingers and a thumb.

When they were still again, all five digits were stretched out in the same direction, pointing west.

"That is where you will find the child, Logan," Two Bears said softly. "Somewhere west. That is where you must go."

He gathered up the bones, wrapped them in the black cloth, and gave the bundle to Logan. "The bones will lead you to the child. Cast them as often as you need to. When you have found the child, give it the bones of its mother and it will know what to do from there."

Logan stuffed the cloth and the bones into his jacket. He wasn't sure if he believed all this or not. He guessed he did. The world was a strange place now, and strange things were a regular part of it.

"After I find the child and give it the bones, then what?" he pressed.

"You are to go with it wherever you must. You are to protect it with your life." The Sinnissippi's eyes were strangely kind and reassuring. "You must remember what I said and believe. The child is humankind's last hope. The child is humankind's link to the future."

Logan stared at him a moment, then shook his head. "I'm only one man."

"When in the history of the human race has one man not been enough, Logan?"

He shrugged.

"You will have help. Others will find their way to you. Some will be powerful allies—perhaps more powerful than you. But none will be better suited to what is needed. You are the protector the child requires. Yours is the greatest courage and the strongest heart."

Logan smiled. "Pretty words."

"Words of truth."

"Why don't you do this, Two Bears? Why bother with me? You are stronger and more powerful than any Knight of the Word. Wouldn't you be better suited to this task?"

O'olish Amaneh smiled. "Once, I might have been. Before the Nam and the breaking of my heart. Now I am too old and tired. I am too soft inside. I no longer want to fight. I am filled with the pain and sadness of my memories of the battles I have already fought. The history of my people is burden enough. I am the last, and the last carries all that remains of those who are gone."

Logan folded his scarred hands and placed them on the table. "Well, I will do what I can."

"You will do much more than that," the big man said. "Because there is something else to be won or lost, something of which I have not told you. What is it that you want most in all the world?"

He frowned, a darkness clouding his features. "You know the answer to that. It hasn't changed."

"I need for you to tell me."

"I want to find the demon that led the assault against the compound where my parents and brother and sister were killed."

"If you are successful in your efforts to find and protect the child," Two Bears said softly, "you will have your wish."

He rose and held out his hand. "We are done here, and I must go. Others need me, too."

Logan was staring into space, coming to terms with the promise he had just been given. To find the demon that had killed his family had been his goal since Michael had saved him. It was what he lived for.

Aware suddenly of the hand being offered, he rose and gripped it. "When will I see you again?"

The Sinnissippi shook his head. "You won't in this life. My time is almost over. I will pass with the old world into memory. The new world belongs to others."

Logan wanted to ask if it belonged in any way to him, but he was afraid to hear the answer. "Good-bye, then, O'olish Amaneh," he said instead.

"Good-bye, Logan Tom."

Logan released the other's hand and turned away, walking back toward the Lightning. When he had reached the edge of the circle of firelight, he paused and glanced back. The last of the Sinnissippi had vanished, disappeared as if he had never been. Even the old knapsack was gone.

Logan Tom stared at the clearing with its empty picnic table and burning metal grill, then turned and kept walking.

5

HAWK WOKE EARLY the next morning, restless with anticipation. That night he would meet with Tessa, and meetings with Tessa always made him run hot and cold. He lay quietly on his mattress, staying warm beneath his blanket, thinking of her. As he did so, he listened to the boys sleeping around him, Bear snoring like some great machine while Panther, Chalk, and Fixit added harmonic wheezing sounds. He envisioned the same scene playing out in the other bedrooms, the girls sleeping in the one farthest away, Owl in the middle room with Squirrel, keeping the little boy close until he got better. Cheney would be curled up somewhere out by the entry door, a fly wing's rustle away from coming awake to protect them.

He sat up slowly and stared off through the darkness to where the faint glow of the night candle lit the common room. He liked waking before the others and listening to them, knowing they were all safely together. They were his family and this was their home. He was the one who had discovered it. Had discovered the whole underground city, in fact. Not before the Freaks, but before the other

tribes, the Cats and the Gulls and the Wolves. He had found it five
years earlier while exploring the ruins of Pioneer Square after arriv-
ing in Seattle and quickly deciding he was not going to live in the
compounds. Not that any of them would have taken him in anyway,
another orphan, another castoff. Tessa might have persuaded them
at Safeco, but he had known early on that life in a compound wasn't
what he wanted. He couldn't say why, even now. In part, it was his
abhorrence of the idea of confinement in a walled fortress, a claus-
trophobic existence for someone who had always run free. In part, it
was his need to be responsible for his fate and to not give that responsibility over to anyone else. He had always been independent,
always self-sufficient, always a loner. He knew that, even though the
particulars of his past were hazy and difficult to remember. Even the
faces of his parents were vague and indistinct memories that came
and went and sometimes seemed to change entirely.

It didn't matter, though. The past was of no significance to him;
the future was what mattered. All of the tribes accepted this, but the
Ghosts especially. Their greeting to others said as much: *We haunt
the ruins.* It was a constant reminder of the state of their existence.
The past belonged to the grown-ups who had destroyed it. The future belonged to the kids of the tribes. Those in the compounds did
not understand this, nor would they have accepted it if they had understood. They believed themselves to be the future. But they were
wrong. They were just another part of the problem. Hawk knew
this. He had seen the future in his vision, and the future was
promised only to those who would keep it safe.

His thoughts wavered and broke, and he was left alone with the
darkness and the sounds of the sleepers around him. He sat motionless for a moment longer, then rose and pulled on yesterday's jeans
and sweatshirt. Tonight was his turn to bathe, and tomorrow he
would get a fresh change of clothes. Owl kept them all on a strict
schedule; sickness and disease were enemies against which they had
few defenses.

Dressed, he walked out into the common room to sit where the
candle burned and he could read. But Owl was there ahead of him,
curled up under a blanket on the couch, an open book in her lap.
She looked up as he entered and smiled.

"Couldn't sleep?"

He shook his head. "You?"

"I don't sleep much anyway." She patted the couch next to her, and he sat. "Squirrel's fever broke. He should be up and about by tomorrow. Maybe even yet today, if I let him." She shook her head, her sleep-tousled hair falling into her face. "I think he was lucky."

"We're all lucky. Otherwise we would be dead. Like that Lizard. Like maybe Persia will be if I don't get the pleneten from Tessa." He paused. "Think she'll give it to me?"

He watched Owl's soft face tighten and worry lines appear across her forehead as she considered. He liked her face, liked the way you could always tell what she was thinking. There was nothing complicated about Owl; what you saw was what you got. Maybe that was what made her so good with the others. It made him like her all the more.

"She loves you," Owl said. She let the words hang in the air. "So I think she will get you the medicine if she can." She pursed her lips. "But it is dangerous for her to do so. You know what might happen if she's caught."

He knew. Thieves were thrown from the walls. But he didn't believe such a punishment would be visited on Tessa. Her parents were powerful figures in the compound hierarchy, and she was their only child. They would protect her from any real harm. She might be exiled from the compound, though, if her transgression was severe enough. He would like that, he thought. Then she could come live with him.

"Persia is dying," he said finally. "What am I supposed to do?"

"A child is always dying somewhere." She brushed back the unruly strands of hair from her forehead. "But I believe we must do what we can to stop it from happening—all of us, including Tessa or anyone else who has a chance to help, inside the compounds or not. Just be careful."

She put the book aside, careful to mark her place with a scrap of paper, drawing her withered legs farther up under the blanket as if to find deeper warmth. He glanced over at the dark shape of Cheney sprawled in the corner by the door, thinking that he didn't need to be told to be careful; he was careful all the time anyway.

But he let it pass, his mind on something else. "Why did you tell that story last night?"

"About the boy and the evil King?"

"About the boy leading the children to the Promised Land. What were you doing?"

"Reminding them of your vision. Candle knew that right away. She told me so afterward. Maybe some of the others knew it, too. What difference does it make?"

He shook his head. "I don't know. Maybe it was the way you told it. You changed things. You made things up. It felt like you were stealing."

She stared at him, genuinely surprised. "I'm sorry. Maybe I shouldn't have told it the way I did. But it needs to be told, Hawk, and last night telling it just felt right. I wanted to reassure everyone that we have a goal in our lives and the goal is to find a better, safer place to live. That is your vision, isn't it? To take us to a better place?"

"You know it is. I've said so often enough. I've dreamed it."

She reached out and placed her hand over his. "Your dream is an old one, Hawk. Guiding others to safety, finding the Promised Land. As old as time, I imagine. It has been dreamed and told hundreds of times over the years in one form or another. I don't pretend to know all the particulars of your vision. You haven't shared them with anyone, have you? Not even Tessa. So how can I steal them from you? Besides, I would never do such a thing."

"I know." He flushed, embarrassed by his accusation. "But hearing that story made me uneasy. Maybe its because I don't know enough about what's supposed to happen. I don't know how we'll know when it's time to leave. I don't know how we'll know where we're supposed to go. I keep waiting to find out, waiting for someone to tell me. But my dreams don't. They only tell me that it *will* happen."

"If your dreams tell you that much, then you have to believe that they will eventually tell you the rest." She patted his hand. "I won't tell the story again. Not until you tell me to. Not until you know something more yourself."

He nodded, realizing he was being petty, but at the same time feeling a need to be protective, too. The dream was all he had. It was the bedrock of his leadership, the reason he was able to hold the Ghosts together. Without the dream, he was just another street kid, orphaned and abandoned, living out his life in a postapocalyptic world where everything had gone mad. Without the dream, he had nothing to give to those who relied on him.

"You'll dream the rest one day soon," Owl reassured him, as if reading his mind. "You will, Hawk."

"I know that," he replied quickly.

But, in truth, he didn't.

● ● ●

IT IS TESSA *who brings Owl to him when he is still new to the city and living alone in the underground. He is just fourteen years old, and Owl, who is called Margaret then, is an infinitely older and more mature eighteen. Hawk has gone to meet Tessa for one of their nighttime assignations, and she surprises him by bringing along a small, plain, quiet girl in a wheelchair.*

They are standing in the lee of the last wall of an otherwise collapsed building, not a hundred yards from Safeco, when Tessa tells him what the older girl is doing there.

"Margaret can't live in the compound any longer," she says. "She needs a different home."

Hawk looks at the girl, at the chair, and at the outline of her withered legs beneath a blanket. "It's safer in the compounds," he says.

Margaret meets his gaze and holds it. "I'm dying in there."

"You're sick?"

"Sick at heart. I need air and space and freedom."

He understands her right away, but cannot believe she will be better off with him. "What about your parents?"

"Dead nine years. I have no family. Tessa is my only real friend." She keeps looking at him. "I can take care of myself. I can help take care of you, too. I know a lot about sickness and medicines. I can teach you."

"She is the one you are looking for," Tessa says suddenly.

She cannot walk, Hawk almost says, but keeps the words from slipping out, realizing just in time what sort of judgment he will be passing.

"Tell her what it is you want to do," Tessa presses. "Let her tell you what she thinks."

He shakes his head. "No."

"If you don't, I will."

Hawk flushes at the rebuke. "All right." He speaks without looking at Margaret. "I want to start a family. I don't have a family, and I want one."

"Tell her the rest."

She wants him to speak of his dream. She is determined about this, he sees. She is like that, Tessa.

His gaze shifts back to the older girl. "I want to gather together kids like myself, and then I want to take them away from here to a place where they will be safe." He feels like a small boy as he speaks. The words sound foolish. He has to tell her something more. He takes a deep breath. "I saw that I would do this in a dream," he finishes.

Margaret doesn't laugh at him. Her expression does not change at all, but there is a flicker of recognition in her eyes. "You will be the father, and I will be the mother."

He hesitates. "You believe me?"

"Why shouldn't your dream be as real as anyone else's? Why shouldn't you do what you say you will? Tessa says you're special. I know what she means. I can tell by looking at you. By listening to you. I don't have dreams anymore. I don't even have hope. I want both again. If I come with you, I think I will find them."

He shakes his head. "It is dangerous in the ruins, outside the compound walls. You know what's out there, don't you?"

"I know."

"I can't be with you all the time. I might not be there to protect you when you need it."

"Or I you," she replies without blinking. "Life is a risk. Life is precious. But life has to be lived in a way that matters. Even now." She reaches out her hand. "Take me with you. Give me a chance. I don't ask for anything else. If you decide it isn't working out, you can bring me back or leave me. You are not bound to me. You owe me nothing."

He does not believe this for a moment, knowing that if he agrees to take her with him, he is accepting responsibility for her on some level. But the force of her plea moves him. The intensity of her eyes captivates

*him. He sees strength in her that he has not often found, and he believes
it would be a mistake to underestimate it.*

"She does not belong in the compounds," Tessa says quietly.

"Nor do you."

*But in the end it is Margaret who goes with him and Tessa who stays
behind.*

● ● ●

IT WAS MIDMORNING when he departed with Cheney for the
waterfront. The day was overcast, but not rainy, the air thick with
the taste of chemicals and the smell of putrefaction. The wind was
blowing off the water, the ocean waste spills making their presence
known. It was like this on the coastlines when the wind was blowing the wrong way. The spills, which had taken place even before
the start of the wars, had all but overpowered the natural cleansing
ability of the oceans and left millions of square miles fouled. Their
poisons were dissipating, but the detritus washed back up regularly
through the estuaries and inland passages to clog the shorelines and
remind the humans that the damage they had done was mostly ir-
reparable. Some of those poisons were carried onshore by the wind,
which was what Hawk could taste on the air. He closed his mouth,
put a cloth over his face, and tried not to breathe.

A futile effort, he knew. The poisons were everywhere. In the
air, the water, and the land, and the things that lived in or on all of
it. There was no escaping what had been done. Not for the humans
alive now. Maybe for those who would be born a hundred years
down the road, but Hawk would never know.

He had waited with Owl until the others awoke, eaten
breakfast—a meal consisting of oatmeal, condensed milk, and sugar,
all of it salvaged from packaging that time and the weather had not
eroded—then called the others together to give them their marching orders. Panther was to take Sparrow, Candle, and Fixit and try to
retrieve the stash of bottled water that the latter had discovered
with Chalk on the previous day. Bear was to take Chalk up on the
roof and retrieve the water storage cylinders, which would have ab-

sorbed their purification tablets by now. River was to stay with Owl to help look after Squirrel. He had given strict warning that no one was to go outside alone or to become separated from the others if out in a group. Until they found out what had done such terrible damage to the Lizard they had stumbled across yesterday, they would assume that everyone was at risk.

"So that changes things how?" Panther had sniffed dismissively as he headed out the door.

Hawk had waited until Panther's group was gone and Bear and Chalk had departed for the roof, then warned Owl again to keep the door barred until she was sure who was on the other side. Just to be certain, he had waited on the other side of the metal barrier until he heard the heavy latch click into place.

Now he stood outside in the street, waiting while Cheney relieved himself, thinking of the dead Lizard, still bothered by the mystery behind the damage it had incurred and determined to find out what had caused it. To do that, he needed to visit the Weatherman. The sky had turned darker and more threatening, as if rain were on the way. And it might be, but it was unlikely. Days like this one came and went all the time, gray and misty and sterile. Rain used to fall regularly in this city, but that wasn't true anymore. Nevertheless, he wore his rain jacket, the one Candle had found for him. In one pocket, he carried a flashlight; in the other, two of the viper-pricks. It was always best to be prepared.

He looked around for a moment, seeking out any signs of movement, found none, and headed downhill for the waterfront, Cheney leading. The bristle-haired dog padded along with his big head lowered and swinging from side to side, his strange walk familiar to the boy by now. It might seem as if Cheney weren't entirely sure where he was going, but the look was deceptive. Cheney always knew where he was going and what was in the way. He was just keeping watch. Cheney knew more than any of them about staying alive.

He had found the big dog when he was a burly puppy, foraging for food in the remains of a collapsed building in the midtown, half starved and unapproachable. The puppy growled at him boldly, warning him off. Intrigued, Hawk knelt and held out a scrap of dried meat he was carrying, then waited for the dog to approach. He watched him for a very long time without doing anything, gray eyes baleful and hard and suspicious. Hawk waited, meeting the other's dark gaze. Something passed between them, an understanding or recognition, perhaps—Hawk was never sure. Eventually, the puppy came a bit closer, but not close enough to be touched. Hawk waited until he was bored, then threw him the meat, turned, and started off. He had other things to do and no place in his life for a dog, in any case. He had only just brought Sparrow and Fixit into the underground to join Owl and himself, the start of his little family, and finding food for the four of them was a big enough problem without adding a dog to the mix.

But when he had looked back again, the puppy was following him, staying out of reach but keeping close enough so that he would not lose sight of him. Three blocks later, he was still there. He tried to shoo him away, but he refused to leave. In the end, his persistence won him over. He had stayed with him all the way back to the entrance to the underground, but refused to come inside. Finding him still there the following morning, he had fed him again. This had gone on for weeks until one day, without warning, he had decided to go down with him. On reaching their home, he had looked around carefully, sniffed all the corners and studied all four kids, then picked out a corner, curled into a ball, and gone to sleep.

After that, he had stayed with them inside. But he had never become friendly with anyone but Hawk. He allowed the others to touch him, those bold enough to want to do so, but he kept apart except when Hawk was around. The boy couldn't explain Cheney's behavior, other than to attribute it to the fact that he was the one who had found the dog when he was a puppy and fed him, but he took a certain pride in the fact that Cheney, to the extent that he was anyone's, was clearly his.

He glanced over at the big dog now, watching the way he scanned the street, sniffed the air, kept his ears perked and his body loose and ready. Cheney was no one to mess with. He was big to begin with, but when he felt threatened he became twice as big, his heavy coat bristling and his muzzle drawing back to reveal those huge teeth. It wasn't just for show. Today Hawk was carrying one of the prods for protection. But once, when he wasn't, less than a year after he had found Cheney, he had gotten trapped in an alley by a

pair of Croaks—zombie-like remnants of human beings who had ingested too much of the poisons and chemicals that had been used in
the terrorist attacks and misguided reprisals that followed. Half
dead already and shut out of the compounds, the Croaks roamed
the streets and buildings and waited to die. Croaks were extremely
dangerous. Even the smallest scratch or bite from one could infect
you. This pair was particularly nasty, the sum of their rage and frustration directed toward Hawk when they saw he couldn't escape
them. But they were so intent on the boy that they hadn't noticed
Cheney. It was a fatal mistake. The big dog had come up on them in
a silent rush and both were dead almost before they realized what
had happened, their throats torn out. Hawk had checked out Cheney
afterward, fearing the worst. But there wasn't a mark on him.

After that, Hawk was convinced that Cheney was worth his sub-
stantial weight in daily rations. He quit worrying when he had to
leave Owl and the smaller children alone. He quit thinking that he
was the only one who could protect them.

The street sloped downhill in a smooth, undulating concrete
ramp that was littered with car wrecks and debris from collapsed
buildings. On one side lay a pile of bones that had been there for as
long as he could remember. You didn't see bones often in the city;
scavengers cleaned out most of them. But for some reason no one
wanted any part of this batch. Cheney had never even gone over to
sniff them.

Ahead, the waterfront opened up in a series of half-collapsed
wooden piers and ruined buildings that left the concrete breakwater
and pilings exposed. The waters of the sound spread away in a black,
oily sheen clogged with refuse and algae, disappearing offshore in a
massive fog bank that hung from clouds to earth like a thick, gauzy
curtain. There was land beyond the fog, another piece of the city
that stuck out south to north in a hilly peninsula dotted with houses
and withered trees. But he seldom saw it these days, for the fog kept
it wrapped tightly, a world far removed from his own.

He reached the waterfront and stood looking about for a moment, Cheney working his way in front of him, left to right, right to
left, nose to the ground, eyes glittering in the thin light. Left, the

steel skeletons of the shipping cranes rose through the mist like dinosaurs frozen in time, dark and spectral. Right, the buildings of the city loomed over the dockside, their windows thousands of black, sightless eyes whose glass had long ago been broken out. The waterfront itself was littered with old car hulks and pieces of the buildings that had come down with the collapse of the piers and the concrete viaduct that had carried traffic through the city long ago. A dark figure moved in the shadows of a building front, one of the few still standing, there for just an instant, then quickly gone. Hawk waited in vain for another look. It was something more scared of him than he was of it.

He started down the waterfront toward the places where the Weatherman could usually be found. He kept to the open spaces, away from the dark openings and rubble where the bad things would sometimes lie in wait. Croaks, in particular, were unpredictable. Even with Cheney present, a Croak would attack if given a chance. Of course, anything would attack street kids because they were the easiest of prey.

He had walked perhaps a hundred yards north when he heard the Weatherman singing:

A tisket, a tasket,
The world is in a casket.
Broken stones and dead men's bones,
All gathered in a basket.

The Weatherman's voice was thin and high and singsong in a meandering sort of way that suggested his mind wasn't fully focused on what he was doing. Hawk suspected the old man's mind hadn't been fully focused on anything for years. It was a miracle that he had survived this long on the streets, alone and unprotected. Almost no adults lived outside the compounds; only kids and Freaks lived on the streets.

Mary had a little lamb, little lamb, little lamb.
Sweet and kind and slow of mind, it really didn't know.

That everywhere that Mary went, Mary went, Mary went.
Everywhere that Mary went, bad things were sure to go.

"Which accounted for its untimely demise the day Mary decided to visit the waterfront and ran into the big, bad wolf. Hello, Brother Hawk."

The Weatherman emerged from the shadow of a partially collapsed building along the dockside, his ravaged face like something out of a nightmare—the skin pocked and mottled, the strange blue eyes as mad as those of any Croak, and the wispy white hair sticking out in all directions. He wore his trademark black cloak and red scarf, both so tattered it was a wonder the threads still managed to hold together.

"Are you the wolf that Mary should have stayed away from?" Hawk asked him. You never knew for sure what the Weatherman was singing about.

The old man hobbled over to him, giving Cheney a passing glance but showing no fear. Cheney, for his part, kept his gray eyes fixed on the scarecrow but did not growl. "Hadn't given it much thought. Do you think I might be?"

Hawk shrugged. "I think you're the Weatherman. But you could be a wolf, too."

The old man came right up to him. He reeked of the streets, of the waterfront smells, of the poisons and the waste. His eyes were milky and his fingers bony as he lifted them to his scraggly beard and tugged on it contemplatively.

"I could be many things, Brother Hawk. But I am only one. I am the Weatherman, and my forecast for you this day is of dark clouds and cold nights and of a heavy wind that threatens to blow you away." The mad eyes fixed on him. "My prediction calls for a Ghost watch. Keep a weather eye out, boy, until I have a chance to provide an update."

Hawk nodded, not understanding at all. He never understood the Weatherman's predictions, but out of politeness he pretended he did. "We came across a Lizard yesterday. It was all torn up. You know something out there that could do that, Weatherman?"

The ragged head cocked and the gaunt face tightened. "Something searching for food or establishing its territory. Something like us. The times we live in—who would have believed they would come to pass? Do you know, Brother Hawk, that this city was beautiful once? It was green and sparkling, and the waters of this bay were so blue and the sky so clear you could see forever. Everything was lovely and new and filled with color and it could hurt your eyes just to look at it."

He smiled, the gaps in his teeth showing black and empty. "I was a boy like you, long ago. I lived over there, beyond the mist." He pointed west, glanced that way as if he might see something of his past, and then looked back at Hawk, his face stricken. "What we've done! What we've allowed! We deserve what's happened to us. We deserve it all."

"Speak for yourself," Hawk said. "I didn't do anything to deserve this. The Ghosts didn't do anything. Grown-ups did. Tell me what you know about the Lizard."

But the Weatherman wasn't ready to move on yet. "Not all grown-ups are bad, Hawk. Never were. Not all are responsible for what happened to the world. Some few were enough to cause the destruction—some few with power and means. It was different then. Do you know that people could speak with each other and see each other at the same time through little black boxes, even though they were thousands of miles away? Did you know they could project images of themselves in the same way?"

Hawk shook his head. "Owl reads to us about that stuff, but what's the difference? That's all gone now, all in the past. What about the Lizard?"

The old man stared at him as if he couldn't believe what he was hearing, then nodded slowly. "I guess it really is gone. I guess so." He shook his shaggy head. "Hard to believe. Sometimes I think about it as if it never really happened. An old man's dreams."

He sighed. "There are things coming out of the earth, Brother Hawk. Things big and dark, birthed by the poisons and the chemicals and the madness, I expect." One eyebrow cocked. "Haven't seen them myself, but I've seen evidence of their passing. Like your

Lizard, a whole nest of Croaks, down by the cranes at the south end, torn to pieces. They fought back, but they were no match for whatever got them. That sound similar?"

Hawk nodded. Most creatures simply avoided Croaks, especially if there were more than one. What would attack several and not be afraid?

The Weatherman bent close. "It's not safe in the city anymore. Not on the streets and not in the buildings. Not even in the compounds. There's a change in the weather coming, Brother Hawk, and it threatens to sweep us away."

"It won't sweep me away," Hawk snapped, angry at having to listen to yet another bleak prediction. His lean face tightened and his patience slipped. "You make these forecasts, Weatherman, like they don't have anything to do with you. But you're on the streets, too. What are you going to do if one of them comes true?"

The other's smile was gap-toothed and crooked. "Take shelter. Ride it out. Wait for the storm to pass." He shrugged. "Of course, I'm an old man, and old men have less to lose than boys like you."

"Everyone has a life to lose, and once it's gone, that's it." Hawk didn't like what he was hearing. The Weatherman never talked about dying. "What kind of weather are you talking about, anyway?"

The old man didn't seem to hear. "Sometimes it's best to get far away from a storm, not try to ride it out."

Hawk lost the last of his patience. "I'll be leaving here one day soon, don't you worry! Maybe I'll leave now! I'll just pack up and go! I'll take the Ghosts out of this garbage pit and find a new home, a better home!"

The words came out of his mouth before he could stop himself. He didn't really mean to speak them, but the old man was always predicting something dire, always forecasting something awful, and this time it just got to him. What was the point, after all? How much worse could things get than they were now?

The Weatherman didn't seem to notice his distress. He turned away and looked off into the mist that hung over the bay. "Well, Brother Hawk, there's better places to be than here, I guess. But I don't know where they are. Most of the cities are ruined. Most of the country is dust and poison. The compounds are the way of things now, and they won't last. Can't, with what's coming. The worst hasn't reached us yet, but it will. It will."

Hawk shifted his feet, suddenly anxious to be gone. He glanced around the waterfront, then back at the old man. "You better watch out for yourself," he said. "Whatever's out there in the city isn't anything you want to run across."

The Weatherman didn't reply. He didn't even look around.

"I'll come back down in a few days to see if you've seen anything else."

No response. Then suddenly, the old man said, "If you leave, Brother Hawk, will you take me with you?"

The question was so unexpected that for a moment Hawk was unable to reply. He didn't really want to take the old man with him, but he knew he couldn't leave him behind.

Taking a deep breath, he said, "All right. If you still want to come when it's time." He paused. "I have to go now."

He walked back down the dockside, unhappy with himself for reasons he couldn't define, irritated that he had come at all. Nothing much had been accomplished by doing so. He glanced over at Cheney, who was fanned out to his right, big head lowered and swinging from side to side.

From behind him, the thin, high voice tracked his steps.

Happy Humanity sat on a wall.
Happy Humanity had a great fall.
All of our efforts to put him to mend
Couldn't make Happy be human again.

Without looking back, Hawk lifted his arm in a wave of farewell and walked on through the mist and the gray.

6

AFTER HIS MEETING with Two Bears, Logan Tom climbed back into the Lightning AV and drove it out into the country to a spot off the road where the prairie stretched away in an unobstructed sweep on all sides. There he parked, set the perimeter alarm system, crawled into the back of the vehicle, and fell asleep. His sleep was deep and dreamless, and when he awoke at dawn he felt fresh and rested in a way he hadn't felt for weeks. He stripped naked outside the AV in the faint light of first dawn and took a sponge bath using water from the tank he carried in the back. The water was purified with tablets, clean enough for bathing if not for drinking. No one had drunk anything but bottled liquids in years, and when the stockpiles that remained were exhausted, it was probably over for them all.

Dressed, he ate a breakfast of canned fruit and dry cereal, sitting cross-legged on the ground and staring out across the empty fields, his back against the AV. On the horizon, the windows of the farmhouses and outbuildings were black holes and the trees barren sticks.

As he ate he thought about Two Bears, the task the Sinnissippi had given him to accomplish, and the impact of what it meant. In particular, he thought about something O'olish Amaneh had said and passed over so quickly there hadn't been time to take it in fully until now.

A fire is coming, huge and engulfing. When it ignites, most of what is left of humankind will perish. It will happen suddenly and quite soon.

Logan Tom stopped chewing and stared down at his hands. It wouldn't matter what any of them did after that, demons or humans. If he was to make a difference as a Knight of the Word—if anyone was to make a difference—it would have to happen before that conflagration consumed them all. That was what Two Bears was telling him; that was the warning he had been given. Find the gypsy morph and you find a way to save the remnants of humankind from what is coming.

He wasn't sure he believed that. He wasn't sure he knew what he believed. It seemed to him that the world had already come to an end for all intents and purposes, that even a conflagration of the sort the Sinnissippi was foretelling couldn't make things worse. But he knew as soon as he thought this that it wasn't true. Things could always get worse, even in a world as riddled by madness as this one.

He finished his breakfast, took out the finger bones of Nest Freemark, and cast them on the black square of cloth in which they had been wrapped. The bones lay motionless for a moment, then began to wriggle into place, forming up as fingers. Creepy. He watched them shift until they were pointing west. He stared down at them for a few moments longer, then scooped them up and stuffed them back in his jacket pocket. He had his marching orders; he might as well get started.

He drove slowly through the early morning, following the broken ribbon of highway across the remainder of the state under overcast and hazy skies. It was not yet midday when he reached the Mississippi River. The waters of the Mighty Miss flowed thick and sluggish between their defoliated banks, the waters clouded and gray and choked with debris. He could see the shells of old cars and trucks jammed up against the far bank. He could see parts of houses and fallen trees. He could see bodies. He could smell death and decay, a heavy sickening odor hanging in the windless air. He shifted his gaze to the bridge again, a broad concrete span stretching ahead into Iowa.

The bridge was littered with bodies.

The smell wasn't coming from the dead in the river; it was coming from up there.

He stared in disbelief for a moment, not sure that he was seeing things correctly. The makeshift crossing gate told him that this had been a checkpoint for the river, a place staffed by militia serving some local order or other. But the number of bodies and abandoned vehicles and accumulation of debris told him that everyone had been dead for a while now. It told him, as well, that the end had come suddenly.

He took a moment to scan his surroundings in all directions, cautious of what might be hidden there. Finding nothing, he eased the S-150 ahead in a crawl, weaving carefully through the makeshift obstacle course that blocked his path. On the bridge, nothing moved. He began to cross, passing bodies with arms and legs flung wide, fingers clutched in agony, heads thrown back and necks stretched taut. Then he saw the first of many faces turned black and leathery, and he knew.

Plague.

This strain was called Quick Drain for the speed with which it stole life from the body. It was carried on the air, a human-made recreation of what centuries earlier had been labeled the Black Death. It was chemically induced, contracted through the lungs, and fatal in less than an hour if you weren't inoculated against it beforehand or treated afterward at once. From the quickness with which it had obviously overtaken those on the bridge, it must have been a particularly virulent variety. It would have dissipated by now, its life span short once released. There was no way of knowing where it had come from, whether released on purpose or by accident, whether by attack or mistake. It was deadly stuff; he had seen the results of its work several times before when he was still with Michael.

He drove on, trying not to breathe the air, even though he knew it didn't matter by now. He drove on, and as he did so his thoughts drifted to an earlier time.

• • •

HE LIES IN *his bed, so hot he can barely stand his own body. Sweat coats his skin and dampens his sheets. Pain ratchets through his muscles in steady waves, causing him to jerk and twist like a puppet. He grits his teeth, praying for the agony to stop. He no longer cares if he lives or dies; he will accept either fate willingly if only to put an end to the pain.*

His eyes are squeezed shut, but when they blink open momentarily he is still in darkness. He hears voices drift through the partially opened doorway from the adjoining room.

". . . should be dead anyway . . . fever too high . . . can't understand what's keeping him . . ."

". . . tougher than you . . . seven days now, when anyone else would . . . just keep him warm and . . ."

One of them is Michael Poole, the other Michael's companion, Fresh. But which is which? He cannot tell. The fever clouds his thinking, and he can't match the voices to the names. It is ridiculous. He knows Michael the way he knows himself, has been with him now for almost eight years. He knows Fresh almost as well as Michael. But the voices blend and the words shift so that they seem one and the same.

". . . recovery from this doesn't happen . . . as you know better than most . . . better to let things take their course instead of flailing about with all these . . ."

The voice drones on, lost in the buzzing in his ears, in the hiss of his own breath through his clenched teeth, in the sweep of his jumbled thoughts. He has the plague. He doesn't know which strain and doesn't care. He has had it for days. He can't remember how he contracted it or what has happened since. He drifts in and out of consciousness, out of dreams and into reality and back again, always fighting for breath because his throat is so swollen that his windpipe has all but closed up. The pain keeps him breathing because it keeps him awake and fighting for his life. If he sleeps, he thinks, he will lose consciousness and die. He has never been so afraid.

"... have to move camp soon ... close, and no stopping them once they know ..."

"... can't just leave him to die alone ... know what they would do, animals ..."

"... what do you expect us to do if things don't ... sacrifices have to be made ... one against the many ..."

He hears only these snippets, but he gets the gist of the conversation nevertheless. They are arguing over what to do with him, still so sick, perhaps contagious to the others, a danger to them all. They need to move camp because they are threatened anew by the demons that track them, searching constantly for a way to trap them once and for all. One of them is arguing for leaving him behind, the way they have been forced to leave others—for the good of the whole. One of them is arguing for waiting to see if his constitution is strong enough to pull him through. The argument is low-key and rational, not heated and intense. He finds it odd that the matter of his living or dying is being talked about so calmly. He wants to tell them how he feels about it. He wants to scream.

Suddenly there is silence. He squints through a tiny gap in his eyelids and sees that the light in the doorway is blocked. They are standing there, looking at him. He tries to speak, but the words become lodged in his throat and emerge as groans. The pain sheets through him, and he shudders violently.

"See?" says one.

"See what? He fights it."

"A losing fight. It consumes him."

"But hasn't yet overpowered him."

They move away, leaving him alone again, feeling abandoned and betrayed. Which of the two wants to save him and which wants to leave him behind? They are his closest friends, but one of them argues for his death. His eyes sting with tears, and he is crying. This is what dying is like, he thinks. You do it alone. You are debased by it. You are exposed to your own weaknesses and to the harsh reality of what it means.

He draws a deep, pain-filled breath that is mostly a sob and waits for his life to end.

● ● ●

BUT HE DIDN'T die that night. The fever broke, and by morning he could be moved. He was weak still, but he was healing. Michael and Fresh came to him and told him how encouraged they were by his recovery. They reassured him that everything would be all right. He still didn't know which of them had argued for leaving him behind—had given him up for dead. He told himself at the time that it must have been Fresh, that Michael would never abandon him. But he couldn't be sure. Especially now, knowing what he did about what would happen with Michael later.

It was odd, the way he felt about Michael. His parents would never have left him, not even if it had cost them their lives. Yet he remembered them only vaguely, more indistinctly with the passing of every day. He recalled his brother and sister even less well; their faces had become faint images, blurred around the edges and leached of color. Yet he remembered Michael as if he were still there—the strong features, the wide, sloped shoulders, the sound of his deep voice as clear as yesterday's meeting with Two Bears. Even now, Logan knowing what he did, Michael retained his larger-than-life image. He knew it had something to do with the amount of time he had spent with Michael, the impression Michael had made on him while he grew, and the impact of Michael's strong personality. Yet he had never loved Michael as he had his blood family. He had never been as sure of Michael as he was of them. It didn't seem right that it should be this way, but there was no help for it.

The buildings of the city slipped away on either side of him. There were more bodies in the streets, and the smell of death was everywhere. There was no movement in the shadows of the buildings, no sign of life. According to his sensors even the feeders had departed, a sure sign that nothing remained. He scanned doorways and windows, alleyways and side streets as he made his way through, but the city was deserted.

He came out the other side at midday, the weather turned gloomy and the skies dark with heavy roiling clouds. Maybe it would rain today, although he doubted it. The skies frequently looked as if they might open up, but they seldom did.

He drove through the outskirts of the city, past endless dwellings, past schools and churches. There was no one anywhere. When plague struck, you didn't take chances; you got out. Not that there was much of anywhere to go, but fleeing sickness and chemical attacks and armed strikes was pretty much instinctual. You ran because it was your last defense against things too overpowering to try to stand and face.

It wasn't always so. In the beginning, men had stood their ground, even in the face of certain destruction. It had been in their nature to stand and fight, to refuse to be intimidated, to give their lives for what they believed. Even when governments began to disintegrate or simply vanished altogether, the people stood fast. Their faith would protect them, they believed. Their courage was a shield against the worst of it. But they were wrong, and in the end most of them died. The ones who survived were the ones who understood that while faith and courage were necessary, they weren't enough. Good judgment and sound reasoning had to be exercised as well. When the world was collapsing around your ears, you had to know when to stand fast and when to turn and run. There was a time and a place for both.

Even for him. Even for a Knight of the Word.

He pulled off the road at the edge of the city into what had once been a small park and was now a barren stretch of ground with a few broken picnic tables and some rusted playground equipment. Parked with the hood of the Lightning facing west, he sat in the vehicle and ate his lunch. Eating no longer held much pleasure for him. The food was prepackaged and uninteresting. He ate to keep strong and to stay alive. It was the same with sleep, which was rough and troubled. He slept because he had to and wouldn't have otherwise because he hated the dreams that surfaced like phantoms, dreams of his past, reminders of the madness he had endured. But it did not matter what he wanted; the dreams were an unpleasant fact of his life.

As was so much, he thought. As was almost everything.

He was still eating when the men appeared from behind him. He had forgotten to set the perimeter alarms on the S-150 and was lost in his thoughts when they materialized suddenly on either side of the vehicle, their weapons pointed at him. They had crept up on him like predators, careful to mask their approach and to take their time. It didn't hurt their efforts that he had been so self-absorbed, he'd failed to pay attention to his surroundings. They were a sorry-looking lot, soiled and ragged and smelling of sweat. They carried a mix of rifles and handguns, older weapons from before the rise of the once-men. They smiled as they surrounded him, satisfaction a bright gleam in their mad eyes. They had caught him unprepared and they knew it.

Stupid, he chastised himself. *Stupid and careless.*

"Get out," the one standing next to him ordered, touching him on the shoulder with a long-barreled automatic.

He already had his right hand on his staff as he opened the door with his left and levered himself out of the Lightning, pretending that he needed the staff for support. He limped away from the vehicle, glancing from one man to the other, counting heads. There were four of them—hard-featured and wild-eyed, looters and thieves. They would shoot him without a second thought if he gave them even the slightest excuse. They would shoot their own mothers.

"We're confiscating your vehicle for official purposes," said the speaker, keeping the automatic leveled on him.

"Iowa militia?" he asked, backing away.

"Whatever," one of the others muttered, running his hands over the smooth surface of the AV.

The first man smiled and nodded. "Official business," he repeated. "We'll return your vehicle when we're finished."

He seemed to enjoy the charade, the man in charge, the leader, turning now to the others and motioning them to climb in. Logan stood watching as they did so, waiting. His hand tightened on the staff, and the slow build of the magic began to take hold deep inside, working its way through his body and limbs. He could feel its heat, could sense the impending adrenaline rush. He was suddenly eager for it, anticipating the satisfaction it would give him, his one small pleasure in an otherwise disappointing existence.

He took another step back. "What happened to the people here?"

"They got sick," one answered.

"Real sick," said another.

"So sick they died," said the first, grinning.

"The lucky ones, anyway," said the second.

The men were settling themselves in place, looking around with obvious admiration at their newfound acquisition. Kids in a candy store, they had gotten their hands on something better than they had ever imagined possible. But the driver was having trouble figuring out what to do with the controls, which were clearly unfamiliar to him.

He looked over, pointing the automatic at Logan. "Show me what to do," he ordered.

Logan came forward, leaning on the staff. "The lucky ones got sick, you say? What about the unlucky ones?"

"What do you care?" the driver snapped.

"Taken to the slave camps," another answered.

The driver gave him a look, but the other man just shrugged. Logan stopped several feet away and pointed to the AV's dash. "Punch that button to the right of those green levers. That turns her on."

The driver glanced down at the dash, located the button Logan had indicated, and pushed. Nothing happened. He pushed again. Still nothing. Angry now, he tried several more times without success. He looked up finally, glaring at Logan.

"Here, let me show you," Logan said, coming forward.

He reached into the cab, locked his fingers on the man's gun hand before he knew what was happening, tightened his grip until the gun dropped away, then yanked the man bodily from the vehicle and flung him a dozen feet into the air. It cost almost no effort at all. The magic of his staff gave him the strength for this and much more. The other three stared in disbelief, but before they could react he swept the staff in front of them, the magic jetting forth in a blue sheet of fire that picked them up and flung them clear. In seconds, all four lay dazed on the ground. He walked over to them, took their weapons from their nerveless fingers, and smashed them against a light pole that had long since lost any other possible use.

"Shame on you," he said quietly. He yanked the leader into a sitting position and squatted before him. "Where is this slave camp?"

The man stared at him with a stunned expression, then shook his head. "Don't know."

"Yes, you do. You probably helped those that were hunting them." He tightened his hand about the other's throat and squeezed. "Tell me where it is."

The man gasped frantically, fighting for breath. "West . . . somewhere. Never . . . been . . . there!"

Logan nodded in response. "You should go sometime. It would do you a world of good." He flung the man down so hard that his head slammed against the hard earth. "If you're lying, I'll be back to show you the error of your ways. Do you understand me?"

The man nodded, eyes wide, swallowing hard. "I can't make my arms move. What did you do to me?"

Logan straightened. "I let you live. That's more than you deserve. If I were you, I'd find a way to make the best of my good fortune, you and these other animals." He stood up, looking down at the man. "If I ever come across you again, I'll not be so generous."

For just a moment, he considered the possibility of not being so generous right then and there. These men were the worst of their kind, the dregs of the humanity that the once-men preyed upon. They were little better than the once-men themselves, lacking only organization and a little deeper madness to qualify. That was what the world had come to, what civilization in its terrible collapse had birthed.

The man must have seen something of what he was thinking in his eyes. "Don't hurt me," he said. "I'm just trying to stay alive like everyone else."

Logan stared down at him. Trying to stay alive for what? But it didn't bear thinking on. He turned away, climbed back in the AV, and started up the engine. With a final glance at the men on the ground, he drove from the park back onto the roadway and then west toward the midland flats.

7

L ATE THAT AFTERNOON, with the other Ghosts safely returned to their underground home, Hawk departed for his meeting with Tessa. He told Owl to feed the others, and that he would eat when he returned. She gave him the look she always gave him when he was going out so close to nightfall, the one that both despaired of his insistence on tempting fate and warned him to be careful. She did not try to dissuade him; she never did. Even at only twenty-three, she understood his needs better than he did, and she knew that telling him not to go would make no difference. Not in this case. Not with Tessa.

The gray mistiness of earlier had darkened further with the night's approach, and the ruins of the city were layered thick with shadows as Hawk emerged from the underground with one of the solar-charged prods in hand and Cheney in tow. He always took Cheney on these visits, not so reckless as to go alone. It was dangerous for anyone to be out after dark, although he was better equipped than most to take the risk. Blessed with night vision that enabled him to see as clearly in the dark as in the light, he was also possessed of unusually acute hearing. But the darkness could be treacherous, and there were things hiding in it that could see and hear much better than he could. The Ghosts were forbidden to go out at night for that very reason, even in groups. Hawk went because it was the only time Tessa could risk meeting him.

But he was especially mindful tonight of whatever it was that had killed those Croaks down by the waterfront and the Lizard at midtown. Something big and dangerous was loose in the city, and it was hunting. If it could kill a full-grown Lizard and a pack of Croaks, it probably could dispatch a street kid without much trouble. Even a street kid with a dog like Cheney.

The light was failing, but it was not yet so dark that Hawk couldn't see down First Avenue through the jumble of abandoned cars and collapsed buildings. He made his way quickly through the debris, keeping to the center of the roadway, letting Cheney take the lead and set the pace. The city was silent and empty feeling, but he knew there were things living in it everywhere. Some he had encountered, like the community of Spiders living in the warehouse complex that sat just above the compound and the small family of Lizards that occupied what had once been a residential apartment building. There were Croaks down this way, too, but not many because of the compound. The Croaks were bold, but they were wary of open places. Croaks preferred the darker, more isolated locations for their hunting. Even in packs, they avoided the compounds.

But Hawk was alone and outside, so he knew he was fair game. The Croaks would be watching.

His lean, ragged shadow lengthened as he walked and the air grew cooler. It was midyear sometime, though he didn't know exactly when. Owl might, but she made little mention of it because it didn't matter. Clocks and calendars were for those who lived in the compounds and wanted to maintain some sense of a past they refused to recognize as dead and gone. Those living on the streets, like the Ghosts, found comfort only in the moment, not in memories. Most of them didn't even talk about their parents anymore, those who could remember their parents at all. Their old families were like stories once told and then mostly forgotten. Their old families were no longer real.

Some of them could still recall a little of their past lives. Hawk wasn't one of them. He remembered almost nothing, and what he did recall was so fragmented and disconnected from his current reality that he could not give a context to it. His father was a faceless shadow, but every now and then he could catch glimpses of his mother—an image of her face on a smudged wall, a beckoning of her hand in the movement of shadows, her laugh in the cry of a gull. He could never put the pieces together, though; could never make her whole. Even the particulars of his past life were vague. He remembered swimming on the Oregon coast. He remembered the beach. Not much else. It was almost as if he had not had a life until he came to this city.

He gave a mental shrug. Life before coming here didn't matter anyway. The Ghosts had reinvented their lives in more ways than not. Customs and rituals were all new. Owl set the rules for eating, sleeping, and bathing. Hawk assigned chores. Routine kept them focused on staying alive. They did not celebrate holidays. No one except for Owl could even name more than one or two. They celebrated them in the compounds, he knew. Sometimes Tessa talked glowingly of those celebrations, but to him they sounded perfunctory and forced. There even seemed to be disagreement on the kinds of holidays worth remembering. It was just more clinging to the past. The Ghosts did celebrate birthdays, even though most of them no longer knew when their birthdays actually were. Owl had assigned birthdays to those who had forgotten them, and she marked them off on a makeshift calendar she had drawn on the wall. She didn't know what day it was or even what year. She just made it up, and it became a game they could all play.

Off to one side, deep in the shadows of a mostly whole building, something moved. Cheney went into a crouch, faced the black opening of the doorway, and growled softly. Hawk stopped where he was, holding the prod ready. After a few tense moments, Cheney turned away and started off again. Hawk swung in behind him, and they continued on.

Sometimes he thought that it would all be so much simpler if they lived in the compound with Tessa and the others. Not that it would ever be allowed after they had lived on the streets for so long, but just for the sake of argument. There was safety in numbers. There was less to be responsible for and less to worry about on a daily basis. Food and shelter and medical supplies were easier to come by. Some of the people in the compounds still had special skills that street kids would never have. But there was something so abhorrent about compound life that it overshadowed everything that made it appear desirable. Too many restrictions and rules. Too little freedom. Too much conformity of the few for the benefit of the many. Too much fear of everything outside the walls. It was the old world in miniature, and if Hawk was certain of one thing in this life it was that the old world was dead and gone and should remain that way. Eventually, a new world would be born from the ashes of the old, and living in a walled fortress was not the way to make that happen.

Darkness was almost complete when he emerged from the ash- and soot-blackened ruins of the city's south end and could see clearly the dark bulk of the compound outlined against the gray sky-line. Walls several stories high surrounded what had once been an arena and playing field, stretching away on four sides to occupy sev-eral city blocks. A raised metal roof rested atop a network of steel girders and wheels that had once allowed it to move back and forth on a track to open the playing field to the sky, but now was rusted permanently open. Barbed wire rimmed the tops of the walls and the perimeter of the compound in thick rolls. Watchtowers dotted the corners and heavy barricades blocked those entrances that hadn't been sealed completely. A wide swath of open space sepa-rated the compound from the rest of the city; everything close had been torn down to prevent enemies from approaching without being seen.

A sign with bits and pieces of its letters broken off and its smooth surface blackened and scarred proclaimed that this was SAFECO FIELD.

Rumor had it that there had once been an adjacent arena that oc-cupied the open space between the city and the compound. But ter-rorists had bombed it when it was one of the last active playing fields in the country and still fighting to maintain its traditions. More than two thousand had died in the attack, and much of the building had collapsed. Shortly after, the first of the plagues struck, wiping out fifty thousand in less than a week, and that was pretty much the beginning of the end of the old ways.

Hawk made a circuitous approach to the compound, keeping to the concealment of the rubble and shadows. His destination was some hundred yards east of where he worked his way forward in a crouch, Cheney close beside him. Nothing lived in this part of the city because the men on the walls kept watch day and night; if anything was seen, they were quick to send out a sanitation squad to destroy it. Twilight was the hardest time for the watchers to spot movement in the debris, even on the more open ground, which was the main reason Hawk had chosen this time of day for his meetings with Tessa. He met with her on the same day each week with no deviation. If either failed to show, the meeting was automatically rescheduled for the following night. The time and place were always the same—nightfall in the ruins of an old shelter that had once connected to an underground light rail system.

Hawk scanned his surroundings as he proceeded, searching through a mix of old bones, desiccated animals, and the occasional human corpse. He didn't look closely at any of it; there wasn't any reason to. Dead things were everywhere, and there wasn't anything anyone could do about them. He found the remains of street children almost every week, loners or outcasts or just plain unfortunates who had fallen victim to the things that hunted them. He no longer found the remains of adults; except for the Weatherman, those few still living outside the compounds had long since fled into the countryside, where your chances were marginally better if you possessed a few survival skills.

Hawk had lost two of his own family in the five years he had been living in the underground. The Croaks had gotten one, a little girl he'd named Mouse. The older boy, Heron, had died in a fall. He could still see their faces, hear their voices, and remember what they had been like. He could still feel the heat of his rage at having failed them.

It took him a long time to reach the outbuilding, working his way slowly and carefully through the ruins to keep out of sight of the compound guards, which sometimes required that he change directions away from the place he was trying to reach. Cheney stayed close to him, aware of his caution. But Cheney knew enough about staying alive to avoid being seen in any case. Hawk was always amazed at how anything so big could move so quietly and invisibly. When Cheney didn't want to be seen or heard, you didn't see or hear him. Even now, he would come up on Hawk unexpectedly, appearing from the shadows as if born of mist and darkness. If the boy hadn't been so used to it, he would have jumped out of his skin.

When he reached the shelter leading to the rail system, he slipped down the darkened stairwell to the underground door and rapped three times, twice hard and once soft, then stepped back and waited. Almost immediately the locking device on the other side of the door released, the door opened, and Tessa burst through.

"Hawk!" She breathed his name like a prayer answered and threw her arms around him. "I almost gave up! Where were you?" She began kissing him on his face and mouth. "I was so sure that this time you weren't coming!"

She was always like this, desperate to be with him, convinced he wouldn't appear. She loved him so much that it frightened him, yet it made him feel empowered, too. She gave him a different kind of strength with her love, a strength born of knowing that you could change another person's life just by being who you were. That he felt the same about her reinforced his certainty that by being together anything was possible. He had known it almost from the moment he had first seen her. He had felt it deep inside in a way he had never felt anything else.

He kissed her back now, as eager for her as she was for him.

When she broke away finally, she was laughing. "You'd think we'd never done this. You'd think we'd been waiting to do it all our lives."

She was small and dark, her skin a light chocolate in color, her hair raven black and close-cropped in a silky helmet that glistened even in the darkness. Her eyes were large and wide with surprise, as if everything she was seeing was new and incredibly exciting. She exuded energy and life in a way that no one else could. She made him smile, but it was more than the way he felt about her. She had an enthusiasm that was infectious; she could make you feel good about life even in the bleakest of times and places.

"Look at you," she whispered. "All ragged and dirty and mussed up, like Owl hasn't made you take a bath in a month! Such a boy!" She grinned, and then whispered, "You look wonderful."

He didn't, of course, especially compared with her in her soft leather boots and coat and bright, clean blouse. Compound kids always had better clothes. His jeans and sweatshirt were worn and his sneakers falling apart. But she would never tell him that. She would only tell him what would make him feel good about himself. That was the way she was. She made him ache inside and want to tell her all the good things he had ever thought about her all at once, even the things that he didn't think he could ever tell.

"How is everyone?" She steered him over to the concrete bench set against the far wall and sat him down.

"Good. All safe and sound. Owl sends her love. She misses you. Almost as much as me."

Tessa bit her lip. "I wish she could come back. I wish things weren't so difficult."

He nodded. "You could make things easier. You could come live with us. We don't have a compound, but we don't have a compound's stupid rules, either." He seized her hands. "Do it, Tessa! Come tonight! Become a Ghost! You belong out here with me, not inside those walls!"

She gave him a quick, uneasy grin. "You know the answer, Hawk. Why do you keep asking?"

"Because I don't think your parents should dictate what you do with your life."

"They don't dictate what I do with my life. The choice to stay with them is mine." Her lips compressed in a tight line of frustration. "I can't leave until . . . My father would survive it, but my mother . . . well, you know. She isn't the same since the accident. If she could use . . ." She shook her head, unable to continue. "If she could just use . . ."

She was stumbling all over herself, trying to get the words out. Stone blocks had crushed her mother's hands when a wall in the compound kitchen had collapsed during an earthquake more than a year ago. It was an event that had changed everything for Tessa, who could barely bring herself to talk about it even now.

Hawk dropped his gaze. "If she could use her hands again," he finished, "she would have a purpose and they wouldn't have an excuse to put her outside the walls."

Tessa nodded. "But it's more than that. She's crippled on the inside, too. She's broken emotionally. Daddy and I are all she has. It would kill her if she lost either one of us." She reached up and touched his cheek. "You know all this. Why are we talking about it? Why don't you change your mind, instead? Why don't you come live with me? If you did, they might let Owl and the others come inside, too."

His hiss of frustration betrayed his impatience. "You know they won't let anyone come in from the streets. Especially kids."

She gripped his hands. "They would if you married me. They would have to. It's compound law."

She held him spellbound for a moment with the force of her grip and the intensity of her gaze, but then he shook his head. "Maybe they would allow me in, but not the others. A family sticks together. Besides, marriage is a convention that belongs in the past. It doesn't mean anything anymore."

"It means something to me." She refused to look away. "It means everything." She bent forward and kissed his lips. "What are we supposed to do, Hawk? Are we supposed to keep meeting like this for the rest of our lives? Is this what you want? One hour a week in a concrete windbreak?"

He shook his head slowly, eyes closed, feeling the press of her lips on his. It wasn't even close to what he really wanted, but what you wanted wasn't always what you got. Hardly ever, in fact. They'd had this discussion before—had it almost every time they met. She had begun talking about marriage only recently, however. It was a mark of how desperate she was to find a way to bring them together that she was willing to suggest it openly when she knew how he felt.

"Marriage won't change anything, Tessa. I am already as married to you as I'll ever be. Having an adult stand in front of us and say we're married won't make us any more so. Anyway, I can't live inside a compound. You know that. I have to live on the streets where

I can breathe. Someday you'll want that, too. You'll want it enough to come live with me, parents or not."

She nodded more as if to placate than to agree, a sad smile escaping her tightly compressed lips. "Someday."

He wanted to tell her that someday would never come. They had waited on it too long already. Until lately, their hopes and dreams had been enough. Time had slowed and all things had seemed possible. But now he was growing anxious. Tessa seemed no closer to him, no nearer than before. He saw their chances beginning to slip away and the weight of an uncertain world bearing down.

He exhaled in frustration. "Let's talk about something else. I need your help. Tiger's little sister, Persia, has red spot. She needs pleneten. I promised Tiger I would see if I could get her some."

She looked down to where their hands were joined, and then up again. "I get to see you again tomorrow night if I can find some. I guess that's reason enough to try."

"Tessa . . ."

"No, don't say anything else, Hawk. Words only get in the way. Just put your arms around me for a while. Just be with me."

They held each other wordlessly, neither of them speaking, the darkness around deepening with the closing in of night. Hawk listened to the blanketing silence, picking out the faint sounds of small creatures scurrying in the debris and of voices drifting out from behind the walls of the compound. He could feel Tessa's heart beating; he could hear her soft breathing. Now and then she would shift against him, seeking a different closeness. Now and again she would kiss him, and he would kiss her back. He thought of how much he wanted her with him, wanted her to come away and live in the underground. He didn't care about her parents. She belonged with him. They were meant to be together. He tried to communicate this to her simply by thinking it. He tried to make her feel it through the sheer intensity of his determination.

And for the little while that Tessa had asked him for, everything else faded away. Time stretched and slowed and finally stopped entirely.

But then she whispered, "I have to go."

She released him abruptly, as if deciding all at once that they had transgressed. The absence of her warmth left him instantly chilled. He stood up with her, trying not to show the disappointment he was feeling.

"It hasn't been that long," he protested.

"Longer than you think." She hugged herself, watching his face. "But never long enough, is it?"

"Tomorrow night?"

She nodded. "Tomorrow night."

"Do the best you can for Persia. I know it's asking a lot."

"To help a little girl?" She shook her head. "Not so much."

He hesitated. "Listen, there's one more thing. There might be something new on the streets. The Weatherman found a nest of dead Croaks down by the waterfront, by the cranes. He doesn't know what did it. You haven't heard anything about this, have you?"

She shook her head, her short black hair rippling. "No, nothing. The compound sends foragers out almost every day. No one has reported anything unusual."

"They might not tell you. They don't always tell kids everything."

"Daddy does."

Hawk nodded, not all that convinced that her confidence in her father was well placed. Adults protected their children in strange ways. He took her hands in his own and held them. "Just be careful if you have to go out. Better yet, why don't you stay inside for a while until I know something more."

She smiled, quick and ironic. "Until you can go out and take a look around? Maybe you should worry a little more about yourself. I shouldn't have to do all the worrying for you."

They stood close together in the darkness, not speaking, looking at each other with an intensity that was electric. Hawk was the first to break the silence. "I don't want to let you go."

For a long moment, she didn't reply. Then she tightened her fingers about his and said, "One day, you won't have to."

She said it quietly and without force, but with a calm insistence that suggested it was inevitable. "I know I belong with you. I know that. I will find a way. But you have to be patient. You have to trust me."

"I do trust you. I love you." He bent forward to kiss her so that he wouldn't say anything more, so that he would leave it at that.

She kissed him back. "You better go," she whispered, pressing the words against his lips.

Then she slipped through the doorway leading back into the underground and was gone. He waited until he heard the *snick* of the heavy lock, and then waited some more because he ached so much he could not make himself move. He waited a long time.

● ● ●

HAWK WALKED BACK through the city with Cheney at his side, the sky roofed by heavy banks of clouds that left everything shrouded in gloom. The buildings clustered silent and empty about him, hollow monoliths, mute witnesses to the ruin they had survived. There were no lights anywhere. Once, this entire city would have been lit, with every window bright and welcoming. Panther had told him so; he had seen it near the end in San Francisco. Owl had read the Ghosts stories in which kids walked streets made bright with lights from lamps. She had read them stories of how the moon shone in a silver orb out of a sky thick with stars glimmering in a thousand pinpricks against the black.

None of them had ever seen it, but they believed it had been like that. Hawk believed it would be like that again.

He worked his way through the piles of debris, around derelict cars and cracked pieces of concrete and steel, and past doorways too dark to see into and too dangerous to pass close by. The city was one huge trap, its jaws waiting to close on the unwary. It was a place of predators and prey. Their shadows moved all around him, some in the alleyways, some in the interiors of the buildings. They were always there, the remnants of the old world, the refuse left over from the destruction and the madness. He felt a certain sympathy for the creatures that prowled the night, hunting and being hunted. They hadn't wanted this any more than he had. They, too, were victims of humankind's reckless behavior and poor judgment.

He thought of Tessa and tried to figure out what else he could do to persuade her to come to live with him. But her attachment to her parents was so strong that he couldn't see any way around it. He resented it, but he understood it, too. He knew that her feelings for them must be as strong as his own were for her. But things could not continue like this. Sooner or later, something would happen to change them. He knew it instinctively. What worried him was that when it did, Tessa would be standing in the way.

He would talk to her about it again tomorrow night. He would talk to her about it every night until she changed her mind.

When he reached the underground, he paused to take a careful look around, making sure that nothing was tracking him. Satisfied, he went into the building that led down to their home. He went quickly now, Cheney at his side, feeling suddenly tired and ready to sleep. The heavy door was barred and locked, and he gave the requisite series of taps to alert Owl of his presence.

But it was not Owl who opened the door. It was Candle. She stood just inside as he entered, small and waif-like in her nightdress, red hair tousled. Hawk waited for Cheney as he padded over to his accustomed sleeping spot, and then closed and locked the door behind them. When he glanced back at Candle, he saw for the first time how big and scared her eyes were.

He knelt in front of her right away. "What is it?"

"A dream," she whispered. "Owl went to bed, and I stayed up to wait for you and I had a dream. I saw something. It was big and scary."

"What was it, Candle?" he asked. He put his hands on her thin shoulders and found that she was shaking. He drew her close to him at once, hugging her. "Tell me."

He could no longer see her face, pressed close to him as she was, but he could feel the shake of her head against his shoulder. "I couldn't be sure. But it's coming here, and if it finds us, it will hurt us." She paused, her breath catching in her throat. "It will kill us."

A vision, Hawk thought without saying so to the little girl. And Candle's visions were never wrong. He ran his hand along her silky hair, then down her thin back. She was still shaking.

"We have to leave right away," she whispered. "Right now."

"Shhhh," he soothed, tightening his arms to steady her. "That's enough for tonight, little one."

Right now, she had said.

At once he thought of Tessa.

8

ALTHOUGH LOGAN TOM hadn't expected to be able to track down the slave camp—hadn't even been certain, in fact, that it was there—he stumbled on it almost without trying. Daylight was failing and darkness closing all about the countryside as he drove west out of Iowa into whatever lay beyond—he couldn't remember and didn't care to stop long enough to check maps that no longer had relevance—when he saw the glow of the watch fires burning on the horizon like a second setting of the sun. Crimson against the pale shading of twilight, the glow drew his attention instantly, signaling its presence in a way that all but invited him in for a closer look. He had seen this glow before—in other times, at other camps—and he realized quickly enough what it was and drove toward it.

Darkness had fallen completely by the time he arrived at a dirt road that led in from the main highway, driving the S-150 with the lights off and the big engine idled down to a low hum. As he approached, the watchtowers and the barricades took shape and the slave pens became recognizable. The glow emanated from a combi-

nation of lights powered by solar generators and pillars of flame rising out of fire pits. The latter gave the landscape a hellish and surreal
look, as if devil imps with pitchforks might be prowling the countryside. The camp was huge, stretching two miles across and at least
as deep. It had been a stockyard once, he guessed, that had been
turned by the once-men and their mentors to a different use. The
odor of cows and manure and hay was strong, although he knew that
the smell could be deceiving and its source something else entirely.

By the time he cut the engine, still well back from the watchtowers and their lights, he could hear the mewling of the prisoners.
He sat motionless in the AV, ashamed and enraged by the sounds,
unable to stop himself from listening. He could make out shadowy
forms moving back and forth behind the fences in the hazy glow
of the lights, a listless, shuffling mass. Humans become slaves, become the living dead, made to work and to breed by the once-men
and their demon masters. It was the fate decreed for all who weren't
killed outright during the hunts. It was the punishment visited on
humans for their foolishness and inaction when the collapse of civilization began, and it was horrifying beyond imagining.

But, then, he didn't have to imagine it. He had seen it so often
that it was burned into his memory. It haunted him in his dreams
and in his waking. It would not let him be.

He wondered for the first time what he was doing here. He had
come looking for the camp in the way he had looked for such camps
for years, a Knight-errant in search of injustice. He had done so without thinking about it because this was what he was given to do, all
he knew to do to try to set things right. He would attack the camps
and free those enslaved. He would kill the once-men and their
demon masters. He would disrupt the breeding operations and destroy the slave pens. He would do whatever he could to right just a
little of what had been turned so terribly wrong.

But his purpose in coming to this particular camp was unclear to
him. He had been given a task already, one of monumental importance. He was to find the gypsy morph and identify it, then serve as
its protector as it led a small band of humans to a place where humanity would rebuild itself in the wake of an approaching cataclysm
that would finish what the demons had begun. Nothing could be al-

lowed to interfere with that task; Two Bears had made it clear that the future of humanity was riding on whether or not he was able to carry it out. Such responsibility did not allow for deviations or personal indulgences. He could not afford to risk himself in an attack that was, in essence, both. However terrible it was to do so, he must pass by this camp and continue on.

Yet how could he? How could he abandon these people and still call himself a Knight of the Word?

He tried focusing on the reward Two Bears had promised him. If he did as he'd been asked, the demon responsible for the murder of his family would be delivered up to him—that old man in his gray slouch hat and long cloak, that monster with his knowing smile and his eyes as cold as death. It was a bold promise, but he believed the Word would not have made it if it could not be kept. He wanted that demon more than he wanted anything. He had searched for it for years, thinking that sooner or later in the course of his struggle he would stumble on it. It seemed impossible to him that he could not. Even Michael, who had a knack for predicting how things would work out, had believed that eventually they would find it, that they could not avoid doing so.

But he had never seen the demon again, not once, not even the barest glimpse.

Still, he knew it was out there. He knew it the way he knew that the promise would be honored. He knew it the way he knew that the finding of that demon was the end purpose of his life.

He sat staring into the distance, wrestling with his conscience, then started up the engine on the AV once more, turned it around, and drove away from the camp and its smells and its sounds. He drove until he could no longer see its fiery brightness, until the horizon behind him was just a hazy glow. By then he was back near the main highway, alone on the flats in the darkness. He parked in the shelter of a copse of withered trees, set the perimeter alarm system on the AV, ate because he knew he should, and settled down to sleep.

● ● ●

HE STANDS WITH *the others in the shadows that fill the gullies that crisscross the terrain at the rear of the camp. It is nearing midnight, and the world is a black hole beneath a heavily overcast sky. A light rain is falling, something of a minor miracle in this farmland become desert. No wind blows to stir the silt; no breeze cools the stifling heat. Save for the moans and cries of the imprisoned, no sounds disturb the deep night silence.*

He looks down at his weapon, a blunt, short-barreled flechette called a Scattershot. Michael has given it to him to carry, trusting him to use it wisely and safely. He is familiar with weapons, having been trained to use them since Michael took him from the compound on the night his parents and siblings died. The Scattershot fires a single charge that sweeps clean an area of up to twenty feet; it is a weapon meant to create a broad killing ground. He has been told that it will help against the things that will come at him, but that his best protection lies in keeping close to his companions.

"Do not stray, boy," Michael has warned. "This is a dangerous business. If I did not think you needed to learn from it, I would not have brought you at all. Don't make me regret my decision."

He does not wish to disappoint Michael, whom he loves and respects and to whom he owes his life. He has dedicated himself to making certain that Michael never regrets having rescued him that first night. He grips his weapon tightly, waiting for the signal to advance. They have come to attack and destroy this camp, to free the humans imprisoned within, to disrupt the work and breeding programs set in place by the once-men who wield the power of life and death over those brought here from the compounds.

It is his first time on such an expedition.

He is twelve years old.

"Stand ready," Michael whispers to those he leads, and the word is passed up and down the line.

When they attack, they come out of the gullies and shadows like wolves, howling and crouched low against the open ground, racing to gain the fences before the guards have a chance to stop them. Logan stays close beside Michael, shadowing him as he charges through the smoky haze of the fires, weapon leveled, safety off. He howls with the others, then cringes as automatic weapons fire sweeps through the darkness in a deadly rain. Most of the bullets miss, but a few find their targets, and men go down in crumpled heaps. In the towers and at the gates, once-men surge forward to repel the attack.

But the defenders are too few and too slow. Michael's command is well trained and battle-hardened, and they have done this often. They know what to expect and are not deterred by the efforts of those within the camp to stop them. They gain the fences and cut the wires and are through. They gain the gates, set their explosive charges, duck aside as they detonate, and are through. They gain the masses of concertina wire rolled across gaps in the earthworks that serve as loading ramps, throw mattresses across the deadly spikes, and are through.

In a determined rush, Michael and those closest, himself included, burst through shards of wood, scraps of iron, and ribbons of wire, weapons firing. There is no attempt at this point to distinguish targets. It is assumed that anything moving outside the confines of the pens is an enemy. From within the pens themselves, the moans and cries turn to recognizable pleas: Help me, save me, free me! The cries are raw and desperate, but the attackers ignore them. They know what they are doing and how best to do it. Responding to the prisoners is a mistake that will get them killed. To succeed in what they are attempting, they must first eliminate the enemy.

They do so with a single-mindedness that is frightening. They stay bunched in their attack units, protecting one another's backs as Michael has taught them to do, surging forward into the heart of the compound, destroying the once-men as they go. If they should encounter a demon, they will stand their ground and attempt to drive it back; if that fails, they will turn and flee. They do not expect to encounter one this night. Scouting reports say the resident demon is absent. Michael takes a chance that the reports are accurate because he has no choice. Encounters with demons are a part of the risk they all take.

They are lucky this night. No demon surfaces to challenge them.

There are feeders everywhere, but he doesn't yet know what feeders are and can only sense their presence as they rush in a maddened frenzy through the dead and wounded, savoring the taste of pain and death and fear. Now and again, he catches glimpses of them from the corner of his eye, swift and shadowy, and he shivers.

The once-men are driven steadily back until all are dead or have fled into the darkness. When the camp is secured, one set of liberators begins to free the prisoners while another follows Michael. As instructed, Logan stays close to his mentor. He pounds through the darkness toward the cluster of cabins isolated in the middle of the camp while the pens around him are pulled down and the men and women imprisoned within are released. He glances down once at the Scattershot and finds that the metal of the weapon is cool against his skin. He realizes in surprise that he has not fired it.

Michael reaches the first of the cabins and kicks in the door. There is movement within, but Michael does not fire. Other men go to the other cabins and kick in their doors, as well. An eerie silence settles over this section of the camp, all the noise and furor suddenly gone elsewhere. The men who have come here with Michael lower their weapons and, one by one, step inside the cabins they have assaulted. Michael waits until they are inside, glances back to where the boy stands, and beckons him forward.

Together, they enter the cabin in front of them.

Logan thinks he is ready for what he will find, but he is wrong. He stands in the doorway openmouthed, his throat so tight he does not think he can draw another breath. There are children in the cabin, dozens of them, packed close as they huddle together in the darkness, pressed up against the farthest wall. They are dirty and ragged. They are pitiful to look at. Most wear almost nothing. Their bones protrude from their emaciated bodies like sticks bundled in sacks; they are held together by little more than ligaments and skin. They have the look of skeletons, of corpses, of ghosts. They are all ages, many younger than he is. They do not know what is happening. They stare at him in shock and terror. Many are crying.

They begin to beg for their lives.

"Look carefully, Logan," Michael tells him. "This is what we have been reduced to by our enemies. This is our future if we do not find a way to change it."

Logan looks at the children and wishes he had never seen them. He wishes Michael had not brought him here, that he had been left behind. He wishes he could sink into the floor and disappear. He knows he will never forget this moment. He knows it will haunt him forever.

"They are kept alive for various reasons," Michael says softly. "Some for work. Some for experiments. Some for things I cannot bear to speak about."

Logan understands. He draws a long, slow breath and exhales. He thinks he will be sick to his stomach, and he fights it down. He swallows and straightens.

Michael's hand closes on his shoulder and tightens. "We shall set most of them free and hope that some will survive." He pauses. "Most of them, but not all."

He moves to the farthest corner of the room, the corner that is darkest. As he nears, a hissing, mewling sound rises from the shadows.

What happens next is indescribable.

● ● ●

LOGAN WOKE SWEATING and disoriented in the backseat of the Lightning, thrashing beneath the light blanket as if jolted by a charge from an electric prod. The dream of the slave camp, of what Michael had brought him to see, was right in front of him, painted on a canvas of darkness and air, blood red and razor sharp.

Madness, he screamed in the silence of his mind and was filled with sudden, ungovernable anger.

It happened then as it always happened, a sudden shift of emotions that took him from simmer straight to white-hot. The canvas of the dream expanded until it was all he could see. Memories of every atrocity he had witnessed since his boyhood surfaced like a swarm of angry bees from the dark place in his mind to which he had consigned them, and a quick, hard burn of rage tore through him. He was suddenly unable to focus on anything but his horror of the slave camp he had passed by only hours before, unable to think with anything remotely resembling dispassion, unable to bring reason or common sense to bear. His rage was all-consuming. It swept through him in seconds, took control of him completely, and left him with a single thought.

Destroy it!

Without stopping to think about what he was doing, he crawled

into the driver's seat, shut down the perimeter alarms, started the
engine, and wheeled the AV about. Forgotten was his promise to
himself that he would not let anything jeopardize his search for the
gypsy morph. Abandoned was the quest that had brought him to
this place and time. His rage washed all of it away, swept it aside as
if it were unimportant and replaced it with an inexorable determination to go back to that camp and do what he knew was needed.

Because there was no one else to help those imprisoned in that
camp. Because he knew what was being done to them, and he could
not abide it.

He took the highway back to the cutoff, back to where he could
see the glow from the fires of the camp, and turned toward them,
anger flooding through him like molten lava. He switched on the
AV's weapons, setting them to the armed position. His rune-carved
staff rested on the seat beside him, ready to employ. He might have
taken time to make better preparations, but his rage would not allow
for it. It demanded that he hurry, that he act now. It demanded that
he cast aside reason and let impulse rule.

He blew over the flats toward the now-visible camp like an
avenging angel, his inner fire a match for the flames that burned in
the perimeter pits. He had reached the walls almost before the
guards could comprehend what he was about, too close for them to
bring their heavy weapons to bear. He attacked the towers with the
long-barreled flechettes that elevated from their fender housings,
shards of iron cutting apart the walls and occupants that warded
them as if both were made of thin paper. He swung the AV around
after taking down two, left it in idle, and sprang to the ground before
the fencing and rolled razor wire, his staff in hand. They were shooting at him now with their automatic weapons, but he was already
shielded by the magic of his staff, an impregnable force of nature. He
strode forward, his staff sweeping along the fencing and wire in a
line of fire that melted everything it touched. Inside, the prisoners
were screaming and crying, thinking it was they who were under attack, they who were meant to die. He could not stop to tell them
otherwise. He could only act, and act quickly.

He was through the fence in moments, a Knight of the Word in
full-blown frenzy, as savage and unpredictable as the creatures he

hunted. Feeders appeared as if by magic, swirling all around him, hundreds strong, hungry and expectant. Cringing prisoners scattered before him in all directions, howling in fear. Once-men came at him in waves, firing their weapons, trying to bring him down. But ordinary weapons were no match for his staff, and he scattered them like leaves. He moved deliberately from fence to fence, from tower to tower, from one building to the next, sending everything up in flames.

He kept his eyes peeled for a demon, but none approached. He was lucky this night, but then luck was a part of what kept him alive.

The once-men were falling back, losing heart in the face of his wildness and seeming invulnerability. Their mad eyes and sharp faces lost their hard edge and turned frightened. Soon they were fleeing into the night, seeking shelter in the darkness. The camp's prisoners flooded through the shattered fences after them, hundreds of men, women, and children. Strange skeletal apparitions, they fled through the brightness of the flames without fully understanding what was happening or where they were fleeing. It didn't matter to the Knight of the Word. It only mattered that they run and keep running and never come back.

When the camp was in flames and the pens emptied, he turned his attention to the isolated cluster of cabins that sat deliberately untouched at the very center. He stared at the ramshackle structures, and his rage drained away with the slow onset of his horror at what must happen next. He hesitated, a mix of almost unbearable sadness and disgust welling up inside him.

Then Michael's voice reached out to him from the long-ago.

Don't think about it. Don't try to make sense of it. Do what you must.

He took a deep, steadying breath and started forward.

● ● ●

"COME LOOK, BOY. *Come see what hides here in the darkness.*"

Michael stands waiting on him near the shadows from which the hissing and mewling issues, his face carved of granite, his words hard-

edged and commanding. Nevertheless, Logan hesitates before advancing, knowing he should flee, that what he is about to see will scar him forever. But there is no running away from this, and he comes forward as bidden.

As he does so, the things hiding in the darkness slowly begin to take shape.

His breath catches in his throat and his chest tightens.

They are children, he sees. Or what once were children and now are something bordering on the demonic. Their arms and legs have grown disproportionate to their bodies, made long and crooked, and their hands end in claws. Their backs arch like those of cornered cats as they twist and writhe angrily. Their faces are distorted and maddened, cheeks hollow, chins narrow and sharp, noses flattened to almost nothing, ears split as if with knives, eyes yellow slits that are mirrors of their souls, mouths filled with needle-sharp teeth and tongues that protrude and lick the air. They are manifestations of evil, of the monsters to which they have fallen prey.

He tries to ask what has been done to them, but words fail him. He cannot speak, cannot do anything but stare at these creatures that once were children like him.

"They have been changed by experimentation," Michael tells him. "They cannot be saved."

But they must be saved, *the boy thinks, looking quickly at the older man for a better answer.* No child should be allowed to come to this! No child should be consigned to this hell!

Michael is not looking at him. He is looking at the demon children, at the monsters huddled before him. There is such blackness in that look that it seems those upon which it is cast must succumb to its intensity and weight. Yet they continue to arch their backs and hiss and mewl and crouch in the shadows, little nightmares.

Michael points his weapon at them. "Go outside now, boy. Wait for me there."

He does as he is told, moving on wooden legs, wanting desperately to turn back, to stop what is about to happen, but unable to do so. He reaches the door and looks out into the night. The fires of the camp burn all about him, their flames a hellish crimson against the smoky black.

Dark forms rush here and there, faceless wraiths in flight. He hesitates for a moment, realizing with new insight what has become of his world.

Madness.

There is a burst of automatic weapons fire from behind him and then silence.

●　●　●

HE SET FIRE to the cabins when he was finished, working quickly and efficiently, shutting off his emotions as he moved from building to building, taking refuge in the mechanics of his work. The feeders went with him, frenzied shadows in the red glare of the flames. He tried to ignore them and couldn't. He wished them dead, but that was pointless. Feeders were a force of nature. Only when he was done and walking away did they abandon him, content to frolic in the carnage. He glanced back once to be certain that the cabins were burning, that what lay lifeless inside would be consumed, then quickened his pace until he was through the collapsed fence and moving back toward the AV. Neither the prisoners he had freed nor the once-men that had held them captive were in sight. It was as if both had disappeared in the smoke and flames.

He climbed into the AV and sat staring at nothing. The rage that had earlier consumed him was gone. His wildness had dissipated and his emotions had cooled. He felt detached from his dreams and purged of his madness. He could barely remember having come here. The events that had transpired were a hazy swirl of unconnected images that lacked an identifiable center. His staff was a quiet presence at his side, emptied of magic, cleansed of killing fire.

But as he shifted in his seat, metal fastenings scraped against the door and suddenly he could hear anew the hissing and mewling of the demon children.

He started up the AV's engine and wheeled away into the darkness, accelerating back across the flats toward the westbound highway. The roar of the Lightning's big engine drowned out the sounds that had surfaced in his mind, but the damage was done. Tears filled his eyes as he drove, and the momentary peace he had found was gone.

How had Michael endured this for as long as he had? No wonder it had consumed him. It would consume anyone sooner or later, even a Knight of the Word. He wondered if that was what happened to all Knights of the Word whom the demons had failed to destroy. He wondered if it would happen to him, and then he wondered if it mattered.

He had asked it of Two Bears, and now he asked it again of himself.

Was he the last of his kind?

He could provide no answer. Dispirited and weary, he drove on through the night and the silence.

9

CONTRARY TO HIS fears, Logan Tom was not the last of the Knights of the Word. Another remained.

Her name was Angel Perez.

She stood deep in the shadows of a building alcove and looked past the blackened storefronts lining both sides of the street toward the fighting. The Anaheim compound was under attack by demons and once-men, an army of such size and ferocity that it seemed a miracle the defenders had not succumbed months ago when first placed under siege. She had warned them then that they should make their escape and flee north, that they couldn't win if they insisted on holing up behind their compound walls. They couldn't win if they didn't engage in guerrilla warfare. She had told them this over and over, warning them what would happen if they refused to listen.

They hadn't, of course. They couldn't make themselves listen. She was a Knight of the Word and understood the danger far better than they, but it didn't matter. They had made up their minds. They stayed behind their walls, blind to the inevitable.

Now the inevitable had arrived. All of the city's compounds

were gone but this one. She had just come from the Coliseum, one of eight she had spent almost a year trying to help. But she was only one person, and she couldn't be everywhere at once. The Coliseum had fallen last night at dusk. She had been on her feet for the better part of the last three days, for the better part of a week before that, and for the better part of the month before that. She couldn't say when she had last slept more than four hours at a time. Everything about the last several months, about the fighting and the dying and the terror and the madness, was a blur of images and sounds that denied her even the smallest measure of peace. It cloaked her like a second skin, a constant presence, an unforgettable memory.

She should have left months ago. She knew what was coming, and she should have left. Nevertheless, she had stayed. This was her home, too.

She took a moment longer to consider how she could best help the doomed people trapped inside this last compound. She already knew the answer. She had known it for weeks and had made her plans accordingly. She could not save them all, so she would save those who most needed saving. It had been her mission from the beginning, and she had worked hard to fulfill it as the army of demons and once-men overran each compound. This would be her final effort.

She slipped from her hiding place and started toward the chaos. Darting from one hiding place to the next, she scanned the street ahead, searching for movement. The buildings that lined the broken stretch of concrete were silent and empty, their windows broken out, their doors hanging loose or gone completely, walls blackened by fire and soot. Once they had been high-end shops and professional offices, but that was a long time ago.

Angel was small and compact, much stronger than her size would indicate, much better conditioned, fit enough that she could hold her own against almost anyone or anything, a fact she had proved repeatedly. Her battles with the demons and once-men were legendary, although the number of witnesses who could testify to this had dwindled considerably. With her thick black hair, deep brown skin, and sloped features, she had a distinctively Latina look, but she did not think of herself that way. She thought of herself in a different way entirely.

Born in East LA, in one of the poorest sections of the city, she had found her identity early. Her parents had been illegals who had crossed the border when borders no longer meant anything, seeking sanctuary from the madness that had already engulfed their home country. They had lived long enough to give birth to Angel and to see her reach early childhood, then succumbed to one of the plagues. She had grown up on the streets, like any number of others, poor and uneducated and homeless. She should have died, but she had not. She had dug deep down inside herself to find reservoirs of strength she hadn't known she possessed, and she survived.

She caught sight of the feeders now, their shadowy forms flitting past open doors and windows, racing toward the compound's besieged gates. Her mood darkened further. They were always there, always watching and waiting. She had learned to live with it, but not to like it. Even knowing their purpose, she still didn't understand what feeders were or what had created them. Were they made of something substantive? They fed on the darker emotions of human beings, but there was no reason for shadows to require food. There were so many of them it seemed impossible they could avoid detection, yet no human could see them save those few like herself.

She particularly hated the way they swarmed about her when she engaged in battle against the demons and once-men. She could feel them in the way she could feel a spider crawling on her skin. Even though they were only shadows. How could something that was only a shadow—little more than a darkness on the air—make you feel that it was alive?

Her attention shifted to the battle. Thousands of feeders swarmed at the base of the compound walls, climbing over the bodies of the dead and wounded, feeding on their pain and misery. They were everywhere, black shapes twisting and writhing as they fought to get at the living. There were so many that in places it was impossible for her to see anything else. Beneath their dark mass, humans and once-men fought for survival.

And the once-men were winning. Their army was vast and purposeful, their assault inexorable. Makeshift siege towers had been rolled forward, long scaling ladders had been thrown up, and battering rams were hammering at the reinforced iron gates. It was an all-out assault, one that in the end would succeed. In other times and places, this army had possessed artillery and had used it against the compounds it had besieged. But the mechanized weapons had slowly failed or fallen apart as conditions worsened and war matériel was used up or destroyed. Everything was rudimentary now, sliding back toward the medieval. But that didn't mean the army was any less successful. Ask those who had fought against it in the other compounds, if you could find any still alive. It didn't make any difference what kinds of war machines were used; the once-men held the advantage. They were not shut away inside compound walls. They were not afraid of dying. They were not even sane. Their madness and their bloodlust drove them.

And they had that old man to lead them.

She paused in the lee of an alleyway, not two blocks distant now from where the battle raged, close enough that she could make out the rage in the faces of the combatants and see the blood that soaked their clothing. She looked down momentarily at the rune-carved staff she carried in her hands, its burnished surface as black and depthless as a night pool. She could help those men and women who defended the compound. She commanded power enough to scatter the once-men like dried leaves, but she must not give in to the temptation to do so. She had not come here for that and could not afford to allow herself to become distracted. Besides, any summoning of the staff's magic would alert the demons, and the demons were already hunting for her.

Especially that old man.

Robert had warned her of him last year, just before the end, when he had gone to make a final stand with the defenders of the New Mexico and Arizona compounds. The old man had brought this same army to their walls and laid siege, hemming them in, closing off any escape. Robert had done what he could, but a single Knight of the Word was not enough—not then and not now. She had known Robert for five years, had fought beside him in Denver and might have fallen in love if the times had been different and falling in love had been a reasonable thing to do. Robert was tough physically and mentally, a better fighter than she was. But it hadn't been enough to save him.

In his final messages, the ones sent by carrier pigeon, he had described the old man so that she could not mistake him when he reached Los Angeles, as Robert knew by then he would. Tall and stooped, wrapped in a long gray cloak and wearing a wide-brimmed hat, he was the personification of evil. The eyes were what you remembered, Robert wrote. Hard as steel, so cold you could feel them burn your skin, but empty of everything human when they looked at you.

There were rumors about him even before Robert's letters. A demon whose special skills lay in tracking down Knights of the Word, he had been hunting and killing them for years. She did not know how many the old man had dispatched besides Robert, but it was more than a handful. Eventually he would come hunting for her.

But she would not be so easily trapped, she thought, and her hands tightened anew on her staff.

She darted from her hiding place and sprinted back down the street and then onto a side street, dodging debris and the shells of burned-out cars to reach the entrance to the hotel that lay just outside the Anaheim compound perimeter.

● ● ●

FIFTY YARDS BACK from where the once-men battered at the main gates of the compound, the old man stood watching. Wrapped in his gray cloak and shadowed by his slouch-brimmed hat, he had the look of Gandalf until you got close enough to see his face and feel the weight of those eyes. Then you knew for certain he wasn't a wizard seeking to convey the One Ring to Mount Doom, but a creature fallen under its terrible spell, his soul forever lost.

The old man didn't know about Gandalf or the One Ring and wouldn't have cared about either if he had. He was a demon, and humans were his prey. He had been there at the fall, when the first real cracks had begun to appear in civilization's weakening façade. He had been there in the time of Nest Freemark, when the gypsy morph had come into being. He had been there for centuries before that, a constant presence in the fabric of the world. He had been there long enough that he had forgotten completely the shedding of his human skin. As a demon, he viewed humankind as anathema, a plague upon the earth, an infection that required eradication.

But the old man was different from others of his kind. He was driven not by base instincts. Most demons self-destructed early and spectacularly, turned mad by their emotional excesses. His own struggle was of a different kind. He was not motivated by a desire for revenge or personal gratification or to prove himself or leave his mark upon the earth. What drove him, what consumed him as no fire could, was an insatiable desire to expose the deep and pervasive failings of humanity, and so prove irrefutably that his choice to remove himself from the species had been the right one.

He had made the decision early on to trade his humanity for a demon soul. He had never felt comfortable in his temporal skin, never accepted that he was meant to be nothing more than a brief presence in the firmament of life, here for only a moment, gone forever. Embracing the Void was a fair exchange for the depth of power his new identity offered, and he had never regretted his decision. He found his demon life fascinating. He was given countless opportunities to explore the nature of his former species. Peel back the layers of their skin and the discoveries proved endlessly surprising. All that was needed on his part was to figure out fresh ways to go about testing his theories.

It had taken him centuries to find the perfect way, but in the end, with the collapse of civilization, he had done so.

The slave camps had been his idea, his laboratory for experimentation. Breeding and genetic alteration could tell you so much about a species. The possibilities were unlimited; the results were quite astonishing. It was amazing to him even now what he had been able to do. Destruction of the human race was the ultimate goal, but there was no reason to rush the process.

Still, he was growing weary. His studies had been long and difficult, and he no longer possessed the physical or mental strength that had served him so well in the beginning. Neither the intensity of his purpose nor the hard edge of his determination had diminished. But time had drained the reservoir of his energy and, in truth, his interest in humans was waning. He was beginning to see them differently these days. They had become more of a distraction than an opportunity. There were only so many ways you could examine them, force them to reveal themselves. Sooner or later, they simply ceased to have importance.

He had even put aside his Book of Names, the list he had so carefully compiled of all those he had killed or caused to be killed over the centuries. Somewhere along the way, not so long ago, he had simply lost interest in record keeping. The dead no longer mattered to him. Now it seemed that even the living didn't matter. He was reaching the point at which he'd have to forgo experimentation and simply get on with extermination.

He looked at the once-men that attacked the compound gates. Although the screams and cries of the wounded and dying formed a wall of white noise in the background of his musings, he was barely aware of it. He cared nothing for what was taking place at this compound or at any of the compounds he had destroyed. He cared nothing for the army that followed him. He led because the other demons and the once-men feared him. They believed him to be the chosen of the Void, the one to whom they must all answer for any failure. He did nothing to discourage this thinking, although in truth he did not know if the Void had chosen him or not. He knew that what he did to the humans on his own time fit nicely with the Void's larger vision of the world. As long as his efforts continued to succeed, he did not think anyone would dare to challenge him.

Which was not to say that some among those he led would not see him dead in an instant, if they could find a way to make it happen.

One among them, the one he found the most dangerous, appeared now at his elbow, a looming presence that instantly took his mind off everything else.

"Lost in your memories of the dead, Old Man?" the female demon asked softly, bending close so that only he could hear.

Old Man. No one else would have dared to call him that. But she was fearless—or just plain crazy, depending on your point of view. Whichever it was, she was the only one among those he led that he knew he must watch closely.

"Have you found her yet, Delloreen?" he replied without bothering to look at her.

If he had looked, he would have found himself staring at her chest. Delloreen stood well over seven feet tall, one of the biggest women, demon or human, that he had ever seen. She was broad in the shoulders, narrow in the waist, and strong as an ox. There wasn't an ounce of fat on Delloreen, not an inch that wasn't muscle. He had seen her pick up one end of a car to move it out of the way like a toy. He had seen her break a man in half. No one ever crossed Delloreen, not even the Klee, which wasn't afraid of anything.

If he had looked up from her chest to her face, he would have found himself staring at features flattened and shaved to almost nothing, eyes the color of lichen, spiky blond hair, and patches of scales that coated her neck and chin. The scales were new in the past few years, small blemishes that had spread and grown thick and coarse. As if she were going through a biological change, maturing into a new species.

She had been with him for almost a dozen years now, his good right hand, the one who made certain his wishes were carried out. She was the only one strong enough to do that, which made her both useful and dangerous. At first, he hadn't seen her as a real threat. Delloreen didn't want what he had. She wasn't interested in leading. Leading required an assumption of responsibility, and she was too independent for anything as restrictive as that. She didn't want to have others relying on her; she liked going it alone. The old man understood. He gave her the freedom she sought, allowed her sufficient time to satisfy her special demon cravings, and required in turn that she watch his back. It was an arrangement that had worked well enough up to now.

Of late, however, she had begun to show signs of growing restless with her situation, and he was beginning to suspect that he would need to make a change.

"Have you," he repeated when she didn't answer him right away, "found her yet?" This time he looked directly at her. "Are you listening to me, Delloreen?"

Her broad flat face broke into a wide smile that showed all of her pointed teeth. "I always listen to you, Old Man. No, I haven't found her yet. But I will."

"Do you even know if she is still here?"

"She was at the Coliseum yesterday. She took the children out while we were breaking down the doors and killing the parents." Her demon smile widened. "Clever of her."

He shook his head reprovingly. "Escaped you again, did she?"

"She'll try the same thing here, sneaking the children past us while we concentrate on the adults." She paused. "This time it won't work."

"That remains to be seen. You've had three chances already and nothing to show for it."

Delloreen's smile twisted into something unpleasant. "Too bad about the children, isn't it, Fin-Fin? They would have kept you amused for hours. All those lost opportunities to make a fresh batch of little demons. Such a waste! It must make you very angry that she took them away."

He managed a disinterested shrug. "I've no need of more children, Delloreen."

She laughed. "Of course, you haven't. All you need are your memories of the ones you've already played all your hateful little games with. Isn't that right?"

She was deliberately taunting him, something she had made a habit of doing over the years, but which today, for reasons he couldn't explain, set his teeth on edge. The way she said it told him that things had changed between them in a way that couldn't be set right. It wasn't so much what she said as the tone she used, as if daring him to do something about it. She had never come at him like this before. No one challenged him—no one in his right mind.

She smiled at him as she might have a child. "Stop worrying, Old Man. You'll have what you want soon enough. You'll have your precious Knight of the Word to play games with."

He was still thinking about the way she had spoken to him a moment earlier, but he nodded agreeably. "Will I? I don't know. Perhaps she is too much for you. Perhaps I should send one of the others this time. The Klee, for instance?"

He did not miss the flush that blossomed like blood between the patches of scale. "The Klee is an animal. It doesn't think. It won't know what to do with her."

He looked at her questioningly, showing nothing of malice or disgust or the half a dozen other things he was feeling. His seamed, weathered face was an unreadable road map. "Perhaps an animal is what's needed."

He turned away before she could answer, giving her a moment to think about it. The gates of the compound were beginning to splinter. The once-men were advancing in a steady wave, the living climbing atop the bodies of the dead. A pyramid of corpses was forming at the base of the walls; here and there limbs still twitched. It was what made the once-men so useful: they didn't think, didn't feel, and didn't care about dying.

"The fact remains, she needs to be eliminated," he continued.

"I told you. I can manage it."

There was an edge to her words, but he kept his eyes on the battle at the compound gates. "I fear you underestimate her, Delloreen."

"As you once did Nest Freemark?" she snapped. "Hold the mirror up to your own face before you hold it up to mine, Old Man!"

He knew in that instant that he was going to have to kill her, but he did not change expression or react in any way. He just nodded and kept looking at the fighting in front of him, his mind working it through.

"Well," he said finally, "I expect you are right. I shouldn't be judging you. The fact of the matter is I'm doing too much of that lately. It's because I'm tired of this business. I've been at it too long. Someone younger and fresher is needed." He looked at her and saw the wariness in her lizard eyes. "Don't look so surprised. You were right about me. There's no use pretending otherwise. I've been alive a long time, and my enthusiasm for most things has been used up. My only real pleasure now comes from the children and the experiments. If I were to do nothing else, I could be happy."

He looked away again, letting her chew on that. Then he said, "Are you eager to take my place, Delloreen? I think maybe you are.

I think it's time you did. But it has to be handled right. My declaration of support will help, yet it isn't enough by itself. You must provide your followers with reassurance that you are the right choice to lead them. Just a little something to instill fresh confidence."

She hadn't said a word, still listening.

"Bring me the head of that girl on a stake, Delloreen," he said suddenly, almost as if he had just thought of it. "The head of a Knight of the Word—what better proof could anyone offer? When you do that, I'll step aside." He nodded slowly. "Yes, I'll gladly step aside."

Even without looking at her, he knew what she was thinking. She was thinking she would like to mount *his* head on a stake. Fair enough. But she wouldn't try it now, not while she wasn't quite sure of herself. She would wait until she was on firmer ground. She would wait for her chance.

"Listen to me, Old Man," she said suddenly, stepping so close he could feel her breath on his neck. "I don't want to take your place. I don't want to lead this rabble." One clawed hand fastened lightly on his shoulder. "I will bring you the girl's head because I'm tired of listening to you carp about it." The hand tightened. "But that's the end of it. You keep what you have and I'll do the same."

Then she turned and was gone. He did not look after her, but continued to stare at the fighting. He did not mistake her intentions, whatever she claimed. Nor did he think for one minute that things could remain the way they were. Once the line was crossed, that was the end of it. Or, in this case, the end of her.

He did not know yet how he would make it happen, only that he would. But getting her out of the way long enough to think about it was the first step. She would find herself fully occupied tracking that female Knight of the Word. She might even find herself in over her head. It wasn't the ideal solution, but it would suffice.

He heard her voice again in his mind, taunting him about Nest Freemark, reminding him of the only mistake he had ever made. It was not a mistake he was likely to repeat. It was a mistake, in fact, that one day he would set right. Because at some point in time, the gypsy morph would reveal itself, and when it did, he would know and he would find it and crush the life out of it.

He stared at the carnage in front of him and smiled bleakly as the gates gave way and the once-men poured through, screaming in anticipation of the bloodbath that waited. He would join them soon. He would immerse himself in the heady mix of killing and subjugation that was about to take place. He wasn't too old or tired for that.

Delloreen had called him *Old Man*.

But his demon name was Findo Gask.

10

ANGEL PEREZ MOVED quickly through the deserted lobby of the hotel, stepping past the trash and broken furniture, her eyes on the dilapidated stairway across the room. The lobby was in ruins, its walls stained and its carpet either torn out or worn through. Rats scurried in the walls, loud enough that she could hear them. Shattered glass littered the floor, and scraps of paper were piled up against the walls in heaps. The smell of dead things was everywhere.

She glanced around quickly, scanning the shadows. There were no feeders to be seen. A good sign.

Outside, the sounds of battle continued, drifting in through the broken windows. The intensity of the fighting was increasing, an unmistakable indication that time was running out. The compound would fall within the hour. She could not delay or her chance at helping the children trapped inside would be gone.

She reached the stairway, a wide circular ramp with carpeted steps that were worn and soiled and a wood-capped banister that wound upward through particles of dust and ash that floated on the air like tiny insects. Ignoring the stairs, she moved past their upward march to the back wall, where a small door stood closed and locked. She checked to make certain that the lock was still intact and the magic that warded it still in place, reassuring herself that no one had discovered her secret entrance to the compound. When she found that the door was secure, she used her staff to force it open.

Inside, she closed the door behind her, retrieved the solar-powered torch she had hidden in the walls weeks earlier, and started down the narrow stairwell that led to the underground passageway. Her footsteps echoed softly in a silence broken only by the distant boom and thud of the compound battle. She reached the basement level quickly, staying alert for any sign of danger. She had managed to get in and out of the other compounds without trouble, and she wasn't about to spoil her record here.

While she had failed to convince most of the Anaheim population, there were a few—mostly women—who understood that the end was inevitable. They had listened and accepted that what she was trying to tell the others was true, and that the best that they could do was to help Angel save the children. Working together, they had made a plan more than two months ago in preparation for this day. The children would be gathered together in a prearranged place, and Angel would take them away. Those among the women who chose to could go as well. Mothers and caregivers would be needed. Those who chose to could stay with their husbands and sons.

She knew that some would be undecided right up to the moment she appeared. She knew, as well, that some would help her and some would stand in her way. All would believe they were doing the right thing.

It was the same every time; it would be the same here.

She would have preferred not to have anything to do with this business. She was a Knight of the Word, and it was her mission in life to destroy the demons and those they led. But that was only half of the responsibility she had been given. The other half was to protect the humans the demons sought to enslave. She had found it to be the harder of the two jobs. Those she tried to help would have been happy to have her stand and die along with them, but they refused to change their minds about hiding behind their compound walls.

That left the children and the old and sick and sometimes the women, so she did what she could to help those and tried not to think about the rest. It was hard, because she knew what would happen to them. She had witnessed it over and over again. She had come upon the compounds after they had fallen; she had raided the slave camps where the survivors had been taken. She had viewed the results of the experiments the demons performed and heard the stories of the survivors. The memories were burned into her mind.

She slipped down the corridor to where a sealed door blocked her way. Again, she tested the locks and found them secure. Satisfied, she opened the door with her staff, a swift and subtle exercise of its magic, and was through. The corridor beyond was much broader and lit with solar-powered lamps. She was beneath the compound now, working her way toward the rooms where the children would be waiting. She could no longer hear the sounds of battle and therefore had no indication of how much time remained to her. She would have to hurry.

She followed the corridor for several hundred yards, ignoring the branching passageways and closed doors to either side. The safe room, where the children would be hidden, was ahead, buried another level down, protected by heavy steel doors and traps designed to collapse the passageway. She knew them all, and she knew how to avoid them. The demons and the once-men would not be so lucky, but in the end it wouldn't be enough to save the children and their protectors. It never was.

"Angel!"

She stopped abruptly as a woman's form emerged from the shadows ahead. "Are they all right?" Angel asked.

Helen Rice nodded. Small, slight, and full of energy, she was the leader of those who had promised to help when the day to do so arrived. Angel had met with Helen last week, warning her that it would happen soon. "We have them all together in the safe room. Almost two hundred children and a dozen women and men to shepherd them. A few others are there, too, the ones who won't allow it. I couldn't do anything about them until you came."

Angel started ahead once more, taking Helen's arm and turning her about. "They won't be a problem. But we have to hurry. The once-men are breaking through. They'll be down here soon."

"Where are the children from the other compounds?" Helen asked, breathing hard as they practically ran down this small, dark corridor that was deliberately disguised to look as if it lacked any importance at all. "Did you get them all out?"

"Most." She tried not to think about the ones she hadn't, the ones she'd lost. "As many as I could. It wasn't easy. They're hidden up in the hills north, waiting for us."

Helen shook her head. "I can't believe this is happening. I tell myself it is, know for a fact it is, and I still can't believe it. Sweet Heaven!"

They went down a set of steps and along a second corridor that ended at a steel wall with a metal keypad recessed into its surface. Helen punched a sequence of numbers on the pad, and a set of hidden locks released. Angel pushed against the wall, which swung open far enough to allow them passage. The women stepped through into bright light and eerie silence.

Dozens of children sat cross-legged around makeshift tables on a concrete floor. The smaller children were drawing and working with puzzles. The older ones were reading. A few not quite old enough to fight at the walls or work in the nursing stations were helping the adults supervise. No one was talking in a regular tone of voice; everyone was whispering. Frightened eyes glanced up as Angel and Helen appeared through the door, fixing quickly on the former with her strange black staff.

A small clutch of women came forward, faces drawn, eyes filled with fear. They knew.

"Is it time?" one asked.

"What do we do?" asked another.

Helen reached for the closest and squeezed her arm reassuringly. "Gather them in their safety groups and put one older child or one adult with each group. Remind them they are not to speak or make any sounds at all once we leave this room."

Those addressed broke away, spreading out across the room and summoning the children to their feet. But now a different woman came charging over, her face flushed and angry, her hands gesturing wildly. "No, no, no!" she cried out, coming right up against Helen and gripping the smaller woman by her shoulders. "What do you think you're doing? You can't take these children out of here!"

She swung around on Angel. "This is your fault. You've caused nothing but trouble with your scare tactics and false prophecies! I'm sick of it! Who do you think you are? These aren't your children! You can't just come in here and take them away!"

She was furious, and now she was joined by several others, all of them looking as if they meant to attack her if she even moved toward the children.

Angel held her ground. "The gates are about to collapse under the weight of the attack. The enemy will be inside in minutes. When that happens, all chance of escape will be cut off. You will be sealed inside. Eventually, you will be found. You know what will happen then."

"I know what you *say* will happen! Anyway, I don't believe you! You'd do anything to get those children!"

"I would do anything to save them, yes." Angel kept her voice even, her gaze level.

"Get out of here! Leave us alone! We're safe right where we are! Our men will protect us from those creatures outside!"

Angel stepped right up to her and seized her by the arms. "Look in my eyes. Tell me what you see. Go on, look!"

Squirming to break free, but held fast by Angel's strong grip, the woman did as she was told. It was impossible to say what she saw there, but Angel knew what the effect would be. It was a skill she had learned when she had become a Knight of the Word, although she was the only one she knew who could do it. She pictured the worst things she had ever been witness to; she conjured the most terrible images of the most heinous acts of the demons and the once-men. Something of that horror reflected in her eyes when she did so, and anyone looking caught a momentary glimpse of Hell.

"Oh, my God!" the woman breathed. She shrank down inside herself as if deflated; she would have fallen if Angel wasn't holding her. Her hands covered her face and tears began running down her cheeks. "Don't show me any more! Please, please don't!"

She was shaking now, completely undone. The others who had

supported her clustered about protectively, hands reaching for her, faces stricken. Angel gave the woman over to them and motioned them back. "Don't interfere further in this. Either help with the children or stand aside."

They stood aside, consoling the demoralized woman, huddling together and whispering furiously. Angel ignored them, sending Helen to those who had agreed to help in readying the children for departure. They were already standing in lines, hands joined, eyes darting this way and that as they waited for instructions. A few exchanged momentary glances with her, but no one tried to speak. She gave it a few more seconds, then moved over to reopen the section of wall that would take them to safety.

"Quietly, now," she whispered.

They went back through the hidden door, climbed the stairs to the basement level, and went down the narrow corridor to the larger, more brightly lit one beyond. Angel, in the lead, glanced back repeatedly, making sure the children and their escorts were keeping up while at the same time listening for anything that seemed out of place. She believed they had not been discovered yet, but there was no point in taking chances.

At the mouth of the corridor, she brought the procession to a halt, letting those in the rear close up the gaps between themselves and those in the front. She took a moment to scan ahead, searching for movement. The corridor seemed empty. She stepped out into the light, beckoned to those who followed her, and moved back down toward the doors and stairs that led to the abandoned hotel and the streets beyond.

She was all the way to the last door, the one that opened onto the stairwell leading up to the hotel, when she sensed the presence of the demon. It was ahead of her, waiting at the top of the stairs. She could smell its stink and feel its heat, and her stomach reacted as it always did when she was in the presence of evil—with a sudden lurch and a queasiness that threatened to bring her to her knees. She stopped where she was, waiting for the feeling to pass, for her training to reassert itself.

Behind her, the line of children and women slowed to a ragged halt. Helen appeared at her elbow. "What is it?"

Angel didn't answer. She stared at the door ahead, trying to think what she could do. The one thing she could not do was to tell Helen the truth: that they were trapped.

● ● ●

WHEN HER PARENTS *die, Angel Perez becomes a true child of the streets. She has no family and no home. She has no one to look after her. She has no skills and no knowledge of how to forage for food and water or how to find shelter or how to survive for more than a day. She is eight years old.*

But luck favors her. She manages to survive for five days by staying hidden and living on the little food and water her parents scavenged before the plague took them. She fights down her fear and spends her time trying to think what to do.

Then Johnny finds her.

His given name is Juan Gonzalez, and like her parents he has come over the border to make a better life. He seems old to her, even though he is only forty-five. His hair is wild and long, his face bearded and scarred, and his hands weathered and gnarled. But his voice is kind, and when he finds her hiding in the rubble of the home her parents made for her, he doesn't try to approach her too quickly or play the sort of games that might frighten her. He simply starts talking to her, calling her little one *and telling her she can't stay where she is, that it is too dangerous, that all of LA is too dangerous for an eight-year-old girl. She must come with him, he says. He has a place not far from there and she can stay there with him. He is tired of living alone anyway, and he wants someone to talk to. She is under no obligation to stay. She can leave whenever she wants, and he will never hurt her or do anything that she doesn't want him to.*

She believes him. She can't say why, but she does. So she goes with him and lives with him for six years. He teaches her to forage and to cook. He teaches her how to defend herself with just her hands and feet. He teaches her how to look out for the things that might threaten her— the scavengers and the mutants and the animals. He shows her places she can run to if anything ever happens to him. He even shows her how to use the short-barreled flechette that he keeps for emergencies he hopes will never arrive. He tells her that she is the daughter he will never have, the daughter he would have wanted if things had worked out differently.

Everybody knows him. Johnny is the man, the one everyone looks up to. The street people like him for the same reasons Angel does: he is respectful of and kind to them and does what he can to help them in their struggle to survive. He watches out for them in the same way he watches out for her, and their little barrio community is tight-knit and protective. Even if the compounds will not have them, with their fear of outsiders and plague, they will have one another.

But it isn't enough to save them. The collapse of civilization has spawned all sorts of human flotsam and jetsam, and some of it eventually finds its way to their hideaway. The gang calls itself the Blade Runners and believes itself the beginning of a new order. Its members are their own law, and their allegiance is to one another and no one else. They go where they choose and take what they want. Where they come from or how they get to LA and Angel's little community is a mystery that she later decides has more to do with perverse chance than anything else.

Johnny stands up to them when they threaten the others, bringing out the flechette, and they back down. But they hover at the fringes of the community, angry and vengeful and determined to get what they want, even if what they want is barely worth the effort. People are crazy then, just as they are crazy now. They do insane, inexplicable things; they do them without reason or they do them for the worst of reasons. Angel knows when she sees these men that they are mad. She knows it the same way that she knows exactly how the madness will end.

One night, Johnny doesn't come home. She knows right away that he is dead, that the Blades have found a way to catch him off guard and kill him. She knows, as well, that they will be coming next for her. She has seen how several of them look at her, and she knows what that means. She cries first because she is sad and afraid and because her life is forever changed with Johnny gone. She thinks about seeking help from some of the others. She thinks about fleeing into another part of the city.

Then she brings out the flechette, hides herself in the crumbling warehouse next to where she and Johnny made their home, and hunkers down to wait.

The wait is short. The Blades appear around midnight, slinking out of the shadows like dogs, creeping up on the now deserted home, ten strong, armed with knives and clubs. They probably think her asleep. They probably think she does not yet realize what they have done to Johnny and will catch her unawares. They are not very good at what they are attempting, making enough noise that their approach would have awakened her even if she had been sleeping. But that doesn't make them any less dangerous or odious, and her mind is made up as to what she will do to them.

She waits until they have crowded inside, all but one who stays at the door as lookout. He leans against the frame and looks bored, glancing inside periodically as he waits for something to happen. She is upon him by then, rounding the corner of the house. The flechette fires ten rounds and cuts a twelve-foot-wide swath with each discharge. She uses the first round on the lookout, blowing him back through the doorway and into the others. She uses the next seven on the ones she catches inside, leaving them shattered and broken. She uses the last on the one who somehow manages to get out through a window, catching up with him two blocks away and taking his head off.

She is left shaking and furious and terrified all at once, and she knows in the aftermath of her retribution that nothing in her life will ever be the same.

● ● ●

HER THOUGHTS OF Johnny and of that night ten years ago when she destroyed the Blade Runners were there and gone in seconds. She wished she had a weapon like the flechette now, something that could open up a path with shards of metal that would rip apart even a demon. But she had only her staff and her skills to protect more than two hundred children and a handful of women, and she was afraid it wasn't enough.

"Angel, what's wrong?" Helen hissed again.

She looked at the other woman, then at the door in front of her, and made up her mind. She had little choice. They had to either go forward or turn around and go back; all the other entrances had long since collapsed or been sealed. Although the situation was different from the one she had faced after Johnny was killed, it felt the same. She knew what she had to do.

"Wait here," she said to Helen. "This door will be open, but don't go through it until you hear me call for you. Then bring everyone at once, as quickly as you can. Don't stop for anything. Especially not for me. Get up the stairs and out of the building; run down the street and out of the city. Go up into the hills and hide. I will find you." She paused. "If I don't come within the next few hours, head north toward San Francisco. You might find those from the other compounds on your way and you can join forces."

Helen started to speak, but Angel stopped her by taking hold of her arms and drawing her close. "Listen to me. There is something very bad at the top of the stairs. I don't think it cares about you or the children. I think it is looking for me. It won't let itself be distracted once it has me. Don't give it a reason to change its mind. Do you understand me?"

The other woman nodded, then shook her head quickly. "I can't just run away and leave you! I want to help. You've done so much for us. There must be something!"

She took a deep breath. "This isn't something you can help me with, Helen. What waits up there is very powerful. It isn't anything human; it is something else. Only I can deal with it."

She released the other's arms and stepped away. "Remember what I said. Do what I told you to do."

Then she moved over to the heavy door, used the magic of her staff a second time to release its locks, pulled it wide open, and stepped through into the gloom of the narrow corridor beyond.

11

SHE SWITCHED ON the flashlight and began to climb. She went slowly and soundlessly, placing her feet carefully. She had been able to sense the presence of the demon, but that was a gift peculiar to her. It was entirely possible that the demon had not yet sensed her. Still, she had to be ready.

When she reached the door that opened onto the lobby of the old hotel, she stopped. Her five senses told her nothing of what waited beyond, but her sixth sense reaffirmed what she already knew. The demon was out there. It had discovered her plan to rescue the children, surmised that she had gone into the tunnels, and was awaiting her return.

Oddly enough, it appeared to be alone.

She took a long time to make sure she wasn't mistaken about this, thinking that her instincts must be misleading her. But they weren't; the demon was alone. This worried her more than she cared to think about. A demon hunting for a Knight of the Word would normally have brought dozens of once-men to help with the effort. This one was apparently confident enough to believe that it could handle the job by itself. Which, in turn, meant that it possessed either great strength or extraordinary skill.

Or, she added with a shiver, it was totally insane.

I'm not going to survive this.

It was a terrible thing to tell herself, but the words were out and swimming about inside her head before she could stop them. She fought them down and locked them away again, but their whisper lingered.

She took a deep steadying breath and closed her eyes, trying to read what lay beyond. She pictured the lobby, its walls and ceiling, the curved stairway, the debris, the broken-out windows and doors, the check-in desk against the back wall, all of it. She formed the picture and studied it and tried to see where the demon would be. It would choose a place where she wouldn't see it right away, but where it could get to her quickly. It would try to kill her before she even knew it was there, thinking to catch her unawares. Where would it wait? She tried to imagine it, seeing it in her mind, searching it out.

Then, all at once, she knew.

It would be waiting on the stairs above the doorway where it could vault the railing and fall upon her as she came through. If it was quick enough, it could break her neck before she even knew what had happened.

She could see it now in her mind, could see it clearly, could see the demon, faceless and formless, crouched and ready.

Big.

But she would be bigger.

Strong.

But she would be stronger.

She tightened her grip on the staff and faced the door. She had left it unlocked. The demon would know that, would have tested it to discover if the locks were back in place. Had they been resealed, it could have relied on the sound of their release as a warning of her approach. Unsealed, they would give no warning. So it would be listening for the sounds of her approach or, failing that, the shadow of the door opening into the room.

She would have to be very quick.

She summoned the magic, let it build, and then blew the door right off its hinges. As she did so, she went through the opening at a slant, angling back against the wall as she broke clear of the doorway, eyes and staff lifted to the stairs above her. The shadow was already dropping toward her, every bit as smooth and supple as she had feared. But it was a fraction of a second too slow. Clawed fingers raked the air she had just passed through, just out of reach, clutching futilely. As the demon landed, the white fire of her staff exploded into it, throwing it across the room and into the lobby desk, smashing the desk into pieces.

She had gotten only a momentary glance at it, but enough to reveal that it was huge. "Helen!" she screamed. "Run!"

She moved quickly to place herself between the doorway and the demon, which was already struggling to free itself from the debris, arms and legs thrashing. She got another glimpse of it as it pulled itself clear—spiky blond hair, scaly patches on its face and neck, tree-trunk body. It was female, barely. She attacked, the staff's fire striking it a second time, knocking it off its feet and sending it sprawling. But the fire seemed to have less effect on it this time, as if it had found a way to deal with the punishment.

Behind her, she heard the pounding of feet and the shrill of small voices raised in alarm. The children were escaping, racing for the freedom of the streets. She didn't turn to look, her eyes on the demon. She advanced on it, looking to gain more impact from a third strike. But the demon was ready this time and came at her like a huge rodent, skittering across the floor with unbelievable speed, dodging her attempted strike, knocking her from her feet, and closing on her with an audible hiss. She felt as if a wall had collapsed on her, but she tightened her compact body into a knot and fought her way free. The demon tried to follow, but she jammed the staff into its throat and the white fire exploded out and thrust it away.

She was back on her feet quickly, the sound of screaming children washing over her, chaos everywhere. She forced herself to ignore the noise, to keep her eyes on the demon as it rolled into a corner before springing back to its feet. It hissed at her and laughed, taunting her. It was as if the fire of her staff was having no effect at all, as if all she was doing was buying time. Perhaps she was, she realized; perhaps that was the best she could do.

The demon came at her again, flinging pieces of debris, sweeping them up and hurling them so quickly she had to use the fire to protect herself. Then it was on top of her, hammering into her with all of its considerable weight, tearing at her with clawed fingers and ripping at the staff. She sidestepped the charge, ducking under the long arms, using the training Johnny had given her to keep her feet as she moved to one side. Even so, the long claws raked her right side, knocking her off balance and flat on her back. Fiery pain ripped down the length of her body as she tried to scramble to her feet. She was too slow; before she could rise, the demon was on top of her again.

This time it picked her up and threw her across the room. She was weightless for a moment, flying through the air, hugging the staff to her chest. Then she slammed into the curved lift of the stairway and collapsed to the floor, nearly blacking out from the impact. It felt as if every bone in her body had been broken. She gasped for air and struggled up again, swinging the staff about and sending the fire in a wide protective sweep. There was blood and dust in her eyes, and she could barely see. She got lucky and caught a glimpse of the huge body leaping for her, and she brought the staff's fire to bear.

The demon went right through it.

She watched the fire engulf it, turn it into a living torch, and fail to halt its momentum. She watched it as if it were happening in slow motion. She could see the madness in the demon's green eyes, could see the glint of its sharp teeth as it grimaced against the pain it was absorbing. She could see it breaking past her defenses, impossibly strong.

In the next instant it had wrenched the staff from her hands and flung it away.

It went into a crouch in front of her then, smiling through a mask of scales and dirt and blood. Its spiky hair was singed and its clothing was in tatters; one arm had been opened to the bone. But it was a demon, and demons felt little pain. Demons could heal themselves of injuries that humans would die from. This one seemed both un-slowed and untroubled by its injuries. This one seemed to revel in them.

It feinted right and then left in mock attacks, toying with her. It was enjoying this, she realized. It was having fun.

She was back on her feet now and had taken a defensive stance. She did not look for the staff, did not take her eyes off the demon. Her training made her reactions instinctive. She knew what to do, even though she knew it was probably over and she was going to be killed. She did not respond to the feints, did not lunge or back away. She held her ground, waiting.

When the demon came for her, its claws slashing, its huge body seeking to envelop her in a ring of muscle and bone, she braced her-self until it was close enough, then hit it with both fists between the eyes. The blow was shocking, and the demon staggered, crying out. Its arms tried to wrap about her anyway, but she ducked under their sweep and struck it again, this time on the right ear. The demon howled, swung about, and caught her fists flush on its nose.

Even then, Angel could not escape. The demon's claws raked her shoulder and back, and one forearm hammered into the side of her face with such force that she was knocked sprawling and dazed. The demon shrieked in fury as its next lunge missed, and Angel regained her feet and sprinted across the room toward her staff. In a single motion she swept it from the rubble, wheeled back, and sent the fire directly into the face of her pursuer.

This time the fire did its work. The demon went over backward, howling and thrashing, twisting so violently that it careened back-ward into the already damaged staircase. Wood splintered, plaster cracked, supports buckled, and the entire structure gave way with shocking suddenness, collapsing on the demon and burying it from view.

Angel stared at the rubble, breathing heavily, waiting. When nothing happened, she wheeled about. The room was silent and empty; the children had disappeared with Helen and the other women. She glanced back at the collapsed staircase, searching for movement. There was none. Had she not been so debilitated by her struggle, she might have taken the time to dig through the debris to finish the job. As it was, she could barely move.

She took a long slow breath and pulled herself together. She was still alive and that was enough. Aching and bloodied, she walked out the door and into the street.

●　●　●

THE GATES TO the compound had given way half an hour earlier, the once-men had poured through, and Findo Gask had waited patiently for the way to be opened. His orders were clear. Everyone who resisted was to be killed. All of the sick and injured were to be killed. All of the old people were to be killed. The rest, the strong and the fit, were to be chained together, but not harmed. The children, in particular, were not to be touched. Prisoners were no good to him if they were damaged. Breeding pens and experimentation labs required healthy specimens.

Once shackled and lined up, the captives would be marched twenty miles east to the slave camp he had established two months earlier. There they would live out their usefulness.

He glanced over at the gates as the first of them appeared through the haze of smoke and ash. They shuffled ahead with their heads down and their hands clasped, and only one or two bothered to look up as they passed him. He gave them a momentary glance, then looked back at the burning compound. It would be looted for whatever supplies, equipment, and weapons they could salvage. Everything left over, including the bodies of the dead, would be burned in the compound center. It would take all day to complete this task. It would take the rest of the week to pull down the walls and level the buildings. Findo Gask was thorough. By the time he was finished, almost nothing would remain to mark where the compound had stood.

Then he would march his army north and begin the process all over again with the compounds on the coast.

Except that he had done something different this time in antici-

pation of bringing his efforts to a swifter conclusion. With precise instructions, he had sent half of his army north two weeks ago to begin
laying siege to the compounds of Seattle and Portland. While his
half of the army worked its way up the coastline to San Francisco,
the other half would begin working its way down from Seattle. Together, the two would form the jaws of a trap that would soon close
on the last outposts of the Pacific coast.

In less than six months, it would all be over.

One of the lesser demons that served him, a still-too-human
creature named Arlen, lean and stoop-shouldered and possessed of
stringy hair and reptilian features, came through the gates leading
two bloodied figures by chains he had fastened about their necks.
Every time they stumbled, he screamed at them and yanked hard
on the chains before allowing them to struggle up again. Bringing
them to a ragged halt, he threw them down at his leader's feet and
kicked them. One was a woman. Findo Gask waited. Arlen beamed
in expectation of his reward, then realized he was expected to say
something.

"These are all that are left, yessir," he said.

Findo Gask nodded patiently. "Left of what?"

"Them that was guarding the children."

"And the children are where?"

Arlen shrugged. "Gone. She took them out while we was breaking down the gates. Took them out some tunnels, says these two. The
whole bunch of them."

"The female Knight of the Word?" He spoke quietly, but from
between clenched teeth. "She took all of the children?"

The other demon nodded eagerly. "Sure enough. Took 'em all.
Must have come in another way."

Findo Gask picked up the length of chain knotted about the
woman and drew her back to her feet. His eyes locked on hers. She
was shaking all over, but she could not look away.

"Where did the Knight of the Word take them?" he said.

"Please," she whispered.

He gave her one moment more, then snapped her neck and
threw her aside. He reached down and yanked the man to his feet.
"Can you tell me where they went?"

"Out the tunnels . . . that lead to the streets," the man gasped. One eye was gone and the other swollen shut. His face was a mask of blood. "She told us . . . this would happen. We . . . should have listened."

"Yes, you should have." He dropped the man in a heap and looked at Arlen. "Where are these tunnels?"

Arlen shrugged—one shrug too many to suit Findo Gask. Quick as a snake, his hand shot out, fastened around the other's neck, and began to squeeze. "Maybe you had better organize a search party to go down into the lower levels of the compound and find them."

He emphasized each word without raising his voice, then threw the hapless Arlen down beside the chained prisoner. "Maybe I should arrange for you to change places with him. Maybe I will if you don't find those children."

Arlen crawled a safe distance away on hands and knees, then came to his feet and staggered off without looking back. Findo Gask let him go. In truth, he didn't really care about the children. There were always other children. What he cared about was discipline and obedience. What he cared about was respect born of fear. Let them think he was soft or indecisive, and they would rip him apart.

There was danger of that happening as it was.

Where, he wondered suddenly, was Delloreen?

• • •

IT TOOK ANGEL a long time to get out of the city. She was too sore and too tired to move quickly, so beaten up from her encounter with the demon that she could barely put one foot in front of the other. If she was to meet resistance from another demon now, or even from a band of once-men, she wasn't sure she had the strength to stand up to them. So she kept to the alleyways and shadows, skirting anything that seemed like danger, conserving what strength remained to try to catch up to Helen and the children.

More than once, she looked back to see if that demon from the hotel was following. She had never encountered anything quite so

ferocious. That the demon was female only made it seem more re-
pellent, made it feel as if it were a perversion of herself as a Knight
of the Word, a monster with no other purpose than to destroy. She
hoped she had killed it, but she didn't think she had. Worse, she
knew that if it lived it would come after her, probably with once-
men to support it this time, probably with that old man as company.

When it did, she wasn't certain what she was going to do to save
herself. If not for the stairway collapse, it would have had her. She
had been lucky this time. She couldn't expect to be that lucky
again.

Behind her, black clouds of smoke billowed from the Anaheim
compound. The demons had broken through the gates and were inside. The last of the defenders were being slaughtered; she could
hear their screams rising with the smoke. Why hadn't they listened
to her? What more could she have done? There were no answers,
and asking the questions only served to point up the futility of her
efforts as a Knight of the Word.

She stopped a moment and looked back at the shattered landscape. It didn't help knowing what was going on now inside the
compound. The lucky ones would be killed; the unlucky would be
taken as slaves. If there were any children left, they would be taken
for experimentation. She hoped they had all gotten out. She wished
she could go back to make sure. She wanted nothing so much as to
save one more tiny life.

The ache and weariness washed through her in a sudden rush
and she began to cry silently. She didn't cry much these days, but
every now and then she couldn't seem to help herself. She grieved
for those in the compounds, men and women who had struggled so
hard to survive. She grieved for everything the world had lost, for
the common ordinary things everyone had taken for granted, for
what had once seemed so dependable and lasting. She had not been
alive then, but she knew something of what it had been like from
the stories the old ones told. A few had been born in those times
and remembered a little of what it had been like. But they were
mostly gone, and the memories of the old ones now were much
darker.

She wondered if she would ever be able to have memories that were sweet and treasured and welcome when they surfaced. They would have to be memories she would make later, she knew. Such memories would have to come from the future.

After a last look back across the broken walls and collapsed roofs of the buildings stretching to the compound pyre, she turned away. With Los Angeles gone, the demon-led army would begin to move north toward San Francisco, where the whole scenario would be repeated. She wondered if there was a Knight of the Word defending that city. She guessed she would find out when she got there. That was where she was going. It was the only place left for her to go.

Ahead, the escaped children and the women herding them appeared in a ragged line. Some of them were clutching favorite possessions as they trudged through the ruined city streets. Some of them were crying and hanging on to each other. She could imagine their thoughts in the wake of losing home, and parents, and everything they had ever known and loved. She could imagine their despair.

She hurried to catch up to them, anxious to do what she could to ease their suffering.

● ● ●

IT TOOK DELLOREEN a long time to extricate herself from beneath the collapsed stairway. She had lost consciousness, knocked senseless by one of the supports that had struck her head. When she woke, everything was black and the weight of the rubble was pressing down on her. She pushed and shoved and finally worked her way free, clawing up from the debris to the air and light and the silence of the hotel lobby. She stood and looked around, already knowing what she would find. The Knight of the Word had escaped her.

She was in some pain, but her pain was secondary to her rage, and her rage gave her renewed strength. She looked down at the tear in her arm, at the white of the bone. Injuries like this would cripple a human, but not a demon. Using her fingers, she pulled the flesh back together and held it in place until scales, which were gradually spreading over her entire body, closed the wound. Her human flesh was weak, but her demon scales were like armor. She hated the human part of herself, but there wasn't much of it left.

When the wound was sealed sufficiently that she didn't have to think about it anymore, she brushed herself off, wiped the blood from her face with her hands, and licked her fingers clean. She thought about her battle with the Knight of the Word. The woman was small, but resilient. She was stronger than she looked. Still, she should not have escaped. If not for the staircase collapsing, she wouldn't have. Delloreen was more than a match for her. When they met again, she would prove it.

She walked to the door and looked outside. Down the street, from the direction of the compound, black smoke billowed into the midday air. The sounds of battle had subsided, and the solitary wails and groans that had replaced them bore testament to the result. She could go back now and resume her place at Findo Gask's side, but she already knew she wouldn't be doing that. She would not go back until she had found and killed the Knight of the Word. She would not go back until she had the Knight's head on a stake.

That was what it would take for her to replace Findo Gask as leader of the army. He had set the conditions, and she had as much as said she would fulfill them. Crawling back to him now would be a clear indication to everyone that she lacked the strength to rule. It would be an admission of failure and a sign of weakness. She knew that. She knew, as well, it would be her death sentence.

But she was not compelled by any of this. She would not go after the Knight of the Word out of either fear or a need to prove anything to Findo Gask—or to the other demons or the once-men that served them or even to the Void, itself. She would go because no one had ever bested her. She would go to match herself against an adversary that might mistakenly believe it was her equal. Her failure to kill this female Knight of the Word was a humiliation that she would not suffer under any circumstances. It did not matter what she had promised Findo Gask, or what anyone else expected of her. It only mattered that she find this creature and set things right.

She looked down the street, away from the compound. The Knight would have gone north, taking the rescued women and children with her to the compounds in San Francisco. She would not be able to travel quickly with children in tow. Not as quickly as Delloreen, who would be tracking her. She would not escape a second time. She would try, of course, but she would fail.

The demon pictured in her mind for a moment what she might do to the woman when she had her within reach again. She pictured the fear and pain she would find in her eyes when she had her in her grasp. She pictured the ways she would break her.

It was only then that she would feel vindicated.

Putting such images aside for another time and brushing off any further concerns about the old man, she began walking north out of the city.

12

IT WAS MIDDAY in the ruins of the Emerald City, and the Ghosts were playing stickball in the streets of Pioneer Square. Stickball most closely resembled baseball, a game none of the Ghosts had ever seen, though they'd read about it in books. They didn't know anything about stickball, either, for that matter, other than what Panther taught them. Panther claimed to have played it on the streets of San Francisco. He showed them what he knew, and they made up the rest.

They had figured out what innings were and how many they should play, but nine innings made the game go on too long so they settled on five. They had figured out that in baseball there were nine or maybe ten players on the field, but they didn't have that many Ghosts, so they settled for teams of three or four. They had a rubber ball, one that was kind of worn and squishy, but no bat, so they used a sawed-off broomstick. The batter just tossed the ball in the air, hit it as hard as possible, and took off running. If someone caught the ball, the runner was out. If it was dropped, the runner could keep going. But you could still touch him with the ball or throw it at him and hit him, in which case he was out, too. The game was played in the open space just north of the old pergola—Owl had looked the name up in one of her history books. There were four bases, old tires laid out in an irregular formation because the open space and surrounding streets were clogged with debris and derelict vehicles. The base paths looked a little like a maze. They hadn't figured out strikes and balls, either, but that didn't matter since there was no pitcher and they had decided early on that the batter should just keep swinging at the ball until he hit it.

They allowed three outs per side per inning, but sometimes they extended that number to four when one of the little kids made an out, like Squirrel or Candle, just because it seemed fair.

It wasn't the stickball kids had played fifty years earlier in the streets of the cities of America, but it worked just as well. It gave them something to do besides forage and scout, and Owl was forever telling them they needed to have fun now and then. Panther, in particular, liked this form of fun, having thought up the game in the first place, and he spent much of his time urging the others to play it.

Just now, it was the fourth inning and he was batting, facing a field that consisted of Chalk, Sparrow, and Bear. Fixit and Candle were waiting for their turn at bat. Owl was acting as umpire, a role she was regularly assigned, as much because she was the only one any of them trusted to be fair and impartial as because of the wheelchair. Squirrel was still in their underground lair, recovering from his fever. While he had insisted he was strong enough to come up and play ball with the others, Owl had told him he needed at least one more day in bed. River was keeping him company.

Hawk stood off to one side, the odd man out in the game and just as happy to be so because he was preoccupied with mulling over the consequences of Candle's vision of the previous night. Cheney dozed in a nearby doorway, big head resting on his paws, eyes closed, ears pricked, missing nothing.

"Better move way back, children!" Panther shouted to the fielders, tossing the ball up casually as he took his batting stance. "Hey, I said *way back* 'cause this baby's gonna fly!"

Then he hit it a ton, his smooth, hard swing catching the ball flush on the end of the broomstick and sending it soaring far out into the square. Chalk and Bear, who were already playing pretty far out in deference to Panther's superior athletic ability, backed up hurriedly. But the ball dropped between them as they misjudged its distance, and Panther skipped around the bases, tossing out taunts about ineptitude and bad eyesight. Unfortunately for him, he was having such a good time that he failed to account for Sparrow, who was waiting at second base for the relay, and he ran right into her. Sparrow, furious, kicked him in the shins and started beating on him. Howling in dismay and at the same time laughing, Panther broke away.

By this time, Bear had chased down the ball. Wheeling back, he gave it a mighty heave. Bear was strong, and the ball flew a long way. Sparrow tried to catch it, but the ball caromed off her hands, took an odd hop, and bounced into Panther, who was just coming into home plate.

"You're out!" shouted Sparrow.

"Out!" Panther laughed. "No frickin' way."

"Out!" Sparrow repeated. "The ball hit you on the base path. The rules say you're out!"

Panther picked up the broomstick, waved it at her threateningly, and then threw it down again. "What are you talking about? That don't count! Bear just heaved the ball in! He didn't try to hit me, so I ain't out! Besides, it hit you first!"

"Doesn't matter who it hit first. It hit you last, and you're out!"

"You're frickin' crazy!"

Sparrow stalked over to him, brushing her mop of straw-colored hair out of her blue eyes, brow furrowed in anger. "Don't talk to me like that! Don't use that street language on me, Panther Puss! Owl, tell him he's out!"

The rest of them came crowding in to stand around Panther and Sparrow, who by now were right in each other's faces, yelling. Hawk watched it for a moment, amused. Then he saw Owl give him an irritated glance as she wheeled over to try to break it up, and he decided that enough was enough.

"Hey, all right, that's the end of it!" he shouted them down, striding over. "Panther, you're not out. You can't be out when the ball bounces off someone or something else first. That's the rule. But," he held up one hand to silence Sparrow's objection, "you have to go back to first for running over Sparrow. Isn't that right, Owl?" He looked over at her and winked.

She gave him a thumbs-up. "Play ball!" she shouted, one of the few things she knew they said in baseball when they wanted the game to resume, motioning Panther back to first base.

Grumbling, the players all returned to their positions. "Still say that's bull!" snapped Panther over his shoulder as he slouched away.

Hawk ambled after Owl as she wheeled back behind home plate, hands in his pockets, head lowered so that he could watch the movement of his feet on the pavement ahead of him. "I don't know about these games," he said.

Owl glanced over her shoulder. "It's good for them, Hawk. They need the games. They need something to take their minds off what's happening around them. They need to get all that energy and aggression out." She gestured at him. "You should be playing, too. Why don't you take Fixit's place for a while?"

He shrugged. "Maybe later."

She wheeled into position behind home plate and reached for his hand as he stopped beside her. "At least tell me what's bothering you. And don't say *nothing* because I know better. Is this about Tessa?"

It was, of course, because everything was about Tessa these days. But it was also about Candle's vision, and he hadn't told Owl of that yet. He wasn't sure he should tell anyone because he didn't know what it meant or what he should do about it. He was still working that through, trying to decide if he should make preparations to leave the city and, if so, where he should think about going.

Leaving meant uprooting everyone from the only stable home they had known. It meant finding another place to go to, abandoning the familiar and striking off into the unknown. It meant finding a way to persuade Tessa to go with them, to leave her parents and her life inside the compound, to give up everything she had ever known.

In short, it meant turning everyone's world upside down. He didn't have the first notion how to go about doing that.

"While you're deciding how much you want to tell me," Owl

said, breaking into his thoughts, "there's something I need to tell *you*. It's about River. She's been going somewhere on her own without telling anyone. Not at night, but during the daytime, when the rest of us are busy with other things and don't notice her absence." She paused. "I think she might be meeting someone."

Hawk knelt beside her, one eye on Fixit, who was standing at the plate getting ready to hit the ball. "How do you know this?"

"Candle told me. You know she and River are like sisters; they don't have many secrets. But this was one. She noticed River sneaking out and when River came back, she confronted her. River wouldn't tell her anything, just said she had to trust her and not to tell anyone. Candle didn't, until yesterday. She became worried after you got back from your visit with the Weatherman and she heard about the dead Croaks, so she decided to tell me."

Hawk shook his head. "Who would she be meeting?"

"I don't know. But Candle says she was taking something with her in a bag when she saw her leave that one time. She thinks she's been doing this for a while. Hawk, I don't know what to do. I don't want to confront her about it. She would know it was Candle who told me, and that would ruin their relationship. They're too close for me to do that."

He nodded. "But we have to do something."

"Maybe you could keep an eye on her, and when she sneaks away again, you could follow her."

That sounded a good deal easier than it was likely to turn out to be, he thought. River was pretty good at looking out for herself, and she would not be caught off guard. If he was going to find anything out by following her, he would have to be particularly skillful about it. It was not something he was anxious to attempt, in any case. Following any of his family secretly was a demonstration of his lack of trust in them and a betrayal of their trust in him.

"I don't know," he said to Owl.

"I don't know, either," she agreed, "but I don't think we can let her go off by herself like this without knowing what she's doing. Being a family means assuming responsibility for each other, making sure that we look out for each other. I don't think we're doing that if we ignore the possibility that she is putting herself in danger."

He knew it was true, but that didn't make him feel any better about it. He resented the fact that this was happening now, when there was so much else that needed his attention. He wanted to confront River on the spot and tell her that he didn't need this added distraction, but he knew that wasn't the way to handle things.

"Let me think about it," he said.

Owl's attention was back on the game. "Don't take too long. I don't think this can wait."

Hawk didn't think it could, either.

● ● ●

WHEN THE GAME was finished, he took Panther, Bear, Fixit, and Candle with him to forage for purification tablets for the catchment system. They had been running low on the tablets for some time, and he had been delaying replenishing their stock because it meant traveling all the way across the city to a supply source nearly two miles away, a distance he didn't normally like to travel. But clean drinking water was a must, and he couldn't put off the trip any longer.

Owl and the others retired to the underground to work on cleaning and mending chores, busywork that would keep them all occupied until the others returned. Hawk took the biggest and the strongest with him, a necessary precaution on a journey into territory that was only marginally familiar. Candle was the exception, but he took Candle because of her ability to sense danger. It would take them all afternoon to go and return, and there was no guarantee they would find what they were looking for, but at least with Candle present they would have a better chance at staying safe.

The day was gray and overcast and the streets deserted. It rained on them as they walked, a misting that left them beaded with water droplets. Panther was still griping about the outcome of the stickball game, which his team had lost. He walked wing on the right with Fixit on the left, Hawk on point, and Bear and Candle in the center. Hawk glanced over at him every now and then, distracted by his mumbling, half inclined to tell him to shut up and knowing it wouldn't do any good. All four boys carried prods. Panther held his like he was hoping for a chance to use it.

Panther was carrying around a lot of pent-up anger.

He had been born on the streets of San Francisco, the youngest of five brothers and sisters. He was called Anan Kawanda. He was mostly African American, but with other blood mixed in, too. His father was dead before he was born. No one ever talked about what had happened to him, and when Panther asked he was told that no one knew. His mother was tough and determined, part of an extended family living in Presidio Park, a group that disdained the compounds and the countryside alike. They lived in tents and deserted buildings and even on platforms constructed in trees. There were several hundred of them, all part of the same neighborhood before the move to the Presidio. Most were black and Hispanic. Most knew more than a little something about staying alive. His mother and the other adults believed that survival depended on adaptation to the altered environment, and that in turn meant building up immunity to the things that threatened you. The changes in air, water, and soil could be tolerated once you developed this immunity, and living behind walls or fleeing to the countryside was not the answer. They were city people, and the city was where they belonged.

Freaks were a threat for which there was no immunity, and some of the bigger, meaner ones—the mutations—preyed on people like them, people living out in the open. But the community was well armed with flechettes, prods, and stingers—dart guns loaded with a particularly toxic poison. They organized themselves into protective units within their enclave, and they never went anywhere alone. Sentries stood watch at all times, and the children were heavily guarded. There were rumors of rogue militias roaming the countryside and attacking the compounds. There were rumors of atrocities committed by creatures that weren't human, that were something less, creatures of a darker origin. Neither of these dangers had surfaced in San Francisco yet, but no one was taking any chances

There was a plan for evacuation from the city when they did appear, but no one really believed they would need it. Panther grew up playing at survival and quickly passed into practicing the real thing. In the brave new world of collapsed governments and wild-eyed fanatics, of plagues and poisons and madness, of bombs and chemical strikes, childhood in the traditional sense was over early. By the time he was seven, he already knew how to use all the community weapons. He knew about the Freaks and their habits. He could hunt and forage and read tracks. He knew which medicines counteracted which sicknesses and how to recognize when places and things were to be avoided. He could keep watch all night. He could stand and fight if it were needed.

He grew up fast, athletic, and strong, a quick study and an eager volunteer. By the time he was twelve, it was already accepted that one day he would be a leader of the community. Even his older brothers and sisters deferred to his superior judgment and skills. Panther worked hard at being the best. In the back of his mind, he knew he'd need to be. Talk of the armies that were sweeping the eastern half of the country continued to surface. Everyone knew that things were getting worse, that the dangers were growing. Once, long ago, there had been talk about things going back to the way they were—a way Panther knew nothing about and could only envision. But that sort of talk had diminished over time. It was accepted that the past was lost forever and nothing would ever be the same.

It bothered the older men and women, the ones who remembered a little of better times. It was less troubling to Panther and his peers, who only knew things as they were and felt comfortable with the familiar, no matter how dangerous. It seemed to Panther that the best any of them could do was to take things one day at a time and watch their backs.

For a while, that was enough.

Then one day, shortly after he turned fourteen, he returned with four others from a weeklong foraging expedition and found everyone he had left behind dead. They lay sprawled all across the park, their bodies rigid with agony, arms and legs flung wide, mouths agape, blood leaking from their ears and noses. There was no sign of violence, no evidence of what had killed them. It looked as if whatever was responsible had disposed of them quickly. It had the appearance of plague.

Panther searched the camp all the rest of the day and into the next, prowling through discarded containers and debris, desperate to find the cause. He did not think he would find any peace until he solved the mystery. But nothing revealed itself. When it finally became apparent that it wasn't going to do so, he broke down and cried, kneeling amid the bodies, rocking back and forth until he felt emptied out. Something changed inside him that day, something that he knew would never change back. Everything he had believed in was turned upside down. Preparation and skills alone weren't what would save you in this life. What would save you was luck. Pure chance. What would save you was something over which you had no control at all.

He buried his family—his mother and brothers and sisters— ignoring the protestations of his companions that he was risking his own health by touching the dead, refusing to listen to their warnings that what had killed them was almost certainly contagious. When he was done, he said good-bye to the others, who had chosen to stay in the city and to seek admittance into one of the compounds, salvaged what he could of weapons and supplies, packed them on his back, and started walking north.

Weeks later, he arrived in Seattle and found Hawk and the Ghosts and his new home.

For the first week after he became a member of this new family, he was willing to talk about what had happened to him. After that, he never spoke of it, consigning it to the past, a part of his life that was over and done with. But Hawk could tell that he hadn't forgotten it; he simply kept it locked away inside, white-hot and corrosive. The pain and anger were always eating at him, and he had yet to find an effective means of dealing with them, of healing himself so that he could put the past to rest.

Sometimes it seemed as if he never would.

Hawk glanced over at him now, at the dark intense features, at the restless, troubled eyes. Panther caught him looking, and he glanced quickly away.

The trek through the city went swiftly and without incident. They encountered no Freaks, no other tribes, and no obstacles that slowed their passage. The day stayed dark and the air damp. Mist rose from the pavement and clung to the buildings, cloaking every-

thing in gauzy trailers. Before long, the skeleton of the Space Needle
came into view over the tops of the buildings, its ragged spire lifting
skyward like a torch gone dark. Once, people could take an elevator
to its top to an eating place and view deck that looked out over the
whole of the city. But that was back in the days before hand-cranked
generators and stairs were the best anyone could hope for, when
there was citywide electricity and the elevators still worked.

It must have been something to see, he thought suddenly. Not
the city—you could still see the city if you climbed to the view-
points on the hills that surrounded it—but the population that made
the city come alive, all the people and the traffic and the movement
and color before everything fell apart.

Their destination appeared ahead, a broad two-story building with
its plate-glass windows broken out and its façade scorched by fire
and scoured by the elements. Hawk had found it by accident on a
foraging expedition two years earlier: a storage and distribution center for chemical supplies, including purification tablets. The stock
was too extensive to carry out in a single load or to try to store in the
limited space of their underground home. But the tablets were precious and difficult to find in a time when retail outlets had long since
been pillaged and emptied of useful goods. So he had taken what he
could pack on his back and hidden the rest in the basement behind
a cluster of empty packing crates. So far, his secret stash had not
been disturbed.

They walked to the front of the building and stood looking
through the broken-out windows for a moment.

"So what's the plan, Bird-Man?" Panther asked in a singsong
voice.

Hawk ignored him, casting about the shadows and the mist, listening to the silence and trusting to his instincts. He peered down
the streets where they tunneled between the buildings and through
the misty haze. Rain had dampened the pavement, leaving it slick
and oily, and the air smelled of metal and old fish. He glanced at
Candle, who met his gaze and shook her head. *No danger so far,* she
was saying.

He turned to the others. "Fixit, you wait just inside, out of sight,
and keep watch. The rest of us will go get the tablets."

They climbed through one of the window frames, avoiding the door, which was barred and chained. Inside, the building opened through layers of deep shadows and long, hazy streaks of gray light to a jumbled collection of shelves, tables, counters, boxes, and debris of all sorts. Leaving Fixit at the front wall, Hawk took the others toward a half wall that separated the front and back of the store. Inside the half wall, a trapdoor opened onto stairs leading down into the basement. Once again, Hawk hesitated. He didn't like the feel of the entry, never had. Then, brushing aside his fears, he switched on his solar-powered torch and started down.

The stairs ended in the very center of the basement, which was ink-black and musty and spread away in all directions to walls only faintly visible in the dim light of Hawk's torch. Packing crates were stacked against the back wall, concealing the supplies they had come for. The wall to their left was partially collapsed, leaving a black hole that opened into the basement of the cavernous adjoining warehouse. The hole was ragged and slick with moisture, and the room beyond so thick with shadows that it was impossible to see anything. A deep, pervasive silence hung over everything.

Right away Candle said, "Something's down here." She pointed to the hole in the wall and the impenetrable blackness beyond. "In there."

Everyone swung about to face the collapsed wall, prods coming up defensively. They stood motionless for a moment, listening. Nothing happened. No movement, no sounds. The seconds ticked away, and the basement seemed to grow stuffy and warm.

Finally, knowing he had to do something, Hawk started forward to take a closer look.

Candle grasped his arm instantly, pulling him back. "Don't go in there!"

Hawk looked at her in surprise. "What is it?"

She shook her head. Her face was pale and drawn, and her eyes wide with fear. She could barely make herself answer him. "We have to get out of here. We have to get out right away."

The way she said it made it clear that she felt there was no room for argument. Hawk looked at the others. "Go back up the stairs, right now."

"Wait a minute!" Panther was right in his face, his voice angry. "We came all the way across town to turn tail and run? You want us to leave the tablets behind?"

"Go back up the stairs," Hawk repeated.

"Go back up the stairs yourself!" Panther snapped, and wheeled away.

As the others watched in disbelief, he started toward the back of the room and the deep shadows, ignoring the looks directed after him, oblivious to Candle's hiss of warning. Hawk started to follow, then stopped as he realized he could not turn Panther around without risking a confrontation that would likely do more harm than good. Not knowing what else to do, he swung the thin beam of his torch after the retreating figure to help light his way. Panther reached the piles of crates and moved through them, neither hesitating nor hurrying.

Then, abruptly, he disappeared from view.

Hawk held his breath and waited. He glanced left quickly. Within the black hole of the collapsed wall, everything was still. But the shadows of the room seemed to coalesce into something huge.

In the next instant Panther reemerged from between the crates, carrying a box of the precious tablets, his prod cradled loosely in the crook of his arms. He crossed the room to where the others waited, went past them without stopping, and started up the stairs.

"Come along, children," he sneered.

No one argued. They went up from the basement with hurried glances over their shoulders, crossed to the front wall of the building where Fixit was waiting, and climbed back through the broken window. Outside, they stood uneasily in the street and stared at one another.

"What happened?" Fixit asked in bewilderment, looking from one face to the next.

"Good thing you got me along to do the tough stuff," Panther declared, giving Hawk a meaningful glance. "Got to have someone who ain't afraid of the dark. Got to have someone to face down the bogeyman when he crawls out of his hole."

Hawk didn't reply, even though he wanted to tell Panther that he'd better not disobey him like that again, ever. Instead, he motioned them into the wing formation and they set off for home, moving back toward the center of the city. Candle walked next to him and stared straight ahead, her young face tight and hard and her thin body rigid. Hawk left her alone. She knew what he was thinking. He was thinking that they had gotten away with something back there, even if Panther didn't believe it. He was thinking that they had been lucky. He was thinking of the dead Lizard and the nest of Croaks and the possibility that there was something new and dangerous in the city.

But he was also thinking of her vision of the previous night—that something was coming for them, something that was going to kill them—thinking that maybe the world beyond their underground home was closing in on them in a way none of them had anticipated.

Thinking that maybe they had better be ready for it when it did.

13

HAWK WAS STILL brooding over the incident in the warehouse basement when he arrived back at Pioneer Square. It was already growing dark, and he could not afford to be late for his meeting with Tessa, so he set out again almost at once. Owl caught the look on his face as he passed through the kitchen and grabbed a slice of the bread she had baked, but said nothing. The others were preoccupied and didn't notice. Except for Candle, who shared an understanding of what they had brushed up against in the darkness and somehow managed to avoid. But Candle didn't say anything, either.

She would later, he thought as he went out the door, Cheney padding silently after him. She would tell Owl everything. Owl was her mother, and she was her mother's little girl.

Theirs was a special relationship, made strong by the circumstances that had brought them together. Owl had been gone from the Safeco compound and living with Hawk and the first of the Ghosts, Bear and Fixit and Sparrow, for almost two years when she found Candle. Confined to her wheelchair and for the most part to the underground, there was no good reason for Owl to ever find anyone. But against all odds, she had found Candle.

She had been outside that day, carried up by Hawk and Bear for a visit to the compound and Tessa, in the days before Tessa and Hawk had been caught together and Tessa had been forbidden by her parents to go out alone. They had arranged to meet just north of the compound at the edge of Pioneer Square in one of the buildings fronting Occidental Park. Tessa had been waiting when they arrived. The four had visited, then Bear had gone off in search of writing materials for Sparrow, who had been left behind with Cheney, and Owl had wheeled her chair out into the square to give Hawk and Tessa some time alone.

She was sitting in a pale wash of sunlight with her back to the building and her eyes lifted to watch tiny strips of blue sky come and go like phantom ribbons through breaks in the clouds when the little girl appeared. One moment she wasn't there and the next she was, standing in front of the building across the way and staring at Owl. Owl was so surprised that for a moment she just stared back.

Then she called over, "What's your name?"

The little girl didn't answer. She just kept staring. She was very tiny and so thin that it seemed she would disappear if she turned sideways. Her clothes were in tatters, her face smudged with dirt. She was such a ragged little thing that Owl decided on the spot that she would have to help her.

She took a chance then and wheeled herself over, taking her time, not rushing it, being careful not to do anything that would frighten the little girl. But the child just stood there and didn't move.

Owl got to within ten feet and stopped. "Are you all right?"

"I'm hungry," the little girl said.

Owl had no real food to offer. So she reached into one pocket, brought out a piece of rock candy, and held it out. The little girl looked at it, but stayed where she was.

"It's all right," Owl told her. "You can have it. It's candy."

The little girl's gaze shifted, her eyes a startling blue that seemed exactly the right complement for her mop of thick red hair. Her skin tone was porcelain, so pale that it suggested she had never seen the sunlight. It wasn't all that unusual to encounter such children in these times, but even so this little girl didn't look like anyone Owl had ever come across.

Owl leaned back in her wheelchair and put her hands in her lap. "I can't walk, so I can't bring it over to you. And I can't throw it, because if I do it will shatter. So you have to come and get it. Will you do that for me?"

No response. The little girl just kept staring. Then, all at once, she changed her mind. She came right up to Owl, reached down and took the candy, unwrapped it and put it in her mouth. She sucked on it for a moment, and then smiled. It was the most dazzling smile Owl had ever seen. She smiled back, so charmed that she would have done anything for the girl.

"Can you tell me your name?" she asked again.

The little girl nodded. "Sarah."

"Well, Sarah, what are you doing here all by yourself?"

The little girl shrugged.

"Where are your parents?"

The little girl shrugged again.

"Where is your home?"

"I don't have a home."

"No mommy and daddy?"

Sarah shook her head.

"No brothers and sisters?"

Another shake of her carrot-top.

"Are you all alone?"

The little girl hugged herself and bit her lip. "Mostly."

Owl wasn't sure what she meant by this, and neither was Hawk when the conversation was repeated to him later. He had reappeared with Tessa to find Owl in her wheelchair and Sarah sitting on the pavement in front of her, staring up in rapt attention as Owl finished another story of the children and their boy leader. By then, it was clear at a glance that the two had bonded in a way that couldn't be undone and that the little girl had joined the family.

But within days of Sarah coming to live with them in their underground home the Ghosts began to realize that there was something very different about her. She dreamed all the time, waking frequently from nightmares that left her shaking and mute. They would ask her what was wrong, but she would never say. Sometimes she would refuse to go into places, especially places that were dark and close. She wouldn't let them go in, either, throwing such a fit that it proved easier just to let her have her way. Neither Owl nor Hawk could figure out what was going on, but they knew it was something important.

Then, one day, Owl was alone with Sarah in the center of Pioneer Square, sorting containers collected from a bin that Bear had dragged from several blocks away. Bear wasn't far away, but he wasn't in sight, either. Hawk and Sparrow were scouting new supply sources in midtown. Owl wasn't paying much attention to what was going on around her, concentrating on the job at hand, and then all at once Sarah hissed as if she had been scalded, grabbed the back of Owl's wheelchair, and pushed her swiftly into the interior of their building. Owl barely had time to try to ask what was wrong when the little girl's hand clamped across her mouth, and she was whispering, *Croaks!*

Seconds later they appeared. Three of the walking dead, slouching out of the darkness of an alleyway, casting baleful glances right and left as they passed through the square and continued down a side street. Had Sarah not gotten Owl out of sight, they would have been discovered. Owl braced the little girl by her shoulders. How had she known about the Croaks? Sarah shook her head, not wanting to say, but this time Owl persisted, telling her that it was all right, whatever it was, but that she had to know, it was important.

The little girl said it was the voices.

She said it was the voices inside her head, the ones that came to her both in dreams and in waking, warning her of danger. They were always there, always watching out for her.

Owl didn't understand. Sarah had voices that spoke to her, that could tell when danger threatened? The little girl nodded, suddenly looking very ashamed. Owl still didn't understand. Why wouldn't she talk about it with the other members of the family? Why did she keep this to herself?

That was when Sarah told her that some people didn't believe in the voices, that some people thought the voices were bad. Which, in turn, made Sarah bad, and she didn't want to be bad. But she couldn't help it that she heard the voices and believed in them. She couldn't help it that sometimes people didn't listen to the voices and they died.

Like her mommy and daddy.

Owl left it alone right there, but she told Hawk the story later, and they took Candle aside and told her that the voices were important and that she must always tell them what the voices said. The voices weren't bad and neither was Sarah. Both were just trying to help, and it was only when you *didn't* try to help that you were being bad.

Hawk wasn't quite sure himself that he believed in the voices at first. But after a few months of watching Sarah, he changed his mind, especially after taking her with him on foraging expeditions where she repeatedly warned him of unseen dangers, keeping him from harm. Keeping all of them from harm. There was no rational explanation for how she could see these things or where the voices came from, but that didn't change the facts. Sarah was quickly renamed Candle, and she became their light in the darkest of places.

He let the memory drift back into the past, turning his thoughts to the present as he emerged from the building above their hideout into the square and the onset of twilight. He would have to hurry to make his meeting with Tessa, and he needed to make the meeting in order to keep his promise to Tiger about the pleneten. Cheney padded on ahead of him, big head lowered, sniffing at the pavement and casting sharp glances at the darkened doorways and windows of the buildings they passed. The city was quiet, its few sounds distant and muffled, lost in the darkness and the haze. The smells of decay and pollution drifted up from the waterfront, but Hawk had grown so used to them he barely noticed. Sometimes he thought about a world in which the smells were all sweet and fragrant, like the wildflower fields and woodlands he remembered from his Oregon childhood. Sometimes he imagined he would take the Ghosts one day to a place that smelled like that.

He moved down First Avenue through the derelict vehicles and piles of trash, through the grass and weeds growing up through cracks in the pavement, and then turned north while still on his side of the compound and made his way toward the old entry to the light rail station. He was thinking again of Candle's vision and her admonition to him that they must flee the city. He was thinking that everything that had happened lately was telling him that he should listen to her. The dead Croaks, the dead Lizard, this afternoon's experience in the warehouse basement, and his own sense of things changing around him all contributed to his growing certainty that Candle's voices were a warning he could not ignore.

But he also knew that he would never leave without Tessa. Even at the cost of his own life, he would never leave her. It wasn't a rational decision, wasn't even a decision he had consciously arrived at. He simply knew it. Maybe he had always known deep in his heart and hadn't wanted to acknowledge it. It really didn't matter. Somewhere along the way, at some point during their time together, he had made the commitment and it was too late even to try to change it. His feelings for her were so strong and so deeply ingrained that he could no longer imagine life without her. He was wedded to her in the only way that mattered—in his heart, in the strength of his affection, and in his determination to be with her forever.

So before he could fulfill what he believed to be his destiny—to save the Ghosts, to take his family away from the city and the danger that threatened—he must convince Tessa to come with them. She had steadfastly refused to leave her parents, but he must find a way to change her mind and he must do so quickly.

He thought of this as he came up to the station entrance and went down the steps, leaving Cheney to prowl the ruins outside. The light was so poor by now that he could barely see the walls of the compound. By the time he was finished here, it would be completely dark on a night in which there were no breaks in the clouds and no light from the moon or stars.

But he brushed his concerns aside, worries for another time, and rapped hard on the steel door that led down into the tunnels, using the prearranged signal, twice hard and once soft.

Seconds later the locks on the other side released, the door swung open, and Tessa slipped through and was in his arms, hugging him close. "Why do you do this to me?" she breathed in his ear, kissing him, then burying her face in his neck.

"I had a long afternoon uptown. I didn't get back until late." He hugged and kissed her back. "Sorry."

"It's okay," she said. "But I worry. Every time, I think that you're not coming, that something's happened. I don't know how to handle it."

She broke away, holding him at arm's length and staring at him as if she had never seen him before, or never would again. Her eyes were black pools in the dim light, and her brown skin was smoothed and darkened by the shadows. "Did you miss me?"

He laughed. "Only enough that I gave up dinner to come see you."

"That's all? Only dinner?"

"That's all I had time to give up. What else do you want?"

She stared at him. "I don't know. Everything, I guess." She smiled self-consciously and reached into her jacket pocket. "I brought the pleneten. Six doses wrapped in cold packs. It should be enough for Persia. Keep them cold until she takes them. Have Tiger do the same while they're stored."

He nodded, accepting the packs and sticking them deep into his side pocket. The pleneten came in tablets that were easily transported. He would take them to Tiger tomorrow at midday, as promised.

She took his hands and led him over to the bench where they liked to sit during their visits. He wrapped one arm about her shoulders and cradled her against him. "Thanks for doing this."

She nodded, but didn't say anything.

He sensed something. "It went okay, didn't it?"

"I might have been seen."

He felt himself grow cold inside, and for a moment he didn't say anything in response. "Seen by whom?" he managed finally.

She sighed and lifted her head from his shoulder. "There was another girl working in the medical supply room. She caught me in the refrigeration cabinet where they store the pleneten. I made up a story about doing an inventory, but everyone knows that inventories are only done by assignment and at certain times."

"Do you think she might tell someone?"

"She might."

"Then you shouldn't go back." *Because you know what will happen if you do and they find out you've been stealing medical supplies,* he wanted to add, but didn't. "You should come with me."

"You know I can't do that."

"I know you *think* you can't."

She drew back from him. "Why must we always have this argument, Hawk? Every time I see you! Why can't we be together without talking about the future?" She squeezed his hands sharply. "Why can't we just be in the present?"

He had thought he would be able to lead into this more gradually, but that wasn't the way things were working out. He bent close, so that their faces were almost touching.

"Because," he whispered. "Because of everything." He took a deep breath. "Listen to me, Tessa. I told you last night that you had to be careful about going out of the compound, that the Weatherman had found an entire nest of dead Croaks down on the waterfront. But there's more. We came across a Lizard two days ago that was just all ripped apart. I've never seen anything like it. I don't know anything that could have done it. Then, earlier today, we were down in a warehouse basement and Candle's voices warned her to get out of there. I couldn't see anything, but I could feel it. There was something there, something big and dangerous, hiding on the other side of a collapsed wall."

She started to speak, but he put his fingers to her lips. "Wait, there's more. Last night, after I came back from seeing you, Candle was waiting up for me. She was shaking, she was so afraid. She'd had one of her visions, a bad one. It was of something huge coming to the city, something that was going to kill us all."

He touched her cheek, then stroked her hair. "Candle doesn't make these things up. The voices are real, and they have never been wrong. I don't think they're wrong this time. But I don't know what to do about it. I haven't told anyone but you. Do you know why that is? Because I can't do *anything* without you. I have to get the Ghosts out of the city to someplace safe. But I won't go without you. I can't leave you. I won't ever leave you."

She nodded, biting her lip and reaching up with her hands to hold his head steady as she kissed his eyes and nose and mouth. There were tears in her eyes. "What am I supposed to do about my mother? You can't ask me to leave her!"

His gaze was fierce. "You're all grown up, Tessa; you're not a child. We belong together—you and me. We're ready to start our own life. To do that, you have to leave her. That's just the way of things. She has your father; he can look after her. You would be leaving her, in any case, if we were to marry. Isn't that what you want for us?"

She shook her head. "I've told you before! You could come live in the compound! You could be with me there!"

He lost control and shook her hard. "What are you talking about? That's nonsense! When they caught us together outside the compound—what was it, six months ago—your father forbid you from ever seeing me again. He told us both that it wasn't something that he would allow, his daughter with a street kid, the member of a tribe. He said that! Others in the compound were even worse. Some wanted you cast out on the spot. They worried you might have picked up diseases that could be transmitted to them. Some would have thrown you from the walls. Do you think that if we tell them we want to get married, it will change any of that?"

He put his hand on her mouth as she tried to speak. "Wait, don't say anything. Let me finish. Let me get it all out. I didn't argue about it at the time. I didn't know what to say. I just knew I didn't want to lose you. So we've been meeting like this ever since, you sneaking out at night, me sneaking down here through the ruins. But we both know how it's going to end. Sooner or later we're going to get caught—unless we find another way to live our lives."

He exhaled sharply, his energy exhausted. "We're right on the edge of something. I can feel it. Step the wrong way, and we are lost. Step the right way, and we will never lose each other. But you have to leave the compound. You have to leave and come with me to wherever it is that we have to go to be safe and together. Your parents won't understand. Nothing you can say will make them understand. We could offer to take them with us, but you know as well as I do that they wouldn't come. What will happen is that they will make sure you don't leave, either."

She shook her head. "You don't know that."

"I *do* know that. I know it as surely as I know how I feel about you."

Tessa stared silently at him, then wiped the tears from her eyes. "I have to think about this. I have to give it some time."

Time is something you don't have, he wanted to say, but he managed to keep himself from doing so. "I know," he said instead. "I know."

They sat together on the bench, holding each other and not speaking, looking off into the dark. Hawk kept wondering if there was something else he should say, something that would better persuade her. But he couldn't think of what it would be. So he settled for keeping her close for the time they had, soaking in her warmth and her softness, giving himself some small measure of comfort before she was gone again.

"A foraging party went out early last week," she said suddenly, not looking at him, her face buried in his shoulder. She didn't continue right away, but then said very quickly, "There were eleven of them, all experienced, all heavily armed. They went south toward the warehouses twenty or thirty miles outside the city, looking for fresh medical supplies and packaged goods to bring back to the compound. It was a five-day expedition." She paused, as if waiting on him, and then said, "It's been a week, and they haven't come back. One of them is my father."

He could hear the fear in her voice now, could sense the deep abiding terror she was feeling. His warnings about Candle's vision and the strange things happening in the city had done that. He wished he had saved it for another time. But it was too late to take it back.

"There are eleven of them carrying weapons," he said, trying to reassure her. "They know what they are doing. They can protect themselves."

He could feel her head shake in disagreement. "The Croaks and that Lizard you told me about would have known what they were doing, too. They should have been able to protect themselves, too, but look what happened."

"It isn't the same. Eleven armed men can stand up to anything. Your father will be all right."

He wished he believed it. He wished he could think of something more reassuring. He knew how she felt about her father and mother and what it would do to her to lose either of them.

You're so stupid, he told himself angrily.

"I have to get back," she said suddenly, breaking away. She rose and went over to the door, then looked back at him. "Will you come again soon?"

He rose. "If you promise to be careful, I will. In two nights, okay?"

She came back to him quickly and pressed herself against him. "You're the one on the streets."

"Sometimes the streets are safer."

"Doesn't sound like it to me."

"I love you."

"I love you more." She kissed him hard, then broke away, her black eyes shining, her face radiant with her feelings. "I want you. I want everything from you. I want to be with you forever."

She kissed him again, and then turned and bolted back through the tunnel door and was gone. He stood listening to the locks fasten and then to the silence. He was flushed with excitement and riven by fear. He could barely contain his feelings. Two words played themselves over and over in his mind.

Don't go.

14

IRISIN," BIAT WHISPERED to him through the crack in the open door. "Aren't you coming to bed?"

The Elven boy looked over his shoulder at his friend and caught a glimpse of his thin, pinched face in the pale haze of the candlelight. "Just finishing," he said.

"Do you know what time it is?"

Kirisin shook his head. "It's not dawn, I know that."

There was a despairing sigh as Biat's face disappeared and the door closed. Kirisin went right back to writing.

He was sitting on the tiny veranda of the home that the six of them shared—Biat, Erisha, Raya, Jarn, Giln, and himself. Four were from the Cintra and two had traveled from other places to participate in the choosing. The greater portion of the Elven nation resided in the Cintra, but other, smaller communities were scattered around the world in similar forests. The Ellcrys could have settled on using only Elves who lived close for her Chosen. But something made it pleasing to her that they should come from all over, and so it had been for as long as anyone could remember. She was who she was, after all, so she could have what she wanted.

When Kirisin saw her for the first time, it took his breath away. There were trees of great magnificence and beauty, and then there was the Ellcrys. She was tall and willowy and had a presence that transcended majesty or grace. Silvery bark and crimson leaves formed an aura about her canopy so that the shimmer of her foliage suggested feathers and silk. She was magic, of course; what tree that looked like this could be otherwise? She was the only one of her kind, created centuries ago to maintain the Forbidding, the barrier behind which the demonkind had been shut away in the time of Faerie. So long as she lived, they could never break free. The Chosen were her servants, selected to safeguard her. It was an honor of immense proportions, but one that did not include questioning her motives or reasons. Service to the Ellcrys required a devotion and obedience that did not allow for satisfying personal curiosity.

Still, Kirisin wished he understood her better. So little was known, and most of that was what had been gleaned from years of service and passed down through generations of Chosen. The Ellcrys had been alive for thousands of years, but almost all of what had been written about her at the time of her creation was lost. Like so much of everything else that was Elven, he reminded himself. Like the magic, in particular. Once the world had been full of magic, and the Elves had commanded the greater part of it. But the Elves had lost their magic, just as they had lost their way of life. In the beginning, they had been the dominant species. Now they were little more than rumor. Humans populated the world now, and they had no understanding of magic. All they understood was how to savage the land, how to take what they wanted and not care about the harm it caused.

Humans, he thought suddenly, were destroyers.

He brushed aside his mop of blond hair and wrote it down, adding it to his other thoughts. He wrote in his journal each night before going to sleep, putting down his musings and his discoveries so that he would have a record of them when his term of service was done. Maybe if others had done the same centuries earlier, there wouldn't be so much no one knew anything about now. Particularly where the Ellcrys was concerned.

The Chosen were the logical scribes to make those recordings, of course, but few did. Their period of service was brief. Selected during the summer solstice from among the boys and girls who had just passed into their first year of adulthood, they served for a single year and then relinquished the duty to a new group. The tree never chose more than eight or fewer than six. Just enough to perform the required duties of tending to her needs and caring for the gardens in which she was rooted.

The choosing itself was ritual. All of the candidates passed beneath the branches of the tree at dawn on the day of the solstice. Those who would become the new Chosen were touched lightly on the shoulder by one of the tree's slender branches, the only time she would ever communicate with them. How she made her choices, how she decided who would serve her for the next twelve months, was a mystery no one had ever solved. That she was a sentient being was not open to dispute. The lore made it clear that she had been created so, and that the nature of her creation, though vague in the histories that described it, required she experience a constant human connection. Thus the presence of the Elves who looked after her daily, and the ongoing protection of the community that relied on her.

He wrote the last few lines of his entry, put his writing materials aside, and rose to stretch. The sun would be coming up in a little more than an hour, and the Chosen would walk down into the gardens to greet the Ellcrys and welcome her to a new day. It was a formality, really. They did it because the Chosen had been doing it for as long as anyone could remember. It was a custom rooted in a need to maintain a connection with the tree.

Odd, really. The Ellcrys was beholden to them, yet for the most part she did not even seem aware of their presence. That didn't seem right. He thought about it and then shook his head in self-admonishment. He was being unfair. She was a tree, and what tree had ever enjoyed a warm relationship with any two-legged creature who might on a whim decide to cut it down for firewood?

"What are you doing, Kirisin?" a familiar voice asked.

Erisha was standing right behind him. He hadn't heard her approach, which irritated him. She was good at sneaking around. She stood with her hands on her hips, a challenging tone in her voice. She was the oldest by five months and the designated leader of the

Chosen. She was also the daughter of the King. Kirisin didn't mind this, but he wished she were a little less impressed with herself.

"Just finishing up on my journal," he answered, smiling cheerfully.

She didn't smile back. That was the trouble with Erisha. She didn't smile enough. She took everything so seriously, as if what they were doing transcended anything else they would ever do in their lives. It was a mistake to take anything so seriously. It aged you too quickly and drained you of energy and hope. He had seen it happen with his parents, who had fought so hard to persuade the King to establish a second enclave on the mountain slopes of Paradise, where there was cleaner air and water. But leaving the Cintra meant leaving the Ellcrys as well, a prospect few felt comfortable embracing. Most had never lived anywhere but close to her and couldn't conceive of doing so now. It didn't matter that only the Chosen were actually needed to care for her. Life outside the Cintra was for other Elves; the Cintra Elves belonged where they were.

His parents had wasted themselves in a futile effort to persuade the King to their cause. The King, after all, was his father's cousin and should have been willing to listen. But Arissen Belloruus had been unreceptive to the idea and instead had made it clear that while he was King and his family rulers of the Cintra Elves, no second enclave would ever be established. Whatever problems the Elves might encounter, they would solve them here.

Not that the Elves were solving any of the problems confronting them, of course. They had made no progress toward stopping the poisoning of the earth's resources. They had done nothing about the wars and plagues devastating the human population. Worst of all, they were ignoring the most dangerous threat of all—the new demons and their once-men soldiers. It hadn't been enough that the Elves had shut away the demonkind of Faerie; a new demonkind, one born of the human race, had taken their place. By absenting themselves from the world's affairs, the Elves had allowed this to happen. These new demons hadn't bothered with the Elves yet; maybe they didn't even realize Elves existed. But sooner or later they would find out, and when that happened the Elves would discover what burying your head in the sand got you.

It made him angry to think about it. It made him angrier still that Erisha wasted her serious attitude on small matters rather than on something that might make a real difference.

That was what daughters of Kings were supposed to do, wasn't it? Turn their attention to important matters?

But, then, cousins of Kings were supposed to be of a responsible disposition, too, so he could hardly complain.

"Do you know what time it is?" she asked him.

He sighed. "Close to dawn. I couldn't sleep."

"If you don't sleep, you aren't rested. If you aren't rested, you can't perform adequately your duties as a Chosen. Have you thought of that? You are distracted all the time, Kirisin. Lack of sleep could explain the problem."

They looked very much the same, these two—slender and Elven-featured, with slanted eyes and brows, narrow faces, ears that were slightly pointed at their tips, and a way of walking that suggested they might take flight on a moment's notice. They had the look of cousins, though Kirisin thought that facial resemblance aside they were nothing alike.

"You're probably right, Erisha," he agreed, still smiling. "I will try to do better starting tonight. But I'm awake now, so I think I will just stay awake until dawn."

"Kirisin . . ."

But he was already down off the veranda and walking away. He gave her a short wave as he disappeared into the trees, just to let her know that there were no hard feelings. But he didn't slow.

The Elves were the old people of the world. Some believed they were the prototype of humans, although Kirisin had always thought that nonsense. Elves, he told himself, were nothing like humans.

Yet they coexisted in a world on which both species had made an impact, for better and worse. At the moment, the impact was mostly human-generated and all bad. The humans had lost control of their world. It had happened over time, and it had happened to a degree that no Elf could comprehend. They had systematically destroyed the resources, poisoning everything, at first locally and eventually globally. They had begun warring with each other with such fero-cious determination that after a century of violence more were dead than alive. Nature had responded, of course. Plagues and storms and upheavals had finished off what humans had begun. At first, the Elves had told themselves that much of what was happening was a part of nature's cycle, that things would eventually be set right. They weren't telling themselves that anymore. In fact, it had gotten bad enough that some were advocating that the Elves come out of hiding to try to set things right.

Of course, much of the fault for what had happened lay squarely at their own doorstep, Kirisin thought darkly. It had been their decision to go into hiding centuries earlier when the human population had begun to proliferate and the Elven to decline. Coexistence seemed a better possibility if the former knew nothing of the latter. Elves had always known how to disappear in plain sight. It was not so difficult for them to fade into the forests that had served as their homes since the beginning of time. It was the wiser choice, the elders of that time had believed.

So they settled for surviving in a human world and did so mostly by keeping hidden. The humans called the Cintra the Willamette, and the land surrounding was called Oregon. It was remote and sparsely settled, and the Elves had little trouble staying out of sight. When humans came too close, they were turned aside. A slight distraction was usually enough—a small noise here, a little movement there. When that failed, intruders often woke from an unexpected fall or unexplained bump on the head. It didn't happen often; there was nothing in the deep woods that appealed to most humans. The Elves warded their homelands against the encroachments fostered by human neglect and poor stewardship, but their efforts of late were proving insufficient. Soon, something would have to be done. The matter was already under discussion in the Elven High Council, but opinion was divided and solutions scarce.

As the Elves were beginning to find out, absenting yourself from the affairs of the world was an invitation for disaster.

Ahead, the crimson canopy of the Ellcrys appeared through the trees, bright and shining even in the pale moonlight, a beacon that never failed to make the boy smile. She was so beautiful, he thought. How could anything be too wrong in a world that had given her life?

He stepped into the clearing where the Ellcrys grew and stood staring at her. He came here almost every morning before the others woke, a private time in which he sat and talked with her alone. She never responded, of course, because she never responded to anyone. But that didn't matter to Kirisin. He was there because he understood somehow that this was where he belonged. His time as a Chosen didn't start at sunrise and end at sunset. For the year that he had given himself over to her service, he owed her whatever time he could give her. That meant he could do as he pleased, so long as he carried out his assigned duties.

It was this lack of recognizable structure that drove Erisha to regard him as undependable. She believed in doing things in settled ways, on an organized and carefully regulated schedule. She did not like what she viewed as his undisciplined habits. But then she was not him and he was not her, something she seemed to have trouble understanding.

He spent these early-morning hours working on small projects of his own devising. Sometimes he worked at smoothing out and cleaning the earth in which she was rooted. Sometimes he fed her organic supplements of his own creation, both of food and antitoxins; that one would really drive Erisha wild if she knew about it. Sometimes he just sat with her. Sometimes, although not too often, he touched her to let her know he was there. He couldn't say why he found this so pleasing, why he actually looked forward to rising early and in secret spending time with a creature that gave nothing back. He just did. His connection with her was visceral, and it felt wrong not to respond to it. He had only one year to do what he could for her, and then it would be someone else's turn. He didn't want to waste a minute.

It helped that he was particularly good at the nurturing and care of living things. He possessed a special gift for such work; he enjoyed making things grow and keeping them healthy. He could sense what was wrong with them and act on his instincts. His sister said it ran in the family. His mother possessed unusual healing skills, and Simralin was uncanny at deciphering the secrets of the wilderness and the behavior of the creatures that lived within it. Trained as a Tracker, she had opportunities to use her gift in her work as an Elven Hunter, just as he had his opportunities here.

Which he had better get busy and make use of, he thought. The other Chosen would be coming along soon. He could picture their faces as they ringed the tree, their hands joined. He could see the familiar mix of expressions—eager and bored, determined and distracted, bright and clouded—that mirrored the feelings of each. So predictable that he didn't have to think twice on it. He kept hoping one of them would surprise him. Shouldn't there be a measurable transformation in the character of each Chosen during the course of his or her service? Shouldn't that be an integral part of the experience?

He thought so, but he hadn't seen any evidence of it as yet. Nor had he himself undergone much of a change. You couldn't very well start throwing stones if you lived in a glass house, although that hadn't stopped him before.

He walked around the Ellcrys for a time, studying the ground, looking for signs of invasive pests or damaging sicknesses in the smaller plants surrounding her. Such things manifested themselves in these indicators first; it was one of the reasons they were planted— to serve as a warning of possible threats to her.

Not that much of anything got that far, given the attention the Chosen gave to the tree and every square inch of dirt and plant life surrounding her. Not that there was any real . . .

Something touched his shoulder lightly.

–Kirisin–

The voice came out of nowhere, sudden and compelling. Kirisin jumped a foot when he heard it. A slender branch was resting lightly on his shoulder. The branch did not grip or entwine, but held him bound as surely as with chains.

–My beloved–

Kirisin felt the hair on the back of his neck rise, and he shivered as if chilled through, although the morning was warm and windless.

The Ellcrys was speaking to him. The tree was communicating.

–Why am I forsaken–

Forsaken? He cringed at the rebuke, not understanding the reason for it. What had he failed to do?

–Pay heed to me. I have not lied. A change is coming to the land. The change will be devastating and inexorable and no one will be spared. All that you know will pass away. If you are to survive, I must survive. If I am to survive, you must help me. Though she chooses not to hear me, you must listen–

The voice was coming from everywhere—from outside Kirisin but from inside, as well. Then he realized that it wasn't an audible voice he was hearing; it was unspoken thoughts projected into his mind, lending those thoughts the weight and substance of spoken words.

Wait a minute. *She?* Who was *she?*

–Your order has served me long and well, my beloved, my Chosen. You have stayed at my side since the time of my birthing, since the moment of my inception. I have never wanted. I have never needed. But I want and need now, and you must heed me. You must do as I ask–

Kirisin was listening intently, even as he couldn't quite bring himself to believe that it was real. The Ellcrys never spoke to anyone save the Chosen, and she only spoke to them once—on the day of their choosing, when she called them by name. That she was communicating with him was mind boggling. What was it she had said? A change in the world? The end of everything they knew?

"What is this change?" he whispered, almost without realizing he had spoken the words.

–Humans and their demons are at war. It is a war that neither will win. It is a war that will destroy them both. But you and I will be destroyed, as well. If we are to survive, we must leave the Cintra. We must travel to a new land, to a new life, where we will find shelter and rebirth–

Was the tree answering him? Had it heard his question? Kirisin tried to decide, and then simply quit thinking about it and said what was on his mind. "What can we do to help?"

–Take me from the Cintra. Do not uproot me, but carry me away still rooted in my soil. Place me inside a Loden Elfstone, and I will be protected. Use the seeking-Elfstones to find it, the three to find the one. Read your histories. The secret is written down–

Kirisin had no idea how to respond. He knew of Elfstones, for they were a part of Elven history. But the Elves had not possessed one for hundreds of years. No one knew what had become of them.

No one even knew for certain what it was they were supposed to do. They were magic, but their magic was a mystery.

He wanted to ask more. He wanted to know all about the Elfstones and everything else he had just heard the tree reveal. Mostly, he wanted to hear the tree speak to him again. But he couldn't think what to ask, and before he could his chance was gone.

–Do not fail me, Kirisin Belloruus. Do not fail the Elves. Do what I have asked of you–

The branch lifted away and the voice went still. Kirisin waited, but nothing further happened. The Ellcrys was silent. He exhaled slowly, his mouth dry and his face hot. Everything that had just happened felt surreal, as if he had been lost in a dream.

"What am I going to do?" he whispered to the air.

* * *

HE WAITED UNTIL dawn, until after the greeting, until the rituals were satisfied, then gathered the Chosen together at the edge of the clearing and told them what had happened. They sat close, listening, their eyes skittering from face to face. When he finished, they stared at him as if he had lost his mind. The doubt on their faces was unmistakable.

"Don't you believe me?" he demanded angrily. He clenched his fists. "I know what I heard!"

"I know what you *think* you heard," Biat said, skepticism clear in his tone. "But maybe you imagined it."

A few of the others nodded in agreement. They *wanted* him to have imagined it. Kirisin shook his head angrily. "I didn't imagine anything! She spoke to me. She told me some sort of change is coming, and it's going to destroy everything. She told me we have to go somewhere else and take her with us. She talked about Elfstones and magic and histories and secrets. I heard her clearly enough."

"Sometimes whole groups of people think they see or hear something that never happened," Giln said quietly.

"The Ellcrys never speaks to anyone," added Raya. She shifted her dark eyes toward Kirisin. "Never."

"Never before, maybe," Kirisin said. "But she spoke today. You can pretend anything you want, but it doesn't change things. Stop talking about hallucinations and dreams. What are we going to do?"

"Erisha," Biat said suddenly. "What do you think we should do?"

Erisha didn't seem to hear him. But when everyone grew silent, waiting on her, she said, "Nothing."

"Nothing!" Kirisin repeated in disbelief. "Don't be ridiculous! You have to go to your father and tell him what has happened!"

Erisha shook her head. "My father won't believe any of this. I don't even know if I do!" She was suddenly angry. "I am the leader of the Chosen, Kirisin. I say what we do and don't do. We need to wait on this, to make certain about it. We need to see if she speaks to any of the rest of us. Then we can decide."

"That sounds sensible to me," Biat agreed, giving Kirisin a look that said, *Be reasonable.*

Kirisin couldn't believe what he was hearing. "What do you mean, wait to see if she speaks to the rest of you? What sort of advice is that? She told me she depends on us for help! What sort of help are we giving her by waiting?"

"You don't really know what you heard!" Erisha snapped. "You just *think* you know! You daydream all the time! You probably hear voices all the time. You would be the first one to imagine something that never happened! So don't lecture the rest of us about what we should do in this matter!"

Kirisin stared at her, and then looked at the others. "Does everyone else think the tree didn't speak to me, that I imagined it?"

He waited for a response. There was none. Everyone looked somewhere else. He couldn't tell whether they were on his side or Erisha's. In truth, it didn't matter. They could sit around talking about this until the cows came home, but it wouldn't help. What they had to do was to find out if there really were Elfstones. They had to discover if anyone had ever heard of a Stone called a Loden. Mostly, they had to do something besides bury their heads in the sand.

He refused the possibility that he might have imagined the Ell-crys talking to him. His mind was made up on that point. The humans and demons had found a way to destroy everything, and the

Ellcrys was warning them that they had to do something about it. It was their job to protect and preserve her. She depended on them for that. Unless they were intending to abrogate their responsibilities toward her, they had no choice. They had to do what she asked.

Kirisin stood up. "The rest of you can do what you want. But I'm going to speak to the King!"

15

ITHOUT GIVING THEM another glance, Kirisin stalked out of the clearing. The other Chosen shouted after him, telling him to come back, warning him that he was acting too quickly, not thinking things through. He was making a mistake, he heard Erisha shout. He ignored her, ignored them all, furious at their refusal to do more than find reasons to delay doing anything. Even Biat, his best friend. He had expected better of him. But then he always expected better of everyone except himself.

He was the one who always prevaricated. He was the one who should have been questioning this whole business.

But he wasn't doing so here. Why was that?

The question almost stopped him in his tracks because he had no answer. He experienced a momentary sense of stepping over a line, of making a decision that he would look back on for a long time to come. But his anger and his forward momentum kept him going when common sense and second thoughts might have turned him around. He had stomped away with such finality that going back now would be the same as crawling back, and he wasn't about to do that. Stopping to debate his reasons for accepting on faith what the Ellcrys had told him was pointless. He couldn't explain it because his commitment to the Ellcrys transcended reason or argument and went to the heart of his service as a Chosen. He couldn't speak for the others, but that was the way it was for him. What the Ellcrys had told him this morning had only strengthened his determination to fulfill his obligations to serve and protect.

Why am I forsaken?

The words chilled him. It was an accusation he could not ignore.

What he couldn't understand was Erisha's failure to act. Why hadn't she agreed to talk to her father? It was almost as if she was afraid to approach him about it. He couldn't think of any reason for that, but he didn't pretend to know everything about their relationship, either. He supposed being the daughter of the King carried with it a set of built-in problems, the kinds that were always hidden from the general public. His father and mother had certainly had their share of troubles with Arissen Belloruus. It shouldn't seem strange that his daughter might have a few, as well.

Still, she had been adamant about not speaking to him.

Again, he almost stopped and turned around, a small whisper warning him to watch out. But his mind was made up.

He passed from the gardens into the surrounding trees and walked uphill through homes that might easily have been mistaken as part of the forest if you were looking at them from a little farther off. Elven cottages and huts burrowed into the earth, formed extensions of the forest old growth, and sat like nests in the trees. They were like spiders in their webs—you had to be close and you had to be looking to spot them. Even the trails Kirisin followed were virtually undetectable, reworked and rerouted on a regular basis to avoid giving them away. Elves had learned long ago to walk lightly in the world.

Of course, walking lightly didn't solve all the problems of the world, especially in these times. Not everyone shared the sensibilities of Elves. Sickness and decay had penetrated even here, a direct consequence of the poisons injected into earth, air, and water by humans everywhere. The fallout from their wars had spilled over into Elven homelands, as well. The Elves knew about healing, but there was only so much anyone could do. Until now, the Elves had fought back using skills mastered over countless centuries, but their efforts were beginning to fall short. The poisoning was too pervasive; it had penetrated too deep. Without the use of the magic that had sustained them in the time of Faerie, they were fighting a losing battle.

Even Arissen Belloruus, famous for his optimism and insistence on Elven ingenuity as a solution for all things, must know this.

The Belloruus home sat astride a heavily forested hilltop; its rooms and passageways were worked deep into the earth so that virtually the whole of the rise was wormholed. There were numerous entrances and exits, dozens of light shafts and windows, but none that were visible until you got close. All were heavily guarded. He was still fifty yards away, coming up the incline toward the main entry, when the first of the Home Guards intercepted him. The Home Guards were the King's personal defenders, an elite unit formed of Elven Hunters whose specific duty was to protect the royal family. He was known to the pair who challenged him, and so he was allowed to pass. He went in through the main entrance, announced himself to the personal aide on duty, and was directed to take a seat along with several others who had come in ahead of him.

There he sat, waiting.

He passed the time by trying to dredge up from memory what little he knew about the Elven histories. *Look there for your answers,* the Ellcrys had told him, so that was what he must suggest to the King. The histories were old, so old they could be traced back all the way to the beginning of the ancient wars between good and evil. It was then that the Elves and their Faerie allies created the Forbidding out of magic and shut away the dark creatures that had plagued them since the Word and the Void had begun their battle for control of all life. It had been a long, bitter struggle, but in the end the Elves had prevailed and the demons and their like were defeated and imprisoned. It was the creation of the Ellcrys that made victory possible and allowed for the confinement of the evil ones. Everyone knew that story, even those who had never read a word of the histories.

He had seen these ancient tomes while visiting Erisha some years ago. They were kept in a special room that was always locked when not in use. The books were watched over by the royal historian, Culph, a formidable oldster possessed of an even more formidable temper. Kirisin had met him only once, and once was enough.

For the most part, the Elven histories were the property and concern of the Kings and Queens of the realm, and lesser folks were not allowed to peruse them. They were too fragile and too easily damaged for them to be made available to all, and perhaps it didn't matter anyway since they were said to be sketchy about much of what had happened in the early years. The books themselves had been recorded and bound only a dozen centuries ago, their contents translated from written notes and oral history gathered together from hundreds of sources. It was impossible to say how much of it was accurate. Certainly some of it was too thin and dated to be of any use. But perhaps the Loden and the seeking-Elfstones were important enough to Elven history and culture that whatever was written about them would be essentially correct.

He had to hope so. Because if there wasn't something in those books about the seeking-Stones and the Loden and the whole business of how to save the Ellcrys without uprooting her . . .

So his thinking went, unraveling like thread off a spool, spinning out into a pile at his feet.

By the time he was summoned, two hours later, he had lost most of his enthusiasm for what he had come to do and all of his patience. Everyone else had been taken ahead of him, even though he was a member of the royal family. He couldn't help but think that this was the King's way of letting him know that he had slid a long way down in the royal pecking order since the confrontation with his parents over splitting the Elves. That hadn't involved him personally, but it seemed he might be paying the price nevertheless. He made a mental note to ask his sister how she was faring as a member of the King's personal guard.

"Kirisin!" the King exclaimed. "What a pleasant surprise!" He was a big man with a booming voice and expansive gestures, and the exuberance of his greeting seemed to refute the possibility of any personal antagonism. "But why aren't you in the gardens with the other Chosen?"

If you knew I was supposed to be there, why did you make me sit in the hall for two hours? Kirisin thought. *Why didn't you take me ahead of those others?* But he didn't say any of that. He wasn't there to pick a fight. He hoped.

"My lord," he greeted, giving the King a respectful bow. "I'm sorry to interrupt you."

"Nonsense! I don't see enough of you. Come in, come in. How is my daughter? Still trying to convince everyone she's all grown up at seventeen? I wish she could learn to take herself a little less seriously. More like you. You always seem so relaxed."

He guided Kirisin over to a couch, sat them both down, and leaned forward conspiratorially. "I would have called you in sooner, but I was stuck in a conference and couldn't break free. All those others who came in first had to deal with one of my aides, but I selfishly kept you for myself. Hope the waiting didn't age you too badly. Tell me how you are."

Conflicted and slightly ashamed of my suspicious mind, Kirisin thought. Arissen Belloruus always did this to him, and it wasn't made easier in this situation where he was already uncertain about what he had come to do.

"Very well, my lord." He cleared his throat. "I'm here because something happened in the gardens this morning. Something I thought you ought to know about. The Ellcrys spoke to me."

Something changed in the King's expression. It wasn't a dramatic change, one that evidenced astonishment or excitement. It was subtler, more calculating. It was there for an instant and then gone. Kirisin registered its presence, but was already forging ahead with his story.

"She said she was in danger, my lord. She said the Elves are in danger. She spoke about a change in the world that would affect all of us. She asked for our help. She wants us to find an Elfstone called a Loden. She is to be placed inside this Stone and taken to a safer place and it is all written down in the histories. I thought someone should tell you, so I decided to—"

"Apparently, my daughter didn't think she should be the one to tell me this?" the King interrupted suddenly.

Kirisin hesitated. "There was some discussion. I volunteered to come tell you because I think something needs to be done."

"But not everyone agrees with you?"

Unfortunately. "No, not everyone does."

Arissen Belloruus arched one eyebrow. "My daughter is one of those who doesn't, I gather?" Kirisin nodded. "Well, then. How many of the others feel the same way she does?"

Kirisin took a deep breath. "All of them."

The King nodded. "Did anyone besides you hear the Ellcrys speak?"

Kirisin shook his head. "No."

"Can you think of any reason why the Ellcrys would speak only to you and not to any of the others?"

Again Kirisin shook his head, not even bothering to answer aloud.

There was a long pause. The King put a hand on his shoulder. "You show the courage of your convictions coming to me like this. But maybe you need to reassess your position."

"Maybe I do. But I don't think it will change my mind. I know what I heard."

The King smiled. "I can't take this before the members of the High Council and ask for their support without something more substantive than what you've told me. I will do as suggested and have a look at our histories. Perhaps there is something written down about this Loden Elfstone and the three others needed to find it. I will have the keeper of the histories begin right away. If something is found, I will act on it. But if nothing is found, I am not sure what I will be able to do to help."

Kirisin wasn't pleased with this answer, but he knew better than to press things further. The King had gotten to his feet, an indication that the conversation was over. Kirisin rose with him. "Thank you for listening to me," he said, not knowing what else to say.

Arissen Belloruus nodded. "I don't want you to speak of this to anyone until I tell you to do so. We don't want to cause needless panic."

Needless panic. Kirisin nodded. "I won't say anything."

There would be panic enough once they found out the truth about the tree's predictions, he was thinking as he left the room and walked back down the hallway and out the front door. He was already chastising himself for not being more forceful about acting on the tree's plea, even understanding that there was nothing more that he could have done. He had to hope the histories would reveal something of the Loden and the history of the Elfstones so that the King could act.

He was well down the trail and out of sight of the Belloruus quarters when he suddenly realized something. The King had said that perhaps there was something written in the histories about the Loden Elfstone *and the three others needed to find it*. But Kirisin had not mentioned the three seeking-Stones.

Yet Arissen Belloruus had known about it.

It stopped him in his tracks. He replayed carefully what he had told the King, just to make sure. There was no mistake. He had not mentioned the seeking-Stones at all. He hadn't had a chance to finish his explanation before the King had interrupted him. The implications of this were so stunning that for a moment he could not make himself believe them. It meant the King had already known about the other Elfstones before Kirisin had told him anything. Which, in turn, meant he had already known about everything else, as well.

How could that be?

His face darkened. Well, it was obvious, of course. Only one other person could have told him. Erisha. Despite her insistence on not going to her father about what had happened, she had left the gardens right after he had and done so anyway. That was why the King had left him sitting there for two hours with nothing to do. He was listening to Erisha and then making up his mind about what he was going to say to Kirisin. The boy stared at the ground in front of him, anger building inside. He had been deliberately deceived, and for the life of him he could not understand why.

Kirisin stood where he was for a long time, thinking it through. This was dangerous ground he was standing on. He knew he had to do something, but if he did the wrong thing he would end up creating more trouble for his family than he could even imagine. He couldn't expose the King's duplicity without embarrassing him. He couldn't brace Erisha about what she had done without revealing what he knew about her father. He couldn't tell anyone about the game being played without risking the possibility that it would get back to the King.

But he couldn't stand by and do nothing, either. He had taken an oath when he had become a member of the Chosen, and by doing so he had committed himself to helping protect and care for the tree in any way he could.

He walked slowly back to the gardens, thinking it over, trying to decide what to do. Nothing much came to mind. It depressed him to find himself so powerless, but rushing into things wouldn't help, either. Like it or not, he had to be patient. He had to take his time and figure out what he could do to turn matters around. There was clearly something going on that he didn't understand, and he had to find out what it was. But if he didn't use care in doing so, he risked finding himself shut out of everything.

He arrived back at the gardens and without a word to anyone went back to work. He knew his duties for the day and didn't need to speak to the others if he didn't choose to. It might be better, he decided, if he waited for them to speak to him.

Biat was the first to approach, coming over as soon as he saw him. "What did the King say?" he whispered, giving a quick glance over his shoulder in the direction of Erisha, who was down on her hands and knees digging out weeds across the way.

Kirisin shrugged. "He said he was glad I told him about it and that he would have a look at the histories. He didn't get angry." He paused. "Did I miss anything here?"

"What do you mean?"

"Well, was anything else said about this after I left? Erisha was pretty mad."

Biat chuckled. "Erisha was *furious*. But she dropped the matter right away and put us all to work. We've been at it ever since. What took you so long?"

"Did Erisha say where she was going when she went after me?" he asked, ignoring the question.

Biat stared at him. "What are you talking about? Erisha didn't go after you. She never left the garden. No one did."

Kirisin bent over his digging implement so that the other boy couldn't see his expression. "My mistake. I thought I saw her." *What is going on?* "You had better get back to work. We'll talk about it later."

Biat moved away, leaving him with what were now much darker thoughts. If Erisha hadn't talked to her father, how had he found out what the tree had told Kirisin?

The answer came to him almost instantly. Arissen Belloruus had learned about it much earlier, even before this morning.

Though she chooses not to hear me, you must listen.

He sat up slowly and stared off into space. *She.* He remembered the tree's words now, how they had seemed an accusation that lacked any basis. But they made perfect sense if this morning's attempt to seek help from the Chosen wasn't the first, if the Ellcrys had spoken to someone earlier.

To Erisha.

His gaze drifted across the clearing and settled on his cousin. She was their leader, the foremost among the Chosen. If the tree had spoken to anyone before him, she would have spoken to Erisha. She would have revealed her fears and asked for Erisha's help, and the girl would have told her father. That was how he would have known about the seeking-Stones.

He went back to weeding while he fought to contain his anger and channel it into something more productive than crossing over to wring Erisha's neck. Could it really have happened that way? If so, why? It didn't make any sense. Erisha might have told her father, but why would she keep it secret from the Chosen? For that matter, why would they both keep secret the tree's perceived danger? Everyone knew how important she was as protector of the Elves.

He knew that he was going to have to find out. But that meant getting the truth out of Erisha without having her run to her father. He took a deep breath. He had no idea how he was going to do that.

He continued with his work, trying unsuccessfully to come up with a plan. He was still trying when she suddenly appeared at his elbow.

"What happened with my father?" she asked perfunctorily, kneeling next to him. She brushed back her long dusky hair. "What did he say when you told him about the tree?"

Something in the way she asked it set his teeth on edge, and as quickly as that, he made his decision. He looked up at her so that he could watch her face. "He already knew all about it," he said.

Her fine, delicate features tightened, and she flushed. Her gaze dropped, and then lifted again to meet his. "What do you mean?"

He knew instantly that he had been right in his suspicions. The Ellcrys had spoken to her before this morning, and instead of confiding in the other Chosen she had gone to her father. Both of them had been hiding the truth ever since.

"You know what I mean," he said quietly, his eyes locked on hers. He could see the mix of anger and fear revealed there; she was visibly distraught. "The Ellcrys spoke to you before today and you told your father about it, but you didn't tell us."

"That's not true." She tried to look away.

"Then how did your father know what I was going to say before I said it? He knew all about the Loden and the Elfstones and the histories. He knew about everything, Erisha." He paused. "What is this all about?"

Her lips tightened, and she looked as if she might cry. He thought for just a moment that she was going to tell him what he wanted to know. But then she regained her composure, and her face closed down.

"You imagine things, Kirisin," she whispered furiously. "You make up stories to suit your own purposes. You have a talent for it. I think you had better go back to your work and let me do the same."

She scrambled to her feet. "You better keep these wild stories to yourself, too, or I won't be responsible for what happens to you!"

She stalked away, arms stiff at her sides, shoulders rigid, long hair swaying. She did not look back. Kirisin waited until she had knelt down again to continue her work, then quit watching. So much for not acting precipitously. He wondered how long it would take for her to tell her father. He wondered what would happen to him then. It didn't bear thinking on too closely. If the King determined to keep what the Ellcrys had revealed a secret, he would do whatever he felt was necessary to keep Kirisin from interfering.

It was a very long day after that. He worked in the gardens all morning, then spent the afternoon studying lessons on caring for plants and trees with old Willum. He was close enough to Erisha the entire time for either to call over to the other, but he never said one word to her, nor she to him. He tried to think of what he should do next, but couldn't come up with anything. It seemed he had burned all his bridges by telling her what he knew. If he now told anyone else, she would deny everything. Would the other Chosen back him up? Maybe, but he couldn't be sure. They hadn't been too eager to back him up so far. They were uncertain of him and would not be quick to want to take a stand.

He could talk to Biat, he decided. Of all of them, Biat was the one most likely to support him.

But when the day ended, he didn't say anything to Biat. He left alone and walked home through the trees without a word to any of them. He found he didn't know exactly what he wanted to say or how he wanted to say it. He wasn't sure what he should do, and he needed time to think it over. So he walked out to one of his favorite places, a promontory overlooking the River Orish, and sat down with his back to one of the old-growth cedars.

He wished Simralin were home. She would know what to do. Or at least she would have an opinion. He could talk to his parents, but they might decide to confront Arissen about it, and what happened to them then would be his fault. Worse, they might decide he was confused or mistaken. He was just a boy, after all. Boys like him were confused or mistaken much of the time. Every adult knew that.

But he had to do something. The Ellcrys was in peril, and time was running out. If she didn't receive the help she was asking for, she might perish. It didn't seem that anyone else was going to do anything if he didn't. So he had better come up with a plan.

He sat there until dusk, looking for such a plan. By the time it was dark and he started home, he still didn't have one.

16

IT WAS LATE in the day, the light turned gray and the world become a place of shadows and mysterious sounds, when Angel Perez finally found what she was looking for. She had marched the compound children and their protectors north all afternoon through a haze of smoke and ash to get clear of the city. She had stopped when rest was necessary and once for a quick bite to eat from their meager supplies, but otherwise she had kept them moving. It was hard on the children, especially the little ones, many of whom had to be carried as the march wore on. But stopping was dangerous. They were still too close to the creatures who sought their annihilation, the demons and the once-men and especially that old man. She didn't know if he had discovered yet that she had escaped him again. She didn't know if a pursuit had been mounted. Yet she knew better than to assume anything but the worst, and took no chances.

So they walked out of Anaheim and into the Chino Hills, a distance of more than twenty miles, a march that left them footsore and weary and ready for sleep by the time they reached the scouts from the guerrilla force who were waiting to lead them on. She had

formed the unit eight months earlier, when she knew that Robert
was gone and the compounds east of the mountains had fallen. She
had culled them from the Los Angeles compounds, men and women
who believed that fortresses could no longer protect them and that
their way of life was ended and another way was needed. She had
joined them together with a ragtag band of outcasts and drifters that
knew something about staying alive outside the compounds, men
and women who had learned how to survive in the open. She had
prepared them for what would happen and the exodus of the children she would try to save. She had given to them the responsibility
for guiding those children north, protecting them on their journey,
and finding them safe haven in another place.

Including the ones she had brought with her from the Anaheim
compound, the children now numbered more than a thousand.

The men and women she had waiting had come with trucks
scavenged from all over the city and repaired, vehicles that could
transport the children to the rendezvous point farther north and
well outside the city proper, where the other children and adults
were gathered. Once joined, the entire force would begin the long
trek toward San Francisco—although Angel had not yet decided if
that was to be their final destination.

There were good reasons it should not be. The army of demons
and once-men, now that they were finished with the compounds of
Southern California, would come after them. Going to San Francisco only postponed the inevitable. She could not envision saving
them all a second time if she allowed them to take refuge in the
compounds there. But if not there, then where? Should they go farther north, all the way to Seattle and the Pacific Northwest? Would
they be any safer there? Could they do anything to better prepare
for the time they did battle with their enemies? Could she expect a
different result when they did?

Just thinking of it drained her. It left her with an unshakable conviction that they were running out of time and space and in the end
nothing would save them. The human race was being ground down,
its once seemingly inexhaustible populace steadily reduced from
millions to hundreds of thousands to thousands. She had no idea
how many were left, only that the numbers were diminishing with

every sunrise. It was a trend that must be reversed or the unthink-
able would come to pass and humanity would be wiped out. But she
had no idea how to accomplish this other than to save the ones she
could and hope that something turned the tide in their favor.

So much had gone wrong that it was difficult for her to imagine
anything going right. The Word had once held the upper hand in this
battle, but now everything favored the Void. How could that have
happened when everyone had been warned of the possibility and
the need to guard against it? The answer was simple, of course. Not
enough of those warned had believed.

She turned her small charges over to those waiting, standing back
while they were loaded into the trucks. She took a moment to look
back at the city, searching for any indication of a pursuit. But she
saw only the encroaching shroud of nightfall. She imagined she
could still hear the cries of the wounded and dying, but she knew by
now that she was only hearing them in her mind. She wished she
could find a way to shut those cries out, to silence them. But she
knew from experience that she couldn't.

The trucks were loaded and beginning to pull away. They were
old and jerry-rigged and ran on batteries that were solar-charged.
They would convey the children far enough to get them clear of the
city, but not much farther. It was four hundred miles to San Francisco, and that was too far to walk. The batteries would have to be
replaced or recharged. She hoped some thought had been given to
this in her absence. She hoped preparations had been made.

But there was nothing she could do about it now.

Too tired to think further on the matter, she climbed into the
back of the last of the trucks, curled up in a corner, and quickly fell
asleep.

● ● ●

SHE SURVIVED A fitful night of rough road bounces and grinding
truck noises amid the small distressed sounds from the children who
shared her quarters. The cessation of the truck's movement coupled
with the sudden stillness woke her at daybreak. She was stiff and

sore and, for a moment, disoriented. She had been dreaming of the compounds and the assault of the once-men. The sights and sounds of battle were still fresh in her mind, a wild mix of horror-inducing struggles that left the smell of death thick and pungent in her nostrils. It felt as if it had just happened, and she had just escaped it.

She climbed down from the truck, greeted a few of the guerrillas who came up to her, and waved good morning to Helen Rice, who was already organizing into groups the children she had brought out of the Anaheim compound. Angel stood watching for a moment, filled with a sense of sadness she could not dismiss. It was all so futile, so hopeless. They were saving these children for what? For a chance to live? But what sort of chance were they going to be given if nothing in the larger picture changed?

They were in the guerrilla camp now, a wooded refuge that allowed entry and exit from several directions and could be watched over from a dozen high points close at hand. The defenders were heavily armed and organized. She did not think they would be caught off guard, but did not intend to linger long enough to test the possibility. By midday, they would be traveling north to wherever she decided they must go. They would do so because she was certain that the old man was coming after them with his armies and his weapons and his insatiable lust to see them destroyed.

Or, more particularly, to see her destroyed.

She thought about that for a moment, walking away from the encampment, moving back into the trees where she could be alone to think. The real target of his efforts, of this hunter of Knights of the Word, was herself. His purpose as a servant of the Void was to eliminate all of the remaining Knights, and she was likely one of the last. Her battle with that female demon today demonstrated how intent the old man was on finding and eliminating her. He would not stop because today's attack had failed. He would come after her again, from a different direction perhaps, in a different way. He would come and keep coming until one of them was dead.

For just a moment, she considered turning the tables on him. She considered going after him before he could come after her. He would not be expecting that. She might catch him unawares. She might kill him before he even realized he was in danger. The thought was immensely satisfying. It would atone for all the lives the old man had taken, all the anguish he had caused, all the evil he had perpetrated. It would be retribution well deserved.

It was also a pipe dream of the first order. Johnny would have been quick to point that out, and she knew enough to be quick to do so in his absence.

"Angel Perez?"

The voice seemed to come out of nowhere. Angel looked around quickly, wondering who had followed her from the camp. But there was no one to be seen. She stood perfectly still, knowing she had not imagined it, that someone had spoken her name.

"Are you Angel Perez?" the voice asked.

This time Angel turned toward the place where the voice seemed to originate, but she could see only trees and leaves and grass discolored by pollution and clouded by haze. "Who's there? Where are you?"

A small, slender figure stepped out of the foliage, materializing like something that had just this instant assumed substantive shape and form. A girl, her skin as white as chalk, her eyes dark pools, and her hair long and fine and colored almost pale blue, stood before her. The girl wore clothing that was diaphanous; it trailed from and might have been a part of her body. She stood quietly before Angel, an ethereal creature of exquisite and exotic appearance, letting the Knight of the Word study her.

"I am called Ailie," she said.

Angel knew her for what she was instantly. A tatterdemalion, a strange breed of Faerie creature formed of the memories of dead children, come alive out of circumstance and chance to live a mayfly existence that was over almost before it was begun. How long was it—a month, two? She tried to remember and couldn't. Those Angel knew about had a single purpose—to serve the Lady, the voice of the Word. Angel had never seen one, but she had been told about them by Robert, who had. Tatterdemalions were among the few Faerie creatures who had survived the unbalancing of magic by the demons and the rise of the dark years of the Void.

"She has sent me to you," the tatterdemalion confirmed, as if reading her thoughts. "She has sent me to ask for your help in the battle with the Void. She knows the battle goes badly, but she also knows that there is still a chance to win it."

Angel stared at the child-like creature, trying to equate the words with the speaker, to imagine what it must mean for it to exist in a world of demonkind and humans.

"I have only seen the Lady in my dreams," Angel said suddenly.

But then it was said that few saw her anymore. Not since the balance of good and evil was tilted in favor of the Void. She did not come to the Knights of the Word either in their dreams or in waking once they had pledged themselves. She was an invisible presence, a legend that no longer had substance, but that all of them who were Knights of the Word still believed in.

Still needed to believe in, she added.

"The Lady sent you to me?" she asked, not quite knowing what to make of it. "What does she want me to do?"

Ailie's voice was soft and singsong. "She says you have served her well, but you have saved all the children you can. She wants you to leave them here and go on alone. She wants you to be her Knight-errant and to go in search of a lost talisman. She believes you are the one who can find it. The people who need its magic are in danger of perishing. They are the ones to whom you must go."

The tatterdemalion saw the confusion reflected on Angel's face and came forward wordlessly, took her hands in her own, and held them. Ailie's fingers were like the wings of little birds, so soft and light they seemed weightless.

"Long ago, in the time of John Ross, there was a gypsy morph that took the form of a child and was born to Nest Freemark." Ailie's voice was soft and lilting. "The demons tried to find it and kill it, but they failed. They have not forgotten its existence because they know that the salvation of the human race depends on what it has been given to do. No one has seen the morph in years, not since before the death of Nest Freemark. No one knows where it is or what it looks like. It has gone into hiding, waiting for its time. That time is upon us, and the gypsy morph will reveal itself shortly. Another Knight of the Word goes to find it now, sent by O'olish Amaneh."

Two Bears, Angel thought, remembering. It was Two Bears who had come to her in the beginning to make her a Knight of the Word.

It was Two Bears who acted as emissary to the Lady, the bearer of the black staff, the giver of the Word's power as its champion. How long ago it seemed now.

"Am I to help this Knight of the Word?" she asked.

The tatterdemalion shook her head, her hair rippling like a length of blue silk. "He goes another way from you; his is a different quest. If he lives, you will see him when you are finished."

If he lives. Sure. And if I live.

"So this talisman I'm being sent to find is not the gypsy morph?" she pressed. She knew the story of the gypsy morph and Nest Freemark. Two Bears had told it to her. She wasn't sure she believed it, Ailie's tale notwithstanding. "Then what sort of talisman is it?"

"It is an Elfstone."

Now Angel was really lost. "An Elfstone?" she asked. "As in Elves?"

"Elves created it, long ago in the world of Faerie."

Angel scowled, angry now. "*Elves* created it? You're saying there are *Elves* out there? What does *that* mean? Look, I don't know what any of this is about. I don't know anything about Elves and their Stones. I'm a barrio girl, a street girl, never even been this far north before in my life, and this Elf stuff is just words that don't mean anything. You want to tell me what you're talking about?"

The tiny hands tightened on her own, surprisingly strong. "There are Elves in the world, Angel Perez. There have always been Elves in the world, even before there were humans. They were of the old people, in the time of Faerie, in the world as the Word conceived it before humans came into it. But the Faerie world faded, until only the Elves remained of the old people, and the Elves went into hiding. They have been in hiding ever since."

Ailie pressed close. "But now they must come back into the world if they are to save themselves. They are threatened as humans are threatened, but their salvation lies in the recovery of an Elfstone called a Loden. The Loden is lost to them and must be found. It will give them a way to leave their hiding place and travel to where they will be safe. But the search for the Loden will be difficult and dangerous, and they lack the use of the magic that once would have protected them. They need a Knight of the Word to keep them safe, Angel."

Angel was still coming to terms with the idea that there were Elves, beings she had always believed to be imaginary, creatures of storybooks and legends. What else was there in the world that she didn't know about—what else that she wrongly assumed didn't exist? Her world had always been one of concrete and steel, the ruins of cities and skyscrapers.

She looked off into the trees, then back at Ailie. Well, she thought, if you'd accepted that tatterdemalions were real, how big of a jump was it to believe in Elves?

"So? The Lady has asked that I do all this? She thinks I'm the right one to undertake this search? There is no one else better suited?"

Ailie smiled sadly. "There is no one else at all."

Angel drew in a quick breath and exhaled sharply. "All of the Knights of the Word are gone?"

The tatterdemalion released her hands, folded her child's arms across her chest, and hugged herself. "Will you go?"

Angel took a long moment to answer. She felt the world sliding away from her—the world of her childhood, the only world she had ever known—and it left her feeling bereft and hollow. Everything she knew of life aside from what she did—the rescue of children, the defense of the compounds—had been gone a long time. Now even the little she had been left was about to be taken away, too. It was difficult to accept, and she didn't know if she could.

"What of these people I lead?" she asked. "These children and their protectors? They depend on me."

"You may see them again in another place and time." Ailie's smile was a flicker of brightness. "But they travel too slowly for you, and their road leads another way. You must tell them to travel north to the Columbia River in the Cascade Mountains. Someone will find them there when it is time."

Angel did not miss the evasiveness in Ailie's response. You *may* see them again. *Someone* will find them. But not necessarily her because maybe she wouldn't be alive to do so. Whispers of terrible danger echoed in Ailie's words—unvoiced promises of confrontations and struggles that would end in someone's death. She would have believed it in any event because she was a Knight of the Word and it was the nature of her life. But the tatterdemalion's responses left no doubt.

She sighed and nodded. "*Muy bien*. How will I find these Elves? Where do I go?"

"I will take you," Ailie answered.

"You will go with me?"

"I will be your guide and your conscience."

Angel blinked. "My conscience?"

The tatterdemalion took a long moment before responding. "It may be that you will misplace your own. It may be that you will need a fresh one. It may be that what you encounter on a journey such as this will require it."

Angel didn't like the sound of this. The tatterdemalion was making a point of telling her that her conscience might become an issue for her. She would not do that if the Lady had not told her to do so. Ailie was acting under orders to prepare Angel for what lay ahead, so that she could not say later that she had not been warned. The implications were not encouraging: it suggested strongly that in the face of future events she might consider turning back.

She shook her head. "What training have you had in the conscience department? Why should I listen to you?"

"Sometimes you cannot hear your own voice clearly and need another to enable it to be understood," the other responded. "I am to be that second voice, there when you need it. But I am not to make your decisions for you. You must do that for yourself."

Angel nodded slowly, understanding the wisdom of this answer. She was being sent out alone; perhaps she would be alone for much of the time. It was not a good thing to have no one to talk to. Given what she was being asked to do, it made sense that the Lady would send someone with her of whom she could ask questions and seek advice. A tatterdemalion, a creature of Faerie, was not the worst choice.

"Your guidance and counseling will be welcome, *amiguita mía*," she said to Ailie. "You and I, we will do what we can for these Elves.

We will travel to where they live and then take them to find their Elf-stone. But," she held up one finger, "when we are done, I will come back for these children and their protectors and take them to where they, too, will be safe. Agreed?"

"Once the Loden is found, the Lady says you are free to do whatever you wish," the tatterdemalion said. "But nothing will change who you are. You will still be a Knight of the Word."

Angel shook her head and brushed back her dark hair. "I don't want to be anything else, Ailie." *Not since Johnny died.* "What happens now?"

Ailie looked skyward, as if searching for something in the clouds and mist. "We leave. We go north."

Angel sighed. "Not until I tell someone what's happening. Wait here. I'll be right back."

● ● ●

SHE WENT TO find Helen Rice because she couldn't think of anyone else to talk to about what she intended. She was still struggling to accept that she had agreed to undertake a search for Elves—*for Elves, ¡dios mío!*—and for a magic that would protect them from the world's destruction. But what choice did she have? The world's misery was an unbearable weight, an accumulation of sorrows and horrors that would in a time fast approaching bury them all. If she could do something more than what she was doing to change things, she could hardly refuse the chance. Still, it didn't make things any easier that what she was being asked to do was almost impossible for her to understand.

Elves and Elfstones. Faerie creatures and their magic.

She found Helen standing apart from the children, who were eating a hasty breakfast before the caravan set out. Already the trucks were lined up for boarding, supplies stacked for loading. The hoods of the trucks were raised as mechanics installed fresh solar-charged batteries. Apparently, someone had been thinking ahead after all.

"Angel, where have you been?" her friend asked, turning to greet her. Helen's face was dirt-smudged and her eyes tired. "Get something to eat while you can."

Angel shook her head. "I'm not going with you. I have something else I must do. It will take me far away from you and the children. You'll have to go on without me and protect yourselves as best you can until I come back. Can you do this?"

Helen stared at her for a moment, then nodded. "I can do anything I have to do." She paused. "Can you tell me what this is about?"

"It's something I have been given to do as a Knight of the Word. It will mean helping others who need it even more than you and the children. But I won't forget you. Take everyone north to the Columbia River and wait at the edge of the Cascade Mountains. Do you know the way?"

Helen nodded. "Others traveling with me know it better than I do. We will find our way."

"Be careful. The once-men will follow you north; they will try to trap you somewhere along the way. You must not underestimate them. If they find you on the Columbia, go farther north and seek shelter in the compounds there."

"But you will come for us?"

Angel took a deep breath and promised what she shouldn't have. "I will come for you."

Helen reached out for her and hugged her close. Her thin body was shaking, and her usually steady voice sounded strained and broken. "You have done so much for us. You are the backbone of our courage, and we can't afford to lose you. Please be careful."

Angel hugged her back. "Care for the children, *amiga mía. Confioenti.* I'm relying on you."

She kissed Helen Rice on the cheek and broke away when she felt the other woman start to cry.

17

LOGAN TOM WAS almost all the way across the Great Plains and in sight of the dark wall of the Rocky Mountains when he encountered the Preacher. He had been driving west for almost two days, following the highway that the finger bones of Nest Freemark had set him upon more than a week earlier. He hadn't slept in two days. He hadn't even tried the first night, after fleeing the fiery ruins of the compound and its monsters. On the second night, terrifying dreams and sudden awakenings plagued him, and he was consumed by an unshakable sense that fate was overtaking him and nothing he did would turn it aside.

His surroundings did not comfort or reassure him. The plains were a dry and empty sweep of land that stretched away from horizon to horizon, a vast dusty carpet that looked frayed at the edges. He encountered no other human beings—not in the towns he occasionally turned in to to explore for supplies, and not on the highway itself. Once or twice, he saw things moving in the distance, but they were too far away to identify. He felt as if he were the last living creature on earth and wondered from time to time if that might not be best. No humans would want to live on a world like this, he told himself.

So it was a surprise and something of a revelation when he stumbled upon the Preacher and his strange flock.

It was nearing dusk at the end of the second day, and he had been driving for more than ten hours. His muscles were cramped and sore, and he was looking for a safe place to spend the night. The land about him seemed empty, but you could never be sure and you never took chances. So when he spied the little town off to his left, he left the highway just past the collapsed interchange and drove through the hardpan fields until he reached its edge.

He stopped then and got out, peering among the ramshackle houses and sheds to the cluster of buildings that formed the town center. One street led in and out. Windblown pieces of paper and old leaves were piled against the walls, and broken branches and scraps of tar paper lay scattered about. A few of the roofs had collapsed in on the houses, and most of the window glass was gone. Derelict cars, trucks, and even tractors sat rusting away in yards and in the surrounding fields. A farm town, probably close to three hundred years old, its life ended perhaps twenty years ago, it sat waiting for someone to reclaim it. But no one ever would.

He was sizing up a grove of withered oak trees for a place to park the AV when the old man walked out of the shadows from between the buildings. He was tall and stooped, with white hair and skin that was leathery and deeply lined. He must have been handsome once, and Logan supposed he still was—in that rough, weathered sort of way old men sometimes were. Even from twenty yards away and with the light failing, he could see the clear blue light of the other's eyes.

"Good evening to you, Brother," the old man greeted. He walked up and extended his hand.

Logan shook it. "Evening."

"Come a long way? You look tired."

"I've been driving since sunrise."

The old man nodded toward the freeway. "Hard work on these roads. See anyone on your way?"

"Just shadows and ghosts."

"That's most of what there is now. Might I inquire of your name? It lends a familiarity to conversation to be on a first-name basis."

His smile was warm and disarming. Logan shrugged. "I'm Logan Tom."

"Brother Logan," the other acknowledged and released his hand. "You may call me Preacher. Everybody does. It defines both my profession and my identity. My own name ceased to have relevance a long time ago—so long ago I can barely recall it. I'm simply Preacher now, a shepherd to my flock."

Logan glanced past him to the deserted town. "Your flock seems as if it might have scattered."

The Preacher smiled. "Well, as they say, looks are deceiving. My flock of fifty years ago, when I was a young minister starting out, is dead or gone, almost the whole of them, along with the church in which I gave my sermons and spoke of my faith. But when you undertake a ministry to those seeking guidance, you don't pick and choose your flock or your pulpit; you take what comes your way and minister where you can."

Logan nodded. "A few of those in need have found their way here, have they?"

The Preacher leaned forward, brow furrowing. "Are you a believer in the Word, Brother Logan?"

Logan hesitated, and the clear blue eyes fixed on him. "I believe in the Word, Preacher," he said, wary now. "Maybe not the same Word you believe in, though."

"I ask not to be rude, but because I have heard that there are servants of the Word who carry black staffs of the sort you grip so firmly in your right hand."

Logan glanced down. He had forgotten he was holding the staff. It was so much a part of him by now that he had taken it with him when he left the Lightning with barely a second thought.

"The staff and its bearer are the Word's own cleansing fire, I am told," the Preacher went on with a hushed reverence. "You are welcome here, sir. In this poor outback, in this withered and dusty gathering place of wounded souls, we still do what we can to serve the

Word and her Knights." He smiled reassuringly. "Can I offer you something of food and drink? We haven't much, but we would be honored to share it with you."

Logan almost said no, then decided that doing so would be an unnecessary insult and a disappointment to the old man. What did it hurt for him to accept the invitation? He had planned on spending the night here anyway, and it would be nice to eat indoors for a change.

"I can only stay a little while, Preacher," he said

The old man nodded. "Let me be honest with you, Brother Logan. This invitation is well meant, but selfish, too. It would mean a great deal to those to whom I minister if they could visit with you. Trial and tribulation and time erode their faith. They have little with which to restore it. You would provide them with a large measure of what is needed, just with a few well-chosen words. We are isolated out here, which is probably for the best. But we are not ignorant of the world, even though the world is ignorant of us. We hear bits and pieces of news from the few who pass this way. Some speak of the Knights of the Word and the demons with which they do battle. We hear of the struggle taking place and understand its source. But the reality is distant and insubstantial for many. It would help give it a face and an identity if a champion of the Word were to grace us with his presence. Knowing this, will you still stay for just a little while?"

Logan smiled despite himself. How could he refuse? He walked back to the Lightning, set the alarm and locks, and then gestured for the Preacher to lead the way. They set off among the buildings toward the center of the town. "How did you know I was here?" Logan asked him.

"Sound carries long distances out here, where so much is silence. We heard you coming across the fields in your vehicle."

They passed between the residences and arrived at the main street. The buildings were weathered and sad, the paint peeling, windows and doors mostly gone, and the roofs stripped of shingles. The walkways and street were cracked and weed-grown, and trash was piled everywhere. There was no sign of life, nothing to indicate that the Preacher's flock consisted of anything more than the ghosts of the dead.

"Used to be a drugstore over there—soda fountain and phar-macy," the Preacher said, turning left down the walk. "Gas station back there at the end of the block. Two pumps, that was it. Clothing store, insurance and real estate office combined, barbershop and hairdresser—they were combined, too—bank and post office."

He shook his head. "The post office was one of the last govern-ment services to close down, you know. Delivered the mail even after Washington was destroyed. It was all done locally, nothing be-yond that. But it was something, and it gave people a sense of sharing a larger community. It gave them hope that maybe not everything was gone."

They had reached a square, single-story building at the edge of the town proper, something that might have once served as a com-munity center. The windows were shuttered and the door tightly sealed. Heavy deadbolts secured against unauthorized entry. The Preacher took a ring of keys from the pocket of his jacket and re-leased the locks one by one.

"Won't stop everything, but it makes my flock feel a little safer," he offered. "Usually, we leave the shutters open to let in the light. But we closed them when we heard your vehicle coming. Almost dark now, so we will leave them closed until sunrise."

He led Logan inside, where a different world awaited.

There was a large room with three long folding tables and chairs set out in its center. A pass-through cut into the back wall opened onto a small kitchen. He could smell food cooking and see trays of glasses sitting out. A door to the left of the pass-through revealed a second large room beyond. Doors marked MEN and WOMEN were set into the wall to his left.

A scattering of faces turned his way; all of them were ancient and worn and framed by dustings of white hair. There were maybe two dozen, all seated at the tables except three who occupied wheel-chairs, ancient eyes giving him an uncertain look, wrinkled hands folded together on the tabletops. Whatever conversation had pre-ceded his appearance had died away. The room was quiet save for a shuffling of chairs and the soft wheezing of labored breathing.

"Everyone, please welcome Brother Logan," the Preacher said.

There was a soft muttering of "Hi, Logan," and "Welcome,

Logan," in response. Logan nodded, thinking there wasn't a person in
the room under the age of seventy-five. He wondered how they had
found their way here. It didn't seem possible that any of them could
have traveled very far. But then perhaps they had all been here
much longer than he assumed.

"Brother Logan will be eating with us tonight," the Preacher said.
"You might notice that he is a bearer of the black staff of a Knight of
the Word. He has come a long way. I hope you will all do your best
to make him feel at peace on his night with us so that he will be well
rested when he leaves us on the morrow."

He guided Logan to the center table and seated him between
two very elderly women who looked at him as if he were something
come out of the ether. He smiled at them, and watched as the
Preacher walked around the table and took the chair across from
him.

"Give thanks for what we have, Sister Anne," he said to the old
woman on Logan's right.

The meal was served and Logan got another surprise. The food
was fresh, not prepackaged—vegetables and pasta, bread, and some
sort of fruit. Tea was poured from pitchers, and he didn't ask where
they had gotten the water. He didn't ask where any of it came from.
It didn't feel right to do so. He just ate and drank what he was given
and answered what questions he could. Most were about what he
had seen of the outside world. He kept his descriptions as positive as
he could, staying away from demons and once-men, from the destruction that was taking place everywhere, and from his own
knowledge that worse times lay ahead. These people didn't need to
hear about it tonight. They had already chosen what to do with the
rest of their lives.

"How long have all these people been here?" he asked the
Preacher at one point.

"Most have been here for close to twenty years. Some were born
and raised here. Some came to be with relatives and friends. They're
the castoffs and leftovers of families splintered and scattered long
since. All the young ones left long ago. The bombings chased most
away. It was bad; there were a lot of missile silos and command cen-
ters in the mountains. They all went. But they took a lot of us who

were standing out in the open with them. Then the water and soil turned bad. That was the end for most; everyone pretty much packed it in. We're the only ones who stayed. Now almost no one comes this way anymore. You are the first in more than a year."

Logan nodded. "I'm surprised you're still here."

The Preacher laughed softly. "Where else would we be? Inside the compounds? Not people like us. We've lived all our lives in the open, most of us in small towns like this one. We're old, all of us. We don't want to change what we know. We've only got a little time left under the best of circumstances, and we want it to feel as comfortable and familiar as possible. Living here gives us that."

"It's not so bad," said the old woman on his left. "We've got what we need."

"No one bothers us here," said an old man across from her.

"No one," the old woman agreed.

They finished their dinner, and the Preacher brought them all together in a circle of chairs. An old man with wild white hair and long, supple fingers brought out a guitar, and they began to sing songs they remembered from their childhood. Their faces brightened with the music and the memories it conjured. Their voices were thin and ragged, but brought life to the songs. Logan didn't sing; he only listened. There hadn't been much singing in his childhood and none since he had gone with Michael. Listening now, he realized how much he had missed. Worse, he realized how much he had lost.

Then the Preacher said, "We will do a song now for Brother Logan, one that speaks to the nature of his life and work." He looked at Logan. "Maybe you will carry something of the words and melody with you when you leave us. Maybe they will soothe you when you are in need of soothing. Maybe they will help you remember that there are those who still have faith in the Knights of the Word."

He looked over at the guitar player. "Brother Jackson?"

The guitar player nodded and his fingers began to pick out the notes.

Amazing grace,
how sweet the sound

That saved a wretch like me
I once was lost,
but now am found
Was blind but now I see.

'Twas grace that taught
my heart to fear
And grace my fears relieved
How precious did
that grace appear
The hour I first believed.

Amazing grace,
How sweet the sound
That saved a wretch like me
I once was lost,
but now am found
Was blind but now I see.

That was the whole of it, and afterward Logan could remember every word. It wasn't his story exactly, but it felt like a close approximation. The music was sweet and haunting and conjured memories that were strong and true. When the song was finished, there was a hushed silence as all eyes turned to Logan to measure his reaction. He looked around at those assembled and found mirrored in their expressions an understanding of what the song had meant to him. Wherever he went, whatever he did, he would never forget it.

"We owe a debt to the writer of that one," the Preacher said quietly. "The words still speak to us, and the music still works magic."

They sang several more songs, the night enfolding the building and its occupants, the darkness deep and unbroken. When the evening ended, the assemblage joined hands and murmured thanks for their day and began to shuffle off to the back room to where they would sleep. Most took time to say good night and thank you to Logan, a gesture that touched him deeply.

The Preacher came up when the rest were gone. "Would you like to sleep here tonight, Brother Logan?"

Logan shook his head. "I don't think so, Preacher. I plan to leave early. I've said my good-byes to your flock. I think I should leave it at that."

"You brought a little light with you on your visit. I hope we gave you a little light back in return." The old man smiled. "I wish we could do more."

Logan wanted to ask him how long he thought they could stay out here like this. He wanted to tell him that it was too dangerous to be alone and unprotected. But he knew what the response would be, and he felt that saying anything would be an insult. Some things you had to accept. Some things you left alone.

"Travel safely," the Preacher said to him, and extended his hand.

Logan gripped it firmly. "I will remember you every time I think of that song."

"Then remember, too, that there are still some of us who believe in what you are doing. We will pray for you."

Logan went out the door into the night and did not look back.

● ● ●

BY SUNRISE OF the following day he was driving into the foothills below the Rockies, winding his way slowly upward toward the barren peaks. There had been snow on these mountains once, long ago before the weather changed. Even in summer, the permafrost had endured and traces of winter had remained. Winter had capped the peaks in a soft white covering that could be seen for fifty miles. He had been told that it was a beautiful sight.

He had come to the Preacher almost broken by what he had done inside the compound two nights previous, consumed by self-loathing and a growing fear of what he was becoming. It wasn't that he hadn't done any of it before; it wasn't even that it was more horrific this time than any other. His mood was the cumulative result of so many compounds and so many encounters with children transformed into monsters. It was the repetition of the killing, however necessary, however well intentioned. It was the crushing weight of the numbers.

He had been doing these . . . he searched for the right word, the least contemptible word . . . these *mercy killings* for almost fifteen years. How many children had he killed in that time? *Children!* He made himself say the word. How many *children* had he killed?

Of course, they weren't really children. They weren't even human by the time he reached them inside the compound walls, not after the demons had altered them. But they had been, and something of that still reflected in their eyes and on their faces, even as he snuffed out their lives. Oh, yes, he had no choice. He had to put an end to them because he understood what was happening.

Demons were breeding demons from human children.

Tears came to his eyes, and he couldn't stop them. *It's all right*, he told himself. *You can cry for them. No one else will.*

But he was crying now for himself, as well. He was crying for what he had turned himself into. He understood better than anyone what too much of something could do to you. He had witnessed it firsthand not that many years ago. He had not believed it possible before then. He thought that once you understood the difference between right and wrong, it was ingrained in you. He thought your moral values were developed early and stayed with you.

As with so many things, Michael had taught him otherwise. It was a lesson he would never forget.

He drove on through the morning, the sun an indistinct splash of brightness above the thick screen of clouds, its light diffused into a dull wash as it filtered down through the mist that shrouded the lower levels of the peaks. The temperature was changing slightly, but the air was still warm and oddly dry, even in the haze. If there was such a thing as dry damp, this was it. He remembered an expression he had once heard—*sunny showers*—which was used to describe bright sun shining down through a rain. He wondered what that would be like.

It was barren and empty in the mountains, more so than on the plains, which was disconcerting. To keep himself from dwelling on it, he sang "Amazing Grace" a few times, repeating the phrases he liked the best, letting the melody take him away. He was feeling better today, after his night with the Preacher and his flock of old people, and he wanted to keep that feeling wrapped about him for as long as he could. The horror of the compound had begun to dissipate, as such horrors always did, even when he feared they wouldn't. The human spirit was remarkably resilient. Were it not, he supposed he would have gone mad a long time ago.

The road tunneled between the cliffs, and he went with it, steering the AV through clusters of boulders and over small slides. If he had been driving anything else, he might not have been able to go on, but the Lightning's huge tires and high-set chassis allowed passage over almost anything. The mountains loomed all about him now, huge monoliths that jutted skyward until they disappeared in clouds and mist. Everything was taking on a hazy look, giving the world about him an indistinct quality that suggested it was fading away. He wondered how much farther he would have to climb in order to reach the crest of the pass.

He got his answer almost as soon as he finished asking the question. The road rounded a curve and simply disappeared. Tons of rock had collapsed in a slide that had brought down an entire cliff face. He drove right up to it, stopped, and got out. The slide was fifty feet high if it was an inch. It angled down across the road from what remained of the cliff and tumbled over a drop. There was no way around or over unless he proceeded on foot. The slide had formed a wall he could not get past.

He would have to find another way.

There is no other way!

The familiar voice screamed at him in the silence of his mind, the words cutting at him like a razor and triggering a memory he knew he would never escape. He felt the world drop away beneath his feet as the memory surfaced in a swarm of harsh, angry images.

And suddenly, he was reliving the final moments of his last night with Michael Poole.

18

H E CROUCHES WITH *the others in the concealing shadows of a skeletal forest and peers through the hazy darkness of the moonless night at the Midline Slave Camp. The
Midline sits squarely on the border of what used to be the states of Indiana and Illinois, just below Lake Michigan. A hundred yards of open
ground surrounds the camp, land cleared by the once-men as a precaution against what is about to happen. Watch fires burn in pits along the
barbed-wire fences surrounding the camp, and torches flicker at its
heavy gates. It is a slave camp like all other slave camps, and yet it is
something more. It is the one slave camp that Michael Poole has steadfastly avoided attacking, the one camp he has said it would take an
army to break into.*

*Nevertheless, here they are, preparing to do what he has sworn they
would not.*

*There is no reason for them to do this. There are other, easier com-
pounds against which they could mount an assault. The Midline is formidable. Three buildings that were once steel mills form the compound—
huge, cavernous structures built of corrugated metal sheets and surrounded
by double rows of mesh steel fencing strung with concertina wire. Ditches*

deep enough to swallow Michael's Lightning S-150 pockmark the open ground outside the fences in all directions. The buildings are tightly sealed, their doors and windows barred and shuttered. The slaves of the once-men who come here are taken inside and do not come out again until they are carried out. The work that is done here is infamous. It is widely regarded as the most impenetrable of the slave camps.

Michael says it doesn't matter, that it is an abomination and must be destroyed. Michael says they have put off doing so long enough.

Logan looks at the camp, assessing its defenses and its sheer size, and shakes his head slowly. This is suicide, he thinks.

But Michael has decided, and once he has done so, that is the end of the matter. Even Grayling, who isn't afraid of anything, won't cross Michael Poole. Michael is a legend. He is a living talisman; nothing can kill him. He has survived against impossible odds. He has led his men on successful attacks again and again. He has never failed.

No one thinks he will fail tonight, either.

Still, Michael is not the same man since Fresh died. It took something out of him when he lost Fresh, and while most had not noticed, Logan could tell. It was an accident, a truck's hand brake giving out, and the truck rolling slowly downhill, gathering speed, and finally crushing Fresh against a wall. There was blood everywhere. Fresh had taken two days to die. There was nothing anyone could do; the injuries were too extensive. Michael had kept vigil the entire time, even when Fresh lapsed into a coma and no longer knew who he was.

Michael told the driver of the truck afterward that it wasn't his fault. Accidents happen. He told the driver he bore him no grudge and thought no less of him. Logan was there and heard what he said and how he said it. Another wouldn't have recognized the rage Michael was hiding. But no one knows Michael better than he does. Michael is so tightly controlled that he never lets anything show that might reveal or compromise him. Still, he gives himself away through small gestures and an emphasis on certain words. He saw the telltale signs during Michael's conversation with the driver and knew instinctively what it meant. The driver was a dead man. Logan almost told him as much, and then decided it was too dangerous.

A week later, the driver disappeared while foraging and was never seen again.

Fresh might have tried to do something about it. But Logan is not Fresh. He is not Michael's equal. He is Michael's adopted child. Even though he has just turned eighteen years old and is technically a man, that is the position to which Michael has relegated him. It is odd to feel so close to someone and at the same time so distant. They share so much that no one else shares, and yet there are boundaries that Logan knows he cannot cross.

Questioning the wisdom of tonight's assault is one. He knows he should say something because on the face of things the attack is foolish and because it is clear to him that Michael has changed. He thinks the change began before the death of Fresh, but it has evolved into something dangerous since. Michael has grown reckless in his efforts to destroy the once-men and their camps. He seems increasingly heedless of the dangers into which he leads them. His leadership decisions are uncomfortably spontaneous and made with less and less consideration for the consequences. So far, he has gotten away with it. So far, his aura of invincibility and his luck have carried him over the rough spots. But Logan knows that sooner or later even these will fail. If that happens before Michael recovers himself, the consequences will be disastrous. But what is he to do? No one will listen to a boy barely turned a man. No one wants to believe that Michael is no longer invincible.

Nor will he be the one to run from what the rest of them go willingly to face. Michael saved his life. Michael gave him everything he has. He will never abandon Michael, even if it means his death.

He tries to push such thoughts out of his mind as he stares at the compound and waits for Michael to give the order to attack. But the thoughts will not be banished; the thoughts persist.

"Logan," Michael says to him suddenly, turning around so that he can see the other's face. Michael's expression is chilling, alive with a terrifying wildness. "I want you to lead the assault on the right wing, on the first building. If you can't handle it, tell me now."

Logan would never tell him that, and Michael knows it. He nods without speaking.

"Just remember what you've been taught. Wilson, you take the left. Grayling, you stay with me. The center building will be the most heavily guarded. The experiments are carried out there."

On the children, Logan thinks. On the old and sick and helpless.

There are demons in residence here, two of them at least. But Michael's information tells them that the demons are absent this night, gone on a hunt that will keep them away until the end of the week. Michael's information has never been wrong. Logan hopes it is right tonight. Once, he would not have thought to question it. But Michael is not the same, and Logan can no longer be certain that anything he does is well considered.

He feels an unexpected sense of despair. How did this happen? When did Michael lose his way? He understands how it could happen, given the terrible work they do. Live long enough in a madhouse, and you risk going mad yourself. But he had always believed Michael could rise above it. Michael is the ultimate warrior, hardened to everything, strong enough to withstand the horrors they encountered no matter how often or how terrible. Even losing Fresh shouldn't have been enough to change him.

Yet something did. Somewhere along the way he failed to recognize that he was slipping away, that an erosion of his soul was taking place.

Logan looks down at the Scattershot he has carried since Michael gave it to him on his first raid. If it can happen to Michael, it can happen to him. Will he recognize it if it does? Will he know enough to do something about it?

He realizes suddenly that Michael is talking to him, and his gaze shifts quickly. "Boy, are you with us or should I find someone to take your place?" Michael snaps. "You look like you've got your head in the clouds. Pay attention when I am talking to you!"

"I'm listening," he says quickly.

Michael sneers. "Then there is no need for me to repeat myself, is there? You know what to do. So be sure and do it. Don't run from it if things get tough. I hate cowards, Logan."

He turns away dismissively, and Logan says nothing. A year ago, Michael would never have spoken to him like this. I should have seen it coming, *he thinks.* I should have done something to stop it. His eyes close, and he vows that as soon as the opportunity presents itself, he will.

"All right, let's go," Michael says suddenly, and they are off.

They spread out through the trees toward the waiting vehicles, trucks modified with snowplow rams and thick protective shields to get them safely through the gates. The trucks are modified four-tons, big and *heavy, and not even gates as strong as those of Midline Slave Camp will stop them once they gain sufficient momentum. Heavy automatic weapons are mounted on the cabs and in the truck beds, each capable of firing hundreds of rounds in seconds. They are better prepared than they have ever been, and Logan feels a rush of excitement at the prospect of what it will mean to destroy this camp.*

He climbs into the cab through the passenger's door and sits next to Jena. She is tight-faced and focused, ten years older than he, more experienced and better trained. By rights, she should be the one leading and he the one driving. But she doesn't say anything. She just looks straight ahead, waiting for the signal.

When it comes, a flare from the middle truck, she engages the clutch and the truck lurches forward through the trees and onto the flats. She whips the heavy vehicle left and right, dodging the pits and the traps, closing quickly on the fence. Weapons fire sounds from the walls ahead, and bullets ricochet off the shields. He peers through the spiderwebbed windshield to find dozens of once-men lining the fences, all of them with weapons, all of them firing.

All we need is a little luck, *he thinks.*

Then everything goes wrong at once. To his left, past Jena's tense face and the hurtling bulk of Michael's vehicle, the truck driven by Wilson misjudges and runs into one of the ditches. Its front wheels catch, its momentum flips it end-over-end, and it explodes. Shards of twisted metal and shattered glass rain down everywhere. Bodies tumble from the truck onto the ground, but only a few. The rest remain trapped inside.

There is no time for him to think about it because they have reached the fence and are tearing through the heavy wire. The once-men scatter, but only far enough to turn and try to shoot at them through the cab windows. The men hunkered down in the truck bed shoot back, and bodies fall all across the compound yard.

"Logan!" Jena yells in warning.

An explosion rocks their truck, sending Logan sliding into her with such force that she cries out. The gates of the south building loom directly in front of them, and they struggle frantically to untangle as they careen toward a collision. Locked together, they steer the truck into the gap between the heavy doors, and as the ram strikes them the doors explode in-

ward with a shriek of metal tearing free. The truck lurches to a stop, and the attackers tumble out, firing into the defenders that come at them.

Too many and too organized, *Logan realizes suddenly.* They have been waiting for us. It is a trap.

He fights with a ferocity he does not know he possesses, lost in a haze of smoke and ash, in the staccato rip of automatic weapons fire, and the harsh scream of his own desperation. He shoots at everything that moves and at the same time keeps moving himself. He does not know how long the fighting continues, but it seems endless. Twice he is wounded, but neither injury stops him. At one point a rush of once-men overwhelms him, and he loses his grip on the Scattershot as he fights to break free. Someone—he never discovers who—comes to his aid and tears them away. Even so, he is left dazed and battered and weaponless. He scrambles about on his hands and knees, searching for the Scatter-shot, for any weapon at all. He thinks that this is the end. He thinks that this is the day he will die.

Then suddenly everything quiets. The shooting is all distant now, off in the other buildings and outside. Low moans and cries for help reach out to him from close at hand, but the smoke trapped inside the building is so thick he cannot find anyone. His ears ring from the weapons fire and bomb concussions, and he feels disoriented and weak. He stumbles about, still searching for the Scattershot, needing to feel a weapon in his hands. He finds it finally, lying not five feet away. When he picks it up, the barrel is so hot that the heat radiates down through the wood grips of the stock.

He gropes his way through the smoke. Where is everyone?

Then he trips over Jena, lying faceup on the floor, her eyes open and staring. He finds most of the others close by, all dead. There is no one left, he thinks. He has lost them all.

The moans and cries continue, and he makes his way blindly toward the sounds. He comes up against a cage, and inside the cage are dozens of imprisoned humans, a part of Midline's slave population. Faces press up against the steel mesh, eyes and mouths beseeching, begging. He pulls away from the hands and fingers that seek to hold him and gropes his way along the mesh in search of the cage door. The smoke is beginning to thin now, and outside the shooting has quieted to a few distant dis-

charges punctuated by shouts and cries. The battle is ending. He must hurry.

He finds the door secured with a heavy chain. He looks around for something he can use to break the lock. He locates a metal bar that will snap the chain—and suddenly Michael appears through the smoke.

"What's happened?" he demands. "Where are the others?"

He is bloodied from head to foot, a walking nightmare, a corpse come out of the grave. It is impossible for Logan to tell if the blood is Michael's or not. One arm hangs limp, the sleeve of his heavy jacket shredded. He carries his Ronin Flechette cradled in the other, smoke curling out of its short, wicked black barrel.

"Did you hear me?" he snaps at Logan, angry now.

"All dead, I think," Logan answers. "I'm not sure. I haven't had time to check."

Michael shrugs. There is a dangerous glint in his eye. "Wilson's group is gone, too. Mine is hacked to pieces. They really made a mess of us." He looks at the prisoners, shakes his head, and mutters something unintelligible. Taking it as an indication he should continue with his efforts, Logan places the iron bar back inside the chain loop and starts to apply pressure. "Leave them!" Michael orders instantly.

Logan turns, not sure he has heard correctly. "But they—"

"Leave them!" Michael roars. He flings his injured arm toward the cage with such force that droplets of blood fly everywhere. "Leave them where they are. Leave them to rot!"

Logan shakes his head in disbelief. "But they're caged."

The other stares at him blankly, and then starts to laugh. "Don't you get it? They're where they deserve to be!" The laughter dies into something that might be a sob. "All we do for them, all we give up, and for what? So that they can run like sheep to be gathered up again? So that they can go back to being stupid and helpless? Look at them! They make me sick!"

"Michael, it's not their fault—"

"Shut up!" Michael screams at him, and all of a sudden the Ronin is pointing at his midsection. "Don't defend them! They killed your friends, your comrades, all the people who made a difference in your life! They killed them just as surely as if they pulled the trigger!"

Logan doesn't know what to do—except that he knows not to make any sudden moves with the Ronin pointing at him. He could argue that it is Michael who has chosen to attack Midline. He could point out that they all came here willingly, knowing the risk. But Michael's face tells him that he isn't going to listen to those arguments. He is barely listening to anything at this point.

"All right, Michael," he says gently, lifting one hand just a fraction of an inch in a placating gesture. "Let's just go. Let's gather everybody up and get out of here. We can talk about it later."

But Michael shakes his head slowly, and the insanity reflected in his eyes is bright and ungovernable. "No, it all ends here, Logan. It all ends tonight. This is as far as we go." He shakes his head, and the Ronin dips slightly. "I've had enough, boy. I don't want to live another day in this damned world. I don't want to endure one more moment of it. I should have killed us both years ago for all the difference it's made."

Logan feels a chill in the pit of his stomach. "Michael, that's crazy! Listen to what you're saying!"

"I saved your life; I can take it away." The Ronin is pointing directly at him again; Michael's arm is steady as he aims it. "Think about it. Think about how hopeless it is! We've lost everything tonight—people, weapons, machines, all of it. Look at me; I probably won't live another day, and if I do I'll never be the same. If we don't end it here, we'll be caught and thrown into the camps. We'll end up just like that!" He gestures again toward the prisoners in the cage. "I made up my mind a long time ago that I wouldn't let that happen."

"But these people need our help! What about all the others like them?"

Michael shakes his head once more. "I don't care about them. What happens to them doesn't matter. What happens to us does. You and me, now that Fresh is gone. I have to protect us. I promised you I would, when you were still a boy. We've had a good run, but the time has come to step out of the race."

Logan is holding the Scattershot down by his side. Michael is going to kill him, and there isn't a chance in the world he will be able to raise his weapon and fire it in time to save himself. He catches glimpses of the prisoners huddling at the back of the cages, eyes wild with fear. No help there. He watches the smoke of battle ebb and flow through the building's deep interior, but nothing else moves. No help there, either.

"*Michael, don't do this,*" *he begs.* "*Put down the weapon and talk to me. Think it through. There has to be another way.*"

"*There is no other way!*" *Michael screams.*

Logan doesn't stop to think after that. He simply acts. He shifts his gaze past Michael's left shoulder, as if catching sight of something, and says in a hushed voice, "*Demon.*"

Acting instinctively, Michael wheels and fires, the Ronin spraying bullets everywhere. Logan does not hesitate. He brings up the Scattershot and levels it. Michael is already turning back, realizing he has been tricked, when the Scattershot discharges its load into his chest. The force of the blow throws him back half a dozen feet and leaves him sprawled on the concrete floor.

For a moment, Logan cannot move. He cannot believe what he has done. The echoes of gunfire and the moaning of the prisoners waft through the building. "*Michael,*" *he whispers.*

Maybe there is still time to help him. Maybe he can still be saved.

But by the time Logan reaches him, Michael is already dead.

$$\bullet \quad \bullet \quad \bullet$$

IN THE AFTERMATH, *it feels to him as if he has lost everything. Unable to make himself leave, he kneels next to Michael's body for much longer than is safe. Finally, hearing shots in the distance, he regains sufficient presence of mind to realize that he needs to flee. Then he remembers the prisoners still locked in the cages, still trapped and helpless. Using the iron bar, he snaps the chains, flings open the doors, and watches them bolt. When the last of them disappears, he slings Michael's body over his shoulder, picks up the Scattershot and the Ronin, and walks through the drifting smoke and the bodies of the dead into the night.*

He finds Grayling outside, another man hanging on to him for support, the two of them working their way toward the only truck still intact. Grayling looks at him, sees whom he is carrying, and stops. When Logan gets close enough, the big man asks him where he is going. Away, he answers. It's over. And keeps walking as the other calls after him, Good luck.

He finds the Lightning parked back in the trees where Michael has left it. Michael always drives it on these raids, to the attacks and then back, his own personal transport. Sometimes he lets Logan ride with him—more often than not since losing Fresh. Once or twice, he has even told Logan that one day the Lightning will be his. One day, it seems, has arrived. Logan knows the codes that release the locks and disarm the security system, and he uses that knowledge now. Then he puts Michael in the back and drives away.

When he is far enough out in the middle of nowhere—so far out that he doesn't know for sure where he is—he parks, takes out a shovel, digs a grave that is both deep and wide, and lays Michael within. After he has covered up the body, he sits by the grave site and tries to think things through.

Had it really been necessary to kill Michael? *He asks himself this question over and over. He agonizes over the possibility that there might have been another way, a way he should have found, a way that would have kept the one person he cared about alive. But it happened so fast, and at the time he had been so sure. If he didn't kill Michael, Michael was going to kill him. Michael had gone native; he had gone over the wall and into the wilderness, and he wasn't coming out. His mind had snapped for reasons that Logan could only guess at, and nothing he did on that night—and perhaps for many nights before then—had been rational.*

Logan would have done anything to save Michael. Anything. But he failed to act quickly enough, and so Michael is gone. He cries, thinking of it. It seems unfair, wrong. Michael did so much for others, for all those men, women, and children consigned to a living hell in the camps, to lives of slavery and worse. Only Michael tried to do anything to help them, to give them a chance at life. Someone should have done something for him in return.

No, not someone, he corrects quickly. Himself. He should have done something for Michael. But he didn't. Didn't know what to do. Didn't know how to do it. And now it is too late.

When dawn breaks in a thin leaden line across a sky so overcast it feels as if it is pressing down against the earth like the hand of judgment, he is forced to confront his future. With Michael dead and his followers dead or scattered, Logan has nowhere to go. He doesn't even know what to do, for that matter. Carry on Michael's work? Attacking the slave camps seems endless and ultimately not enough to make a difference. One man is not enough to attack the slave camps in any case. One man is not enough to do anything in this world.

So he wanders for weeks, driving aimlessly, until finally the Lady appears to tell him what it is that he is needed to do.

●　●　●

THE MEMORY CAME and went like the passing of a cloud's shadow across the earth, and Logan Tom found himself staring once more at the wall of rock that blocked the pass. A gust of wind blew sharp and chill against his face, and the deep silence of the mountains pressed close in the wake of the memory's passing. He stood where he was for a moment, collecting his thoughts, then turned away. Memories could take you outside yourself, but they couldn't keep you there for long. He walked back to the Lightning, climbed inside, and started the engine. In minutes, he was winding his way back down the mountainside. His mouth tightened against his thoughts. One thing he had learned that Michael had not. No matter how bad things looked, there was always another way.

He descended out of the pass, traveling east back down through the foothills toward the flats. He drove as swiftly as the condition of the highway would allow, watching the daylight begin to fail with nighttime's approach. He would have to decide soon whether to turn north or south to find a way through the mountains. He knew there were several major passes that led over, but not which ones were still accessible.

When he reached what appeared to be a major crossroads, he stopped and threw the finger bones once more. The bones writhed and wriggled on the square of black cloth and formed themselves into fingers that by compass reckoning pointed northwest. He put the bones away and turned the Lightning north. This road was smaller, its surface badly eroded by time and weather. He had to travel more slowly as a consequence, and the light soon faded to a thick, hazy gray, leaving behind a world of shadows and furtive movements.

He had almost decided that he had gone as far as it was possible to go without unnecessary risk when the road ahead turned into a morass of dark obstacles that forced him to slow to a crawl. Old vehicles, pieces of fencing, and farm equipment littered a road surface already pocked and cracked. There was room to get around, but only barely.

Then there was no room at all, as dozens of dark, furtive figures materialized out of the dark to surround him.

19

THE FIGURES SEEMED to rise out of the earth like wraiths, their insubstantial forms composed of shadows and secrets, their movements quick and furtive. They did not approach in upright fashion, but in a crouched, crab-like scuttle. It was dark enough by now that he couldn't make out their features, hazy enough that it was like peering through smoke. He was not using the AV's headlights, and there was little natural light to provide any other form of illumination. As the figures drew nearer he could tell that they were human in shape, but lean and corded and crooked-limbed. They wore ragged clothing and clutched staffs and clubs rather than automatic weapons. They seemed curious rather than threatening, so he sat quietly and waited for them to reach the AV.

As the first of them did so, tentatively running slender hands over the smooth metal of the hood, the light from the sunset revealed a face and arms covered with patches of dark hair, suggestive of a creature more simian than human.

Spiders, Logan realized.

He hadn't seen any since Chicago, but he knew of them. One of several kinds of mutants, Spiders were humans infected by poisons or chemicals or radiation—depending on whom you believed—and physically altered as a consequence. Some claimed their minds had been altered, as well, but he had never seen any proof of this. Then again, Spiders were shy and reclusive, so it was difficult to know for sure. In Logan's twenty-eight years, he had encountered them no more than a handful of times. He had never spoken to one, or even seen one this close up.

The face peered in at him, features still clearly human within patches of black facial hair that coated everything from forehead to chin. Blue eyes regarded him with a mix of curiosity and hidden intent. Although the face had a feral, animalistic look to it, the eyes revealed intelligence.

He took a chance and lowered the window. He didn't say anything; he just nodded his greeting.

A dozen faces pressed close, and hands reached out to touch his. He did not try to draw away. He let their gnarled, hairy fingers brush against his skin and clothing. He let them peer past him inside the AV. He let them look at everything, giving them time and space.

At last, the one standing closest asked, "Who are you? Why are you here?"

The words were intelligible, the speaker's voice clear. "My name is Logan," he replied. "I am looking for a way over the mountains."

There was a murmuring among the Spiders that he couldn't follow. The speaker pointed back in the direction from which he had come. "The way over the mountains is behind you."

"I couldn't go that way. The pass I intended to take is blocked by a slide and I cannot get around it. I was hoping to find another. Do you know of one? Is there another north of here?"

The murmuring resumed, then faded. The speaker leaned in and whispered. "No one can go into the mountains north. That is sacred ground."

It was a simple statement of fact, but it was a warning, as well. "Why is it sacred?" he pressed.

The Spider leaned close. "The spirits live in the mountains. Some are as the wind. Some are flesh and blood. They speak with us when we chant their names. They tell us of their will. We give them offerings and make sacrifices so that they will protect us."

The others, standing close behind the speaker, nodded in agree-ment. Logan could tell that this was serious business for them, that these people regarded their relationship with the spirits of the mountains—whatever they might be—as they would a religion.

"Will they let no one pass to the other side?" he asked.

The speaker shook his head, hands making a warding gesture. "You must turn back."

Logan sighed. He didn't know what to do next. He didn't think reasoning was going to work here. He would have to take a different approach. Or maybe he should just turn around and try to find an-other way, one that would allow him to avoid this blockade.

"Do you have an offering so that we may permit you to go?" the speaker continued.

Oh, so now it's blackmail, he thought in disgust. He shook his head. He didn't have time for this. But he wasn't going to get into a fight if he could avoid it. "Let me get out and see," he said.

He opened the door and stepped out of the AV, bringing the black staff with him. As soon as the Spiders got a look at the staff, its carvings clearly visible against the polished surface, there was a col-lective moan. The entire body moved back from him as if it had been scorched by fire, a scattered few dropping to their knees, one or two actually covering their eyes. Logan froze instantly, not sure what was happening.

The speaker hunched forward a step, bowing deeply. "You are a magic wielder! Forgive us, please. We did not know."

Sorry, sorry, sorry, whispered the cringing forms. Logan looked from face to face in disbelief.

"Do you require our lives as payment for our foolishness?" the speaker asked softly.

"No," Logan said quickly. "No, I don't require anything. It's all right." His mind raced. "I just need you to tell me how to find my way through the mountains."

The speaker, head bowed until now, risked a quick glance up. "You would visit with your own kind? I should have realized what you wanted. Of course, of course. We can help you. We can show you where they are. Come this way."

He set out at once, the others hastening after him, casting anxious glances back at Logan and the AV. Logan climbed back in the vehicle and started forward once more, working his way through the obstacles, following the dark gathering that flowed ahead of him. Maybe this was going to work out after all.

They continued up the road for another two or three miles, the Spiders moving smoothly and easily over the terrain, seemingly tireless, their dark forms scattering out ahead in the deepening dark. He thought to turn on the running lights, but he was afraid that would frighten them. They were clearly a highly superstitious bunch, if they believed in mountain spirits, and he couldn't be sure what else might disturb them. All he needed to do was find his way into the mountains, and he could leave this business behind. Besides, the sky was sufficiently clear that slivers of moonlight cut through the cloud cover and washed the landscape in a pale soft glow that brightened the path ahead.

As they traveled, more Spiders joined those already leading the way, until there were easily more than a hundred. They were of all shapes and sizes, probably of all ages, big and little, old and young, and it became clear that word of his coming had spread to the larger community. More appeared with the passing of every minute, materializing out of the dark, come to see the magic wielder. He found himself wondering how large their community was and how distant their village. Did they even have a village? How did they live?

He knew so little about Spiders, he realized. Tiny splinter groups of mutants ostracized by everyone, they had been forced to make their own way in the larger world. They had survived by burrowing, Michael had told him once. Humans, they had gone to ground when the bombs fell and the radiation poisoned everything. They had survived by living on earth, air, and water that should have killed them, but instead had caused them to mutate. Like the Lizards and the other breeds. Normal humans wanted nothing to do with them; normal humans could not imagine living as mutants did, would not have dreamed even of touching them. Humans had gone one way, mutants another. It remained to be seen how it would all come together down the road.

If it ever came together at all.

It was more than an hour later when they reached another crossroads, a new highway intersecting the one on which they traveled, this one running east to west from the plains into the mountains. The speaker came back to the AV and bowed. "The pass lies that way," he said, pointing up the crossroads and toward the peaks. "Should we come with you?"

Logan shook his head. "You have done more than enough to help me."

"The other man asked us to go with him so that he could be certain of the way," the speaker explained.

Logan frowned. "Have others like me come through here?"

The speaker nodded. "Only the one, more than two years ago. He carried a staff like yours. We did not recognize him. We did not understand who he was. We challenged him, and he revealed himself to us through use of his magic. Thirty lives were taken in payment for our foolishness. It was a necessary lesson, he said."

A rogue Knight. Logan had heard of them, a few only, men and women who had lost their way and their belief and become demons themselves. It was rare, but in the madness of the apocalypse, it happened.

"No lives are required here," he assured the speaker and those others pressed close enough to hear.

A murmuring rose from those gathered, borne on a wave of gratitude. Logan shook his head.

"Will you tell the spirits when you see them that we remain faithful?" another asked, one whose face beneath the patches of hair was deeply wrinkled and spotted with age. "Will you tell them we are grateful for their protection?"

Several answers came to mind, but he said only, "I will tell them."

He left them clustered at the base of the mountains, gathered together at the crossroads, a collection of strange creatures with strange ideas. He felt oddly ashamed of himself for playing into their fantasies about mountain spirits, but he couldn't think of a better way to handle things. They seemed convinced that such spirits existed, and it would have been foolish for him to try to convince them otherwise. Even so, he didn't like pretending at things he knew weren't true.

He drove ahead through the darkness along a road that was mostly clear, a two-lane concrete ribbon that wound upward through foothills toward a black massing of jagged peaks. He should have waited until daybreak to attempt this drive, but he was anxious to get on with things. He could see well enough by moonlight to find his way, and if he drove slowly and carefully he should be able to reach the other side before morning and could sleep then.

"As long as there isn't another slide blocking my way," he muttered. Then he smiled. "Or unfriendly mountain spirits who don't appreciate my passing through."

He considered throwing the finger bones again, but it didn't seem necessary at this point. What he was looking for was somewhere on the other side of the Rockies, so he might as well wait until he had crossed to reevaluate which way he needed to go. Unless something drastic changed, he was headed into the northwest part of the country or maybe even into Canada. There was nothing to say that the gypsy morph hadn't chosen to hide outside the United States. Boundaries didn't mean much at this point. Less still, if you were a creature of magic.

Or a wielder of magic, like himself. That was what the Spider had called him. But he knew what he was. He was a hollowed-out shell that had been infused with fresh purpose and a cause. He was a dead man brought back to life by an encounter with the Word. He was an orphan lost in a world of orphans, but unlike so many, he had been found. He was not a wielder of magic; he was its servant.

He ate a little and drank from a water bottle as he drove, keeping his eyes on the road and his attention on the task at hand. The road twisted and turned through the rocks, and now and again he encountered massive boulders hunkered down like predators to block his path. The air turned sharp and cold as he ascended, and breathing became more difficult. He was up about a mile by now, and light-headedness brought on by the thinning air forced him to concentrate harder. He was deep in the mountains, no longer climbing but simply navigating through narrow defiles and towering peaks, a solitary sojourner in an empty land.

Then fog began to gather and settle in about him, a thin blanket at first that quickly thickened to something much more unsettling. There was no reason for fog to appear this high up on a night that had been clear and in weather that had been untroubled. He watched it tighten like a shroud, shortening his vision to less than fifty feet, then thirty, and finally to ten. He slowed the AV to a crawl, switched on the fog lights, and waited patiently for the heavy mist to break. It did not; if anything, it got worse. Time passed, a steady unraveling of minutes that left him numbed and weary. He blinked against his sleepiness, sipping at the water bottle, humming tunelessly. His thoughts drifted and scattered like dried leaves blown in the wind.

You should have listened to them, a voice said suddenly.

He glanced over and found Michael sitting in the passenger's seat, rigid and unmoving, eyes directed straight ahead. He stared for a minute, and then looked back to the road.

"You aren't here. I'm imagining you," he replied.

There was no response. He glanced over, and Michael was gone. He felt a chill run down his back as he realized what had just happened. The change in altitude coupled with exhaustion was causing his mind to play tricks on him. He took a deep, steadying breath and let it out, nosing the car ahead. The fog couldn't go on for much longer; it had to break soon.

I wouldn't be too sure of that, boy, Michael said.

He was back in the passenger's seat, his craggy profile expressionless as he sat staring out at the night, hands resting comfortably in his lap atop his Ronin. Logan risked a quick glance over, unable to help himself, feeling the cold seep back into his bones. There was a pale light all around Michael, a hint of something otherworldly, of an ethereal quality that living things did not possess.

Mountain spirits, he thought in disbelief, then cast the thought away.

"You're dead, Michael," he said. "Have the decency to stay that way."

Beside him, Michael shimmered and vanished. Maybe that was all it took, he thought. Just tell them to go away and they would. He smiled despite the shiver that swept through him. Very accommodating, these mountain spirits.

He glanced back at the empty seat several times after that, trying to prevent any reappearance by telling himself that if he kept watch, it wouldn't happen. He was anxious to get clear of this fog and these mountains now, to get far away from them. Then he could get some sleep and stop hallucinating. He hadn't realized how tired he was, and when he coupled that with the traveling conditions and his mental state, he could understand why he was seeing dead people.

I don't think you should keep going this way, a new voice said. *I think you should turn back. This road doesn't belong to the living, Logan.*

His father was sitting next to him now, a less clear apparition than Michael, but real enough that it caused him to start. His father wouldn't look at him, staring straight ahead as Michael had, an ethereal presence that suggested he could vanish in an instant's time. As Logan continued to stare at him, he did just that. He shimmered, melted into mist, and was gone.

And Logan looked back at the highway just in time to slam on the brakes and swerve to avoid a huge boulder blocking the center of the road. The Lightning skidded along the moisture-dampened road toward a low guardrail and a drop that fell away into blackness. Logan pumped the brakes and pulled the wheel all the way over so that the vehicle was sliding sideways and out of control.

It stopped beside the guardrail with inches to spare. The engine killed with a grunt, and the steady hum turned to a soft ticking in the night silence. Logan sat without moving, staring at nothing. He closed his eyes and waited for his heart to slow and his breathing to steady. It was all right now, he told himself. But maybe he had to stop after all. Maybe there was nothing for it but to wait for morning and to try to sleep until then.

No rest for the wicked, whispered Michael.

No rest for the living, said his father.

He sighed and opened his eyes. There was no one there. He was alone, locked inside the AV, the soft lights of the dash and the slow ticking of the engine the only signs of life.

Outside the AV, the fog was closing in like a living thing, tendrils tightening about the vehicle, shutting off the sky and the earth, wrapping like a spider's webbing. At first, he thought he was mistaking what he was seeing. It was so deliberate, so purposeful. But then everything disappeared in a sheet of damp white, and he knew that despite what common sense and reason told him, there was something out there and it was trying to take control.

Should have turned around, said Michael.

Never should have come, said his father.

Faces began to appear outside the AV, ghostly apparitions that materialized one by one and then pressed close to the window glass. Eyes as blank as bare walls peered from faces etched by pain and suffering. Such eyes could not see, and yet it felt as if they did. Hands reached out and brushed the glass, and he flinched. They were all around the Lightning now, and their numbers were increasing by the minute. He reached quickly for the starter, intending to get out of there. But the motor would not catch. It would not even turn over. The vehicle was dead.

He sat staring at the controls, and then looked up again at the faces. He recognized the ones closest. They were the faces of men and women he had fought beside while he was with Michael. They were the faces of slaves and victims he somehow remembered out of so many he had tried to free. All of them were dead now. He knew it instinctively, not just from their apparitional appearance, but from what he felt inside, too. They were ghosts, and they were there to haunt him.

But what did they want?

Two new faces came into view, sliding through the crowd until they were right up against the driver's window. His throat tightened. It was his older brother Tyler and sister Megan, gone all these years, their faces unchanged, frozen in time. They stared at him blankly, dead-eyed and directionless, but aware, too. They knew he was there, inside the Lightning. Like all the others, they had come looking. Like all the others, their need was a mystery he could not decipher.

He squeezed his eyes shut. They were not going to disappear like Michael and his father. They were more than smoke and mist, more than insubstantial specters, more even than ghosts conjured by imagination. They were creatures of magic and spirit life, brought to him to achieve something, and they would not depart until he responded to their presence.

He opened his eyes and stared out at them. Sometimes you had to confront the dead as well as the living, the past as well as the future. Sometimes the two were so inextricably interlocked that there was little to distinguish between them. It was so here. Mountain spirits or something more insidious, there was a joining that reasoning and common sense could not undo.

He seized his staff, opened the door, and stepped outside the AV to confront whatever waited.

The outside air hit him with a blast of cold that nearly knocked him backward, an icy rush that cut right to his bones. The wind was blowing hard, something he hadn't realized before because its force was having no effect at all on the ghosts crowded around him. They neither advanced nor gave way as he emerged, but held their ground and swung their blind gazes in his general direction. A few lifted their hands as if to touch him, but their efforts were feeble and more demonstrative of need than intention. Shivering in the sharp chill of the wind, he brought the black staff around in front of him, letting the natural light reflect off its surface. The wind howled in response—or perhaps it was the ghosts—and the deeply etched runes flared with inner light, with their infused magic, fiery and bright.

The spirits of the dead fell back, and for an instant Logan believed they would disperse. But in the distance behind them and farther up the road, a strange darkness had begun to gather. More ghosts were emerging from its roiling mass, pressing forward to join those already surrounding him. He watched them approach, half disbelieving what he was seeing, half recognizing the inevitable. The dead had not appeared of their own volition; the dead never did. They were either summoned or sent; he knew that much from his time as a Knight of the Word.

But what was the source of the darkness to which they were responding?

He gripped the black staff and started forward, pushing through the gathering of spirits, their white emptiness giving way, their ephemeral presence dissipating and re-forming as he passed. Only a confrontation with their source would resolve what was happening. If he was to break free of this—whatever *this* was—he would have to face down the thing that was causing it, the darkness from which these spirits emerged. It hung thick and impenetrable as he approached, but even as he reached its edges he still could not put a name to it.

He brought up the staff, its magic already summoned and flowing over him in a bluish light, encasing him in its armor. He felt the warmth of its protection enclose him and was reassured. He lashed out at the blackness, ripping at it as he would a piece of cloth. It split apart easily, unable to hold together, collapsing before him, and a fierce joy engulfed him, a sense of empowerment.

But the split lasted only a moment, and then almost effortlessly the blackness repaired itself, the jagged tear resealing. More ghosts emerged from its dark breast. More faces pressed forward. Again, he attacked. Again, the blackness split apart and again quickly resealed and re-formed, unaffected. If anything, the roiling mass appeared to be an even larger and more inexorable presence.

Now the hands of the dead were touching him. He could feel them stroking his body, their fingers as cold and icy as the mountain wind. He could feel their chill dampness against his skin; he could feel it through his clothing. The effect was unpleasant and oddly debilitating. He could feel his strength eroding, bleeding away.

Angry now, he tried a different approach. Instead of a tearing, rending attack, he used the magic like a huge windmill in an attempt to sweep the blackness away. His efforts worked. The wind he generated exploded the dark mass, and the fire burned what remained to shards of smoke. He stood watching in the aftermath, breathing hard. Nothing of the darkness remained. The way forward was clear.

But then the ghosts of the dead pressed up against him anew, touching him everywhere, more insistent now, more demanding, and he saw that the blackness was beginning to re-form. He stood stunned as it tightened and grew ever larger, pressing toward him, the empty-eyed ghosts pouring from its opaque center in knots. There were so many now that they were tumbling over one another in their efforts to reach him. The entire pass was filled with them.

He experienced a sudden panic, and he understood its source immediately. He had thought he would always be ready for the unexpected when it surfaced. He had told himself that he would know instinctively what to do when threatened. But he was lost here; he was adrift without a lifeline. His attempt at attacking the blackness, at causing it to dissipate or erode, was yielding nothing at all, and he did not know what to do about it.

He took an involuntary step backward. Something about the way he was fighting this battle was doing more harm than good, and if he didn't discover what it was, he was going to lose.

He gathered his thoughts, tightened his resolve, and pushed back the feelings of fear and doubt. He had survived too many fights to lose this one. He was a Knight of the Word, and he would not give way.

He stared at the darkness, and then turned his attention to the white, empty faces surrounding him. Perhaps the spirits of the dead were not as invulnerable as their source. He went into their midst, fighting back against his revulsion, armoring himself against the touch of their fingers, speaking words of magic to banish them. He used the fire of the staff to sweep aside each as he passed, and to his satisfaction they began to disappear, one after the other. He did not look to see how many were still coming, but kept his eyes on those pressing closest, looking at each, recognizing each, knowing he must acknowledge them if they were to be sent back to where they belonged.

He did not know for how long or to how many he did this; he lost track of time and numbers and simply kept pressing ahead. The faces came and went in a wash, so many he remembered, so many he had known. He said good-bye to each as the fire consumed them, facing down the emotions that welled up within him. What he felt was a cold certainty, a hard-edged understanding of what he was doing to himself by banishing them. He was losing his past; he was giving up his memories. With the disappearance of each white face, he let go of a little more of what he remembered.

He understood now that he was the one who had summoned them, perhaps without realizing it, perhaps with help from whatever lived in these mountains. The darkness was his, the past carried on his shoulders, memories of the dead, of those he had known and cared about and could not forget. They weighed on him; they haunted him. He had kept them shut away until tonight, then set them free. There would be no peace for him until they were locked away again, this time for good.

The mass of white faces thinned to only a few. His brother and little sister were before him now, their blank stares sad and lost in a way he could hardly stand. He reached for them and touched them fearlessly, letting the terrible sensation of their presence wash over him as he sent the fire of the staff through their empty forms until they slowly faded away. Dead and gone, he realized, never to return. Already, their faces were so vague in his mind that he could not reconstruct their features.

When he stood alone finally, the darkness that had blocked the pass had dissipated entirely. Nothing remained but rock and cold and black night. He stood looking at nothing, and then turned back to the AV. His father and Michael stood beside it, white and ephemeral, the last of his ghosts. They were staring not at him, but at something beyond him, something he could not see. He did not hesitate, but walked over to where they waited and touched each in turn with his magic, saying good-bye. They did not speak to him or look at him. They simply stood before him as if awaiting the inevitable. Then the staff swept through them, and they, too, were gone.

In the aftermath, he thought about what the Spiders had told him. He did not know if their mountain spirits were entities that had given life to his ghosts or if they were manifestations of the ghosts themselves, but he had been wrong to disparage them. He had not believed they existed, but now he understood that they did. Not everything that was real in this world could be seen.

He looked around for other ghosts, but the last of them had disappeared. He could feel his memory of their faces slipping away. Although he tried, he could not seem to hold on to it. Perhaps he would remember a few of them, the ones he had known best, but most were gone forever. He had banished them with the Word's magic, and he knew that by doing so he had made it impossible for them to return.

Their absence left an ache in his heart, a void so huge that he could not fathom how he could endure it. But when he tried to dispel that ache, he found he could not. For an agonizing moment, he was eight years old again and had just lost his family for a second time.

Only this time, he discovered, there were no tears to be shed. As he stared out into the darkness and the sweep of the land, his eyes were dry.

20

NOON WAS LESS than two hours away, and Hawk was thinking about who he would take with him when he went to his meeting with Tiger. Midday today was the designated time for delivery of the pleneten, and while Hawk was anxious to get the serum into Tiger's hands so that he could help Persia, he was troubled by everything that had happened over the past few days. He might have been willing to dismiss both their encounter with the dying Lizard and the Weatherman's discovery of the nest of dead Croaks as all-too-familiar occurrences in a world where death and dying were commonplace. But Candle's vision of something bad coming their way, coupled with their chilling experience in the warehouse basement, had left him convinced that things were changing in the city and not for the better.

So he spent more time than he normally would considering who to take and who to leave behind, not wanting to put anyone at risk when he already knew there was no avoiding it. In the end, he settled on taking Panther and Bear and leaving the rest behind with Cheney. If they carried prods and viper-pricks, the three of them would be safe enough. The meeting would take place on the open streets and in daylight and would be over quickly. All that was needed was for him to deliver the pleneten and return home. Then he could begin deliberating anew about how to persuade Tessa to leave the compound and come with him.

But he had no sooner come to a decision than Owl appeared at his elbow. Her eyes were troubled as she took him aside where the others could not hear.

"River is gone again. She slipped away right after breakfast. I thought she had gone to retrieve water from the roof, but Candle says she went out into the streets. She's been gone for more than an hour."

Hawk glanced over at Candle, who was cleaning up the breakfast dishes. "River didn't tell her where she was going? She has no idea?"

Owl shook her head. "It's the same as before. She goes out on her own and won't tell anyone what she is doing." She paused, and one hand rested lightly on Hawk's wrist. "I think you'd better go after her this time. I think we have to find out what she is doing."

He almost said no. He almost said that he already had something he had to do and shouldn't be wasting his time chasing after an irresponsible child who couldn't be trusted to do what she had been told to do and who lied on top of it. But he recognized a voice he didn't care for in that kind of thinking, a voice that spoke out of frustration and impatience and not out of caring. Owl was clearly worried about River, and he knew that Owl did not worry easily.

He nodded. "All right, I'll find her."

He glanced around the room, rethinking his earlier plans. He would have to take Cheney if he hoped to track River. That meant he would have to leave Owl and the little ones with someone else and send someone besides himself to the meeting with Tiger.

He settled on Bear to stand watch in the underground. He could rely on Bear to keep everyone safe—Bear, so steady and unflappable, never acting out of haste or panic. He wished he had a dozen Bears in his family, but families don't work like that.

That meant Panther would have to take the pleneten to Tiger. There was no one else old enough or smart enough to send out alone to a meeting like this. It was chancy, sending Panther. He despised the Cats, and Tiger in particular. The source of his dislike was not entirely clear to Hawk, but it didn't make it any less potent or potentially volatile.

He walked over to Panther, telling himself to keep calm. "There's been a change of plans. You're going to take the pleneten to Tiger without me."

Panther didn't exactly glare at him, but his displeasure was clearly reflected on his dark features. "Why do *I* got to do this, Bird-Man? Why not someone else?"

"Don't you think you can handle it?" Hawk pressed.

Now Panther did glare. "I can handle anything, and I can do it better than the rest. You know that."

Hawk nodded. "I do know it. That's why you have to be in charge. I can depend on you to be ready for whatever happens. Take Chalk and Fixit with you. For a show of strength."

"You think those pussycats would try something with me?" Panther sneered. "Like to see them try. Like to see them even think about it. Anyway, I don't need Fixit and Chalk. I can do it alone."

"You know the rules. No one goes out alone to a meeting. If you don't want Chalk and Fixit, take Sparrow."

"Huh! Don't want nothin' to do with Sparrow. Lemme take Bear. At least he takes up some space."

Hawk shook his head. "Bear has to stay here and look out for the others. I need Cheney with me."

"For what? What you doin' that's so important, taking Cheney away now?"

"I'll tell you later. Just get the pleneten to Tiger. I know you don't like him, but we made an agreement and we stick to our agreements. We keep our word."

"I know that. But I don't have to like it."

Hawk nodded. "Just get it done. Take Chalk and Fixit with you. The pleneten's wrapped in brown paper in the cold storage."

Panther shook his head and made a snorting noise. "Frickin' Cats."

Hawk moved over to the storage locker, selected a prod, pocketed two of the viper-pricks, and slipped on his heavy-weather jacket. Owl wheeled over to where he was standing and watched him get ready.

"What do I do when I find her?" he asked quietly.

"You find out what's wrong, you try to help her make it right, and then you bring her home."

He looked at her wise, cheerful face and caring eyes. Her smile told him that she was only reaffirming what he already knew. She gave him such confidence just by her presence that it was impossible for him to measure its importance. She always knew what needed doing and how it could be done. Once, he had thought of her as crippled and helpless. He didn't think of her like that anymore. He thought of her as the strongest among them. Of all of them, she was the most indispensable, the most necessary to their survival.

"I won't be long," he promised.

"Be as long as you need to be," she told him. "River needs to feel safe again. I don't think she feels that way now."

She was saying that River needed to know that she could tell them anything, that she didn't need to hide whatever it was she was doing. Hawk wasn't sure Owl was right, but he had sense enough to keep quiet and hope she was.

He called to Cheney and went out the door and up the stairs to the streets. The day was clear and bright, the sky a blue dome empty of all but the wispiest of clouds. He glanced up at it, squinting despite himself, the brightness unexpected and somehow out of place. The world shouldn't look so clear when life felt so cloudy.

A sudden gust of wind brought him back to reality. The air was chilly and biting and sharp with cold. He hunched down into his jacket and called Cheney over to him. Taking out an old T-shirt that belonged to River, he let the big dog sniff it, and then told him to track. Cheney never hesitated. He wheeled away and started down the street, big head swinging from side to side, muzzle lowered in concentration. Hawk followed, eyes shifting steadily to the darkened doorways and alleys between the buildings they passed, keeping watch. He knew they would find River. He'd had Cheney track things before; once he had the scent, the big dog always found what he was searching for.

They moved down First Avenue toward the center of town, and then Cheney abruptly turned left toward the waterfront. Together, the boy and the dog made their way through the rubble and along the cracked pavement toward the oily shimmer of Elliott Bay, its surface glaring sharply in the bright sunlight. A pair of Spiders appeared in a doorway and disappeared back inside instantly. Hawk and Cheney continued on. A gull lay dead on the street in front of them, its graceful form broken, its sleek feathers matted with dirt and blood. There was nothing to show how it had died. Hawk glanced at it, thought about flying things brought low, and looked away.

Cheney went straight down to the piers, never deviating, working his way ahead at a steady pace, shadow-dark even in the bright sunlight. Hawk stayed close, cautious and alert. The wind blew off the bay like the coming of winter, bringing tears to his eyes as he squinted against its sharpness. The smells of decay filled his nostrils, causing him to duck his face deep into the collar of his coat in an effort to escape them. He found himself wondering if the waters of the bay would ever recover. He guessed that in time, if left alone, nature would find a way to heal them. But he couldn't be sure. He couldn't be sure there was any healing to be found.

Cheney stopped suddenly, freezing in place, hackles raised. Hawk stopped with him, eyes sweeping the streets in all directions. Then he caught sight of movement on the waterfront south, down by the cranes. A cluster of dark figures wearing what looked like red armbands were working their way through the trash, headed away. Another tribe, one he did not recognize. Some came from outside the city to forage, tribes that lived in the hills behind the city, in what were once the residential communities. Some were very dangerous, as bad as the Croaks. One had moved into the city a year or so back, hard-eyed street kids with no compunction about killing. It would have been bad for the rest of them if the group hadn't made the mistake of angering one of the Lizard communities. When it was over, only the Lizards were left.

He waited until the cluster of armbanded figures had disappeared from view, then urged Cheney ahead again. They walked out onto the flats at the foot of James Street and toward the docks. Cheney was sniffing the ground again, returned to his task.

He swung south, and then stopped, casting about in some confusion. A moment later, he started away again, headed north toward the remains of the aquarium. Hawk found himself wondering what River was doing down here. This was where Sparrow had found her nearly four years ago, an orphan rummaging through the buildings in search of food.

Cheney padded along, then turned toward one of the larger piers and nosed his way over to the crumbling building. He stopped at the door and waited, not looking at Hawk, barely lifting his head as Hawk came up beside him.

River was inside, he was saying.

Hawk hesitated, and then moved in front of Cheney. He held the prod in front of him as he stepped through the door. Inside, light streamed through broken windows and collapsed sections of the upper flooring and metal roof to chase back the shadows. There were two floors and dozens of rooms, and the building was deep and high. Again Hawk hesitated, wary of entering a largely unfamiliar place. He had been in this building once or maybe even twice, but not for long and only to look for useful supplies. It had been several years since he had last entered it.

There was nothing he could do but continue. He sent Cheney on ahead, hoping he would find a trail. It wasn't all that easy given the amount of trash and the confluence of smells that permeated every surface. The building smelled of the bay, but also of dead things, mildew, and defecation. There didn't seem to be anything living in it, but you never knew. Shadows rippled in the corners of the rooms he passed, disturbed by the sunlight. Hawk kept the prod in front of him. He couldn't imagine what River was doing here.

They wound their way to the back of the building and finally outside again. Now Hawk really was confused. But Cheney kept moving forward, heading for a large storage shed set back against the edge of the dock inside a barrier of heavy metal fencing. It was a structure that seemed somewhat sturdier than the building they had just left, although its metal surfaces were badly worn and rusted.

Cheney stopped before the fencing and growled.

Instantly River appeared in the doorway of the shed. "Cheney!"

she exclaimed, shock mirrored on her child's face. Then she saw Hawk and gave an audible gasp. "No, Hawk! You can't come in here!"

She said it with such force that for a moment Hawk felt as if she might be right, that he had somehow trespassed and would have to turn around and leave. Her words sounded dangerous, and she had gone into a defensive crouch that suggested she was ready to fight.

"Tell me what's wrong, River," he answered.

She shook her head fiercely, then broke into tears and stood shaking in front of him. "You told me . . . the rules," she sobbed. "I know . . . what I've done. But I . . . had to!"

He had no idea what she was talking about. "River," he said quietly, "let me come in. What's going on in there?"

"Just . . . go away, Hawk," she managed. "I won't come . . . back home . . . or anything. Just go away."

Leaving Cheney where he was, Hawk walked the perimeter of the fence, found the hidden section that swung open, and stepped inside. River rushed to stop him, but he was through before she reached him. She brought up her fists as if to knock him back through the opening, then simply collapsed in a heap on the heavy planking, crying harder than ever. Hawk had never seen her like this. He knelt beside her, stroked her dark hair gently, then put his arm around her shoulders and sat next to her.

"Shhhh," he soothed. "Don't cry. There isn't anything we can't work out between us; you know that. Nothing we can't solve."

She cried some more, and then said suddenly, almost angrily, "You don't understand!"

He nodded into her hair. "I know."

She didn't say anything more and didn't move; she just sat there as the sobs died away. Then she stood and without a word started for the shed. He rose and followed. It was dark and cool inside, but there were brightly colored hangings on the wall and stacks of packaged goods and blankets. Ropes hung from hooks, and books were stacked to one side on makeshift shelves. Someone had lived here recently.

A low moan from the shed's deepest recesses caught his attention, and he peered into the gloom.

The Weatherman lay on a mattress suspended atop a low wooden bed frame, his ancient face twisted with pain, his hands moving under the blankets tucked about him. Hawk took a quick look at the blotches on his face and backed quickly away.

"He has the plague," he said. "You can't stay here, River."

She replied in a whisper so soft he could barely hear her. "You don't understand. I have to."

"He's an old man," Hawk objected. "I like him, but it's—"

"No," she interrupted quickly. "He isn't just an old man." She paused, struggling to get the words out. "He's my grandfather."

●　●　●

SHE TOLD HIM her story then, of her family and of how her grandfather had brought her to Seattle.

Even before there were only the two of them, she was always his favorite. A quiet, introverted girl with a waif's big eyes and a skinny, gawky body that she found embarrassing, she followed him everywhere. For his part, he seemed to enjoy her company and never told her to go away like her brothers always did. He enjoyed talking to her and told her things about herself that made her feel better.

"You are a special little girl," he would say, "because you know how to listen. Not many little girls know how to do that."

When she cried, he would say, "There is nothing wrong with crying. Your feelings tell you who you are. They tell you what is important. Don't ever be ashamed of them."

He was tall and strong then, even though he was already old, and she had heard that he had once been a professional athlete back before they stopped having teams. She imagined that must have been a long time ago, years before she was born, but he never talked about it. He mostly talked about her, and he was the only one who did so. No one else ever even paid attention to her except when they needed something. Her brothers ignored her. Her mother was a strange, distant presence, physically there, but mentally off in a place only she could visit. She barely acknowledged the rest of the family, lost in distant stares and words spoken so softly that no else could hear. River's grandfather said it was because her father had broken her mother's heart.

River didn't know if this was so, but she supposed it was. She remembered very little about her father. She remembered that he was a big, noisy man who took up a lot of space and made her feel even smaller than she was. She was only three when he left. No one ever knew what caused him to go, but one day he simply walked out the door and never came back. For a long time, she thought he would. She would stand in the yard and look for him in the trees, believing he might be hiding there and daring them to find him. Her brothers laughed at her when she told them what she was doing, and eventually she tired of the game and gave up.

They lived in a small woodlands community north of the big Washington State cities, out on the Olympic Peninsula where it was still heavily forested and mountainous and empty of people and their problems. Their isolation protected them, they believed, and so they stayed in their small community, a group of about thirty families, waiting for things to change back for the better, keeping hidden and secret as the rest of the world slowly receded into a distant furor they knew about only from listening to radio and from infrequent encounters with travelers.

But her grandfather was wary.

"You must never go out alone," he would tell her, even though the others said it was safe and nothing would happen to her.

He didn't explain, and she didn't ask. She believed what he told her, and so she was careful not to go anywhere by herself. She was reminded of the disappearance of her father, even though she did not believe anything bad had happened to him. But when her youngest brother vanished one sunny afternoon without even the smallest trace, she knew that it was because he had ignored her grandfather's warning. The others laughed, but she knew.

Then, two months later, when the red haze passed overhead, even though it was gone in less than a day, he told her not to eat or drink anything taken from the earth. She did as he said, but the others didn't listen. When they began to get sick and die, he warned them they would have to leave, but they didn't listen to him then, either. They refused to leave their home, insisting that things would get better, that the sickness would pass. They believed themselves protected in their sheltered enclave, so far removed from the rest of the world. They believed themselves safe from its horrors.

Even though she was only nine by then, she knew they were wrong in the same way they had been wrong every time before.

It was only after all but fifty of them had died, her mother and brothers included, that they acknowledged that her grandfather was right and made preparations to leave. They built rafts to ferry themselves down the waters of Puget Sound in search of a new place to live. There were islands all along the western shoreline; one of them would provide them with a safe haven to disembark and start over.

They set out in good weather, four rafts in all. Within twenty-four hours, a storm caught up with them. Winds reached fifty miles an hour on the open water in a matter of minutes. The trailing raft was lost, capsized with all its goods sunk and its passengers swept away. Plague surfaced on the second raft a day later, and the passengers on the other two made the decision to abandon it, leaving those aboard to fend for themselves. Some talked afterward about the need for sacrificing the few for the good of the many. Fear set in as the journey wore on, and everyone began to realize how much danger they were in. It was going to get much worse, her grandfather told her privately. Bad enough that they were going to have to leave the others because sooner or later their behavior would turn irrational and everyone left alive would be at risk.

Two nights later, while the rafts were tied up in a small cove and the others were sleeping, her grandfather woke her, held his finger to his lips, and led her into the dark. She looked back once or twice as they slipped away, but no one saw them go. They walked inland through forests and fields, past empty farms and houses, skirting the towns and keeping to the countryside. They foraged for food, which her grandfather seemed to know something about. Most of what they found was bottled or packaged, so they were not afraid to consume it. They slept in empty buildings when they could and outside when there was nothing else. Her grandfather had stuffed blankets and medicines and changes of clothes into a backpack, and they were able to get by.

Then, five days into their journey, somewhere west of the islands that dotted the waters across from Seattle, her grandfather came down with plague. He turned hot and feverish, and his skin darkened in broad purplish patches all over his body. She didn't know which form of plague he had contracted, and it wouldn't have made any difference if she had because she was too little to understand which of the medicines would help. She tried them all, one at a time, but none of them seemed to make any difference. She washed him with cool water to help keep his temperature down and tried to make him drink so that he wouldn't become dehydrated. For a time he tried to coach her by telling her what he thought would help, suggesting what she might do for him. But his sickness turned worse, and he became incoherent. He raved as if he had lost all reason, and she became afraid that someone—or something—would overhear. She gave him sleeping medication because she didn't know what else to do. She kept bathing him in an effort to lower his fever, kept trying to get liquids into him, and waited for him to die.

But, against all odds, he recovered. It took weeks, and it was a slow, torturous process. Afterward, he was never the same. His hair had gone white. His face was marked by the struggle he had endured, his once strong visage lined and pinched and gaunt. He was frail and gnarled in a way old men become when all of their youth has been bled out of them. It happened in the span of about four weeks, and even after he was sitting up and eating and drinking again, he was only a ghost of himself.

She looked at him warily and tried to hide how afraid she was for him. But she could tell by the way he looked back that he knew.

They set out again, but he was no longer her grandfather of old. He sang ditties and spoke in odd rhymes. He talked incessantly about the weather, about forecasts, storms, fronts and pressure ridges, and things she had never heard him speak of before. None of it made much sense; it frightened her in a way even the ravings hadn't. He only rarely spoke of anything besides the weather. Nothing else seemed to matter to him.

At night, he would wake her sometimes with his muttering, talking in his sleep of black, evil things coming to get them. She would wake him, and he would look at her as if she were a stranger.

When they reached the shores of Puget Sound, they began walking south until they found a rowboat. Without so much as a word about what he intended, her grandfather loaded their few possessions, placed her aboard at the stern, climbed in after her, and pushed off. It was nearing sunset, and darkness was almost upon them. He didn't seem to notice. He rowed them toward the islands, seated with his back to them, facing her, his haunted eyes fixed on her face. He rowed all night without stopping, and even though it was black all around them, the weather stayed calm. They reached an island sometime just before dawn, pulled the boat ashore, and slept. When they woke, her grandfather rowed them around to the other side of the island, where they stopped again. The following day, he rowed them all the way across the channel to the city.

She could have run from him at any time while they were on the island. She was quicker than he was; she was probably stronger and possessed of more endurance. She could have slipped away while he was sleeping, as well. But she never considered leaving him. He was her grandfather, and she would stay with him no matter what.

In Seattle, they lived in derelict buildings on the waterfront, scavenging supplies and foraging for food. She waited for him to tell her it was time for them to leave, but he seemed to have lost interest. He barely acknowledged her presence now, growing more distant by the day. He never spoke her name, even when she called him Grandfather. He would wander the waterfront for hours and sometimes days before returning. She tried to go with him, but he refused to let her, telling her there was a storm coming or a change in the weather and she needed to stay close to home. Their home was an old container down by the cranes. Her life had turned to ashes.

Then, one day, when she thought things couldn't possibly get any worse, he went out and didn't come back. She waited for a week for his return, but there was no sign of him. In desperation, she went looking for him and was still searching ten days later when Sparrow found her and brought her home to live with the Ghosts.

● ● ●

"THREE MONTHS AFTER he disappeared, I found him down by the docks. He looked at me and didn't say anything. I could tell he didn't know who I was. I spoke to him, but he just smiled and said something about the weather."

River looked away from Hawk to her grandfather. His breathing was ragged, and sweat soaked his clothing. She moved over to a bucket of water, wet a rag, and wiped his brow carefully.

"I know the rules," she said. "No adults can be Ghosts. I didn't want to leave him alone, but I didn't want to leave the Ghosts, either. I didn't know what to do. I went back to check on him when I could, but sometimes I couldn't even find him. Sometimes I thought he was dead. He wasn't, but I thought so. It was okay until now. It was a little like having him live next door. I could still go see him. I could pretend he was still a part of my family."

"You should have told me, River," Hawk said softly. "You should have told someone."

She shook her head, her lips compressing into a tight line. "No adults, you said. Only kids could be members of our family. Ever."

The words felt like a condemnation. He had said it because he blamed adults for so much, said it because he didn't want the Ghosts ever to be dependent on adults again, said it to keep them from even thinking that adults had a place in their life. It was easy to say it when they were all orphans and street kids and there wasn't any real family left and no one wanted anything to do with them anyway.

"I found him two days ago, lying in his bed here in the shed. He'd been well for three years, but the sickness has returned, same as before. I still didn't know what to do." She looked at him, her eyes solemn and depthless. "What if he dies?"

"We won't let him die," Hawk said at once, even knowing it was a promise he could not keep.

"In a way, he already has," she whispered. Tears ran down her cheeks, and she wiped them away quickly.

"I said no adults in the Ghosts, but I didn't say we wouldn't ever help an adult if one needed it. I didn't say that." He tried to think of what to tell her. "River, remember when I went down to the docks maybe a week ago? I went down to speak to your grandfather about the dead Lizard, to see if maybe he knew something. You know what he did? He asked me to take him with us when we left the city. Like he knew we were going." He hesitated. "I told him I would."

She stared. "You did? You said that? Did you mean it?"

Did he? He couldn't remember for sure. He thought about the way the Weatherman had asked him, almost as if it was an afterthought, a throwaway. He lifted one eyebrow at River. "Sure, I meant it. I was thinking, though. Maybe, somewhere deep inside, he still knows who you are. Otherwise, why would he have asked to go with us?"

She seemed doubtful, but didn't disagree. "Can we give him some medicine?"

He nodded. "But we have to ask Owl what to do for him. Maybe one of her books will tell us what sort of sickness this is and how to treat it. She knows a lot. Let's go ask her."

But River shook her head. "You go, Hawk. I don't want to leave him all alone."

Hawk considered arguing the matter, then decided against it. Instead, he reached into his pocket and handed her one of the precious viper-pricks. He left his prod leaning against the shed wall as he moved to the doorway.

"I'll be back as soon as I can," he promised. He gave her grandfather a final glance as he went out. The old man looked like a bundle of sticks lying beneath the thin blanket. "It will be all right," he said.

But in his heart he felt that maybe it wouldn't.

● ● ●

WHEN HE GOT back to the underground, he told Owl what he had discovered about River and the Weatherman. Owl did not recognize the form of plague that the old man had contracted, but she began searching her medical books immediately to see if she could find a sickness that matched what he was describing. He watched her from across the room, absorbed in her work. They had medicines for some plagues, he thought. Or they could get others from Tessa, just as they had done for Persia.

Thinking of Persia, he was reminded that Panther had not yet returned. Leaving Owl to her reading and Cheney to his nap, he went back up the stairs and outside into the streets to wait. Soon Panther reappeared with Chalk and Fixit, his dark face radiating anger that Hawk could detect from fifty feet away.

"What happened?" he asked as the other came up to him.

"Didn't nothin' happen, Bird-Man. We got there like we was supposed to, stood around waiting for those pussycats to appear, and no one showed. We waited more than an hour 'cause I knew you'd say we didn't wait long enough otherwise. Whole thing was a frickin' waste of time."

Hawk blinked. Tiger wouldn't have missed this meeting unless he physically couldn't come. Even then, he would have sent one of the others. Persia was too important to him. He would do anything to protect her.

Something was wrong.

"Wait here while I get Cheney," he said. "We're going back out."

21

As he went back down into the underground, he made a quick series of decisions. He was going to find out what had happened to Tiger, but he had to be careful how he went about it. Finding Tiger probably meant finding where the Cats laired, and all of the tribes were very territorial. If the Ghosts went uninvited into Cat country, even for what they deemed a good cause, they could expect an unfriendly reception. Still, the larger problem was in finding where Cat country was. He knew it was in an abandoned condo building somewhere north of midtown, but he didn't know the exact location. He would need help from Cheney.

By the same token, he had to make certain that Owl and Squirrel, who would remain behind, were sufficiently protected against anything that might threaten them in his absence. Since Cheney would be with him, he guessed he would have to give the job to Bear.

He was almost to the steel door when he realized that someone was following him. He wheeled back to find Panther right behind him.

"Wait up, Bird-Man," the other boy told him, the expression on his dark face reflecting irritation and impatience. "Talk to me. What you plannin' to do? Go lookin' for the pussycats?"

"I told you to wait upstairs."

Panther snorted. "You not the boss of me, Bird-Man. So tell me. This your plan? Huntin' for the Cats?"

Hawk glared. "Cheney can find them."

"How he gonna do that? Don't he need their scent? You got that? You got a piece of clothing or something?"

Hawk just stared. He didn't, of course.

"Tole you before. This ain't none of our business."

Hawk took a deep breath. "Not everything we do in this world is about us, Panther. Sometimes we have do things for other reasons. Sometimes we've got to forget about ourselves and help others. If not, what's the point?"

"The point, man, is that we get to stay alive! You don't think that's what we supposed to be doin' with ourselves?"

"I think that's the point. I just don't think that's the only point."

"Huh! Well, it is for me!"

They were nose-to-nose now, and seconds away from a fight. It had never happened before, although Hawk had suspected for a long time that Panther wanted it. If they fought and Panther won, he would have proved something to himself, although Hawk didn't know exactly what.

He straightened. "Okay, you think what you want. You got the right. But it doesn't matter what you think. I got the pleneten for Persia, and I'm going to find her and give it to her. She's just a little girl and she needs help. You don't want to help her, then don't. Stay here and watch Owl and Squirrel, and I'll take Bear."

"Hey, no one said nuthin' about not goin' with you," Panther said quickly, serious now, no messing around.

"Well, it sounded like it to me." Hawk refused to back off. "You said the Cats weren't any of our concern. You said you didn't care about anything but staying alive. So, fine. You do what you have to do, and I'll do the same."

"I just don't like takin' chances when it ain't necessary. Dangerous enough out there without that." Panther sighed. "Look, you don't need Cheney, but you do need me. I know where they is."

Hawk frowned. "You know where the Cats live? You know how to find them? How do you know that?"

"Tracked 'em. How you think? Look, you might honor that territorial code crap, but it don't mean nuthin' to me. I never did like the way they talked to us, so I waited for my chance one day a few months back and I tracked 'em. Found their little hidey-hole. It ain't far from where we went for the purification tablets a few days back."

Hawk felt a chill run down his spine at mention of the warehouse with its dark corners and sense of evil. "They'll have seen you. They'll have moved on."

Panther grinned broadly and shook his head. "Uh-uh. No one sees me if I don't want it. They still where they was. I can show you."

Hawk hesitated. That would save them all a lot of time. It also meant he could leave Cheney with Owl and Squirrel and take Bear, which he wanted to do. Bear was the biggest and strongest, and he wanted him along. They would be all right without Cheney if they had Bear. Of course, he would take Candle, too, as an added precaution.

He took a deep breath. "Look, you did good." He brought up his fist and Panther rapped it with his own. "We're family, agree or disagree. Nothing changes that."

"I ain't forgot." Panther scowled. "But it don't change how I see things, either."

Hawk dropped the matter, rapped on the door, and was admitted by Bear. He sent him with Panther to collect additional weapons for the outing and went over to where Owl sat watching.

"Tiger didn't show. I think something is wrong. I'm taking the others to see if we can find out what it is."

She nodded slowly, her calm eyes studying him. "Be careful, Hawk. If something has happened to Tiger, it could happen to you, too. Take Cheney."

He shook his head. "No, Cheney stays here with you and Squirrel. I'll take Candle. She'll know if there's danger. We'll be fine." He hesitated, and then added, almost as an afterthought, "I'll leave Sparrow, too. Just so you have another pair of hands."

Without waiting for her response, he called out to Sparrow to stay with Owl, then summoned Panther, Bear, and Candle and went out the door, waiting only long enough to hear the locks click into place before climbing the stairs to the streets.

Once outside, he gathered his little company about him. "Okay, this is what we are going to do," he said. He looked from face to face. "We're going to find out why Tiger didn't come to today's meeting to get the pleneten for Persia. Maybe there's a good reason, but maybe something has happened to him. Panther knows where the Cats make their home, and that's where we're going."

Eyes shifted quickly to Panther with the release of this bit of information, but no one said anything. Panther frowned slightly, but kept his eyes on Hawk and his mouth shut.

"So, Panther, you take the point, be in the lead," Hawk advised, noting the glimmer of excitement that sparked to life in the other's eyes. "Bear and I walk the wings. Fixit and Chalk form the rear guard. Candle stays in the middle. We keep to the center of the streets and we don't break formation unless I say so. We don't take any chances. We stick together."

He paused. "Remember. We're Ghosts, and we walk the ruins of our parents' world. Eyes open."

They set out for midtown, walking down the middle of First Avenue, prods held at the ready, eyes shifting from building to building, peering through the mix of shadows and light. The sun was still out, the day still bright and cheerful, the air still sharp with cold. The road was scattered with the same junk with which it had been scattered for as long as Hawk could remember. He scanned the familiar refuse—the hollowed-out vehicles, the broken pieces of pipe and railing, the splintered boards, and the bones and old clothing and trash.

To one side, up against a building, lay a solitary pink tennis shoe, its silver laces ragged, its bright fabric soiled by what might have been blood but was probably oil. Still bright and new looking, it stood out. He hadn't seen it before and wondered where it had come from.

It was midafternoon by then and later still by the time they passed through the city and reached the north end. They were still a dozen blocks below the Space Needle, but the slender obelisk towered over them, visible through the framework of the abandoned buildings, stark and spectral and oddly sad. Panther took them close by the warehouse that contained the hidden stash of purification tablets, but turned them up into the maze of apartment buildings that filled the blocks above First Avenue before they reached it. The sun had passed well into the west and cast shadows of the buildings down the streets in broad dark stains. It was later than Hawk would have preferred, but there was nothing he could do about it other than to turn back, and he had no intention of doing that.

Finally, as they approached an intersection, but while they were still in the shelter of the buildings to either side, Panther brought them to a halt and pointed ahead.

"Around that corner to the right, second building in across the street, that's their kitty-cat home," he told Hawk. "Big old apartment building with lots of floors."

Hawk nodded. He broke down the formation and put them in a line, Panther and himself in the lead, Bear in the rear, the others in the center. They walked against the walls of the buildings on their right until they had reached the end of the last one before they would have to enter the intersection. Motioning for the others to stay where they were, Hawk peered carefully around the corner at the buildings across the street. The second one in was a huge old redbrick structure with its windows and entry boarded up. There was no sign of life.

"How do they get in and out?" he asked Panther.

The other boy threw up his hands in exasperation. "What do you want from me? I found them; I didn't go in for a visit." He shook his head in disgust. "I saw a couple of them looking out from the windows, up on the higher floors, keeping watch. They thought no one would see them, I suppose. Frickin' idiots."

Hawk studied the building for a long time, thinking about what he should do but unable to come up with anything particularly good. He looked back at the others. "Wait here."

He stepped out from behind his hiding place and walked to the edge of the street where he could be clearly seen. "Tiger!" he called out. "Come down and talk to me! I have the medicine for Persia!"

He was taking a big chance. Street kids were very protective of their hiding places, aware that secrecy was their best defense against the many things that could hurt them, not the least of which were other street kids. The tribes had protection in numbers, but the dangers were the same. None of the tribes ever revealed to the others exactly where they were living. Some of the other denizens of their neighborhoods—Lizards, Spiders, and such—knew of their presence, but left them alone, for the most part. It was only the Croaks that were predatory enough to come hunting you while you slept.

Hawk waited for a response, but none came. He tried again. "Tiger, I have the pleneten! You didn't show for our meeting, so I brought it! Come down and get it!"

Still nothing. He waited several minutes, searching for any sort of sign at all. Time was slipping away. The afternoon shadows were lengthening and the light was fading. He did not want to be up here so far away from home when it got dark.

He considered his options, then called the rest of the Ghosts out of hiding and brought them all into the center of the street. Splitting them into two groups, with Panther taking one and himself the other, they began working their way around the block, searching for an entrance. Fifteen minutes later, they were back, having failed to find one.

"Maybe through one of the other buildings?" Fixit suggested hopefully.

The buildings on either side were not as heavily boarded up as was the brick structure, and they gained entry easily into the one on the left. It yielded nothing; an alleyway separated the two buildings aboveground, and a blank wall closed off any possible access through the basement.

They moved to the one on the right. This one looked more promising: it shared a wall with the building they were trying to get into. It might have been a hotel at one time, its entrance more imposing than those of the buildings surrounding, its ground floor a broad stretch of mostly broken-out windows. There was an eerie feel to the building, the fading light glinting off jagged pieces of broken glass and the darkness gathered inside so thick they could not see past it. They walked up to the entry, glancing at one another for reassurance, and stopped at the revolving doors when they refused to give. Panther moved to one of the side doors, reached through the broken window to release the catch, and slipped inside. The others followed.

They stood in the lobby, an imposing hall with a high ceiling and old furniture set about its broad open space in carefully arranged clusters. The stuffing was coming out of most of it, the leather and fabric cracked and split. They could hear the scurrying sound of rodents, and tiny dark forms shot into view in sudden bursts and were gone.

"Playmates for the pussycats," whispered Panther with a grin, but nobody smiled back.

The silence was deep and pervasive and troubling. Hawk glanced around uneasily, searching for the entrance that would admit them to the adjoining building, but found nothing. They spread out across the room, peering down corridors and up stairways. Because the buildings were connected, the entrance, if it existed, could be anywhere.

Fixit tugged on Hawk's sleeve. "Cats are climbers," he said softly, glancing over at the broad stairway leading up.

Hawk had counted the floors from outside, and there were at least seventeen or eighteen—several more than in the adjoining building. He didn't like the thought of climbing that high with no idea of what he was getting into. He didn't like leaving the relative safety of the open streets. He considered his options, and then gathered the others about him.

"Panther and I are going up. The rest of you wait here. Watch our backs. Don't let us get trapped up there. We'll be quick."

He was just turning away when Candle suddenly doubled over, clutching at her head and sagging to her knees. She moaned softly, her eyes squeezing shut, her breathing turning quick and harsh. Hawk knew at once what was happening and knelt in front of her, gripping her slender shoulders.

"What do you see?" he whispered. He could feel the others pressing close about them.

"Blood everywhere," she whispered.

"That's enough for me," Panther said at once. "I don't like how this place feels, either. Let's get out of here." He made as if to leave, but Hawk and the others stayed where they were. Panther wheeled back. "Are you paying attention, man? Are you listening to her? Are you listening to your own self?"

Hawk ignored him. He stroked Candle's blond head and cradled her against him. "It's all right, sweetie, it's all right. Tell me. Where is the blood? Whose is it?"

The little girl shook her head, then opened her eyes and looked at Hawk. "Here. It's here. But I can't tell whose it is."

Hawk went cold and for an instant thought about doing what Panther wanted and just leaving without taking this business any further. He forced himself not to begin looking around the room for whatever might have caused Candle's vision to come to pass.

"Do you see anything else?" he asked softly, holding her gaze, showing her he was not afraid.

She shook her head again. "I'm sorry, Hawk."

"No, it's okay. You have nothing to be sorry about."

He got back on his feet, bringing her up with him, still holding on to her, waiting until she was steady enough to release. Then he looked at the others. "I'm still going up. I'll do it alone. No one else needs to go. I want to see what's up there, take a quick look around. The rest of you wait here, and I'll be right back. If something happens, get out right away."

"No!" Candle said at once, reaching for him anew, grabbing his wrist. "Don't go up there, Hawk! Don't!"

"Candle, let go," he said firmly, and he disengaged himself, moving her back into Bear's arms. "I'll be careful."

Her head lowered, her eyes closed, and she began to rock. "Don't go, don't go," she said, over and over.

The rest of them kept silent, but they were saying the same thing with the looks they gave him. He turned away quickly and started up the stairs.

"Aw, man!" he heard Panther exclaim. "Wait up!"

Then the other boy was beside him, his dark face clouded with anger. "Can't be letting you go alone. You die up there, who you think gets the blame? C'mon, let's get this over with!"

Hawk nodded, and together they began to climb.

• • •

IT TOOK THEM awhile to get to the top floor. Hawk had decided that it would be best if they worked their way down rather than up. He thought that Fixit might be on to something. Cats liked to climb, so it figured that Tiger and his bunch, true to their name, might have chosen a place on the upper floors. If so, the passage from this building to the next was probably going to be found there.

But the top three floors were higher than the adjoining building, and a quick look out one of the windows on the highest revealed that there were no ladders or ropes allowing for descent to the other building's roof. So they went down to the first floor that allowed direct access and began searching. The rooms were all the same, their windows broken out, their sleeping and living rooms cluttered with decaying furniture and trash, their carpeted floors water-stained and worn, and their papered walls cracked and peeling. Hawk searched them swiftly, aware that the light was continuing to fail, conscious of a quickening in the approach of darkness. He did not like this building. He did not like how it made him feel.

Finding nothing on that floor, they descended to the next. Almost immediately they discovered the makeshift door that had been knocked in the wall of the rearmost sleeping room. After a futile pause to listen for signs of life, they stepped into the adjoining building and found themselves inside a warren of rooms that had once been offices, filled with desks and filing cabinets, with shelving and books, and with machines that no longer ran. The rooms were shadowed and empty of life, and there was no sign of the Cats. They searched the entire floor without success, then went down another floor and started again.

"How many we gonna search?" Panther whispered, his voice conveying a mix of uneasiness and frustration. "This gonna take us forever!"

Hawk agreed. They began moving quickly from floor to floor, not bothering with a thorough search, but settling for a quick scan that would reveal any sign of occupancy. They got all the way down to the ninth floor before they found what they were looking for. *Nine floors, nine lives,* Hawk was thinking before he realized what he was looking at.

"Frickin' hell, Bird-Man," Panther breathed softly.

A huge section of the wall was broken out near the stairwell, and Hawk could tell at a glance that the damage was recent. It hadn't given way on its own; it had been forced. Beyond the rubble of the wall a body lay half buried in the debris. Farther in, doorways and entries had been forcibly broken out and widened, their jambs shattered, the supporting walls ripped apart. Even in the heavy layer of shadows and thin veil of weakening light, Hawk could detect other bodies scattered about.

Everything, for as far as he could see through the damaged walls and entries, was in ruins.

He stepped into the room, climbed over the rubble, and bent down to the first body. He had to pull part of an old curtain off it to make certain it was one of the Cats. It was an older boy, his eyes open and staring, his face contorted in pain and horror. There was a huge swollen purplish mark on his neck with a dark center, as if he had been stung. Hawk had never seen a wound like it. He studied the body for other damage and didn't find any. With Panther following, he moved on.

They found a dozen dead boys and girls of varying ages, some of them bearing the same purplish mark and others simply crushed. One was decapitated and another missing both arms and one leg. The level of violence was shattering; the Cats had been caught unawares and unable to defend themselves. It looked as if they had tried to flee, but there had been no escape.

Despite his revulsion and Panther's whispered insistence that they get out of there, he pressed on. In the very back room, they found Tiger and Persia. Tiger had apparently been trying to protect her, his body half flung across hers where she lay sprawled on a mattress that was pushed up against the back wall. The short-barreled flechette lay on the floor to one side, bloodstained and bent. Hawk picked it up. Both barrels had been fired. Tiger's head was almost torn loose from his body, and his neck bore the same strange purplish mark they had seen on the bodies of the other Cats. He had fought hard to protect his little sister, but in the end it had not been enough. Hawk stared down at him, unable to find the words to express what he was feeling. He could hear Panther mumbling from across the room, the words dark and angry.

He glanced at Persia. She bore the same sting mark, but her face was peaceful. Perhaps she had died quickly and without knowing what was happening to her. Sadness emptied him out. She was only eleven years old. No one should die at eleven. He knew it happened every day, that it had happened every day for as long as he had been alive and much longer before that. But knowing it didn't make witnessing it any less horrific. He wished he had come earlier to his meeting with Tiger. He wished he could have done something to prevent this.

He looked around at the wreckage of the rooms and the scattering of bodies. What in the world had done this?

Then he caught sight of Persia's right leg. It had been severed cleanly at the ankle, and the foot was missing. On the other foot, clearly visible against the white surface of the bloodstained mattress, was a pink tennis shoe with silver laces.

He remembered that on his way here he had seen its mate not two blocks from their underground home, and he felt his heart stop.

Owl!

Shouting frantically for Panther, he raced from the room.

22

OWL SAT QUIETLY in one corner of the common room, poring over another of the medical books she had been researching since Hawk and the others had left, her eyes scanning quickly from page to page. It was the fourth book she had opened, but she still didn't know anything more about the Weatherman's form of plague than when she had started. There just wasn't enough written about the plagues; so many of them had developed in the aftermath of the chemical attacks and poisonings that there hadn't been time to write anything down, let alone find the means to publish it. She was relying on texts that were out of date twenty years ago, but it was all she had—that and her personal experience, which wasn't much better given the rapid evolution of sicknesses all over the world.

She rubbed her eyes to ease the ache of her weariness. She wished sometimes that she could walk, that she wasn't confined to this wheelchair. She wasn't being selfish, although she had her share of those moments, too. She was simply frustrated at being unable to just get up and see what could be done instead of having to rely on others. She wanted to go down to the waterfront and have a look at

River's grandfather, but Hawk would never allow it. He might agree to bring the old man to their underground home, but only if she was able to give him some assurance that doing so would not endanger the family. It was bad enough that River was already exposed to whatever her grandfather had contracted. Hawk would never risk exposing the other children, as well.

She wasn't even sure, thinking on it, that he would allow River back. It seemed inconceivable that he would not, but Hawk could be intractable about certain things, and this might prove to be one.

Across the room, where he lay curled up in his favorite spot, Cheney stirred awake suddenly and lurched to his feet with a low growl. It was the second time he had done so in the last few minutes and the fourth or fifth since Hawk had left, and she knew right away what was happening. The big dog was reacting to the noises in the wall they had both been hearing for the last two hours.

Sparrow appeared in the bedroom doorway, her young face dark and intense. "It's back there now," she said. She gave a quick toss of her blond head toward the rearmost bedroom, which was Owl's. "And it's moved into the ceiling."

Before, it had been under the floor of the boys' bedroom, and before that somewhere outside the walls entirely. Each time, Cheney had leapt up and gone sniffing from corner to corner, hackles raised, a low growl building in his throat. He did the same thing this time, working his way to the back of their quarters, big head swinging from side to side, nose to the floor and then lifting. Owl had no idea what was going on, so she watched Cheney's progress, searching for clues.

"What do you think it is?" Sparrow asked her.

She shook her head. "It's making a lot of noise; it must be something bigger than a rat. Maybe a Spider or a Lizard prowling about, one that doesn't know the rules yet."

That was what she said, but it wasn't what she believed. The sounds didn't remind her of any she'd heard a Spider or Lizard make. They didn't remind her of anything she had *ever* heard. She found herself wishing that Hawk would return, even knowing she was perfectly safe within the shelter of their hideout, behind the reinforced iron-plated doors and heavy concrete walls and with

Cheney to protect them. She knew she was letting her fears run away with her, but she couldn't seem to quite stop them from doing so.

She listened some more, but the sounds were gone. She exchanged a quick glance with Sparrow, who shrugged and went back to reading to Squirrel. She liked it that Sparrow had begun taking such an interest in books. Some of it had to do with her willingness to assume the big-sister role with Squirrel, whom she adored. But some of it was due to a real interest in learning how to read and wanting to learn what all those words could teach her about life. Sparrow had endured a harsh and brutal childhood, one that she had revealed in full only to Owl, and there was every reason to believe that she would never be interested in anything but honing her considerable survival skills. Yet here she was, reading books as if nothing mattered more. Life could still surprise you sometimes.

Owl settled back in her wheelchair and returned to perusing the medical books. She wished she had a better understanding of medical terms. Most of what she knew she had learned through practical experience while still in the compound. She had no formal training. But if someone in your family or a close friend of your family didn't know medicine, your chances of survival lessened considerably. Owl had always been interested in seeking out ways to protect the lives that others would be quick to write off.

"Can Squirrel have a cola?" Sparrow called out from the other room.

Owl said yes, watching Cheney reemerge from her bedroom and wander back over to his spot on the floor. He had an uneasy look to him, and even as he settled back down, he kept his head lifted, his gray eyes alert as they stared off into space. She listened again for the strange noise, but it was gone. She looked back down at her book, reading. Maybe Tessa would know something; she would have Hawk ask her at their next meeting. She wished those meetings didn't have to take place, that Tessa would just come live with them as Hawk wanted. It was too dangerous to meet in violation of compound law. It would take only one mistake for them to be discovered, and if they were, retribution would be swift.

The sound came again, a scrabbling this time, directly overhead. Cheney was on his feet at once, thick fur bristling, muzzle drawn back in a snarl. Owl glanced up, tracking the scrabbling as it moved across the ceiling from the front of the room to the back and toward the rear bedrooms. Cheney tracked it, as well, hunching after it in a crouch, gimlet eyes furious. Owl turned her wheelchair in the direction of the noise and waited. The noise ceased.

Then, all at once, it began anew, a furious digging sound this time, a ripping away at things that suggested a determination bordering on frenzy. Sparrow appeared in the doorway once more, mouth agape as she stared at the back rooms. She was holding Squirrel by one hand. The little boy's face revealed his uncertainty.

Owl didn't know what was happening, but she didn't think it was good. "Sparrow," she said as calmly as she could. "Get several prods from the locker and bring them to me."

She wheeled herself over to the front of the room, close by the iron-plated door, and beckoned Squirrel to come join her. The little boy hurried over and climbed into her lap. "There, there," she cooed, soothing his fears as he buried his head in her shoulder. "It's all right."

Sparrow removed three of the prods from the locker and brought them to Owl. She took two and propped them against the wall behind her. She let Sparrow keep the other. At the far end of the room, Cheney was all the way down on the floor in his crouch, so agitated he was shaking as he inched forward, then crabbed slightly to one side, muzzle lifted toward the sound of the scrabbling.

Cracking sounds resounded through the underground like gunshots, sharp and unexpected, followed by a slow shifting of something big. Cheney backed away toward the center of the room, keeping his eyes on the bedroom ceiling. Then, all at once, the entire ceiling in Owl's room gave way. It happened so fast that she barely had time to register the event before it was over. Heavy chunks of plaster, wooden beams, and wires and cables embedded in the mix came crashing down under the weight of a huge dark presence. Dust billowed into the air, momentarily obscuring everything. Squirrel screamed, and even Sparrow jumped back in shock. Owl was already thinking that they had to get out of there.

But it was too late. The dust settled and a nightmarish creature emerged from the debris. At first, Owl couldn't believe what she was seeing. The creature was a long, jointed insect that looked to be a type of centipede, but one that was hundreds of times larger than it should have been, stretching to twenty feet and rising four feet off the floor. Its reticulated, armored body was supported by dozens of crooked legs and undulated from side to side in a snake-like motion as it advanced. Feelers protruded from atop its shiny head, and a pair of wicked-looking jaws opened and closed from below. There were spikes everywhere, and bits and pieces of clothing and debris hung off the tips like strange decorations. A series of bulbous eyes dotted its flat, hairy face, eyes that were blank and staring.

Cheney was on it at once, tearing at the spindly legs, ripping them off as fast as jaws could close and teeth could shred. The huge insect whipped about to snare him, using mandibles and body weight to try to crush the big dog, but Cheney was too quick and too experienced to be so easily trapped. The battle raged back and forth across the far end of the common room, the combatants smashing everything from furniture to shelves to dishes to lights. Owl and Sparrow watched in horror, transfixed by the ferocity of the struggle. Squirrel just hid his head and begged someone, anyone, to take him away.

For a time it seemed that Cheney would prevail, darting in to tear off legs and rip at armor plates, then darting away again. But the giant centipede was not affected by the damage done to it. It was a creature Owl instantly decided must have been mutated by the chemical and radiation attacks that had taken place as much as five decades earlier. How it had grown to its present size or why it had appeared here was fodder for speculation, and the answers would probably never be known. What mattered was that its alterations had given it tremendous strength and stamina, and not even the considerable wounds that Cheney was inflicting seemed to affect it.

Eventually, the effort began to tell. Cheney was tiring, and the centipede was not. The razor-sharp jaws were beginning to find their mark, ripping at the big body, tearing off chunks of fur and flesh and leaving the big dog's mottled coat matted and damp with blood. Owl could tell that Cheney was slowing, that his attacks were less ferocious and driven more by heart than by muscle. But Cheney would never quit, she knew. He would die first.

When he went down, it happened all at once. He was savaging still another leg, searching for still another weakness, when the creature's jaws finally got a solid hold on him and clamped down viciously. Snarling and snapping, Cheney twisted furiously. Slippery with his own blood, he broke free, but the effort sent him tumbling all the way across the room where he slammed against the wall and went down in a heap. Gasping for air, his flanks heaving and his legs scrambling for purchase on the concrete flooring, he struggled in vain to rise. Blood welled up from the wounds caused by the insect's jaws, and Cheney snapped at them furiously, as if in terrible pain.

The centipede advanced toward him, jaws wide.

Owl turned quickly to Sparrow. "Take Squirrel and get out of here. Get as far away as possible. Try to find Hawk and warn him."

She knew she had just pronounced a death sentence on herself, but she also knew that Sparrow could not get her to safety in time. Sparrow would be lucky if she managed to escape with Squirrel, and that was the best they could hope for.

"Sparrow!" she hissed when the other failed to respond.

But Sparrow was staring straight ahead at the centipede, her hands tightening about the handle of the prod, her lips compressing into a tight line. Owl realized suddenly what she was going to do. *No!* she tried to say, but the word caught in her throat.

Sparrow stepped in front of her, a shield against the thing approaching, and brought up the prod.

●　●　●

BY THE TIME Sparrow was five years old, she already knew that she was expected to grow up to be like her mother. It wasn't just that everyone hoped for it; it was that they talked as if it were an inarguable certainty and the completion of her transformation awaited only her achieving maturity. Physically, she was already a miniature version of her mother, with the same lanky body, big hands, mop of straw-colored hair, crooked smile, and fierce blue eyes that could pin you to the wall when they were angry. She even walked like her mother, a sort of saunter that suggested great confidence and a readiness and willingness to act.

She liked being thought of this way, as the daughter who would one day become her mother. Her mother, after all, was a legend. Her mother was a furious fighter and canny leader. Her mother was a warrior. Growing up to be like her was what any little girl would wish for.

But her mother never spoke to her of any of this. Her mother did not seem to have these expectations for her—or if she did, she kept them to herself. Her mother did not once tell her that hers was the path that Sparrow must necessarily follow. Her mother only told her that she must be her own person and find her own way in the world. What she would give her were the skills and the training that would let her survive. But her heart would have to tell her where she was meant to go.

Sparrow wasn't certain if she believed this or not. What she knew is that she adored her mother. She did not know who her father was; he had been gone before she was born and no one ever spoke of him. Her mother was the seminal figure in her life, and everything she was or hoped to be was a product of that relationship. She thought about her father, but only rarely and never with more than passing interest. She thought about her mother all the time.

Her mother was as good as her word. She trained Sparrow to fight—to attack and to defend. She worked her until Sparrow was ready to drop, but Sparrow never complained. She was a good student, and soon she had mastered the exercises her mother had given her to do. Her dedication was complete. She was not yet big enough to be effective, but she knew she would grow and when she did, she would be ready. She trained every day that her mother was not away, and she practiced on her own when her mother was gone. She was determined to be the best; she was set on making her mother proud.

They lived in the mountains, high up on the slopes in a fortified camp that her mother had established years before Sparrow was born. It was from there that her mother led her raiding parties on the slave pens and the slavers that terrorized everyone. Most of the villages surrounding were small and poorly defended—easy prey for the ravers and the madmen. The larger compounds, the safe ones, were in the cities, miles away from where she lived. Her mother didn't trust them. Her mother believed in freedom and independence; she placed her trust in speed and mobility. Her camp was settled on a cliff shelf accessible only by a series of narrow trails that no one but those who followed her knew about and which could be easily defended. The shelf was fronted by a sheer cliff wall and backed by heavy forest leading up to the impassable slopes of the mountain behind it. It was a good location; it had kept them safe for a long time.

But, as it so often happened in the postapocalypse, their success caused resentment, resentment turned to treachery, and treachery gave them away. Word of their existence spread; vivid descriptions of their raids on the slave camps and the slavers traveled far and wide. Eventually, their enemies began to hunt for them in earnest, and found out where they were. Then one among their number grew jealous and betrayed them. It was a foolish act, one born of anger and poor judgment and not of deliberate intention to cause harm. But the result was the same. The slavers found the path leading in and a way to get past the guards and laid their plans carefully.

They came at night, when most were sleeping. They advanced in silence until they had overcome the guards, and then they charged in screaming and firing their automatic weapons. They were on a mission of destruction, and they were ruthless in their efforts to carry it out. They killed everyone they came upon—men, women, and children—making no effort to take prisoners or to distinguish those who resisted from those who tried to surrender. There were dozens of them, all heavily armed, fed by chemicals or their own peculiar madness, and without a single drop of remorse to give them pause.

Sparrow woke to the sounds of weapons fire, and then her mother was beside her, snatching her up and bearing her from their shelter and into the eye of the maelstrom. Without speaking a word and without slowing, her mother carried her through the camp—

past the dead and dying, past the fires burning everywhere, past shadowy forms that flitted through the night like ghosts. Sharp bursts of gunfire rose all around, and Sparrow closed her eyes and prayed for it to stop. She was terrified; she wanted to cry, but she would not let herself.

Then they were huddled together in the darkness, and her mother was kneeling in front of her, their faces only inches away. Her mother wore a backpack and carried her Parkhan Spray. "I need to have my hands free to use my weapon. Stay close to me. I will not leave you behind, no matter what." She paused. "I love you, little one."

A moment later she was back on her feet, holding the big, black-barreled Spray in front of her, swinging it about and yelling at Sparrow to run. Together they raced across a short stretch of open ground between two of the burning shelters, her mother firing the Spray in short bursts at the dark forms that rushed toward her. Sparrow heard the hiss and whine of bullets as they flew past her head and saw the muzzle flashes of the enemy weapons in the shadows. The sounds were terrifying, and she ran as if she were on fire and only the rush of the wind could extinguish the flames.

They reached the woods behind the camp, the weapons fire tracking them all the way, and suddenly, just as they passed into the trees, she felt a fiery sting on her arm and another on her leg. She heard her mother grunt and saw her falter, then straighten and continue on. Biting her tongue against the pain of her wounds, she followed. They ran deep into the trees, away from the carnage of their home, the sounds of death slowly receding behind them as darkness and shadows closed about.

They ran a long way after that before her mother slowed, and by then they were deep into the woods and climbing the slope behind them into the mountains. Her mother glanced back at her, saw that she was holding her injured arm, and stopped at once to take a look. As she did so, Sparrow saw that the whole front of her mother's shirt was wet and slick with blood.

"Mama, you're hurt!" she whispered, reaching for her.

Her mother intercepted her hands and held her away. "No,

there's nothing wrong," she said quickly. "Are you all right? Can you walk?" Sparrow nodded. "Then we have to keep going."

They climbed high into the mountains, and soon all they could see of the camp was a fiery dot burning out of the blackness below. But the sounds of the killing were still audible, shrill and terrible, and Sparrow was forced to listen. She knew what was happening. All of her friends, all those people she had grown up with, were gone. Only she and her mother and perhaps a handful of others had escaped. Tears flooded her eyes with the realization that she would never see her friends again. She wiped at the dampness and tried not to let her mother see.

It was only an hour or two before dawn when her mother finally allowed them to stop. They had come through a pass and were on the other side of the mountain, and the camp and its horrors were left behind. They sat together on a grassy berm that provided them with shelter, facing west across a plain dark with night and a sky filled with stars. Her mother had abandoned the Spray sometime back, but she still wore her backpack. She stripped it off now and pulled out clothes and boots for Sparrow to change into. She was breathing heavily, and the blood from her wounds coated both the front and back of her shirt. She seemed unaware of it as she watched Sparrow change out of her nightdress, but her eyes were filled with pain.

"We'll rest here until morning, little one," she said. "Then we will walk west to the ocean. It will take a couple of days, but we will go slowly and carefully and watch out for danger." She reached into her pack and pulled out a flechette handgun. "This will be yours until we reach our destination. Don't use it unless you are in real danger."

Sparrow listened and nodded, not knowing how to reply. Finally, she said, "You have to stop the bleeding, Mama. You have to bandage yourself so it will stop."

Her mother smiled and reached for her hand, pulling her down beside her. "I need to rest a little while first. You should rest, too. We have a long walk ahead of us. Can you make that walk? Are you strong enough to walk all the way to the ocean?"

Sparrow nodded, staring into her mother's clear eyes. "I can walk anywhere you want me to, Mama."

Her mother squeezed her hands. "Then everything will be all right." She sighed heavily. "I have to rest now. I'm very tired. Don't forget, little one. I love you. I will always love you."

She lay back against the wall of the berm, and her face was pale and drawn in the starlight. Her eyes closed and her breathing slowed. Sparrow lay down next to her, pressing close, still holding her hand. She looked over at her mother's face and thought how much she loved her in turn. She told herself that she would be strong for her mother and would not complain. She would do whatever her mother wanted her to do.

Moments later, she fell asleep.

When she woke, it was morning. The stars had gone and taken her mother with them.

● ● ●

"SPARROW!" OWL HISSED.

But Sparrow didn't hear her. She was remembering her last night with her mother. Almost five years had passed, yet it might as well have been yesterday. She would never forget what her mother had done for her—how she had carried her from the killing ground of the camp, entrusted her with a weapon to protect herself, told her where to go to find safety, and given her a chance at life. It was all her mother had been able to do for her at the end, but it was enough.

I will grow up to be like my mother, Sparrow had promised herself afterward. *I will make her proud.*

The words recalled themselves now as she stepped in front of Owl, holding the prod at port arms, her finger on the charging trigger. She would have preferred the flechette her mother had given her or the big Parkhan Spray, but both were long since gone. The prod would have to do.

"Sparrow!" Owl pleaded a second time. "Get out of here!"

Sparrow heard her this time, but ignored her, her eyes fixed on the giant centipede. She had already seen how quick it could be, how fast it could strike. Cheney had done well to avoid its jaws for as long as he had, and she was neither as swift nor as agile as Cheney. She would probably have only one chance at the creature, and she would have to make it count. She wished she knew something that would give her an edge—a weakness or a way around its formidable defenses. Tearing off its legs had barely slowed it. Its body was armored from head to tail, and even with his huge teeth and tremendous strength Cheney hadn't been able to do much damage to it.

You find a weakness in your enemy's defenses and you attack it there, her mother had told her repeatedly.

Its eyes, she thought suddenly. *Its eyes look vulnerable.* But she couldn't be certain without testing her theory, and if she was wrong, she was probably dead.

She tried to move and couldn't. She could feel herself shaking she was so afraid.

But the centipede was gathering itself for a rush at Cheney, who lay thrashing against the far wall, still struggling to rise, his dark coat matted with blood, and there was no time left to be afraid. Sparrow slid sideways down the opposite wall, away from Owl and Squirrel, trying not to draw attention to herself. She noticed how the insect's armor folded back on itself from one section to the next, forming a series of overlapping plates. The plates were designed to protect it from a frontal attack. But if she could get behind it or even to one side of it, she might be able to jam the prod between the plates and get up into the soft inner parts of the creature. It didn't seem nearly enough, but it was all she could think to do.

She was not big and strong like her mother. She was not skilled or experienced. She was only thirteen years old. But she was her mother's daughter, and she had vowed to make her mother proud.

She took a deep breath and charged the centipede from just behind its head, both hands gripping the insulated handle, her index finger locked down hard against the charge trigger. The centipede saw her coming and wheeled toward her, the gaps in its armor where she hoped to attack scissoring shut. The terrible jaws opened, and its feelers reached out like tentacles. She jabbed the prod at its head in desperation, trying to strike the eyes, but the feelers knocked her blows aside. Even so, the prod had a measurable effect, and the insect's huge body shivered as the electrical charge jolted it. Sparrow

struck at it again and again, but she couldn't find an opening between the armored plates and was finally knocked aside by one of
the skittering legs, her arms and face cut and bleeding.

Instantly, the centipede came after her, and she knew she was
dead.

But suddenly Cheney was there, back on his feet and attacking
from the other side, lunging wildly at the vulnerable legs, ripping
and snarling as if gone completely berserk. The attack caught the
centipede by surprise, and it curled back on itself, jaws snapping
at this new attacker. As it did so, it spread wide the plates on Sparrow's side. Seeing her chance, she scrambled to her feet and rushed
in with the prod and jammed it deep into the opening just behind
the head, the prod on full power, the trigger locked down. The centipede jerked as if it had been slapped by a giant hand, and Sparrow
could see flashes of electricity spurting from inside the plates and
could smell something terrible burning. Cheney was down again, his
strength gone, his back toward the wall. But the centipede had no
time for Cheney. It had lost all interest in anything but ridding itself
of the prod, which was lodged now between its body sections.

Sparrow didn't wait. As the creature thrashed across the floor,
fighting to dislodge the prod, she snatched up the spare that had
been resting against the wall next to Owl, powered it on, and
charged in again. It was a more dangerous effort this time, the centipede's body twisting and jerking wildly, its nervous system gone
out of control. One wrong step and she would be pinned beneath it.
But she would not be turned back now. She ignored the blows she
took from the spiky legs, ignored the blood in her eyes and the pain
that racked her body, and found an opening midway back in the
spiky body where she buried the prod all the way up to her hands
between the plates. The centipede reacted at once, writhing in agony
all the way back across the room. Jammed against the wall, it con-
vulsed, shuddered once, and lay still.

Sparrow stood in the center of the room, a roaring in her ears
that she couldn't explain and the smell of death and blood all
around her. She bit her lip against the tears that threatened to flood
her eyes. She would not cry.

I did it, Mama, she thought.

She hurried across the room and knelt beside Cheney, flinching at the angry look of the wounds that covered his body. She was aware of Owl wheeling over to join her and of little Squirrel bending close as she cradled Cheney's big head in her lap, smoothing the rough fur coat with her hands and calling his name softly, over and over again.

"Cheney, Cheney, don't die," she pleaded.

That was how Hawk and the others found them only minutes later when they burst through the door.

● ● ●

IT WAS IMMEDIATELY apparent to all of them that pleas alone weren't going to be enough to save Cheney. The centipede had bitten him repeatedly, and his system was flooded with poison. Owl did her best to draw it out, siphoning and then cleaning the wounds, injecting the big dog with antitoxins to slow or stop the sickening, but even so his condition steadily worsened. The wounds were too severe and the poison gone too deep. Cheney was hanging on by a thread, but his life was slipping away.

Hawk sat with him in the darkness of the underground, holding his head and letting the dog feel his presence. Cheney was conscious, but he wasn't responsive. His eyes were glazed and dull, his breathing thick and ragged, and his strength sapped to almost nothing. He barely acknowledged Hawk. There wasn't anything Hawk could do for him, but he refused to leave him alone, even for a minute. This was his fault, he kept telling himself. He had been careless. He had missed all the signs that should have warned him of the danger. He had left the underground too poorly protected. He had failed in so many ways, and Cheney was paying the price.

It was midnight by now, the underground silent and the other Ghosts asleep. They had cut up the centipede and hauled all the sections into the bedroom where it had broken through the ceiling—Owl's bedroom—and then closed it off. Tomorrow, they would have to begin searching for a new place to live, but it was too late to do anything tonight and they were all exhausted. Most of them had stayed with Cheney until Hawk ordered them off to bed. Sparrow had stayed until she collapsed. How she had kept Owl and the others alive against a thing as monstrous as that centipede was something Hawk would never understand. He knew she was a tough girl with the heart of a warrior, unafraid of anything, but he had no idea how she had survived this. Even with Cheney to help, it seemed impossible.

He stared off into the room's darkness, thinking that nothing should seem impossible after today. The world he had constructed, the family he had gathered, the life he had invented for himself— they were all falling apart. He didn't know if the centipede was the fulfillment of Candle's vision or if something worse was looming on the horizon, but he did know that their time in the underground was rapidly drawing to a close. He didn't feel safe in the city anymore. If things like this centipede were coming out of the earth, then it was time to get out.

Not that there was any guarantee it wouldn't be worse elsewhere. In fact, it probably would. Unless he could find the safe haven he had seen in his dreams. Unless he could make the story of the boy and his children come true.

Cheney, Cheney.

He stroked Cheney's big head and watched his flanks rise and fall heavily. He wanted so badly to help him, to do something— anything—that would make him well. But he didn't know what to do. He knew that if Owl couldn't do anything, there was little chance that he could. He had no medical skills. He had no experience with poisonings. But the fact of it didn't stop him from wanting to try. It didn't change the cold, empty feeling that had settled inside.

He thought of Tiger and Persia and the Cats—all dead because of the thing in the next room. It must have caught them sleeping. It must have been on top of them before they knew what was happening. Or perhaps they panicked. Whatever the case, they hadn't stood a chance, not even with Tiger's flechette to protect them. Maybe even Cheney couldn't have saved them.

His fingers touched the big dog's muzzle. It was hot and dry. Cheney never even blinked; he just stared straight ahead. Cheney was just a dog, but Hawk knew that in many ways he was his most loyal friend. Cheney would do anything for him—for any of them. He shouldn't have to die for that. He had thought that nothing could hurt Cheney, that the big dog was too tough and too experienced to be harmed. It was a foolish way to think, a stupid way. He should have known. He should have realized that Cheney was no less vulnerable than they were, even as big and strong as he was.

He sat in the darkness with his dog and wished he could change places with him.

Don't die.

His eyes filled with tears, and he was crying. He bent over Cheney and hugged him, held him as if by doing so he could keep him alive, could hold back his dying, could turn it aside as he would an evil thought. His fingers dug into the thick fur, and he whispered to Cheney, over and over.

Don't die. Please don't die.

He willed it not to happen. He prayed for it so hard that his mind clamped down on the thought and his entire self went into making it so.

And something strange happened.

He was suddenly warm, heat spreading through him as if he had turned on a switch. He felt the heat fill his body and then his limbs. It should have frightened him, something so strange and unexpected, but it had the opposite effect. It reassured him. He lay pressed up against Cheney and let the warmth flow through and then out of him. It happened slowly, almost incrementally, so that he could feel it building by degrees and then exiting in tiny bursts. It went on for a long time, and he thought he must be having a reaction to his grief.

Then he tasted a sudden bitterness in his mouth, and deep down in his belly he felt a burning sensation. Both lasted only seconds, gone so quickly he barely had time to register their presence. But their passing left him unexpectedly drained of strength, as if he had expended a great effort.

He felt Cheney stir beneath him, a squirming coupled with a series of twitches. He almost let go of the big dog, and then decided not to. His own eyes were closed, so he couldn't see exactly what was happening. But he didn't want to open them for fear of break-ing the spell.

"Cheney," he whispered.

The heat radiated out of him, and Cheney continued to squirm, then to shiver, and suddenly to whine. Now Hawk did open his eyes, and he saw that Cheney's were open, too. But they were no longer dull or glazed; they were bright and alert. The big dog's tongue licked out, wetting his dry nose. He was thirsty. Hawk felt Cheney's breathing change, turning stronger and steadier.

Then the heat pulsating through his body faded. He could feel the change happen, a slow diminishing of warmth, a gradual lessen-ing of its passage out. When he lifted away, no longer able to keep from doing so, Cheney lifted his head and looked at him. Hawk swallowed hard, and then stared at Cheney's damaged body.

The wounds were almost entirely healed.

Hawk could not understand what had just happened.

● ● ●

FAR TO THE south, somewhere along the California coast, sur-rounded by his army of once-men and demons, an old man with eyes as cold and empty as the deepest ice cave that nature had ever formed started in surprise as he felt the wave of magic wash over him. He recognized its source at once; there was no mistaking it. He had been searching for it unsuccessfully for almost a century.

A dark, hard smile creased his weathered features. Sometimes you just had to be patient.

23

ANGEL PEREZ SHIFTED her gaze from the winding ribbon of roadway that stretched ahead to the slowly darkening sky and frowned in frustration.

"How much farther do we have to go?" she asked Ailie.

The tatterdemalion, an ethereal figure in the fading light, looked back over her shoulder and blinked. "Not far."

"It's starting to get dark. It will be night before long." Angel glanced around at the trees and deep shadows bracketing the road. "I don't much want to be caught out here when that happens."

She had lived in the city all her life and had an instinctive dislike of the country. They had been walking for several hours and hadn't seen a single building that wasn't either a shed or a barn. There were broad hills, broken-topped mountains, deep woods, roads that seemed to lead nowhere, and not much else. No houses. No stores. Certainly no high-rises. It wasn't Los Angeles, and it wasn't familiar or comfortable. She was pretty sure they were still in California, but for all she knew they might have walked all the way to Canada.

"You said we would find a quicker way to get wherever it is we're going than by taking one of the trucks. I believed you."

"We will." The tatterdemalion didn't even look back this time. "Be patient."

Be patient, Angel thought in exasperation. She had been patient for almost four hours and look where she was. She should have been more trusting, but she hadn't stayed alive this long by relying on trust. She did not think that the creature she followed meant her any harm, but all too often good intentions coupled with poor judgment was all it took. She knew nothing of Ailie's capabilities. In point of fact, she knew nothing about her at all. She was a Faerie creature sent by the Lady, but she would have a life span of not much more than sixty days, so her experience couldn't amount to much. That, all by itself, was troubling.

What was more troubling, physically speaking, were the wounds she had received in her battle with the demon. The claw marks down her back and along her shoulder burned like fire, and she was battered and bruised from head to foot. She needed to bathe and rest. She was unlikely to get a chance to do either anytime soon.

She kicked at the dirt of the road they were following. What was she doing out here anyway, not only out of the city, but away from anything familiar? *!Dios mío!* Hunting for Elves? She didn't even believe in Elves. Well, she supposed that maybe she did, knowing that there were so many other kinds of Faerie creatures in the world. But still. Hunting for Elves? She should have gone with Helen and the children. She should have told Ailie that this wasn't for her.

After all, how did she even know that the Lady had sent Ailie? She only had Ailie's word for it. She had no way of knowing what was going on, what sort of game she might be a pawn in. How could she know what to believe?

Except that she did. She knew because her instincts told her what to believe and what not to believe, and it had very little to do with common sense or life experience.

She sighed, realizing she was being foolish. Most of what she did as a Knight of the Word required a suspension of disbelief and an acceptance that things you couldn't see were still there. You couldn't see the feeders, after all, unless you were a Faerie creature or a Knight of the Word. But they were there all the same, tracking after you, smelling you out, waiting for you to let your darker emotions gain control before they destroyed you. She had watched it happen to those who couldn't see them. Being unaware of their presense hadn't saved those people. So she might as well stop questioning the presence of Elves. She might as well accept that most of what she thought she knew was only half right.

Nevertheless.

"Are we looking for something?" she asked Ailie with controlled exasperation.

The Faerie creature shook her head, her floating blue hair shimmering in what remained of the fading daylight. "It isn't far now, Angel."

It better not be, Angel thought. She tramped on, maintaining a sullen silence.

It was almost dark by the time they reached the storage complex. It sat near the intersection of the dirt road they had been following and a paved highway, well east of where they had started out. The sun had dropped behind the hills to the west, and the sky had turned gray and flat. Frequently there were glorious sunsets in the world, but not tonight. There was a lessening of color, but nothing more. Angel glanced west, thinking suddenly of Anaheim and the ruined compound, of how the fires and the smoke would be reflecting against the darkness, and then turned her attention to the storage complex.

She had seen others like it many times before. A series of low sheet-metal buildings fronted the highway, receding toward the trees in long rows. Most had been broken into and emptied of their contents, the remnants left strewn about the grounds in ragged heaps. Furniture, clothing, books, housewares—everything imaginable—tossed aside and abandoned. She found herself wondering what had been taken. In a world in which power sources were primitive and difficult to obtain, and in which transportation and commerce were essentially destroyed, what was left that would be worth stealing?

There was only one answer, of course. Weapons. Whatever else might happen in this postapocalyptic world, people would still continue to kill one another.

She caught up with Ailie. "This is it? This is what we've been trying to reach?"

Ailie looked back at her with the eyes and face of a child, her expression serene and nonjudgmental. Then she began moving through piles of junk toward the back of the complex. Angel hesitated, and then followed. She had come this far, after all.

When they were almost to the very rear of the complex, the tatterdemalion turned down a long row of emptied-out units and wove her way through the scattered contents until she reached the end unit. Like the others, the doors of this one stood open, locks broken and contents rifled. Angel glanced at Ailie questioningly. The tatterdemalion gave her a quick smile, then moved inside the unit to the very back wall, where a scattering of empty boxes lay piled up.

"Look, Angel," she said, pointing.

Angel peered into the gloom. She didn't see anything. Ailie beckoned her closer, gave a quick hand motion that illuminated the lower left corner of the wall, and now Angel saw a block lock set into the concrete of the floor, securing the wall in place. A door, Angel realized, disguised as a wall. Ailie smiled, moved over to the lock, and reached down and touched it. Instantly the lock clicked open and fell away. Ailie made another quick motion, and the entire wall slid up into a concealed compartment.

Angel peered inside and caught her breath. Two hulking, cloth-draped machines sat back in the shadows, one much bigger than the other, the wheels of each just visible where the coverings failed to reach the floor. Angel walked over, pulled off the coverings, and stepped back.

She was looking at a pair of triwheel ATVs. Big, sleek machines, they were capable of travel over any terrain and could reach speeds of sixty miles an hour on an open road. The smaller was a Mercury 5 series, the larger a Harley Crawler, either a Flex or Sim model. The Mercury was the quicker and more maneuverable of the two, the Harley the more indestructible. She hadn't seen either since her early days with Johnny.

"How did you find these?" she asked.

Ailie gave a small shrug. "We needed a way to travel north, and I looked until I found these. An owner who never came back for them hid them behind this false wall. They still have their power packs."

Angel walked over to the machines and checked the engine bays.

Sure enough, the heavy fuel cells were set in place, charged and ready for use. Three cells for each machine. Either one would take her a long way.

"Which do you want?" Ailie was smiling, her child's face revealing an unexpected excitement.

Angel thought about it a moment, then walked over to the Mercury. Speed and agility. Better mileage for the cells because it was the lighter machine. "This one."

She wheeled the Mercury out into the open and left it while she took time to remove the power cells from the Harley and hide them beneath a pile of debris several storage units down. She then rolled down the door, concealing the big machine. She had learned never to leave behind anything an enemy might use against you. Then she climbed astride the padded seat and fired up the Mercury. The engine caught instantly, emitting a sound that she thought might resemble the growl of a big cat. She waited for Ailie to climb up behind her. She new what to do. Johnny had taught her.

"Which way?" she asked.

Ailie pointed north up the paved crossroad.

Angel wheeled the Mercury through the debris of the storage yard and out the crumpled gates. As she reached the road, she caught sight of a figure standing back in the shadows to one side, underneath a massive old redwood. She peered at it intently, but the figure disappeared, and she found herself looking at a mailbox on a stake. She blinked, wondering what she had seen—wondering if she had been mistaken—and a memory of an earlier time abruptly resurfaced.

● ● ●

SHE IS LIVING *on the streets of Los Angeles, still making her home in the barrio. Johnny has been dead three years now, and she is no longer a child. She is a young woman—much stronger and smarter, much more experienced. She has been tested many times since Johnny taught her how to defend herself, and his lessons have saved her each time. All who live in the neighborhood she calls her own know her by now; she is the one they look to for leadership and protection. She is feared and respected; she is a force to be reckoned with.*

She walks the streets when she chooses, but never in a set pattern. She goes out both day and night, a soldier on patrol. Even the mutants keep their distance from her. They are not afraid of her; they are simply unwilling to put themselves in her path. The arrangement is simple; she leaves them alone and they leave her alone. A few, a reckless few, will test her limits from time to time. They will attack her people; they will pillage her stores. The results are always the same. She tracks them down and disposes of them.

Her life is full, but mostly pointless. She can never win the battle she is waging. There are too many of them, and only one of her. Still, it is all she knows and all she can think to do. So she continues.

Yet on this day, as she walks her streets—searching, watching, and waiting for the inevitable—she encounters someone she has never seen before. At first, she is not even sure what she is looking at. It appears to be a man, yet the edges are unclear and shimmer like something made of water disturbed. She does not look away, however; she continues to concentrate and, finally, the man takes on a definite shape.

Now she studies him closely. He stands in the shadows to one side between the buildings. He is big, but not threatening. She cannot explain why that is, but she feels it. She cannot make out his features, so she walks over to him to see what he will do. He does nothing. He stands where he is and waits for her.

"Angel of the streets," he greets her in a low, rumbling voice that comes from somewhere so deep down inside him that she cannot imagine how it climbs free. "Do you walk in shadows or in light this day?"

She smiles despite herself. "I always walk in light, amigo. ¿Quién eres?"

He steps out of the shadows now, and she sees that he is Native American, his features blunt and strong, his skin copper, his hair jet black and braided. He wears heavy boots and combat fatigues of a sort she has never seen, and the patches on his shoulders are of lightning bolts and crosses. One hand holds a long black staff carved with strange symbols from top to bottom.

His smile is warm. "I am called Two Bears, little Angel," he tells her.

"O'olish Amaneh, in the language of my people. I am Sinnissippi, but my people are all gone, dead now several hundred years. I am the last. So I try to make the most of my efforts."

She nods. "Is that what you are doing here?"

"In part. I arrived last night from other, less friendly places, searching for a place to hide. Those who hunt me are very persistent. They dislike the idea that there is only one of me. They would prefer that there be none."

"Los Angeles is not particularly friendly, amigo," she says, glancing around out of habit. "It may look it, but what lives here is only resting up for the next attack. There are Freaks of the worst sort. There are street gangs. There are things I cannot even give names to. You might be better off in a smaller, quieter place."

"I might be," he agrees. "I will find out when I leave. But I need to speak with you first. I came to do that, as well."

She hides her surprise, wondering how he would even know of her. "As you wish. But we will not do so here. Are you hungry? Have you eaten today?"

He has not, and so they go to a place where she knows there is food to be salvaged, and they carry the packets to a small open square and sit on stone benches to eat while the sun, hot enough to melt iron, sinks slowly into the maze of buildings that lie between them and the ocean.

"Who hunts you?" she asks him after a few minutes of chewing in silence. She regards him carefully. "Who would dare?"

He smiles at the compliment. "Many more than you would think. Mostly demons and the once-men in their service. Do you know of them?"

She does not, and so he tells her of the history of the Great Wars and of the source of the destruction that has changed life for all of them. He tells her of the Word and the Void and the battle they have waged since the beginning of time. He tells her of how life is a balance between good and evil, and how each is always attempting to tip the scales.

"Each side uses servants to aid its efforts. The Void uses demons, black soulless monsters that seek only to destroy. The Word uses its Knights, paladins sent to thwart the efforts of the demons. Once, they were mostly successful. But humans are an unpredictable, volatile

species, and in the end they fell victim to their own excesses, fostered by
the work of the Void's demons. They succumbed, and civilization succumbed with them."

She doesn't know if she believes him or not; certainly she thinks his
story is as much fable as truth. But the way he tells it lends it the weight
of truth, and she finds herself believing despite her reservations. His
words provide an explanation she finds plausible for all the horrific
things that have happened to the world. She has always known that it
is more than it seems, that the conflict between nations, between peoples,
between beliefs, is augmented in a way she doesn't understand.

"I serve the Lady, who is the voice of the Word," he continues. "It is
given to me to find a handful who will attempt to restore the balance
once more. For a long time, it wasn't possible; the lunacy and rage were
too great to be overcome. But enough time has passed, and now there is
a chance it can be done. Are you interested in serving?"

She is caught off guard by his question, and she stares at him in surprise. "My place is here, with my people," she answers.

"Your people are no longer confined to a small part of a large city," he
tells her. "Your people are the people of the world, near and far. If you
would make a difference, you must look beyond your own neighborhood.
A balance restored in one small place is not enough to change anything.
In the end, it will fail and become a part of the larger madness. It will be
consumed."

She knows this is so. She has been feeling it for some time. She fights
a losing battle because the larger world continues to encroach. But she is
afraid to lose even this; it is all she has left.

"What is it you want me to do?" she asks finally.

The big man leans forward. "It is the Lady who seeks your help. She
would have you become a Knight of the Word. She would have you enter
into her service and give over your life to restoring the balance. She
would have you do battle against the demons and their minions, against
the evil they inflict. She would give you this."

He lifts up the black staff, which has been resting against the bench
beside him. She has forgotten about it since she first saw him holding it.
Now she looks at it closely, sees how deep and pervasive are the carvings
on its surface, how they dominate the sheen of its polished wood. She has
never seen anything like the staff. It attracts her in a way she thought

nothing ever could again. When he holds it out to her, she takes it from him because she thinks that maybe it belongs to her.

"You are to keep it with you always. It is your sword and shield. It will protect you from the things that you hunt and that, in turn, hunt you. It is a talisman of powerful magic. Nothing can stand against it. But its power is finite; it is directly dependent on your own strength. Grow tired, and it will grow tired, too. Grow careless or lose heart, and you will be at risk even with the staff."

"What does it do?" she asks him.

"You will discover that when you use it. You will know instinctively."

She is still not decided about whether she will agree, but then he tells her of the slave camps, of the raids that have already begun on the compounds, and of the fate of humans who are taken captive, and she makes her choice. When he leaves her, she is holding the staff, her new life still only a faint glimmer on the horizon of her understanding, a mystery she will have to unravel one day at a time.

She watches him walk away from her until he is standing in the shadows between the buildings where he first appeared to her, a big, motionless presence. Then a noise catches her attention, and she glances toward the sound out of reflex.

When she turns back again, he is gone. Something in the way he has disappeared—the quickness of it, perhaps—makes it feel as if he was never really there.

●　●　●

IT WAS NEARING midnight when Delloreen reached the storage complex and began a slow search of the pillaged units. She had tracked the woman Knight of the Word all the way from Anaheim, from the hotel lobby where she'd nearly had her, from the ruins of the city to the countryside north, a slow and arduous hunt. It had been difficult to do this, but not impossible. Delloreen could track anything that gave off a scent. She was blessed with animal instincts and habits, with feral abilities that gave her an advantage over others. Demons were humans made over, but she had always been more animal than human.

So when she pulled herself clear of the hotel rubble and began her hunt, she used her nose to smell out her quarry's scent, to find it amid all the others, to taste it, memorize it, and then follow after it. It was easy enough, even mixed in as it was with all the other scents. Hers was a distinctive scent, a Knight of the Word's peculiar scent, recognizable by a demon with Delloreen's abilities, there for the discovering if you knew how to look. Delloreen tracked her all the way to the camp, to where she had met the humans fleeing Findo Gask and his army, and then lost the scent. But after circling about, she had found it again, a solitary trail that meandered off into the woods.

The woman Knight had met someone there, deep in the trees. She was able to tell that much, even though she was unable to tell much else. Whoever the Knight had met had left no scent, no tracks, and no readable traces—nothing that would provide an identity. In the end, Delloreen concluded that it was a Faerie creature and that something of importance had taken place, since it had drawn the woman Knight away from the children.

Delloreen had tracked her down the dirt road to the paved crossroad and the storage facility. The trail went into the facility and ended. There were machine smells everywhere, raw and rank and difficult to sort through. Her quarry's scent disappeared in those. The demon ran up and down the paved road like a wolf, sniffing the ground, searching for tracks. She circled the entire complex twice, hunting carefully. But she found no trace of the woman Knight.

She went back into the complex and began to prowl through the units. Down on all fours, she worked her way along each row, through the discarded contents, in and out of the units, across the grounds and back again. Now and then, she caught a trace of the woman Knight's scent, but not enough of it to determine where she had gone. Another hunter might have given up, but Delloreen was relentless. The harder the search, the more satisfying the death that would signal its end. She was driven by thoughts of how that death would play itself out, how the woman Knight of the Word would be brought down, how she would beg for mercy, how she would gasp out her life.

When she smiled, her pointed teeth gleamed and her muzzle showed red. She flexed her claws and ran them softly over her scaly body. So sweet it would be when it happened.

It took her almost an hour to reach the units in the back and to discover the one with the false wall. The Knight had been so confident—or perhaps so hasty—that she had not bothered to close it up again. Delloreen read the absence of the ATV the woman had taken from marks on the floor. The reason for the intensity of the machine smells was revealed; her quarry had ridden the ATV out of here. But the machine left a distinct smell, one as easily recognizable as the woman Knight's own scent. It would be easy enough to track it if she left now and traveled quickly. Easy enough if she could match the other's speed and exceed her stamina.

But she would need a vehicle, something that would convey her as swiftly and surely as the woman Knight was conveyed.

She looked at the huge Harley Crawler sitting back in the shadows. She checked the engine bay and found it empty, but she caught a whiff of her quarry's scent and tracked it to where she had hidden the power cells. She carried the cells back, slipped them in place, and fired up the Harley's big engine. It caught with a roar that shook her to her bones.

She smiled as the vibrations filled her.

It would do.

24

K IRISIN WAITED AN entire week for Arissen Belloruus
to summon him. He remained patient, telling himself he
must not act in haste or out of frustration, that research of
the Elven histories and conferences with official advisers took time.
It wasn't as if the King didn't care what happened to the Ellcrys and
the Elven people; it was that he must be careful to do the right
thing. Kirisin saw it more clearly than the King did, of course; from
his perspective the decision to do what the Ellcrys had asked was
not debatable. But he was only a boy, and he lacked the experience
and wisdom of his elders.

He told himself all this, but even as he did so he was thinking
that he was dealing with a family of duplicitous cowards.

It was a terrible thing to believe, but ever since he had come to
the conclusion that both the King and Erisha had lied to him he had
been unable to think anything else. Erisha's betrayal was worse, because she was a Chosen. Being a Chosen bound them in ways that
even blood could not, and no Chosen had betrayed another in living
memory.

But Kirisin kept his anger in check and went about his business.

He worked in the gardens with the others, caring for the Ellcrys and the grounds in which she was rooted. He performed at the morning greetings and evening farewells. He smiled and joked with Biat and the others—although not with Erisha, who would barely look at him most of the time—trying his best to make it appear that nothing was amiss. Apparently, his efforts were successful. No one seemed to notice anything out of the ordinary, or said another word about what had happened.

The tree did not speak again. Kirisin was certain she would, that her need, so palpable when she had spoken to him, would require it. He willed it to happen each sunrise when he joined the others to wish her good morning and each sunset when they gathered to say good night. He prayed for it to happen, for some small exchange to take place, a reminder of what had passed between them, even a warning or admonition. But nothing happened. The Ellcrys remained silent.

In the times he was free to do what he wanted, he wrote in his journal of his thoughts and concerns, putting down everything he was struggling with, even his thoughts of the King and his daughter. He tried to imagine the King's thinking, to put himself in Arissen Belloruus's frame of mind so that he could better understand. But it was a miserable failure, a process to find a justification for what he did not believe. All it did was further convince him that something was terribly wrong and needed righting.

He thought to speak of it to his parents more times than he could count, but he could not bring himself to do so. He knew that if he voiced his concerns to them, they would act on their feelings, just as he had, and take the matter directly to the King. That would invite a disaster for which Kirisin did not want to be responsible. His parents were already suspect after their efforts to move a colony of Elves to Paradise. The King would have no patience with an intrusion of this sort, particularly if he was hiding something. The best Kirisin could do for them in this situation was to leave them out of it.

He kept hoping Simralin would come home. He could tell his sister what had happened and know that she would offer a thoughtful response. That was her nature; she was not given to rash acts and emotional outbursts like the rest of his family. Simralin would think it all through; she would know what was needed.

But the days passed and Simralin did not come home, the King did not summon him, the Ellcrys did not speak to him, and his thoughts grew steadily darker and more distressed as he carried out his Chosen duties in mechanical fashion and waited futilely for something to happen.

"You seem like your head is somewhere else lately," Biat told him at one point, squatting down beside him as he worked on the flower beds. "Is that business with the Ellcrys still bothering you?"

Overhead, the sun was high in the sky, a blazing orb burning down on the Cintra. There had been no rain in weeks. Everything was drying up, Kirisin thought, including his secret hopes.

"I've just been wondering how Simralin is," he replied.

"Better than most," Biat smirked. "She's the Tracker all the other Trackers wish they could be. Smart, beautiful, talented—everything you're not. Too bad for you."

Too bad indeed, thought Kirisin as his friend wandered away.

For a long time, he did not visit the tree alone at night as he had for so long. Part of him wanted to, but part of him was afraid to face her. He didn't know which prospect was worse—that she might not speak to him ever again or that she might, and no one would be there to see it or believe that it had happened. Finally, he could stand it no longer. Six nights into his fruitless vigil, when he was sure the others were asleep, he went to visit her. It was a moonlit night, and he found his way without difficulty and stood before her as a supplicant might before a shrine. Her silvery bark shimmered brightly, and the reflection of the moonlight brought out the crimson color of her leaves in startling relief. He stared at her reverentially, trying to think what more he could do. He knew he had to do something. He knew he couldn't wait any longer on the King or anyone else.

He walked up to her finally and placed the tips of his fingers on her smooth trunk. *Speak to me*, he thought. *Tell me what to do.*

But the Ellcrys did not respond, even though he waited a long time, speaking softly, telling her his thoughts, trying to break through the wall of her silence. If she heard what he was saying, if she even knew he was there, she gave no sign of it. When he had exhausted himself and his efforts had yielded him nothing, he gave it up and went off to sleep.

The following day was hot and dry, and as he worked in the gardens with the others, Kirisin felt the last of his patience slip away. It had been a week now since he had gone to Arissen Belloruus, and despite his resolve not to act in haste or frustration, he did. It was a precipitous act triggered by Erisha. After days of ignoring him, he caught her looking at him when she thought he wasn't paying attention. There was nothing overtly offensive about the act, nothing that should have set him off, but that was the effect it had. He climbed to his feet, sweaty and tired and mad enough to eat the dirt he was digging up, and stalked over to where she was standing next to Raya, ostensibly instructing the other girl on the pruning of callisto vines. Erisha saw him coming, read the look on his face, and tried to move away. But he would have none of it. He went after her, caught up to her, and blocked her way.

"What's the matter, Erisha?" he snapped, hands on hips, face flushed and taut. "Is your conscience bothering you, cousin? Is that why you are sneaking looks at me?"

She faced him down for a moment, then brushed quickly at her chestnut hair and turned away. "Grow up, Kirisin."

He was back in front of her immediately, blocking her path. "How about this? I'll grow up when you stop lying. That's a reasonable trade, isn't it? Let's start right now. You tell me the truth about your father, and I'll start acting like an adult."

"I don't know what you are talking about." She tried again to move past him, and again he stopped her. "Get out of my way, Kirisin. If you keep this up, I'll have you disciplined."

"Go ahead!" He shouted the words and threw up his hands, ignoring the others, who were beginning to turn toward them to see what was happening. "Do it now! Do it in front of the others! Let's tell them all about it and see what they think!"

She reached for his hands and pulled them down, her face inches from his own. "You stop this right now!" Cold rage etched her words in ice. "What do you think you are doing? Maybe you better go home for the rest of the day and see if you don't have a fever!"

"Maybe you better stop poisoning your mind with your own lies and try healing yourself with the truth!"

He shoved his face so close that their noses were almost touching. His voice dropped to a whisper. "This is what I know. What I know, Erisha! Not what I imagined or made up out of thin air, but what I know! The Ellcrys spoke to me a week ago today. She told me that she is in danger. She told me that something bad is going to happen. She told me that she would have to be placed in an Elfstone called a Loden, which will be found by using three other Elfstones called seeking-Stones. She told me that if this doesn't happen she won't survive what is coming and neither will the Elves."

His hands seized her wrists, and he held her fast. "You knew this and you told your father about it. You did it secretly, but I found out because when I went to your father to tell him of the tree speaking to me, I did not mention the seeking-Stones. But your father did. He knew all about the three finding the one. He knew! That couldn't have happened if you hadn't told him before I did. Admit it!"

He waited, eyes locked on hers. "All right," she whispered back finally. "I told him. I waited until you left the gardens, and then I sneaked away and told him. I didn't want him to hear it from you; I am the leader of the Chosen. It was necessary that it come from me. Now will you let me go?"

Kirisin stared at her in silence. She was still lying. He was so angry now that he thought he might strike her. Instead, he said, "I want you to take a walk with me, Erisha. Away from the others, where they can't hear what we say."

She shook her head quickly. "Not when you're like this."

He released her wrists, stepped back, and folded his arms. "All I want is for you to listen to me. But if you want to continue this conversation here, then let's bring the others over, and that way they won't have to work so hard at eavesdropping."

Erisha shot a quick glance at the other Chosen and saw all of them watching intently, tools lowered, eyes expectant. She hesitated, and then nodded her agreement.

"Finish your work," she called over to them. "Kirisin and I have something we have to discuss. I'll be right back."

She took his arm at the elbow and practically dragged him from the clearing and into the woods beyond, taking a narrow, little-used path that led to the bluffs overlooking the valleys west. He let himself be led, content to wait until they were well away from the others before he had it out with her. Whatever else happened this day, he was going to get to the truth of things. If she refused to give it to him willingly, he would pry it out of her.

When they were well into the trees, she wheeled back angrily and poked him in the chest. "What happens between my father and me isn't any business of yours, *cousin*." She emphasized the word. "You have no right to question me about him."

Kirisin held his ground. "I do when he lies to me. Or when you lie. Like you just did again back there. I spoke to Biat after I came back from your home. You never left the gardens. You told your father, all right. But it wasn't then; it was much earlier. That's why the Ellcrys asked me why she had been forsaken. That's why she said to me that I had to listen to her: because even *she*—meaning you—hadn't. She told you everything before she ever spoke to me, and you did nothing about it. Why are you lying to me?"

Her face was hard and angry. "I'm not lying!"

But he could tell by the way she said it that she was. He gave her a pitying look. "You know, when this is all over, Erisha, you're going to have to live with the consequences. You seem to think nothing will happen to the Ellcrys, but what if it does? What if she dies? You took an oath to care for her, just like the rest of us. How will you justify failing her?"

She shook her head defensively. "I won't fail her."

"You already have. So have I. All of us have. We haven't done a thing to help her! She has begged for our help, pleaded for it, but we've ignored her. I don't know about you, but I can't live with that. It means something to me to be a Chosen. I accepted that duty, and I won't neglect it just because you or your father or anyone else decides it's all right to do so. What's wrong with you? Don't you feel any obligation for her safety? Why are you acting like this?"

Her lips were compressed into a tight line, and she was still shaking her head. She tried to speak and couldn't.

"Well, you have to do what you think is right," he continued, stepping close again. "You have to answer to yourself for your

choices. But I am going back to your father and demand that he do
something. And if that fails, I will go to the High Council and ask
them! And if that fails, I will go to anyone who will listen. In fact, I'll
start with Biat and the others. Right after I walk away from here, I'll
go straight to them and tell them what you and your father are
doing!"

"You better not, Kirisin!" she said with a hiss. "You don't know
what my father would do to you for that!"

"Oh, so now I'm being threatened? I am not like you, Erisha. I am
not afraid of your father!"

"I'm not afraid of him, either!" she snapped, tears springing to her
eyes.

"You're scared to death of him," he said, and realized suddenly
that it was true, that for reasons he didn't understand, she was.

"You . . . !" she started, but couldn't finish. She had collapsed inside herself, and she lowered her head; her hands came up to hide
the tears and distress. "I hate you," she said softly.

"No, you don't."

"I do!" she insisted.

"Tell me the truth," he pressed.

"You don't understand anything!" she shouted loud enough that
he backed away a step.

"Then why don't you help me understand? Tell my why everyone is lying to me!"

She threw up her hands, her hair flying everywhere. "I can't tell
you! My father . . ." She choked on the words as they left her mouth.
"I mean, I . . . I can't!"

"He said you couldn't tell me, didn't he?" Kirisin guessed. "Isn't
that right? Admit it."

She looked at him, defeated. "You won't give up, will you? You
won't quit asking until you know." She took a long, slow breath and
exhaled. "All right, I'll tell you. But if you tell anyone else, I'll say
you're lying."

It was an empty threat, but there was no reason to point that out.
"Just say it, Erisha," he said.

She compressed her lips, tightening her resolve. "I didn't want to pretend I didn't know about the Ellcrys, but my father said I had to. He said I couldn't tell anyone." She wiped at the tears. "He is not just my father; he is the King. What was I supposed to do?"

Kirisin didn't say anything; he simply waited on her. After a moment, she glanced up, as if to make sure he was still listening, and then just as quickly looked away.

"I love what I do, Kirisin, even if you don't think so. I believe in what I do. I wouldn't trade it for anything, and I . . ." She trailed off. "Sometimes I go to see her at night, just like you do. I like being close to her, being alone with her. I can feel her watching me. I know that's silly, but that's how it seems. I sit in the gardens and just . . . be with her. She never did anything to let me know she was aware of me until two weeks ago. That was when she told me about the danger that was coming and about putting her inside the Loden for protection."

She shook her head helplessly. "I didn't know what to do. I had to tell someone right away. I decided to go to my father. I begged him to do something. At first I thought he was going to help. But then he said it was more complicated than I realized. He said that I didn't understand what I was asking, that I didn't know enough about the Loden to appreciate what would happen if he did as I asked. He said we had to wait until my term as a Chosen was over. Once I was no longer a Chosen, then he would act."

She held up her hands as he started to speak. "I know. I told him I didn't see how we could wait that long. But my father said that in terms of an Ellcrys lifetime, it was nothing. The Ellcrys had been alive for hundreds of years. A few months in the tree's life was little more than what a day would be to us. Less, maybe. It wasn't necessary to act right away."

"He can't know that," Kirisin objected.

"What he *believes* he can't know," Erisha said wearily, "is what might happen to me if he doesn't make me wait."

Kirisin started to respond and then stopped. "What do you mean?"

"I mean that there is more to this than you or I know. The Loden is an Elfstone, a talisman of magic. My father says there is great risk to the one who uses it. He wouldn't reveal the nature of that risk, only that he wasn't going to allow me to take it. I told him I wasn't afraid. I told him that I was the leader of the Chosen, and that I was the one who had to take it."

She saw the look on his face and scowled. "You can believe me or not, Kirisin, but that was what I said to him. It made him furious. He told me that I didn't know what I was talking about. He said that if I persisted in this, he would force me to resign my position as one of the Chosen."

She shook her head helplessly. "When I tried to object, he shouted me down. He was so angry! I have never seen him so angry. What could I do? He is my father! He was insistent about it!"

A long silence settled between them. They stared at each other, neither ready to say anything more right away. Kirisin was unsure how he should feel. He was furious at the King, but on the other hand he understood how Arissen Belloruus would want to protect his only daughter from what he perceived to be the danger of using the Loden. What bothered him most, however, was a nagging suspicion that the King might not have told Erisha everything he knew, that he might be holding something back. He had been duplicitous with Kirisin; there was nothing to say he was being any less so with her.

"What are you going to do?" she asked him finally.

In point of fact, he didn't know. He had thought knowing the truth of things would give him the answer to that question, but it hadn't. He was as much adrift now as he had been before.

"How does your father know that the Loden might be a danger to the user?" he asked.

She shrugged. "When I told him what the Ellcrys had said, he had me wait while he sent old Culph to study the histories to see what they said about it. It was after Culph had done so that he decided I couldn't have anything to do with the matter. He found out something about what would happen if the Loden were used, but as I said, he wouldn't tell me."

Kirisin thought it through some more. Then he said to her, "Don't you want to know what that something is?"

She shook her head doubtfully. "I'm not sure if I do or not."

"At least you would know how dangerous it really is to use the Loden. You would know if your father is right to forbid you."

"Maybe."

"You said you took your Chosen oath seriously. If that's so, don't you have to find out what you're risking if you try to help the Ellcrys?" He paused. "She asked you for help first, Erisha. Not me. She didn't ask me until it must have seemed that you had abandoned her. But you were the one she wanted."

Erisha looked miserable. "I know who she asked, Kirisin. What are you suggesting I do?"

"Have a look at the histories. That way you can make up your own mind. I'll help you. I don't expect you to do this alone. Maybe we'll find the answer faster if there are two of us searching."

She was silent again, thinking. "I don't know."

"Remember when we were kids?" he asked impulsively. He reached out and touched her lightly on the shoulder. "We'd chase all through the woods outside your house and pretend we were on an adventure. Sometimes we would do it at night, when the woods were dark and scary. We pretended we were looking for secret treasure. We were friends, then. I know it doesn't seem like it right now, but I think we still are. I don't know why your father is so worried about what might happen to you, but I want to help you find out. Why don't you give me a chance? Don't you want to know the reason?"

She stared fixedly at him, as if not certain who he was. Then she said, "We would have to sneak into the room where the histories are stored. Old Culph is poking around in there all the time. We would have to get in when he was sleeping or he would want to know what we're doing and would probably tell my father." She paused, thinking. "But I know how to get into the room, even after it's locked."

She was getting caught up in the idea of doing something, of shedding the burden of guilt she had been carrying for obeying her father's wishes and ignoring her duty as a Chosen.

"Are you willing to do that?" he pressed, wanting to make sure she wouldn't change her mind. "If you decide to disobey him, he will probably be pretty angry."

"He will be furious," she agreed, looking doubtful again.

"But you can't worry about that right now," he insisted. He watched her face, measuring her resolve. "Not until we find out what he knows that we don't."

She shook her head. "I suppose not." Her eyes lifted to meet his. "No, not until we find out."

The doubt he had seen a moment earlier was gone. He exhaled sharply in relief. "Can we do it tonight?" he asked.

She nodded, determination plain on her face. "We can do it tonight."

● ● ●

THE REMAINDER OF the day passed slowly for Kirisin. He kept as busy as he could in the gardens, his thoughts drifting constantly to what Erisha had revealed to him. His emotions were mixed. On the one hand, he could understand her father's reluctance to place his only child in danger. On the other, she was the leader of the Chosen and the one the Ellcrys had asked for help. It seemed to him that both her father's and her own duties were clear, but he didn't know how he would act if he were King and Erisha were his daughter, so he tried not to judge them—even as he found himself doing so. Kirisin had always looked up to and admired Arissen Belloruus, but he didn't think he would ever feel that way again. How he would feel about Erisha remained to be seen. It would depend on what happened this night. It would depend on how she reacted to whatever they learned from the Elven histories.

One thing was certain. His parents would be furious if they were to learn that their cousin was willing to endanger the entire Elven nation to protect his daughter. Which is why Kirisin would have to keep it from them, since he knew that they would take the matter right to the King and how that was likely to end for all of them.

Sunset was a long time coming, and he had more than sufficient time to mull things over. By then, he was sick of thinking about it and anxious to act.

But first there was dinner with his parents—with whom he had arranged to spend the night—talk of Simralin and her anticipated arrival home, and household chores he was expected to carry out when visiting. He went to bed early, feigning weariness, and slept restlessly for several hours before waking an hour before midnight. After listening to be sure the rest of the household was asleep, he rose and dressed. Taking his long knife and sandals, he climbed out the window and disappeared into the darkness without a sound.

The Elven community was quiet, most of the people either in bed or on their way. The sky was overcast and shed only a little light, so Kirisin was forced to rely on his Elven senses to help him pick his way through the blackness. The air was still and warm, the night cloaked in silence and hushed expectancy. He moved cautiously down the narrow paths that led to the Belloruus home, picking his way and listening for sounds that would alert him to another's presence. He heard none, and he arrived at the edges of the King's home without incident.

Crouching in the bushes at the prearranged spot, just beyond the perimeter where the guards patrolled, he waited for midnight and Erisha.

Several times it occurred to him that no one knew where he was. If anything happened to him, no one would know where to look for him. It was a chilling thought—that the Elven King might do something to silence him—but he could not help thinking about it in light of what he now knew about the man. If he were willing to risk endangering the Ellcrys to protect his daughter, he wouldn't have much trouble finding an excuse for removing a troublesome boy.

It made him wonder. Would Erisha have gone back on her word and betrayed him to her father?

He was still wondering when she appeared out of the darkness, dressed as he was, a shadowy presence in the gloom. "This way," she whispered, putting her mouth right next to his ear. "The guards won't see us. Their eyes look elsewhere for the next few minutes. Hurry!"

He followed her through the trees, doing his best to place his feet exactly where she did, casting anxious glances all about—for the Home Guard and whoever or whatever else kept the King safe. But no one appeared and no alarms sounded, and in only minutes they were at a side door that gave soundlessly at Erisha's touch and admitted them into the Belloruus house.

Kirisin stood just inside the doorway, breathing hard despite himself. Erisha had stopped in front of him, apparently listening, making sure that it was safe. Satisfied, she took his arm and pulled him ahead. They went slowly, passing through rooms lit by tiny candles that gave just enough light to permit them to find their way without falling over the furniture. Once or twice, Erisha stopped and listened anew before proceeding. They reached a door that opened onto the stairway that led to the library housing the Elven histories and started down. Erisha was carrying a smokeless torch now to light their way. The air grew cooler and the silence deeper. They went down several flights until they reached the bottom level and stood in a small anteroom with a worktable and several chairs. A pair of doors were set into earthen walls shored up with beams and siding.

Erisha walked to the door on the right and opened it carefully, thrusting the torch inside for a quick look. Satisfied, she turned back to Kirisin and beckoned him forward. They entered the room, which was filled with shelves and cabinets crammed with books and papers, all marked by printed labels and numbers. Erisha moved to the back of the room, casting about as she went, searching. She stopped finally and pointed to a set of books that were ancient and dust-covered, bound in leather and labeled in gilt. She took down the first two volumes and passed one to him.

"These are the histories," she whispered. "Do you want to carry them outside to the table?"

He shook his head. "Let's stay in here."

Together, they sat cross-legged on the wooden slat floor, placed the torch between them, opened the books, and began to read.

It was a long, slow process. The order in which the contents of the books had been recorded was confusing; it didn't seem to be chronological or by subject. The writing on the pages was small and cramped, and many of the words were unfamiliar. Kirisin quickly decided it would take too long to read everything and suggested to Erisha that they search for key words such as *Ellcrys* and *Elfstones*, stopping to read the text when they found either. They did so and were able to turn the pages more quickly, but still found only infrequent mention of either word.

Worse, they did not once come across even the smallest reference to the Loden.

They finished the first two books and moved on to the next pair. Time was slipping away. Kirisin found himself glancing at Erisha, who was absorbed in her reading and paying no attention to him. He was surprised that she had come around so completely, but gratified, too. He was thinking better of her already. If they found something and she acted on it, he might even be willing to reassess . . .

"Looking for something?" a voice growled from out of the darkness of the doorway.

Kirisin felt his heart stop. He met Erisha's frightened gaze as her head jerked up, and he could not look away.

25

HANDS SHOOK HAWK'S shoulders hard and brought him awake with a start.

"Wake up, Bird-Man," he heard Panther say.

He blinked his sleep-fogged eyes, trying to focus. It took him a moment to orient himself. He was still on the floor of the common room where he had fallen asleep last night. He could hear voices in the background, hushed and filled with wonder. He sensed joy emanating from their rise and fall.

"Hey!" Panther shook him again, and this time he looked up into the other's eyes. A faint, ironic smile greeted him. "Better come see what your dog is up to."

Cheney. He sat up quickly—too quickly—and everything started spinning. He sat with his head between his legs for a moment, waiting for things to quit moving.

"You worse off than that animal," Panther snorted derisively. "Maybe you got some of what he don't. Get up, will you? You want to miss it?"

Hawk blinked, the spinning stopped, and he looked at Panther. "Miss what?" he asked.

"Over there," the other said, pointing.

The remaining Ghosts were crowded around Cheney, who was on his feet and lapping water from a bowl. He looked a bit ragged around the edges, but his wounds from yesterday's battle had all but disappeared.

Owl wheeled, dark eyes intense. "How did this happen?" she asked, a mix of amazement and deep suspicion evident on her face. "We all saw it. He was dying, Hawk."

Hawk shook his head. He was as confused as she was, although for different reasons. He knew what had happened, knew the part he had played in it, but didn't understand how it could possibly be.

"That dog, that's a devil dog," Panther murmured, looking over at Cheney, his brow furrowed. "Ain't no way he should be walking around. He was all tore up, couldn't hardly draw a breath. Now he's moving like he's just the same as always." He shook his head. "Yeah, he's a devil dog, all right."

Candle glanced up from where she knelt beside Cheney, saw that Hawk was awake, and rushed over to give him a big hug. "Isn't it wonderful?" she whispered.

Hawk guessed it was. He guessed it was a miracle of sorts, although he thought it was something else, too—something more personal and more mysterious, perhaps, than even a miracle. He wanted to understand, but at the same time he was afraid of what he might learn. Cheney had indeed been dying, so far gone that he barely knew that it was Hawk who cradled his big head, his eyes glazed and his breathing harsh and ragged. There was nothing anyone could do for him, nothing that could save him, and yet . . .

Yet Hawk had saved him.

How had he done that?

He detached himself from Candle, climbed to his feet, and walked over to where Cheney lay quietly in place, his drink finished. The gray eyes shifted to find Hawk as he approached, no longer glazed, but sharp and clear. Hawk knelt next to him, running his hands over the thick coat, across the grizzled head, pausing to scratch the heavy ears. Every injury had healed. There were ridges of scar beneath the fur—as if the injuries had all occurred a long time ago—but Cheney's coat was virtually unmarked.

Hawk looked down at the big dog, wondering if he were imagining his part in all of this. Maybe he only thought he had done something by wishing for it. Maybe the injuries hadn't been as severe as they all presumed, more superficial than they seemed, and . . .

He stopped himself. He was being foolish. He hadn't imagined anything about those injuries. No, something had happened last night, something between himself and Cheney that only they had been witness to, something that he didn't yet understand.

Or might never understand.

He rose, feeling alien to himself. He wasn't the same person anymore. He was someone else entirely because only someone else, someone he didn't know anything about, could have done for Cheney what he had done.

"Look at him," Panther murmured. "He knows something, but he ain't telling. Devil dogs don't ever tell."

Hawk put them all to work then, deciding that it was better to just get on with things rather than sit around puzzling over mysteries. Given yesterday's events, he knew instinctively what was needed. For the next few days, they would live aboveground on one of the upper floors of the building. It wasn't as safe as he would have liked, but nothing felt very safe at the moment. He delegated Fixit and Chalk to choose a set of rooms that could be closed off and defended. They would move today, taking with them what they could carry of stores and necessities, and leave the rest for later. They would leave the carcass of the giant centipede, as well. It was too heavy and too cumbersome to try to move, and there was little reason to do so in any case. He hoped there weren't any more of these monsters, that there had been only the one, a mutation that had climbed out of the sewers and underground tunnels. Where it had come from and what had caused its mutation were mysteries he doubted any of them would ever solve. But at least they knew now what they should look for if the killings and mutilations of the Lizards and Croaks and other tribes continued.

As he joined the others for a quick breakfast, served cold and salvaged from amid the debris of the kitchen area, he found himself thinking anew of the signs he had missed. He should have been more alert after encountering the savaged Lizard and hearing of the dead Croaks. He should have known to keep his guard up after Candle's sense of danger in the basement of the old warehouse where they'd retrieved the purification tablets. He felt certain now that the basement had been the centipede's lair. It must have nested there, then gone out searching for food. Somehow it had tracked Tiger and the Cats, caught them off guard, and killed them before they could defend themselves. Then it had tracked the Ghosts back to their underground home, wormed its way in through the old air ducts, and dug down through the ceiling.

He shook his head, a mental image forming of a nightmarish creature, a monster that could burrow through steel mesh, plaster, and concrete.

It made him wonder anew at Sparrow's bravery in standing up to it to protect Owl and Squirrel. He glanced over at her, making sure she was still the same little girl, that she wasn't somehow changed in the way he felt himself changed. She sat eating quietly, not saying much, her face composed beneath her mop of straw-colored hair. She looked the same, but he didn't think she was. How could she be?

She caught him looking. He smiled and gave her a wink. She smiled back uncertainly and then went on eating.

When they were finished, he sent Chalk and Fixit off on their search for new quarters and Panther and Bear down to the waterfront to find River and the Weatherman. After what had happened, he couldn't bring himself to leave the girl and her grandfather out there unprotected, plague or not. He would isolate them in one of the upstairs rooms, somewhere they would be as safe as he could make them. Maybe Owl would know what to do to help the old man, once she saw the symptoms. If not, they would simply do the best they could for him until it was time to leave the city.

And they were leaving, that much he knew for certain. He had been debating it for days now, but the unexpected appearance of the giant centipede had decided him. Staying in the city was too dangerous. Things were changing, some of them visible, some that he simply sensed. He didn't think they should be around to see how it would all turn out. It was time to fulfill the vision, even if he wasn't certain how to do so. It was time to take his family and find the home the vision had promised them.

That meant convincing Tessa to come with them. He didn't know how he was going to do that, either. He only knew he would have to find a way. He would meet with her tonight, at their pre-arranged place, and he would tell her what he was going to do. Then he would convince her in whatever way he could, using whatever means were necessary, to come away with him.

He went to work with Owl and Sparrow, gathering up the supplies and equipment they would need to take with them, making preparations for the move upstairs. Chalk and Fixit returned shortly after to say they had found a suitable place. On going with them to inspect it, Hawk found it adequate, a series of rooms with more than one exit, not too far up, not too exposed, a perfect compromise. It wasn't as secure as the underground, but then the underground hadn't turned out to be all that secure, either.

By the time Panther and Bear returned carrying the Weatherman on a makeshift litter with River trailing after, they were ready to install the girl and her grandfather in a room that was physically isolated from the others, but still close enough that they could be protected. The Weatherman looked the same, still covered in purple splotches, still feverish and unresponsive. River hugged Hawk and told him how much it meant to her that he was doing this, and he hugged her back and reminded her again that they were family and must look out for one another. Panther slouched around muttering that they had all lost their minds, that taking chances was becoming a way of life and he, for one, wanted no part of it. Then he pitched in with the rest of them to haul supplies up the stairs to their new quarters.

It took them all day to finish their work. By then, Owl had examined the Weatherman and done some more reading on types of plagues. She thought she understood the nature of the one the old man had contracted and how best to treat it. She instructed River on what to do, using a combination of medicines she already had, if only in limited quantities, liquids to keep him for dehydrating and cold cloths intended to bring down his fever. It was rudimentary, but it was all they had. Hawk promised to speak with Tessa about it when he saw her that night, already knowing that it wouldn't make any difference, that he was not going to allow her to go back inside the compound, even for additional medicines.

By sunset, the Ghosts had everything pretty much in order and had settled in for the night. Cheney was back guarding the doors, his strength returned at least in part, and Hawk had established a schedule for two-hour guard shifts until dawn. There was no point in taking chances, even knowing how reliable Cheney was. It would only be for a few days, and then they would be gone from the city and everything would change. He tried thinking of what that meant and failed. He knew he couldn't hope to foresee everything, even though he desperately wanted to end the uncertainty. He would have to take their departure and their journey one day at a time and hope that he would discover what he needed to know along the way. It was a big risk, but he had the feeling that staying put and hoping for the best was a bigger risk.

Sometimes, you just had to trust in things. He believed that if they stayed together and looked out for one another, that would be enough.

It was deep twilight when he left the building for his meeting with Tessa. From the weapons locker, he took one of the prods and a pair of viper-pricks along with his hunting knife. He considered taking Cheney, as well, but he was worried that the big dog might not be fully recovered and did not wish to put him in harm's way until he was. He had made this journey many times, and he knew how to go in order to stay safe. He would just have to be extra careful.

"Keep everyone inside," he told Owl, bending close so that the others couldn't hear. "If anything goes wrong, don't separate—stick together. I'll try to be quick."

She gave a small nod, but her eyes reflected her misgivings. "What will you do if she won't come back with you?"

He hadn't talked to her about what he intended, but Owl could read his thoughts as easily as she could read her books. She knew what he was going to attempt and what he was up against.

He smiled reassuringly. "She'll come."

"Promise me that if she chooses not to—no, wait, let me finish—

if she chooses not to, you will come back anyway. You won't go into the compound and you won't hang around waiting for her to change her mind."

Her eyes searched his, waiting. When he hesitated, she said, "We need you, Hawk. We can't do this without you. Promise me."

He understood. He bit his lip, looked at his feet, then said, "I'll come back, I promise."

He said his good-byes to the others, went out through the heavy door that Fixit had rigged to protect their common room, and descended the stairs to the street. Standing just inside the door, he looked out at the shadowy shapes of the derelict vehicles and rubble mounds.

Then, taking a deep breath, he set off toward the compound, wanting to get this over with. He moved to the center of the street, giving a sweeping glance to his surroundings as he went, but not slowing as he did so. He had an uneasy feeling about being out here alone in the dark in violation of his own rule that no one should ever go out alone at night. He shivered as the wind blew in off the sound, chill and cutting. It felt wrong going without Cheney, despite what he had told himself. But there was no help for it. He would have to rely on his own instincts.

But his instincts weren't like Cheney's.

Besides which, he was tired and preoccupied.

Which was probably why he missed seeing the shadowy figure standing in the doorway across the street, watching him go.

• • •

THE WALK UP First Avenue toward the compound was still and hollow-feeling and filled with shadows and ghosts. Hawk held the prod ready to use in front of him and stayed in the center of the street, away from places where predators might lurk. He kept up a steady scan of his surroundings, searching out movement and strangeness and unexpected sounds that could signal danger, but found nothing. He knew he wasn't alone in the night, but it felt to him as if he might be. He was content with that, and his thoughts drifted.

Mostly, they found their way to mulling over what had happened with Cheney the night before. He could not stop thinking about it. He kept remembering how he had begged for a miracle and how that miracle had happened. He kept remembering the way his body had changed when the healing had begun, turning hot from the inside out—how a kind of energy had flowed out of him and into the big dog. He kept remembering how Cheney had responded, almost instantaneously, and then begun to recover right before his eyes. Had he really been responsible? Accepting this changed everything he believed about himself and his place in the world. If in fact he had healed the big dog, then he was possessed of a power that transcended anything he had imagined possible. It meant that he really didn't know himself at all, and that was disturbing. He had never been anything special, never anything but an ordinary boy trying to survive in a world where boys were eaten up and spit out regularly. Now he had to consider the possibility that he was something more than a boy with a special vision.

He thought about that for a moment, wondering if it were possible that the vision was in some way connected to what had happened to Cheney. Even accepting that Cheney had been healed because of something he had done or something inside him that had responded to his desperate need to help his dog, it was a stretch to believe that this had anything to do with his vision. But he couldn't quite discount it, either. The two marked him as different when nothing else did, so it was possible that they had a similar source.

But what was the nature of that source? Had he been born with it? Had he acquired it? Everything about it—whatever *it* was—was a mystery.

He slowed, still aware of his surroundings, but caught up in his exploration of what might be the truth. It occurred to him that he had never experienced a clear and complete elucidation of his vision. It had only come to him in pieces and only occasionally since that first time. It had never revealed itself fully, not even enough so that he knew where it was supposed to take him and those he led. He had trusted in it, but in truth he had never really understood it.

Did that make him a fool? He had never thought so, had never believed he was being misled or deceiving himself about what he was meant to do. He had acted on faith, and that had always seemed enough. But a closer examination gave him pause. Following a vision that was incomplete and unsupported by anything concrete did not seem all that intelligent.

And yet he believed in it. Even now, despite everything—or maybe even because of it—he still believed.

Ahead, something moved in the shadows off to one side, something that walked on two legs. He slowed further, moved away from it, and then watched it fade back into the darkness and disappear. Another creature of the night, like himself. Hunting. Trying to find its way, perhaps. Seeking a place in the world, just as he was.

He shook his head. He was being foolish with that sort of poetic thinking. Everything was predator or prey. Everything hunted or was being hunted. The only unknown at any given moment was your own place in the food chain. It was as simple as that.

He shrugged against the chill of the wind as he passed out of the shelter of the buildings and into the openness that surrounded the compound. He was too far away to be seen, but he would have to be more careful as he got closer, would have to make certain he blended in completely with his surroundings. The compound was still a dark featureless bulk ahead with only a scattering of lights visible against its black surface, tiny eyes looking out. He could hear voices, faint and distant. It always felt vaguely surreal, looking in from the outside, as if he were newly arrived from a faraway place. It always reminded him that he could never fit in.

He dropped into a crouch and began working his way toward the transportation shelter where Tessa would be waiting. He crossed the open ground in short spurts, pausing often to look at and listen to his surroundings—watchful, ready. But there was no sign of movement on the compound walls, no indication of anything out of the ordinary. He passed through a frozen landscape, empty and lifeless. Or seemingly so, like so much of the rest of the world. He wondered again how it had felt when the city was alive and bright with lights and filled with the sound of voices and laughter. He could not imagine it.

Off to one side, deep in the shadows, a scraping broke the veil of stillness, causing him to freeze in place. He waited, listening. But the sound was not repeated, and he saw nothing move. He waited some more, watching the lights on the walls of the compound, searching for any change in his surroundings.

Finally, satisfied that it was safe, he began to move forward once more.

The concrete apron surrounding the old bus station was clogged with piles of rubble, and he was able to move easily from one pile to the next with only brief moments in the open. It was dark enough that he couldn't be seen from the walls, so mostly he worried about what might be hiding close at hand. It was unlikely that predators would lie in wait here, a place so empty of life and so close to the compound walls. It was simply too dangerous and unproductive to do so. In all the times he had met Tessa, he had never once encountered a Freak, let alone a human being. He did not expect that to change tonight.

He reached the bus shelter and slipped noiselessly inside, hunkering down as he took a quick look around. Nothing. He turned to the steps leading to the underground tunnel door, easing forward until he was below the lip of the stairwell and hidden from view. He paused again, staring at the door and gathering his thoughts, trying to think through what he was going to say to Tessa. He had to persuade her, had to convince her that coming back with him was the only sensible thing to do. But with her father having disappeared, would she be willing to leave her mother alone? His thoughts spun like windblown leaves. Perhaps her father had returned. Perhaps her mother had already told her she should do what she thought best. Perhaps Tessa had come around to his way of thinking already.

Perhaps he was dreaming.

He brushed aside his misgivings and moved all the way down to the bottom of the stairs, where he stood before the doorway. Something made him hesitate, something about the way the closed door made him feel. He couldn't identify its origin, but it was strong enough to make him pause.

Then he rapped sharply on the door, two hard and one soft.

Instantly the locks on the door released and the door opened into blackness. Hands appeared out of the dark—two pairs, three, more— seizing his arms and fastening on the prod's insulated handle so that he could not bring it to bear. Bodies surged through the opening and slammed into him, knocking him to the floor. He fought like a wild beast, knowing what was happening, desperate to break free. But the hands had a firm grip on him, and he could not escape.

He had time to shout once in dismay, then something crashed into his head and he tumbled into blackness.

26

LOGAN TOM STOOD motionless in the deep shadows across the street as the boy emerged from the doorway, looked around carefully, and then started walking. He could tell, even in the bad light, that it was only a boy he was looking at and not a man. The boy seemed to know where he was going; he did not hesitate in choosing his path and picking his way through the rubble-strewn landscape. This was familiar territory to him. A street kid, Logan thought. How many others were hiding inside the building this one had come out of? Which one was the gypsy morph?

Because he was certain by now that one of them was.

He could feel the finger bones shifting restlessly in his pocket. They had begun doing so earlier in the day, when he had first reached the edge of the city. He had thrown them again to make certain he was on track, watched them gather and point right at the heart of the downtown, then pocketed them once more. Almost immediately he had felt them begin to shift and stir, making a faint clicking sound as they knocked together. It had startled him so he had been forced to fight down a strong sense of revulsion.

By now, hours later, he was used to it. Evidently, they were responding to the closeness of the morph. It was a strange sensation,
having them move around like that, but it meant that his journey
was almost over, his search nearly ended. His last cast of the bones
had brought him directly to this square and the empty buildings surrounding it, but he had known immediately where the morph was
to be found.

He thought momentarily about going after the kid on the street,
and then decided against it. Any attempt to confront him here
might cause him to cry out and alert the others. He didn't want the
whole bunch of them scattering to the four winds. Better to let this
one go and concentrate on the others.

He watched the boy disappear into the gloom, remained where
he was for several minutes more, then stepped out of the shadows
and started across the street.

His instincts and the force of his magic told him that the building he was about to enter was occupied. He could hear movement
within. The finger bones seemed to know it, too. Their rustling inside his clothing grew almost frantic.

He reached the doorway from which the boy had emerged and
paused. Nothing seemed amiss. He could still hear the scurrying
sounds of the occupants inside, somewhere upstairs from where he
stood. He turned and looked around carefully, making certain he
had missed nothing in his approach. But the night was empty and
still, the square a graveyard of old vehicles, fallen walls, and windblown trash. There was a parched and bitter quality to everything
that matched what he had found in the countryside he had passed
through to get here. The feelings it engendered were the same—of a
time and place, of a world and its inhabitants, passing into dust.

He thought back momentarily to three nights earlier, when he
had encountered the ghosts of the dead in the mountains. The deadening he had experienced coming out of that strange and terrible encounter had lessened by now, and he had come back to himself from
the dream world of the mist. Ghosts, he knew, must be relegated to
the past; the future was for the living. Knights of the Word lived
with one foot in the past, the legacy of their dreams, but their purpose in waking was to serve the future. He struggled with this. He

knew he always would. There was a joining of sleep and waking, of past and present, that could not be completely sorted out. Yet his mission in coming here, in finding the gypsy morph, transcended the confusion and misgivings and fears to which such a joining gave birth. What he would do here might change the destiny of the human race. His belief in that possibility demanded that he put aside everything else, everything personal, until he had done what he had been sent to do.

Inside his head, the ghosts chattered and laughed like small animals, and the steel of his determination shivered.

He proceeded through the doorway into the near blackness of a small entry, found the stairway beyond, and began to climb. He went slowly and silently, not wanting to alert the street kids to his presence, not wanting them to have a reason to bolt and scatter. It wasn't that he was afraid of losing the morph. But tracking down the morph, if it fled, would consume time he was not sure he had. Other forces were at work, and sooner or later he would come up against them. He did not want that to happen before his quest was complete.

He found the street kids on the night-shrouded fourth floor, barricaded behind a heavy iron-sheeted door. By then, they had gone quiet, alerted to his presence. Perhaps they had heard him approach. Perhaps they had simply sensed him. One or more possessed preternatural instincts or they would not still be alive. He looked up and down the hallway through the gloom for clues and found none. He looked again at the door. He could hear them breathing, right on the other side of the barrier. Interestingly, they had not fled. That meant they were prepared for intruders and not afraid. He would have to be careful.

"My name is Logan Tom," he said to the door. "Can one of you talk to me?"

No answer. He waited awhile longer, and then said, "I am not here to harm you. I am looking for someone. I have come a long way to find this person. I think you can help me do that."

Still no answer. But there was a faint stirring, a whispering that was almost inaudible, and the sound of a very big animal's low growl.

"Are you from one of the compounds?" a voice asked.

It was an older girl or a young woman, her voice steady and confident. He took a chance. "No, I'm not from the compounds. I serve a higher order. I am a Knight of the Word."

More whispering, including someone's inadvertently sharp query, "What's that?"

"Do you have any weapons?" the first speaker asked.

He had left everything in the Lightning, which was parked and secured on the main north–south highway, perhaps a mile east. "I am unarmed," he said.

"What about your staff?"

So they could see him. Even in the near blackness. He showed no reaction, deliberately not looking for the peephole through which they were viewing him. "It is a symbol of my order. It is not a weapon."

A white lie, because it could be a weapon, of course, even though he would never use it against them. He waited, but no one spoke. He started to ask them if he could come inside, but stopped himself. It would be better to let them make that decision without any pressure from him.

"Tell us who you are looking for," the speaker said.

"I'm not sure. I have never met this person. I have something that will tell me who it is. A talisman. That is what led me here to you. It tells me that the person I am looking for is inside."

"Can you describe who it is?"

He shook his head, and then said, "No. The talisman will point the person out to me. If you will give me a chance to use it."

Further muttering, longer and more intense this time. An argument was taking place, but it was difficult to tell its nature. He tried to think what else he could tell them that would make them open the door.

"We don't know whether to believe you or not, but it doesn't matter. We don't let anyone inside but members of our own tribe." The older girl's voice was firm. "One of us might agree to come out, but you will have to convince us that it's a good idea."

Logan nodded, mostly to himself. "What can I tell you that will help?"

"Tell us everything. Tell us how you came by your talisman. Tell

us how you knew what it would do. Tell us why any of this matters."
A pause. "We will know if you are telling us the truth, so don't lie.
We will also know if you mean us any harm."

He thought about it a moment. Was there anything he couldn't
tell them? He scanned it through in his mind, then decided there
wasn't. What difference did it make what they knew about his purpose in coming here? What mattered was that they let him inside so
that he could throw the finger bones and discover whether the
gypsy morph was there or not.

"All right," he agreed.

He told it all to them. Of his mission as a Knight of the Word, of
his meeting with Two Bears, of the origins of the gypsy morph, of his
search to find it, of his journey west and his arrival here, in the city.
It took him awhile, but he didn't rush it. There were no interrup-
tions from the other side of the door. There was only silence.

But when he was finished, a new voice spoke out instantly, a little girl's voice. "It is the vision, Owl! Hawk's vision!"

"Your story, Owl!" another voice said, this one male, young. "Of
the boy and his children!"

There were hurried whispers and urgent warnings of "hush" and
"be quiet"—five or six voices, at least, all speaking at once. Logan
thought he heard the name *Candle*, as well, but he couldn't be certain. He waited for the muttering to die down, trying to stay patient.

Finally, the older girl said, "I don't know, Logan Tom."

Another voice, darker sounding, older, too, said, "Frickin' bunch
of bull! I don't believe any of it!"

Everyone began talking at once, but he could tell that they were
all kids, none of them, save perhaps the girl who had spoken first, old
enough to be called a grown-up. Any attempt at keeping their numbers hidden had been forgotten, and all the talk now was about
whether or not he was to be believed.

Then the little girl—Candle, he guessed—shouted at them suddenly. "Open the door! He is here to help us. He is not here to hurt
us. I would know. We have to let him in and see what his talisman
tells us!"

The argument resumed for a moment, and then one of them—
the older girl, perhaps—hushed the others into silence.

"Will you put down your staff, Logan Tom? Will you turn around and face away from us so that we can make certain that you mean us no harm? Will you do that? Will you stand there and let us make sure of you?"

It was something that he had never thought he would agree even to consider. His instincts were all directed toward protecting himself—to never give up his staff or put himself at the mercy of another or trust the word of someone he didn't know. He almost said no. He almost decided that enough was enough and he would just go in there and get this over with. But he calmed himself by remembering that with kids you needed to earn their trust. These kids were just trying to stay alive, and they didn't have anyone to help them do that. They were on their own, and they had learned early on that they could only rely on themselves.

He turned around so that he was facing away from the door, laid his staff on the floor, spread his arms out from his sides, and waited. After a moment, he heard the sounds of an iron bar being pulled free and locks being released. The door opened with a small squeal, candlelight seeped out through the opening, and instantly a pair of cold metal tips pressed up against his neck. He stayed where he was, calm and unmoving, even when he saw the dark length of his staff sliding away from him, disappearing from view.

"Look at these carvings," a boy whispered in awe.

"Leave that alone," another snapped. Then to Logan, he said, "Those are prods you feel. You know what they are, what they can do?"

Logan smiled faintly. "I know."

"Then don't move unless you are told to."

There was a hurried discussion and a brief argument about what to do next. Hands patted at his clothing, searched his pockets, and came away with the black cloth that held the finger bones. "Yuck!" someone said, and stuffed the cloth and the bones back in his pocket. "He's carrying bones!"

"Maybe he's a cannibal," another whispered.

The older girl said, "Turn around."

He did and found himself staring at nine dirty faces backlit by the candles burning within: five boys, four girls, all of them sharp-eyed and wary. The youngest boy and girl couldn't have been more than ten years old. The oldest boys, one big and burly, one dark-skinned and hard-eyed, held the prods against his neck. Another of the boys, his skin almost white, was kneeling in front of the staff, running his hands over its polished surface. One of the girls, the one whom he now believed to have done all the talking, was in a wheel-chair. Another girl, her straw-colored hair sticking out everywhere, her face and arms marked with angry scratches and dark bruises, held a viper-prick. Her blue eyes were steady and unforgiving as she peered up him. They were a ragged, motley bunch, but if how they looked concerned them in any way, they weren't showing it.

Crouched just behind all of them, gray eyes baleful, was the biggest dog he had ever seen, some mixed breed or other, its mottled coat shaggy, its body heavily muscled, a huge and dangerous-looking animal. It was no longer growling, but he knew that if he moved in a way it didn't like or threatened these kids, it would be on him instantly.

Almost incongruously, the girl with the straw-colored hair moved over to it and patted its head affectionately. "He won't hurt you if you don't do anything stupid," she said.

The girl in the wheelchair announced quietly, "We are the Ghosts. We haunt the ruins of our parents."

He looked at her. She sounded as if she were reciting a litany she had memorized. "Are you Owl?"

She nodded. "Why should we believe anything you've said? None of us has ever heard of Knights of the Word or demons or this gypsy morph. It sounds like the stories I tell, but those are made up."

"Not about the boy and his children," the smallest girl declared, her red hair framing her anxious face in a fiery halo. Her eyes fixed on him, and he realized that she was the one who had persuaded the others to open the door to him.

"Hush, Candle," Owl said. "We can't be certain yet of his purpose in coming here. He must convince us further before we can trust him."

Her plain, ordinary features masked a fierce intelligence. She was the leader, the one the others looked to, not only because she was older, but because she was the smartest and perhaps the most knowledgeable, too.

"I will say it again," he said. "The end is coming for all of us. Something terrible is going to happen, something that will destroy what remains of this world. Weapons, perhaps. But maybe something else. The gypsy morph is the only one who can save us. The morph is the child of one of the most powerful magic wielders of all time. Nest Freemark is a legend. Her child carries her promise that there is a chance for all of us."

"Her so-called child would be maybe sixty or seventy by now," the dark-skinned boy pointed out. "Kind of old to save the world."

"Her child would not have aged as we do," Logan answered him. "A gypsy morph is not subject to the laws of humans. It is its own being, and it takes the shape and life it chooses. It was a boy once before, when it was brought to Nest. It may have taken that shape again."

"Well, it ain't me," the boy snapped, his lip curling. "Ain't them, either."

He pointed at the other three boys, who seemed inclined to agree with him, their faces reflecting their doubt.

"What of your talisman?" Owl asked him. "What does it tell you?"

"My talisman points me toward the gypsy morph," he said. "But it does not speak. The bones you took from my pocket, they're the finger bones of Nest Freemark's right hand. When cast, they point toward the gypsy morph. If the morph is here, the bones will tell us."

The kids looked at one another with varying degrees of suspicion and doubt. "These bones alive?" the dark-skinned kid demanded incredulously.

"They have magic," Logan answered. "In that sense, yes, they are alive."

The kid looked at Owl. "Let the man throw them. Let's see what they do. Then we decide what we do with him."

The older girl seemed to consider, then looked at Logan. "Are you willing to try using these bones from out there?"

"I will need you to separate enough that I can pick out which one of you the bones are pointing to." He looked at the boys with the prods. "You will have to trust me enough to take the prods away so that I can move."

The dark-skinned boy looked at his burly companion and then shrugged. He moved his prod back from Logan's neck about two feet. "Far enough for you, Mr. Knight of the Word?"

Logan waited until the other boy had followed suit, then knelt slowly. The kids crowded closer as he took out the black cloth and spread it on the floor. The light from the candles barely illuminated the space in which he worked, blocked in part by the crush of bodies.

"Move back," Owl ordered when she realized his difficulty, motioning with both hands. "Let him have enough light to see what he is doing."

Logan glanced up, then took out the finger bones and cast them across the cloth. Instantly, the bones began to move, sliding into place to form fingers, linking up until they were a recognizable whole. The street kids murmured softly, and one or two shrank back. *Now we will find out*, he thought.

But the bones turned away from the circle of children and pointed instead toward Logan, the index finger straightening as the others curled together.

"So, guess *you* be the gympsy moth or whatever," the dark-skinned boy sneered. "Big surprise."

Logan stared, perplexed. This didn't make any sense. Then, abruptly, he understood, and a sinking feeling settled into the pit of his stomach. He moved to one side, away from where the bones were pointing. The bones did not move. They continued to point in the same direction—away from him, from the children, from the room, and off into darkness. He stared at that darkness, feeling it press in about him like a wall, closing off his hopes for ending this.

"The bones are telling us that the gypsy morph isn't here. Is there someone missing—someone who might have been here earlier?"

He looked back at Owl, then at the other kids, already anticipating the answer to his question. Candle's small hands curled into fists and pressed against her mouth.

"Hawk," she whispered.

● ● ●

WHEN HE REGAINED consciousness, his head pounding with the pain of the blow he had absorbed, Hawk was alone in a black, windowless room with an iron-clad door that provided just enough light under the threshold to let him measure its size. He sat up slowly, found that he wasn't bound, tried to stand, and sat down again quickly.

He took a moment to recover his scattered thoughts. The first of those thoughts left him filled with regret. *What a fool I've been.* He should never have come without Cheney, should have waited another day for the big dog to recover, should have realized the danger to which he was exposing himself . . .

Should have, should have, should have . . .

He took a deep breath and blew it out. What was the point in chastising himself now? It was over and done with. They had caught him out, and he was their prisoner. He thought about how they had captured him. They hadn't just stumbled on him; they had been waiting. That suggested that they knew about his meetings with Tessa. In all likelihood, she had been found out, too. If so, she would face the same fate they decreed for him.

For the first time he felt a ripple of fear.

Fighting it down, he climbed to his feet and began exploring the door to see if there might be a way out. They had taken all of his weapons, even the viper-prick, and he had nothing with which to spring the lock. Nevertheless, he kept searching, running his fingers along the seams and across the door, then all along the base of the walls, hoping that his captors might have left something useful lying around.

He was still engaged in this futile effort when he heard their footsteps approaching. He moved back to the center of the room and sat down again.

The door opened, flooding the room with daylight that spilled through high slanted windows from across the way. His captors numbered four—big and strong, too many for him even to consider attacking. So he let them bind his wrists and lead him out into the hallway and from there down several different corridors and up a series of steps to a room filled with people.

The only face he recognized was Tessa's. She was seated in a chair facing a long table occupied by three men. An empty chair sat next to hers, and he was led to it. No one said anything to him. No one in the room did more than murmur softly. There must have been two hundred people gathered, perhaps more. The men leading him released his wrists and pushed him down in the chair.

One bent close. "If you try to run or cause trouble, we'll tie you up again. Understand me?"

Hawk nodded without replying, his eyes on Tessa. His captor hesitated a moment, then moved away.

"Are you all right?" he asked her quietly.

Before she could answer him, the man seated at the center of the table across from them slammed his hand down on the tabletop so hard that it caused Hawk to jump. "Be quiet!" he said. "You will not speak unless asked to. You will not speak to each other. This is a trial and you will obey the dictates of this court!"

The man was big and craggy, his face and voice unfriendly, and his eyes dark with anger. Hawk looked at him, then at the other two, and his heart sank. Their minds were already made up about what they intended to do to him. The best he could hope for was to deflect their anger from Tessa.

"State your name," the man said to him.

He took a deep breath. "I am Hawk," he answered. "I am a Ghost, and I haunt the ruins of my parents' world."

There was subdued laughter from the audience, and the big man reddened. "Is it your intention to mock this court, boy? Do you think this is a game?"

"Your Honor, he is only stating what is true," Tessa said quickly. "He is a member of a tribe called Ghosts. Hawk is the name he has taken."

The judge looked at her, glanced at the two seated next to him, and nodded. "We will call him whatever he wishes to be called so long as he remains respectful. He is accused—you are both accused—of stealing stores from the compound for personal use. The evidence is clear. Tessa, you were observed in the medical dispensary when you had no right to be there. Medicines were found missing. You claimed to have been conducting an inventory, but no inventory was authorized. You met this boy outside the compound walls without permission, a secret assignation, and you gave these medicines to him. If any of this is wrong, say so now."

Tessa's mouth tightened, and she straightened in her chair. "I took the medicines to save a little girl who was dying. Why is that wrong?"

"Your reasons for what you did are not relevant to this trial. Just answer the question. Is any of what I have recited wrong?"

Tessa shook her head slowly. "No, it is correct."

"You, boy. Hawk." The judge gestured at him. "What was your part in this? What did you do with the medicines?"

Hawk glanced at Tessa. "I used them to help the little girl."

"A street child?"

He nodded.

"Answer me!"

Hawk felt his cheeks burn with anger. "Yes."

The man bent close and whispered to the other two, then looked back to Hawk. "There is no defense for what you did." His gaze shifted to Tessa. "No defense for either of you. The law of the compound is clear in this instance. All violators are—"

"Your Honor," Tessa interrupted quickly. "I claim the right and protection of marriage bonding."

There was a muted exclamation from the crowd, and some of them began to mutter angrily. Hawk forced himself not to look at them, knowing what he would find in their faces.

"Are you saying you married a street boy, Tessa?" the judge asked quietly.

Her beautiful, dark face lifted defiantly. "I did. I took him to me, and I carry his child."

Cries of outrage exploded from the assemblage. Hawk glanced quickly at Tessa, but she was looking straight ahead at the judges. He wondered if what she had just told them was true. Was she carrying his child? He stared at her, trying in vain to read the truth in her face.

The judge presiding signaled for quiet, then said, "Compound law does not recognize marriages made to those who live outside the walls. It does not matter that you carry his child. Even if your

marriage were sanctioned, it would not save his life. He is an outsider and he has broken our law. In any case, I am not sure that I believe you. Clearly, you are infatuated with him and would lie to save
him."

"Where is my mother?" Tessa cried out. "I want her to come forward and speak for me."

The judge hesitated, and then glanced toward the crowd. There
was a moment's pause, and then a small, dark-clad woman who bore
more than a passing resemblance to Tessa appeared out of the
crowd. A few hands reached out as if to assist her, but she brushed
them away with her crushed, gnarled fingers, with her hands turned
withered and streaked with vivid red scars. Hawk cringed as he
glimpsed them, thinking of the pain she must have endured. He had
never seen her before, but there was no mistaking who she was.
Once, when she was younger, she must have been beautiful like
Tessa. Now, however, her face was pinched and tight, and there was
no warmth in her dark eyes.

Those eyes shifted momentarily to find his, then slid away again.
She walked up to her daughter and stopped.

"Is it true," she demanded. "Do you carry his child?"

"Mother, please tell them—"

"Do you carry his child!"

Tessa flinched, her face crumpling. "Mother—"

Her mother spit on her, her face contorted with rage. "You have
disgraced us, Tessa. Betrayed us! You were told not to see this boy
again. You were forbidden! If your father . . ."

She was unable to finish the thought. She took a deep breath.
"Do you know what you have done? Do you have any idea? What
will happen to me, Tessa? Have you thought of that? Your father is
gone. Now you abandon me, too. I am crippled—useless to all! Do
you know what that means? Do you?"

Her face turned hard and set. "If your father were here, he would
not speak for you, and neither will I."

Tessa looked stunned, her blank eyes filling with tears. Her
mother held her gaze a moment, and then turned away and disappeared back into the crowd.

"Wait!" Hawk leapt to his feet. "I know what you intend for me, but you can't blame her! She did it because I threatened to hurt her if she didn't do as I said!"

The judge barely glanced at him as two of his captors took hold of him and forced him back into his chair. "Tessa and Hawk, you have been found guilty by this court. The penalty for stealing stores is death. You will be taken to the walls of the compound at sunset today and thrown over. We grant you forgiveness for your acts and wish you a better life in the next world. This court is adjourned. Take them away."

Shouts rose from the crowd, mingled with scattered applause. The guards descended on Hawk once more, seized his arms as he tried in vain to break free, and swept him from the room.

The last thing he saw, looking back over his shoulder, was Tessa sitting where he had left her, weeping into her hands.

27

LOGAN TOM SPENT the remainder of the night keeping watch in the hallway outside the door he had tried unsuccessfully to pass through earlier. Realizing that the gypsy morph was in all likelihood the boy called Hawk—the one he'd unfortunately let pass him by on the street before coming into the building—he had determined to wait for his return. Hawk would be back soon, Owl had insisted. He had gone to the compound to visit his girlfriend. She would not say anything more than that. No one quite trusted him yet. Candle, more than the others, believed he was there to help. But it was Owl who made all the decisions, and she was taking no chances.

So, despite everything—or perhaps because of it—she had steadfastly refused to let him enter their quarters. All she had been willing to agree to was letting him remain in the hallway outside the door. She promised that they would not make up their minds about him until Hawk's return. She promised that they would not try to slip out the back or flee into the city and that they would let him cast the finger bones again when Hawk returned.

Then, having left his staff lying on the floor where he could reach it, they had backed into their lair and closed and locked the door. There had been no argument from any of them, including Candle, that he should be allowed to come inside.

So he sat in the hallway all night with his back against the far wall, facing the door and waiting. He slept off and on, but never deeply and never for very long. He had time to think about what he would do once he had determined if the boy Hawk was, in fact, the gypsy morph. How hard would it be to persuade him of his lineage? It was one thing to offer your help; it was another to gain acceptance. None of these street kids knew anything of Knights of the Word. Why should they? But it made his job just that much more difficult. There was no reason for the morph to trust him any more than these other street kids did.

There was another problem, a potentially bigger one. Would the morph even know what it was supposed to do once it had been told what it was? O'olish Amaneh had seemed confident that all the pieces would fall into place once the morph was found. But Logan was suspicious. In his experience, few things ever seemed to work out the way you expected. Mostly, something went wrong.

Dawn broke, and Hawk had not returned. Logan rose and went down to the street and looked around. There was no one in sight. He stood there for a long time, willing the boy to appear. But the street remained empty of life.

He took a deep breath and exhaled. Something was wrong, and he was afraid that it was going to change everything.

He needed a bath and something to eat, but he gave up on both and went back into the building. He climbed the stairs to the fourth floor and knocked on the door to the lair of the Ghosts. This time the door opened immediately and Owl wheeled into view, the other street kids trailing silently.

"He hasn't come back?" Logan asked.

Owl shook her head. "Will you try to find him?"

"I don't know. Has this ever happened before?"

She tightened her lips. "No. He meets Tessa secretly, and then comes back before it gets light. Usually, he takes Cheney, but Cheney is hurt, so he left him behind. Hawk has been taking chances lately with Tessa. Someone in the compound might have found out about them. I've warned him that these meetings are dangerous. The people in the compound don't like street kids."

Logan nodded. "I know how they think. I've encountered it before. They don't like anyone who lives beyond the walls. They can be very hard on outsiders."

"It might be worse here. Tessa was stealing medicines from the compound stores to help street kids. Hawk asked her, and she agreed. If they found out about that . . ."

"Can you get inside the compound to find out?" asked the girl with dark hair and intense eyes.

"Maybe." He shrugged. "Maybe not. They don't have any reason to help me. A lot of them don't even like me."

The dark-skinned kid pushed forward and looked back at the others, blocking Logan off. "We don't need him. He ain't got nothin' useful to offer us. Ain't got nothin' but that staff. At least we got weapons. We can find out for ourselves about the Bird-Man."

"Shut up, Panther," snapped the slender girl with the straw-colored hair and the fierce eyes. She looked back at Logan. "Will you try to find him? Will you go to the compound and ask?"

Straightforward and to the point. "All right," he agreed.

"Do you want any of us to go with you?"

He shook his head. "Stay here. Let me see what I can learn on my own first. If that doesn't work, I'll come back and we'll try something else."

He went down the stairs without waiting for their reply, his mind made up about what he was going to do. He had come a long way to find the gypsy morph, and he wasn't about to give up on it now. The Ghosts meant well, but they would only get in his way if Hawk was inside the compound. His best chance of reaching the boy was to speak with the compound leaders.

Assuming Hawk was still alive.

He got a block away before he stopped to throw the bones, unable to wait any longer to make certain there was still a reason to go on. But the bones formed up on the square of black cloth, pointing down the street and toward the sports complex that he already knew was serving as shelter for the compound members. He had seen it from the highway coming in and recognized it for what it was—another futile attempt by a dying civilization at staying alive, another false hope that protection from the world could be found by hiding behind walls.

He picked up the finger bones and put them back in his pocket. He wished sometimes he could find a way to convince those who lived in the compounds that they were inhabiting their own tombs. He wished he could make them see that there was no longer any safe place in the world, and that their best bet was to keep moving. But he knew that thousands of years of conditioned thinking was standing in the way of any real change, and the advice of one man wasn't likely to overcome that.

He caught sight of some of the other denizens of the city as he went, their furtive, shadowy movements giving them away. Another would have missed them entirely, but his training and the magic of his staff revealed their presence to him. Mutants: some of them dangerous, some not. Some were solitary, some tribal, but the humans who had not mutated shunned them all. He wondered what would become of them in the future that Two Bears had prophesied.

He reached the compound without incident and walked up to the main gates, not trying to hide his approach. If he was to get anywhere, he must be direct. Guards atop the walls challenged him when he came into view, and he stopped where they could see him, calling up his name and order of service. One of the guards, at least, knew what it meant to be a Knight of the Word and told him that someone would be right down. He waited patiently, studying the complex, noting its defenses. It was heavily fortified; its inhabitants would be well armed. An attack would have to be massive and sustained if it was to succeed. Not that it wouldn't. Eventually, they all did.

A small, metal-clad door opened to one side of the main gates, and a man stepped through into the daylight.

"Morning," he called out, walking toward Logan. "I'm Ethan Cole, Chairman of the Compound Directorate. What brings a Knight of the Word up this way?"

His voice was flat and perfunctory, and his manner was brusque. There was no offer of anything to eat or drink, no invitation to come inside and rest, no small talk, and no time wasted. Get it said and get it done. It wasn't difficult to get an accurate measure of Ethan Cole. He was perhaps fifty years of age, of average size and ordinary looks, nothing unusual about him, nothing odd. But he spoke and walked in the way of a man used to wielding authority. Logan had met men like him before. They were always the same.

Logan leaned on his staff and waited for the other to get close, then said, "I'm looking for someone."

Cole frowned. "Here?"

Logan nodded. "I've come halfway across the country to find him. I think you might have him inside. He's just a boy. His name is Hawk."

"Hawk," the other man repeated and shook his head. "No, I don't know anyone by that name."

Logan studied him a moment, letting the weight of his gaze settle. "Something you should know about Knights of the Word. Whatever you might think of us, we always know when we are being lied to. Maybe you have a good reason for doing so here, but I would appreciate it if you would stop wasting my time. I am tired and hungry. I haven't washed in days. I don't have a lot of patience for this. What's the problem?"

Ethan Cole hesitated, and then shrugged. "No problem. I'm just being careful. You say you are a Knight of the Word, but how do I know what you are? Things have been a little uncertain around here. We lost an entire foraging party last week. They went out fully armed and equipped and they didn't come back. Just disappeared."

"It happens. I'm sorry about your people, but my presence has nothing to do with them. I've been following a trail, and it led me here. I don't know anything about the boy's history with this compound or even this city. I just know he's inside your compound. He is, isn't he?"

He waited. "All right, he's here," Cole admitted.

"Is he a prisoner?"

"He is."

"What has he done?"

Cole took a deep breath and blew it out in exasperation. "He and one of our young girls stole some medical supplies. They've been meeting outside the compound for some time—a violation of our rules, of course. We found out about the girl a day or so ago and caught the boy trying to meet up with her again last night. It wouldn't matter so much if they hadn't stolen the supplies. But they did, so it does."

The way he said it suggested that things were not going to end well for Hawk and the girl. Logan glanced past him to the gates and walls. "I would like to speak with the boy."

The other man pursed his lips. "I don't know about that."

"What is it that you don't know, Mr. Cole? I told you I've come a long way to find him. I need to make certain he's who I think he is."

"It won't make much difference if he is or isn't. Stealing from our medical stores is treason and punishable by death. He and the girl will be thrown from the walls at sunset."

Logan hid the twinge of fear that tightened his throat. "Then it won't hurt to let me see him for a few minutes now, while there's still time."

Cole shifted his weight. "We don't usually allow outsiders inside our walls."

Logan straightened. "Is that how you see me? As an outsider? I guess I find that hard to understand given the nature of my work. In any case, it shouldn't matter here. My request is a simple one. You shouldn't find it difficult to grant."

"I don't know you. I don't know anything about you. But I do know something of Knights of the Word. I'm told you possess unusual powers, magic or arcane skills. Given that, letting you inside our walls seems an unnecessary risk. I don't see what purpose it will serve to let you speak with this boy. You can't help him. The law is quite clear about what's to be done in these cases."

Logan nodded as if he understood, although the only thing he really understood was that Ethan Cole was starting to irritate him. "I'm not interested in your compound laws or what they mandate for offenders," he said. "I'm here to determine if this boy is the one I have been looking for. It seems he is, but I need to speak with him to make certain."

"But if he is who you've been looking for, what then? Will you then demand we set him free? Will you try to take him by force if we don't?"

Logan sighed. "You're getting ahead of yourself. I'm not looking to make trouble. Just let me speak with him. When I'm finished, I won't ask anything further of you."

The other man studied him, undecided. "I won't let you bring any weapons inside."

"I have my staff of office," Logan said. "Nothing else."

"You'll be searched. I'll need to have you speak with the boy in his holding cell." The other man shook his head. "I'll say it again. I don't like this. I don't see why I should agree to it."

Logan folded his staff into the cradle of his arms. "You should agree to it because it is the right thing to do. I told you the truth. I don't know this boy. I don't care about the girl or the medical supplies or any of the rest of it. I am here for one reason and one reason only—to find out if this boy is the one I am looking for. I can't do that if I don't speak to him. He can tell me what I need to know, and then I will be gone from here." He paused, staring at Ethan Cole. "Why are you so afraid?"

Cole flushed at the rebuke, looked as if he was about to make a retort, then thought better of it and simply nodded. "All right. Come this way."

They went back through the doorway and into the compound corridors. Logan allowed himself to be searched, permitted the guards to run their hands over him. But when they tried to take his staff, he stopped them, telling them that his oath of office wouldn't allow it. Cole shrugged the matter away, seeing the staff as ordinary humans were meant to see it, and beckoned him ahead impatiently. Having made up his mind to allow this, Cole clearly wanted to get it over with. A phalanx of guards accompanied them as they wound their way down a series of corridors and then descended into the bowels of the complex. Everything was formed of concrete and steel, smooth and functional and indestructible. Logan hated places like this, found them stultifying and deadening, tombs for the living. He found no comfort in walls and gates, gained no sense of peace or reassurance from their vast bulk, and felt disconnected from the world whenever he was inside them.

But he kept his feelings to himself, focusing on what he was here to do, a small excitement beginning to build at the prospect of completing his journey. He did not allow himself to think beyond the possibility that Hawk was the gypsy morph. He would not worry yet about what he would need to do if he was. The nature of this undertaking, grave and dangerous, required that he not think past the moment. This was difficult for him to do. He had learned to stay alive by thinking ahead. But thinking too far ahead here might result in a mistake that would reveal his intentions to Cole and the others who warded this compound. They must not be given any reason to look on him as a threat.

They were deep inside the compound when Cole halted before a steel door, one of several that lined the corridor in which they stood. He signaled to the guard on duty, and the man produced a key that unlocked the door. The door swung open, the guard stepped back, and Cole gestured for Logan to go inside. Logan almost hesitated.

"I'll need a light," he said. "So I can see after you've closed the door."

Cole handed him a battery-powered torch. "Make it quick. Just call out when you're done. Someone will be right outside."

Logan took the torch wordlessly, switched it on, and walked past him into the cell. The door closed behind him with a soft *thud*, and he could hear footsteps receding into the distance.

Hawk stood directly in front of him, not six feet away, squinting against the brightness of the light. He was slender and not very tall, with a shock of ragged black hair and eyes so deep-set they seemed black until the light revealed a hint of green. He wasn't imposing in any way, didn't appear at all impressive, and gave no indication that he might be anything other than what he seemed to be. Logan directed the torch beam toward the floor, letting the boy's eyes adjust.

"My name is Logan Tom," he said. He turned the beam on himself to let the boy have a good look, keeping it in place as he talked. "I'm a Knight of the Word. Do you know anything of our order?"

The boy shook his head, said nothing.

"Your friends told me where to find you," Logan continued. "Owl said you had come here to meet Tessa. I guess that meeting didn't work out."

The boy made no response, watching Logan closely.

"Your name is Hawk?"

The boy nodded.

"I'm looking for someone. I think you might be him." He waited, and then gestured at the floor. "Sit down with me. I'll show you something interesting."

He sat cross-legged on the floor, and after a moment or two, the boy joined him. Logan placed the light to one side, its beam directed across the floor in front of them so that the pale wash illuminated them both. Then he lay down the black staff, reached into his pocket, and extracted the black cloth and finger bones of Nest Freemark. He spread the cloth on the floor carefully, smoothed out the wrinkles, and looked at the boy.

"This is how I found you," he said.

He tossed the finger bones onto the cloth, and they scattered like bleached sticks. For a moment, they lay where they had fallen. Then they began to move, forming up into fingers and a thumb, taking shape as Nest Freemark's right hand. Logan saw the boy start in shock, then settle back to watch, wonder on his lean face.

The bones came together, a slow connecting of joints, a fitting together of pieces until the entire hand was in place.

The index finger extended, pointing at the boy.

Logan took a deep breath and held it, waited a moment to be sure, then moved the cloth so that the finger was pointing away. As soon as he did so, the bones shuddered and began to move again, readjusting so that they were pointing at the boy once more.

Logan exhaled softly. "There you are," he whispered.

Hawk looked at him, uncomprehending. Leaving the bones where they were, Logan leaned forward, resting his elbows on his knees.

"Let me tell you a story, Hawk," he said.

● ● ●

IN THE HALLWAY outside, the guard stationed on watch was pressed against the door, his ear at the crack between door and jamb, listening. Ethan Cole had told him to do so, to try to learn what this man wanted with the street boy. Ethan didn't trust him, even though he had agreed to let him come inside the compound. Ethan didn't trust any outsiders, which was probably what had helped keep the residents of the compound safe. Best not to trust anyone you didn't know; the guard knew that much about the world. When it came to outsiders, you could never be sure.

He listened hard in the near silence, but all he could hear was the sound of his own breathing. The steel door was too thick; it muffled all sound from within. It would have been better if they had left it open a crack. Then he might have been able to hear something. But Ethan would never agree to take a chance like that. The door had been opened to let the man in and it would be opened to let him out again, and those were the only times it would be opened until sunset.

The guard shivered as he thought about what would happen to the boy and the girl when the sun dropped. He thought about how they would be taken to the highest walls of the compound and pushed off into the fading light. He thought about how they would scream helplessly as they fell. He thought about the sounds they would make when they struck the concrete at the base of the walls. He had seen and heard it all before, and he had hoped not to have to do so again.

He waited a moment longer, and then stepped back impatiently. Trying to listen was a waste of time. He walked a few yards down the corridor to where his folding chair waited and sat down.

●　●　●

WHEN LOGAN HAD finished his story, the boy said, "Are you telling me I'm not human?"

Logan hesitated. "I really don't know what you are. You were born to a woman, so I guess that makes you human. But you were something else first, a creature of magic, and she was always gifted with magic of the same sort." He shrugged. "What difference does it make? What matters is what you're supposed to be now."

The boy looked at him a moment, and then shook his head. "I don't believe any of this. I guess you do or you wouldn't have come this far. But those bones could be telling me anything."

Logan nodded. "Maybe, but I don't think so."

Hawk was silent a moment. "Didn't you say I was supposed to know what to do after the bones found me? If I'm this . . . whatever it is."

"Gypsy morph."

"Gypsy morph. But I don't know anything more now than I did before. I don't have any idea at all what it is I'm supposed to do. Or what everyone thinks I'm supposed to do."

"You have visions. Candle said so. You have dreams about the boy and his children. Maybe that's some of it."

Hawk sat motionless, staring off into space, his thoughts unspoken. He was working it through, trying it on for size, but not finding anything that fit. Logan could see it in his face, in the shifting of his eyes. He was a boy sitting in a cell waiting to die, and this latest twist of fate was too much for him. Why he didn't seem to know who he was or what he was supposed to do surprised Logan. He thought it would all be made clear once he found the morph. Logan wondered suddenly if there was something he had forgotten.

Then, abruptly, he remembered. He gathered up the bones and held them out. "Take these. If you are the morph, they belong to you. They are your mother's bones. They might help you remember."

Hawk looked at the bones, then at him, and shook his head. "I don't want any part of them. I just want you to take them away."

"If I do that, what will happen to you then? They're going to kill you." Logan kept his hand outstretched. "And Tessa. What about her?"

The boy said nothing for a long time, sitting back, looking at the floor. "She told the judges that she was carrying my child," he said finally. He looked up again, meeting Logan's gaze. "I don't know if it's true or not." He shook his head slowly. "Doesn't matter, I suppose. None of it matters. Even if I am who you say, even if the bones are my mother's, it doesn't change what's going to happen to me or to Tessa."

"Or to the Ghosts?" Logan asked. "They seem to believe in you. The boy and his children. They mentioned that right away when I told them I was looking for the gypsy morph and what the morph was expected to do. They say you are a family. What happens to them?"

"I don't think I can do anything for them." Hawk's words were laced with bitterness. "I can't save them or Tessa or anyone. I can't even save myself from this."

He looked at the floor again. "Or my child, if there is one."

Logan gave him a minute, and then said, "Take the bones. Hold them. Let's see if they give you any answers."

"No," Hawk repeated. Then his eyes lifted and met Logan's. They stared at each other for a long time. "All right," the boy said finally. "Give them to me."

Logan leaned forward and dumped the bones gently into the boy's palm. Hawk looked at them, a glimmer of whiteness against the dirt-streaked flesh of his hand. Then slowly he closed his fingers over them.

Logan waited expectantly.

"Nothing," Hawk said finally. "It's all a . . ."

Then his eyes snapped wide, his mouth fell open in shock, and his slender body went rigid, his muscles cording, straining against what was happening to him. Logan started to intervene, then checked himself. Better to let this play out. The boy was shaking now, his body jerking in whiplash fashion. He was trying to say something, but the words came out as small whimpers. He clasped the fist that held the finger bones to his breast, hunched over as if to find a way to absorb the bones into his body, and began to rock forward and back.

"Hawk?" Logan whispered to him.

A white light bloomed from the center of the boy's body, a small blossom at first, and then a bright cloud that all but enveloped him. Logan backed away despite himself, edging toward the darkness, not understanding why, but feeling that his presence was invasive and perhaps even dangerous. He watched the light steady and then begin to pulse in a rhythm that matched the rocking of the boy. Hawk continued to make indecipherable sounds, lost to everything about him, gone completely into whatever catharsis the bones had generated.

The rocking and the pulsing continued for a long time, and then died away in an instant, leaving the boy hunched over like a fetus, pressed down against his hand and the bones and the floor with the wash of the electric torch casting his shadow in a tight, dark stain across the concrete.

"Hawk?" Logan tried again.

The boy's head lifted slowly and his face came into view, his features stricken and his skin damp with his own tears. The green eyes were filled with a mix of wonder and recognition, of understanding that only moments earlier had been lacking. He stared at nothing, and then at Logan without seeing him. He was looking somewhere else, somewhere only he could see.

His throat worked. "Mother," he whispered.

* * *

OWL WAS SUPERVISING preparations for moving, organizing and dispatching the others on tasks designed to gather together their stores and belongings. She had decided that morning, when Hawk failed to return and Logan Tom set out to find him, that whatever else happened the Ghosts were leaving. She no longer trusted Pioneer Square, no longer felt safe, no longer believed they belonged in this part of the city. She had half decided this before, after their terrible battle with the centipede, but now she was determined. They would move to higher ground, farther back from the waterfront, up in the hills behind the city where they were out of the underground tunnels and sewers and away from the tall buildings. There might be less concrete and steel to protect them inside the residences and low-rises, but there might be fewer monsters, as well.

Besides, she thought, they were at the start of the journey Hawk's vision had foreseen. The boy and his children were about to set out, just as she had told them in her stories. There was no reason to think about staying any longer.

She glanced around their temporary living quarters, trying to determine if she had forgotten anything. She regretted having to leave some of what they had built and scavenged, the heavier appliances and equipment, the things that had made their lives marginally easier. But they would find and build others and make new accommodations. She looked at Cheney, lying in one corner, head lowered between his paws, one eye partially open and staring at her. Nothing wrong with Cheney; he was back to his old self. He looked asleep, but he wasn't. Sometimes she thought the big dog never really slept, that he only half slept and was always just this side of dreaming.

Panther trudged through the door, dropping a pile of blankets and clothing in front of her. "Got us two wagons, carts, whatever, to haul this stuff. Can't take too much, though. We got to pull it uphill, and even the Bear can't do that for long." He looked around expectantly. "Any news? He back yet?"

She knew who he was talking about. "No. Can we take some of the drinking water containers off the roof? We might have trouble finding new ones. Or even drinkable water."

Panther shrugged. "We can take what we want. We just have to make choices." He paused. "What if he don't come back? What if something's happened to the Bird-Man?"

She started to answer him, already knowing that she didn't have the answer he needed, when she saw Cheney's big head lift from the floor, his dark muzzle pointing toward the open door. Then he was on his feet, his look expectant and eager.

Hawk, she thought at once.

Panther, seeing the shift in her eyes, turned to look. "What?" he said.

Logan Tom appeared in the doorway, holding the black staff of his order in both hands, his visage dark with knowledge and foreboding.

"Hawk is the gypsy morph," he announced before the question could be asked. "But he's also a prisoner in the compound. Tessa, too."

"You couldn't get them out?" Owl asked, wheeling her chair forward until she was right in front of him.

Logan Tom shook his head. "Not without a fight. They caught Hawk trying to meet her, but they already knew about them. They found out about the medical supplies she was stealing for him. They held some kind of trial. They've sentenced both of them to be thrown from the walls at sunset."

"Today?" Owl exclaimed. "That's only four hours from now!"

Panther stalked forward. "You said you was supposed to protect the morph! What happened to that?"

Logan shrugged. "They were expecting me to try to break him out. Maybe they were even hoping I'd try."

"So you gonna do nothing, Mr. Knight of the Word?" Panther was furious.

Logan met his gaze and held it. "No, Panther, I'm going to do what I came here to do. I'm going back and get Hawk out. Tessa, too, if I can manage it. Because now they won't be expecting it."

He reached out and tapped the boy on his shoulder. "And you're going to help."

28

ANGEL PEREZ AND Ailie were three hundred miles up the road on their first day after starting north to find the Elves when the tatterdemalion said, "Something is following us."

Not anything Angel wanted to hear. She was hunched forward over the handlebars of the Mercury 5, the throb of the engine rippling through her body, wind tearing at her face. Even at the slower speeds they were forced to travel on the dangerously debris-strewn highway, her eyes were tearing.

She glanced over her shoulder at her passenger. The tatterdemalion clung to her like a second skin, bluish hair flying out behind her. She was so insubstantial that Angel could barely feel her presence. "Are you sure? How do you know?"

The dark eyes blinked. "I sense when the demonkind are near. One of them is near now, following."

It was that female demon from the compound. Angel knew it instinctively. She should have found the reserves of strength she needed and killed her when she had the chance. Johnny always told her not to leave enemies alive; they would always come after you later. They would always think you were weak. Johnny knew.

"How far back?" The wind tore the words away and the roar of the ATV engine buried them.

The dark eyes met her own. "I can hear the sound of another ATV engine."

Angel gritted her teeth, then throttled back the Mercury 5 and pulled over to the side of the road. She cut the engine and waited as the ringing in her ears faded and the throbbing in her body eased. She climbed down and stood in the middle of the roadway, listening. All around her, a steadily darkening sky was pressing down to meet the twilight shadows, the world empty and gray.

Within seconds she heard the other engine's roar, big and powerful and instantly recognizable. A Harley Crawler.

Stupid, stupid girl! She chastised herself in fury. First for not killing the demon and second for not destroying that other machine. She had thought that taking its cells and hiding them would be enough, but the creature that hunted her was no ordinary demon. It had tracked her down and found her once, back in the ruins of Los Angeles, and it clearly intended to do so again.

She glanced over at the Mercury and the dark length of her staff, tucked down in the buckled grips of the storage slot. She did not think she was ready to do battle with this creature again so soon. It wasn't that she was afraid; it was that she recognized a hard truth about herself that she didn't much care for. She had been lucky to escape from her pursuer the first time. She might not be so lucky again.

It gave her pause that the demon was so intent on catching up to her. It had worked hard at finding her back in LA. It had discovered what she was doing to save the children in the other compounds, then ferreted out her secret entry into the one in Anaheim and set its trap for her. It hadn't bothered with bringing help to destroy her; it had sufficient confidence—and likely pride—in its own abilities to want to do it alone. As it almost had. Luck had saved her. Luck, and a determination that matched that of the demon's.

Still, to have it tracking her like this . . .

She glanced around quickly at the highway ahead and saw where it branched off into what must have once been an old logging road. Little more than a dirt track, the road dipped down off the embanked highway and disappeared into the trees. So, she thought. Easy enough to drive a hulk like the Harley Crawler down the middle of a paved road. Maybe it wouldn't be so easy down a narrow, rutted trail.

She returned to the Mercury, where Ailie sat watching her, climbed back onto the seat, and restarted the engine. She felt Ailie's slender arms come around her waist. "Hold tight, *pequeñita*," she said to her.

She ratcheted the throttle forward and the ATV shot ahead to the dirt road. She turned down it without slowing, anxious now with twilight settling in and night coming on, knowing how hard it would be to get much of anywhere after dark. The Mercury coughed and labored as it hit the weed-grown interior of the trees, but she kept it on track, the dirt road a navigable ribbon that wound ahead into the woods.

In seconds the highway had disappeared behind her and the dusk had thickened to massed shadows and inky gloom. She throttled the Mercury's engine back again, picking her way carefully, searching out the track where it sometimes faded into waist-high walls of brush and heavy grasses. These woods here were not as sickened as some, the foliage still plentiful and mostly green amid signs of wilt and some heavy stretches of decay. Hardwoods mingled with conifers, and in the deepening gloom it became possible to believe that the forest had never experienced the damaging effects of the chemical poisonings of the earth and atmosphere. Maybe some places were still healthy enough that they would recover in time, Angel thought, steering the ATV down the twisting path, eyes searching out the way. Maybe some places, like this one, would survive.

But uncertainty clouded her hopes, and she put the matter aside where it belonged.

They rode on for the better part of an hour without speaking, their progress slowed by the conditions of the road and the onset of night, but steady nevertheless. The logging road wound on mile after mile, sometimes splitting off into side trails, sometimes disappearing into open stretches in which the trees had been leveled to stumps and a star-strewn sky filled the horizon end to end. When she could, she took roads that narrowed down to almost nothing and angled through trees and stumps grown so close together that the big Harley couldn't pass between them. Once, she took the Mercury into a stream and ran it down the waterway for more than a mile before coming out again onto a bedding of crushed rock and flat stone. Whatever she could do to hide their passing, she did it.

Finally, she slowed and stopped and turned off the engine. "Now what do you hear?" she asked Ailie when the silence had deepened anew.

The tatterdemalion shook her head. "Nothing."

"Do your senses warn of demons close by?"

Again, Ailie shook her head.

Angel smiled. "*Bueno*. Even so, we will ride on for another hour or two before we sleep. Just to make certain."

She climbed back into place on the Mercury, turned on the engine, and set out into the dark.

● ● ●

DELLOREEN KNEW SHE was getting close. The smells she was using as her marker to track the female Knight of the Word were getting stronger, fresher in her nostrils. She could not yet hear the other ATV over the deep, powerful roar of her own, but she knew it wouldn't be long. She had been tracking it all day, choosing not to rush her pursuit, having waited all night before setting out so that she wouldn't miss anything that the light might reveal. The female had no reason to know she was being tracked and would not take much time or effort to hide her trail. She had taken almost none so far, even in her efforts to hide the Harley's solar cells. Her decision to leave the children she had rescued indicated clearly that she had something of more importance with which to deal, and it was preoccupying her thoughts. Her passage through the trees and onto the highway had been straightforward and direct. She had a destination in mind and incentive to reach it, and she was not going to deviate in her efforts to get there.

All of which had made her very easy to track.

Because the Knight of the Word was not trying for extra speed or taking chances with the road and because Delloreen was, she was slowly catching up. If things continued as they were, she would have her by tonight and the chase would be ended.

Then, with her quarry's head in her possession, she would go back to that old man and settle things once and for all.

She flexed her cramped fingers on the grip of the heavy handlebars, and beneath her scaly skin her muscles rippled. The mutation was advancing more rapidly now, her reptilian appearance obliterating the last vestiges of her humanity. Her spiky blond hair was falling out in clumps, her facial features were smoothing out to a sleek, nondescript sameness, and her limbs were elongating. She was becoming something else, something much more efficient and deadly. It had been happening incrementally for the past year, but just recently it had taken on a new urgency. In part, she thought, it was because she was willing it to quicken, anxious to be rid of the last of her human skin. She despised her human self; when the last of it was gone, she would shed no tears.

Others might, when they found out how much more dangerous she was in her new form. That old man, for instance. He might. Findo Gask, when he realized that his time was up.

She had been rethinking her declaration of disinterest in leading the once-men. Perhaps she had been too hasty in dismissing the old man's offer. Why shouldn't she lead them? Wasn't she better equipped, better able, than he was? How much more quickly the annihilation of the human race would go if she were to take control. Then, when the demons and once-men controlled everything, they would begin to rebuild and resettle to suit themselves. Shouldn't she be the one to make that happen?

She was so caught up in the idea that she was surprised when she discovered all at once that she had lost the scent she had been tracking. She was still roaring down the highway, still listening for the sound of the other ATV, certain she was closing in, but the sharp smell of its exhaust fumes and the more subtle smell of the woman herself were suddenly absent.

She pulled the Harley Crawler over to the side of the road, shut down its engine, waited for the silence to settle in, and listened. Nothing. She walked out into the middle of the highway and back across several times, dropping down on all fours to sniff the cracked pavement, the clumps of wintry roadside brush, and the twilight air. Nothing there, either. Somewhere farther back, the Knight of the Word had turned off.

She took a moment to consider what that meant. Either her quarry had reached her destination or she had discovered she was being followed and taken evasive action. Delloreen favored the latter. She had to assume that somehow she had given herself away. The idea infuriated her, and she clenched her fists so hard her claws bit into the scaly hide of her palms. She stalked over to the Harley and turned it around with a furious wrench of its handlebars, and in a shower of gravel and dust she tore back down the highway.

It didn't take her long to discover the dirt road turnoff that the Knight of the Word had taken. Ten miles back, there it was. You could see the ATV tracks in the dirt. A rough, narrow trail, unlikely to lead to anything, which only confirmed her suspicion that the other knew she was being followed. How she knew, Delloreen couldn't say. No one should be able to tell if she was tracking until it was too late. Especially not a human, Knight of the Word or not.

Growling her anger, she turned the big Harley down the dirt road and rocketed ahead, avoiding tree trunks and stumps and swinging wide of the narrow corridors her quarry sought to use as barriers. It would take more than a few trees to stop her. Foolish girl, thinking the forest would hide her. If anything, they betrayed her passage. Even better, the moon was up and its light provided a brilliant beacon by which Delloreen, with her demon-enhanced senses, could find the trail easily.

But the darkness was getting so deep that despite her resolve she was forced to slow to a crawl to make out the tracks of the other machine in the soft earth. The trees thickened further, as well, so much so that it became steadily harder for the Harley to find a path between them. Eventually she was detouring so far off the path before coming back again that it was taking longer for her to make progress on the bike than if she walked. But she pressed on anyway, refusing to be stopped.

It was nearing midnight when she gave it up. She had reached a creek and followed it for almost a mile before finding the Knight's trail again, and her patience was exhausted. She shut the Harley down, climbed off, and stared into the darkness. Her choices were clear. She could stop for the night and see if the Harley would do better in daylight, when she could see the trail better and choose easier terrain to travel, or she could abandon it and proceed on foot.

She could track the woman like an animal.

She smiled at the idea, at the sudden rush of excitement that it generated, and her teeth gleamed. She might actually do better that way. She was mostly animal herself by now, able to go down on all fours, to sniff out the scent of her quarry, to see the impression of her prints. She was lean and quick and much, much stronger than the creature she hunted. How much difference would not having the use of the ATV make to her efforts to catch up to the other? Not that much, she thought. Not that much at all.

She stripped off her clothing and stood naked in the moonlight, all scales and claws and muscle. Exhilarated, she wanted to howl like a wolf. But no, not yet. Not until she was close enough for the female to know she was coming. Not until the sound of it would make clear that there was no escape.

She stretched and preened. Then she went down on all fours and began to run.

• • •

"ANGEL! WAKE UP!"

The words surfaced through a deep fog of sleep and dreams, vague and disembodied. She tried to make sense of them and failed. Her consciousness lifted momentarily, and then fell back again, adrift.

"Angel, please! You have to wake up!"

A child's voice. A little girl's. She blinked this time, the dreams and sleep fading. Her eyes opened. It was dark still, but the sunrise was a silvery brightening of the eastern sky. She remembered where she was. She had crossed out of the woods and reached another paved road sometime after midnight, then followed it to an old roadside shelter. She had hidden the ATV in the trees, left Ailie—who apparently didn't need sleep—on watch, and gone right to sleep.

"Angel, say something!"

Ailie. The tatterdemalion was bent over her, practically shouting in her ear.

"What is it?" she murmured, sleep-fogged and vaguely irritated.

"It's found us! The demon!"

She sat up quickly then, shock galvanizing lethargic muscles and numbed responses into action. She rolled quickly into a sitting position, reaching for the black staff, her eyes sweeping the darkness of the surrounding woods. She listened to the silence. No distant roar of an ATV. No sounds of any kind at all.

"I don't hear anything," she whispered.

"It's not coming that way!" Ailie's face was back in front of her own, blue hair wild, eyes bright with fear. "It's coming on foot!"

On foot? Angel rose quickly, grasping the staff in both hands now, taking a defensive position, her body reacting automatically, out of habit, even though her thinking remained clouded and sluggish. *On foot?* The words didn't make any sense. Even a demon couldn't have caught them on foot, and besides why would it . . .

A blur of white and blue flashed in front of her as Ailie rushed past, sweeping aside deliberation and confusion in a moment's time. "Angel, it's here!"

In the next instant something big and dark burst from the forest, bounding into the clearing in a terrifying rush, down on all fours and grunting and huffing like some monstrous wild animal. Angel barely had time to bring up the staff, the magic surging through it in response to her needs, quicker than thought. She went down on one knee, one end of the staff pointed out like a lance, catching her attacker in the chest as it leapt for her, pinning it in midair. The force of the attack threw her backward, and the staff vaulted the demon right over her head and sent it tumbling away.

She came back to her feet, fully awake now. The demon was already turning, a huge, sleek gray shape in the mix of shadows and half-light, its limbs impossibly long and disjointed, its head hunched down between its massive shoulders like a wolf's. She searched for a hint of the features that had identified the demon as female only days before, but everything recognizable was gone. No spiky blond hair, no human face or body, no skin, nothing. This creature was covered with scales, its fingers and toes were claws, its face was a muzzle split wide to reveal gleaming teeth, and its eyes were yellow lanterns. Yet it was *her* nevertheless, Angel knew. It was the demon from the compound, come to finish her off.

"*¡Diablo!*" Angel muttered as she braced herself for the next attack.

The demon screamed suddenly, a bone-jarring, frenzied wail that reverberated through the trees and froze Angel where she stood.

Then the monster rushed her, so swift it was on top of her almost before she could respond. But respond she did, sending the white fire of the staff surging into her attacker in a rippling, jagged-edged strike that burned the other's scaly hide despite its obvious toughness, knocking the demon backward and aside. It screamed again, as if the sound gave it special strength, and renewed its assault. Again it charged Angel and again she used the fire to throw it back.

It's too strong, she thought as she watched it bound up anew, its hide smoking, but its madness undiminished. *I can't win this.*

This time the demon got through her defenses far enough to backhand her so hard that she flew off her feet and halfway across the clearing. Her ears were ringing as she scrambled up, her head swimming with the blow. She fought off another attack, and then another.

"Ailie!" she shouted.

She didn't expect help from the tatterdemalion, but she needed to know where Ailie was. She was already eyeing the ATV, thinking that her only chance was to get away, to put enough distance between herself and the demon that it couldn't get at her. It felt like a coward's choice, not the right choice for a Knight of the Word, but it might keep her alive to fight another day.

She caught a glimpse of Ailie as the other peeked out from behind the Mercury. The tatterdemalion was thinking the same thing, but there was little she could do to help make it happen. Tatter-demalions were Faerie creatures, lacking sufficient substance to engage in physical combat. They were mostly air and light. She might reason and counsel, but she was not going to do much to fight off a demon.

Which right now was back on top of Angel, slamming her backward, striking at her as though the staff's terrible fire were thin paper. It was as if the pain was making it stronger, giving it fresh energy, while Angel's strength continued to diminish. Angel blocked the follow-up attack, sidestepping the other's shredding claws, trying not to look into the terrible yellow eyes. There was a hypnotic quality to the demon's gaze, the kind that predatory creatures used to freeze their prey in place while they ripped out their throats. Look too closely into that gaze and there was no escape. Angel concentrated on the elongated arms with their razor-sharp claws, still reaching for her, slashing. She was aware that she was wounded anew, fresh blood running down one shoulder and arm. Somehow the demon had gotten through her defenses. It would continue to find ways to do so, she realized. It would continue until she collapsed.

Until it was over.

She took a chance. She attacked. Mustering all the strength she could, she launched a fiery strike at the sleek form, hammering into it with everything she had, sending it flying backward into the trees. Even as it was tumbling out of view, she was racing to gain the Mercury. She leapt astride and slammed down the ignition button. The engine caught and roared to life.

Already the demon was bounding out of the trees, coming for her anew, shrieking in fury.

"Ailie!" she cried, and felt the tatterdemalion's arms come around her waist.

She turned the black staff on the demon once more and sent the Word's white fire lancing into it. But this time the demon kept coming, arms raised protectively, taking the brunt of the attack, the scaly hide smoking and burning as it fought its way through Angel's defenses. Angel held it off as long as she could, maintaining the fire in a steady stream. Then, as she felt the fire begin to collapse, her strength exhausted, she wrenched the Mercury's throttle forward and launched the ATV directly at the demon.

It was a bold move. The demon was too big and strong for her to simply drive over it. But she reacted to the situation, and it probably saved her. The demon could have stood its ground, but the maneuver surprised it. It saw the big machine tearing toward it and instinctively leapt out of the way. Before it realized that it had made a mistake, Angel was past it and tearing down the highway at full speed.

The demon gave chase at once. It came bounding out of the trees after the Mercury, enraged. Angel opened the throttle a notch further. But she could not risk going any faster because this highway, like all the others in the world, was littered with debris. If she hit a big enough obstacle, she would flip the bike and go over and that would be the end of her.

"Faster, Angel!" Ailie cried in her ear, pressing close.

She gritted her teeth, bent low over the handlebars, and ratcheted the throttle up another notch, eyes on the road. When she couldn't stand it any longer, she glanced back at their pursuer. It was farther away now and fading, unable to keep up the pace.

But still coming, still giving chase.

The last she saw of it before it receded into the distance was the gleam of its yellow eyes in the mix of woodland shadows and light.

29

H AWK DIDN'T KNOW what he was supposed to do.
Even after Logan Tom was gone and he was alone in
his prison and could think about it at length, he still
didn't know. Oh, he understood the nature of his reaction to the finger bones; that much of it was clear. Taking the bones from Logan
Tom, closing them into his fist, and, most especially, feeling the press
of them against the flesh of his palm had triggered a very unexpected awakening inside him. Where before he had not believed
himself to be anything of what Logan Tom thought him, suddenly
he discovered that he was all of it and much more.

His awakening came in the form of visions so sharp and hard-
edged that he did not even think to question that they were real.
They exploded in his mind like fireworks; they came to life in star-
bursts.

The first was of a woman, tall and slender and athletic, her face
instantly familiar. She had his green eyes, his build and angular features. He knew her instinctively, without having to be told, without
a word having been spoken.

Nest Freemark. His mother.

The knowledge of it, the certainty, ripped through his doubts and left him breathless with realization. In his vision, she spoke to him of their shared relationship, of who he was and how he had come to be. He saw himself a boy in the company of another Knight of the Word, a man called John Ross. He was still the gypsy morph then, still transitioning out of the magic that had birthed him, still searching for his identity.

Then he was inside her, her unborn child, his magic mingling with hers to begin the forming of a new life.

And after he was born, he lived with her until he was old enough to leave, and then . . .

Then everything grew very vague and uncertain. She was there and then she wasn't, alive and then gone back into the earth, the ether, and the shadows. He was alone again, perhaps for a long time, and the world in which he existed was another form of shadows . . .

You were made safe, she said to him. *You were kept in a place where your enemies couldn't reach you.*

He didn't understand, and perhaps he wasn't meant to. He looked into his mother's eyes as she spoke to him, explaining, revealing, and investing him with the knowledge of his identity.

Then he saw himself coming into the city of Seattle and into the lives of the Ghosts, and all the connections were made clear to him. His mother smiled and leaned down and touched him gently on his cheek. He could feel how she loved him. He understood that his memories of his parents were vague and uncertain because they had never truly existed. Perhaps he had manufactured them to give himself a sense of belonging. Perhaps they had been manufactured for him. But Nest Freemark was his true mother, and his memory of her, now recovered, was the only one that mattered.

A disembodied voice spoke next, one he did not recognize. There was no face attached to this voice, no presence to identify its source. The voice sounded very old. It told him the story of the boy and his children, the one Owl had told the Ghosts piecemeal. Only this version, while essentially the same, was different, too. It was more complicated and larger in scope. He was still the boy and the Ghosts were still his children, but there were others, too. Together, they traveled a long way to find a place where the walls were built of light and the colors were no longer muted but bright and pure. In this place, there was a sense of peace, a promise of safety and a reassurance that the bad things in the world couldn't reach them. He heard his name spoken over and over. *Hawk. Hawk.* He didn't know what it meant, and he couldn't see who was doing the speaking. But the sound of it made him feel wanted.

Further images appeared. He saw monsters and dark things rising up to confront him. He saw himself running from them and saw them giving chase. The Ghosts ran with him, and with them a scattering of others. The pursuit went on, a long and arduous race against a death that rode on the back of a fiery wind that followed in the wake of his pursuers.

There were other visions, as well—other voices—coming together out of the awakening that the finger bones had generated, out of the resurfacing of his memories and the foretelling of his future. Some of them stayed with him; some of them were lost. He understood that this was necessary, that it was all part of restoring his identity. Revelations came in the form of small touchings, in the form of fingerprints of his life's passing. But where the past was fixed, the future was fluid and could not yet be fully defined. He understood why this was so and was not troubled by it.

When it was done, his mother was there again, bending close to kiss him on the cheek, to reassure him anew, to let him feel her presence, which she would not deprive him of again.

Trust in me, she whispered to him as she faded.

Mother, he called after her.

Yes, the nature of his awakening was perfectly clear to him afterward—the visions and voices, the story of his birth and parentage, and the arduous nature of the journey that lay ahead. He even understood for the first time what it was that had happened between Cheney and himself when the dying animal's wounds had mysteriously healed in his presence. As the gypsy morph, as a creature of magical origins, he apparently possessed some innate ability to heal. Although why that ability had never manifested itself before still confused him.

But what wasn't made clear to him, what he didn't understand, was what was expected of him. He was trapped in this cell with only a few hours of life left. Logan Tom had told him on leaving that he would be back for him, that he would not let him die. But Hawk wasn't sure about this. Logan Tom did not seem strong enough to break down walls and gates of concrete and steel. He did not seem powerful enough to take on the entire population of the compound. He was one man, and however well intentioned or determined he might be, however formidable his skills, it did not seem possible that he could do what was needed.

Yet Hawk's future was there in the visions, and it did not end with his death at the bottom of the compound walls. For that future to happen, he would have to break free of his prison.

Was he meant to do this on his own?

He tried to make sense of it, to determine if there was something that he could do, but he couldn't think of anything. If he had magic at his disposal, he didn't know how to use it. He kept coming back to the image of his mother speaking those three small words—*trust in me.* For reasons he couldn't explain, they formed a powerful web of faith that was wholly lacking in any concrete source of support but that refused to let him be. How was his mother supposed to help him? How was he, in turn, supposed to help Tessa?

There were no answers. He slipped the finger bones into his pocket and lay back, weary from all he had experienced. Maybe, he thought, Logan Tom would come for him as he had said he would. Maybe he just needed to have the faith his mother's words suggested.

But he was powerless within this dark room, behind these compound walls and in the hands of people who hated and feared him. He didn't feel like anything special, whatever his supposed origins. He was just someone who had tried to find a home and a family to belong to.

What more was he supposed to be?

Trust in me, he heard his mother whisper one last time.

Then he fell asleep.

●　●　●

LOGAN TOM STOOD with Panther in the deep shadows just inside the building doorway that fronted Pioneer Square. The others were upstairs completing their preparations for leaving. When informed of her plans, Logan had agreed with Owl; whatever happened, it was time for them to get out of there. She had told him about the giant centipede, a creature he had never even heard of, let alone encountered. Too many strange things were coming into the world, and Logan knew what that meant. If there was to be any civilization in the future, any human presence, it was time to start thinking about how they would make it happen.

"This is what you are going to do," he told Panther. "After we get in sight of the compound, you will walk up to the front gates and start yelling for them to let Hawk out. Stay well back when you do. Don't do anything to suggest you are carrying a weapon. If they even think you have a weapon, they will shoot you. All you have to do is yell at them for about five minutes or so. Got it?"

Panther nodded. "What's the point?"

"While you're yelling at them, they'll be looking at you. That will let me get through the rubble to the underground tunnel Tessa used to meet Hawk. That's how I'm going to get into the compound."

The boy shook his head. "That door gonna be locked. Plus, they might see you anyway."

"Let me worry about that. All you need to do is keep their attention for those five minutes. Then get out of there. Don't stand around waiting for something to happen. If you see them start to come out or do anything that even looks like they might be coming out, you run for it." He paused. "No wild stuff. No heroics."

The boy grinned. "So where do I run to?"

"Back to the edge of the square so that I can find you again when I'm done."

He reached down to button the heavy jacket he was wearing and turned up the collar. The day was growing chilly. He crooked the black staff in his arm as he straightened his clothing. Panther glanced at the staff, then at him. "What about you?"

"What about me?"

"Where's your weapons? You ain't going in there with no weapons, are you?"

Logan almost smiled. Once, he would have carried a Tyson Flechette, a brace of Arrow Stunners, and a K-Bar Classic. He would have worn body armor and a helmet with night vision built into the visor. But that was a long time ago, before he became a Knight of the Word.

He took the staff out of the crook of his arm. "This is all I need. Let's go."

The sun was already sinking into the far reaches of the western sky as they walked out the door and into the street. They would have perhaps another two hours of light, two hours in which to get to Hawk and Tessa before the death sentence was carried out. Logan knew it was barely enough time, even if things went the way they should. They would have to hurry.

He said a quick good-bye to Owl, mostly to reinforce his earlier instructions. She was to make certain that the Ghosts left Pioneer Square as quickly as possible, taking whatever they could either carry or haul in the carts. If he were successful in rescuing Hawk and Tessa, the compound would dispatch armed guards to bring them back. They would begin their search in Pioneer Square, and the Ghosts had better not be there when they did. They were to go up to the freeway to where the Lightning was parked and wait for him there. He had given her directions on how to find the vehicle and had warned her against approaching it. If they could find an abandoned trailer of some sort in which to load and pull both kids and possessions, it would be helpful. But they were not to do anything else or leave the area for any reason other than to find safety. They were to stay put and wait for him.

If he didn't appear by midnight or if they heard or saw any signs of a pursuit, they should assume the worst. They were to take what they could carry and go into hiding.

Owl, somber-faced and steady-eyed as she listened, promised that his instructions would be carried out. She didn't question or argue with him.

She spoke only three words: "Please save them."

With Panther at his side, Logan Tom went down First Street and out of Pioneer Square toward the compound, the air off the bay sharp and pungent with the smell of the fouled water, the afternoon sun glinting off its surface like light off metal. Neither the man nor the boy spoke as they reached the edge of the square and faced out from the shadow of the buildings toward their destination.

Logan caught his breath. There were thousands of feeders gathered before the west-facing wall, all of them squirming to get closer, a writhing, surging black mass of bodies. The humans inside the compound couldn't see them, didn't know they were there. Panther couldn't see them, either. Only he knew they were there and what it was that had drawn them.

He felt a shiver ripple the skin at the base of his neck. He had seen feeders massed before in his time as a Knight of the Word, but never like this. If he'd had any doubts about Hawk's identity, the presence of the feeders removed them instantly.

He turned to Panther. "This is where we split up. You go on ahead toward the main gates. Make certain they see you coming. Don't look back for me under any circumstances. We want them to think you are alone in this. Can you do it?"

"Sure. Can you?" Panther grinned at him and was on his way without a backward glance.

Logan waited until the boy was close enough to the compound that the guards would notice, then slipped from the shadows and began to move at a steady pace toward the old bus shelter, keeping the piles of rubble between himself and the walls, taking advantage of the long shadows of the nearest buildings where they spread their black, concealing stains. He did not look in the direction of the compound, even after he heard Panther begin yelling at the guards, until he was only yards from the bus shelter. Then he risked a quick glance at the north-facing wall, a huge steel-and-concrete barrier blocking away the southern horizon. He searched its perimeter and its craggy openings for movement and found none. No one had seen him.

He gave the matter no further thought as he went into the shelter and down the steps to the door leading into the underground tunnels. From somewhere around the front gates, Panther continued to yell wildly, his voice strident and insistent. Logan smiled. The boy was good. He tried the door and found it sealed, but a touch of his staff against the lock and it was burned through in seconds. He pushed the door open and, after stepping inside, pushed it closed again. He went down the tunnel without slowing, his eyes adjusting to the darkness as he went. He chose his path when the tunnel branched, using his wrist compass to guide him, moving ahead until he had passed beneath the walls of the compound and was inside its underground hallways. He had mapped his route to Hawk's cell in his mind, a skill he had perfected over the years while serving with Michael. Their raids on the slave camps often required that they descend into tunnels. If you couldn't remember how you went in, you might not be able to get out again. It was more complicated here, but he recalled enough from his earlier visit to know approximately where he needed to go. The problem was in finding the right level, but he knew it would be somewhere near the basement of the complex.

Twice he was forced to stop and wait in the shadows while someone passed by only yards away. Once he had to backtrack and go around a place where men were working. There was little traffic this deep underground, this far down in the lower levels, so the risks were not as great as they would have been if he had been forced to climb to the surface.

He began to recognize corridors, their walls and doors and entries. He was close.

Then he rounded a corner and came face-to-face with the guard who had admitted him into Hawk's cell only hours before. They stopped instantly, facing each other, and Logan said, "Hello again," snapped one end of his staff against the side of the other's head, and dropped him in his tracks.

He found an open door, dragged the guard inside, took his keys from his belt, and left him. He moved ahead quickly, searching for the cell that contained Hawk, a search that took him no more than another five minutes. A quick glance ahead and behind confirmed that he was alone. He inserted the key into the lock and opened the heavy metal door.

The cell was empty.

* * *

"ARE YOU ALL right?" Hawk whispered when they brought Tessa over and sat her down beside him.

She nodded without speaking. Her face was ashen and tear-streaked, her hair disheveled, and her hands shaking. She had the look of someone who had been struck a sharp blow and was still in shock.

He looked out over the top of the compound wall to where the sun was sinking toward the mountains in the western horizon. Another fifteen minutes, no more. They had brought him up early, trying to unnerve him, he thought, trying to see if he would break down. They hadn't said or done anything to him, but he couldn't think of any other reason to make him sit and wait like this. In any case, it didn't matter. He had come to terms with the future. Escape seemed out of the question. Either someone would come to save them or they would die.

"I'm sorry about your mother," he said to her.

She exhaled sharply. "Did you see her face? Did you see how she looked at me?" She shook her head. "What's happened to her?"

He scuffed the toes of his tennis shoes against the concrete. "Maybe you just saw a side to her you didn't know was there."

She closed her eyes. "I wish I had never seen her like that. I'll never forget how she made me feel. In front of all those people. In front of you. I will never forget."

Hawk said nothing, bent forward with his elbows on his knees, looking at his feet. He breathed in the taste and smell of the bay, of the coldness blown in off the water, and the hard edge of the coming night. The year was winding down, and while the seasons no longer behaved in recognizable ways, lacking identity of the sort people had once known, he could feel winter's bite in the air. He watched the sun begin to press down against the mountains to the west. Time was almost up. He glanced around, thinking again of escape, searching for a way. But there was nowhere to go. A dozen armed guards stood close by. All the exits down off the wall were blocked. They were unfettered and could try to break free, but their chances were almost nonexistent. They would be seized and hauled back to their seats before they got ten steps. The only way open to them was forward, over the edge.

He looked at Tessa, and the soft line of her face brought tears to his eyes. It seemed impossible to think that they were going to die.

"Is there a child?" he asked.

She shook her head. "I only said that to try to buy us some time, to make them rethink what they were going to do."

He nodded. "It was a good try."

"It was a waste of time. They had already decided."

"Even if we were married, I guess."

"Even if."

"I would have married you if it would have changed things. If they would have let us."

"That decision isn't theirs to make. It's ours."

The sharpness in her voice surprised him. "We waited too long, in any case," he said.

Her hand closed over his wrist. "No, we didn't." Her words were whispered and urgent. "We still have time. Say the words to me." She looked at him, her eyes pleading. "Say you take me for your wife."

He hesitated, and then repeated, "I take you for my wife."

"And I take you for my husband," she replied.

He held her gaze. "I don't want them to throw us from the walls. I don't want them to put their hands on us."

She nodded. "I know."

His hand tightened over hers. "I want us to jump."

She stared at him, transfixed. "Jump?"

"Before they can throw us off. Before they can touch us. I want us to do it on our own. I want us to be free when we go over."

She started to say something, but the words seemed locked in her throat. There were fresh tears in her eyes. "I don't think I can do that," she whispered.

He looked out to where several birds were winging their way across the color-streaked sky. One of them, he thought, might be his namesake. He wanted to fly, to soar above everything, to lift away to somewhere he could never be reached.

He took a deep breath. No rescue was at hand. No one was

coming. To one side, four of the guards were clustered around the compound Chairman, a man named Cole who had told Hawk earlier that he was sorry about what was going to happen, but hadn't meant it. The men were whispering and glances were being cast in their direction. They were getting ready to carry out the sentence.

He looked back at Tessa. "Now," he said.

Her hand locked tight on his wrist. "I can't."

"I love you, Tessa," he said.

"I love you, too." Her head lowered into shadow. "But I can't."

"Just don't look. Just hold on to me."

They were too late. The guards were coming toward them, grim-faced in the failing light. Hawk started to his feet, tried to pull Tessa up with him, but she refused to follow, sitting where she was, crying softly. The guards seized them by their shoulders, yanked them to their feet, and began walking them forward.

"Don't do this," Hawk pleaded, glancing from face to face, and then in desperation back at Cole, who stood watching impassively. "Cowards!" he screamed at them.

No one responded to him. He looked around wildly. Was there really no one coming? His mother's words recalled themselves anew. *Trust in me.* His free hand went to his pocket and closed about the bones.

Then they were at the edge of the wall, the world spread away below them in a vast, shadow-streaked carpet, the distant horizon crimson with the sunset. Behind them, Cole spoke sharply, words that sounded more guttural than human. Hawk tried to break free, then tried to reach Tessa, but his captors held him tightly. He caught a quick glimpse of her stricken face as she sagged against the hands holding her. He tried to speak her name, but the word lodged in his throat.

Then the hands gave them a hard shove and together they went tumbling into the void.

● ● ●

ON THE ROOFTOP of the building the Ghosts once had called
home, Sparrow took a last look around. Acting as the legs and eyes
of Owl, she performed a quick check of the catchments to make
certain the necessary pieces had been dismantled and carried away.
The others were down in the street and heading for the freeway,
Bear pulling the heavy cart, Chalk and Fixit carrying the Weatherman on a litter, River pushing Owl in her wheelchair, Candle and
Squirrel carrying packs and armfuls of supplies, and Cheney watching over them all.

She had volunteered to stay behind for a last look around and
would catch up to them when she was satisfied.

She brushed at her ragged thatch of hair and looked south
toward the compound, wondering if the Knight of the Word had
reached Hawk yet. Somehow, she believed, he would find a way. She
searched for movement through the shadows that draped the dark
structure and listened for revealing sounds. But she saw and heard
nothing. The sunset splashed across the metal and stone surfaces of
the compound, a vivid and garish crimson. She didn't like the look
of that light. She didn't like how it made her feel.

Then, suddenly, there was a bright flash near the top of the walls,
a soundless explosion that she would have missed entirely had she
blinked. She stared fixedly, searching for its source, waiting for it to
reappear, but nothing else happened. Had she imagined it?

Her brow furrowed. She didn't think so. She didn't make those
kinds of mistakes.

She turned away, finished her survey of the dismantled catchments and pilfered purification supplies, decided she was done, and
moved toward the stairs. She was almost there when something out
on the water caught her eye. She stopped where she was and stared.
Hundreds of small lights had appeared, seemingly out of nowhere,
all across the mouth of the bay, drifting in off the sound. For a second she didn't know what she was looking at, and then suddenly it
registered.

Lights. Torches and lamps were burning on the decks and masts
of hundreds of boats.

She blinked. Why were all these boats here?

Then, as she puzzled it through, she heard the first faint booming of the drums, a steady cadence that signaled clearly the purpose of the inhabitants of the boats.

It was an invasion.

She took only a moment more to let the realization of what was happening sink in, and then she began to run.

To be continued